A Sparkle
on the Water

Suzan Woods

White Wolf Path Publishing

Cover photograph © 1997 Joseph Woods
Cover illustration by Joseph Woods
Cover design by Joseph & Suzan Woods
Translations by Harvey Schwartz, Ph.D.

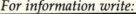

For information write:

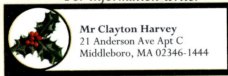

Mr Clayton Harvey
21 Anderson Ave Apt C
Middleboro, MA 02346-1444

Or call: (505) 281-2718
e-mail: WWolfPath@aol.com

For editorial services contact:

Kim Rufer-Bach
P.O. Box 672
Boulder Creek, CA 95006
Kat91@aol.com

If you are unable to order this book
from your local bookseller,
you may order directly from the publisher.

Library of Congress Catalog Card Number: 96-91026

ISBN: 0-9659736-0-3

For Joseph ... without whom this story would not exist.

Acknowledgements

I began writing my acknowledgement list, and soon discovered how lengthy it was! Three pages later, I sat stunned by the love that surrounded this project and which existed in my life. What a gift it was to see how often and in how many ways I had been blessed! Gifts surround each of us in unlimited quantities. If you look, you will see yours right next to you – or perhaps in your heart.

Because my own list is so long, I decided to write a general wish of gratitude. Each person in my life knows how he or she has touched me. How do you thank people who have given you the bounty of insight and wisdom, the warmth of laughter and support, the gift of compassion or the beauty of love?

You give your love in return.

So, to each of you, I give my warmest love,

Suzan

Introduction

Each of us holds a piece to the puzzle of how our universe works. As we share the pieces, the whole becomes clear; the mystery unfolds in all its wonder. We were not meant to find the answers alone, for what a burden that would be to that one individual! We are part of a whole. And each of us, if he or she so chooses, can share a piece of knowledge, making the picture complete for the rest.

This book is our piece of the puzzle, based on what my husband Joseph and I have learned. We offer it with our love, our respect and hoping that our pieces will joyfully fit yours in places, forming a bigger picture for us all.

Suzan Woods 1997

Part One

2000 BC - 800 BC

Prologue

*T*he moonless night sky, clear and dark in its starlit beauty, hung above a small cabin in a forest. Shadowy forms of trees surrounded the rustic building, which sat on the edge of a cliff. Below the cliff a waterfall rushed impatiently over boulders to meet the river, which ran loudly with the heavy waters of a storm that had passed earlier in the evening.

Inside the cabin a young woman slept beneath warm woolen blankets, alone except for a small calico cat who purred softly by her side. Her long dark hair lay about her face in a warm brown halo. Her slender fingers pushed a stray piece of hair away from her face where it tickled her cheek; and then she rolled over and into a deeper sleep.

Her dreams drifted one to another until a view of a blue planet slowly appeared in her subconscious wanderings. Clouds swirled in the atmosphere of the planet, muting the blue into softer gray tones in places. The blackness of space encircled the blue globe with stars, planets, comets, asteroids and mystery. She wondered how she had come to see this image ... and then the image vanished.

She found herself surrounded by tall blond men and women in a circular room. The walls of the room curved inward in a dome shape and were made of a type of metal that looked as if it might be stainless steel. The lighting was artificial and cast a golden glow over everything. The men and women were strangely familiar, and they spoke together casually as they observed a screen on one wall, which displayed a similar view of the planet she had seen only moments ago. She recognized this planet as "Earth," while the other people in the dream called it by an unpronounceable name. One of the tall men turned and spoke directly to her.

"Serra, are you ready?"

Her mind struggled with the foreign name; her heart raced as he smiled at her. His face was acutely intimate and beautiful. Blue eyes stared into hers and touched her in a way that was sensual and loving. His smile widened as he watched her startled expression. His blond hair was shoulder length and brushed away from his face. He was tall, quite tall, but his height seemed natural to her and she realized in that moment that her height matched his. For a brief moment she saw herself reflected in the pale blue of his eyes. Her own eyes were large, gray-blue and puzzled. They stared out of a face that was foreign, and as fair and blond as the man she faced.

She knew this man. But, who was he? Her mind struggled for his name as he patiently awaited her response. He reached and took her hand in a gentle display of affection.

"Serra?" he asked in a puzzled tone.

Her mouth found the name her mind had been seeking. As she said it, she came suddenly awake.

"Lohkan!" She whispered hoarsely while her heart yelled for the man and the dream to remain.

When she awoke hours later, the day awaited her, brilliant and clear after the previous evening's storm. The sky was washed clean to a startling blue and the trees around the cabin stood regally adorned in autumn gold. Drops fell silently from the limbs to the forest floor, which was carpeted with green grass and the first of fall's scarlet and yellow leaves. The waterfall ran peacefully again in a graceful descent as she viewed it it through the kitchen window.

She rushed through her morning routine of breakfast and bathing, and decided to go for a brief walk along the river bank before leaving for work. She stepped carefully down the steep path to the river's edge and walked the well-worn trail along the bank and deeper into the forest, where the river flattened and the waters became more tame. She found her favorite place, a small cove in the river with a still pool where a felled tree bridged the river and gold leaves covered the bank, and draped her coat over the log. She lazily laid on her stomach, reached down and touched the water with her fingers and peacefully reflected on her strange dreams.

The quiet of the morning promised her that no one was about; no one would notice her odd reflections there by the river's edge. As her thoughts wandered through her unfathomable dreams, an even stranger event took place.

An image took form and floated in the water, surreal and opaque. Beside the reflection of her slim, tanned face was a likeness of someone else, a male face, the man from her dreams: the man she had called "Lohkan." The sun crested over the trees, causing the image to fade somewhat. She slowly brushed aside her dark hair as it momentarily fell and obscured the image. She squinted her brown eyes with concentration, hoping to define his features, to remember more.

A light breeze stirred the pool while the waterfall continued to cascade in the distance, giving no advice or explanations for the face she saw. Her cabin lay behind her, back along the trail, offering silence and shelter should she give up this foolish adventure of chasing visions and ghosts in the watery mirror. She breathed in deeply, concentrated on the image that was leaving, drawing to it every detail her memory could add, making the face solid again.

A promise lay in his countenance, a promise of a sweetness, of a deep love, mingled with peace, wisdom and secrets that had been learned through untold tears, breathless beauty, speechless actions and ... years, many years, of experience. Yet, the face was not old. His blond hair had fallen over his clear blue eyes, which stared back at her, winking at her, teasing her to follow him on a journey. To where? And with whom? There was something ancient in his beauty, an otherworldliness in his expression. What had he seen? What was she to him? How did they know each other? And what had they learned?

If only she could remember....

Chapter 1

*S*erra heard the call clearly the first time, but her mind and heart denied its meaning with an intensity of passion that was not typical of her nature. She swam quickly to a large rock that jutted out of the green ocean waves near her, and held onto it while she waited for another call ... and for her heart to stop its panicked beating. The sandy shore with its tall tropical trees was behind her, a few hundred yards away. A gray cloud in the overcast sky opened and a gentle rain fell, making small patterns on the water's surface. And then the call came again.

Serra!

A dolphin swimming next to her squealed in a troubled voice. Her mind as well as her heart knew what this plea meant. Something was terribly wrong. As the dolphin's smooth body touched hers, she grabbed onto his dorsal fin and let him pull her away from the rock, further from the shore and toward what her heart dreaded.

Two miles out to sea, Serra found him floating near the surface of the water. His blond hair swirled around his head like sun-washed seaweed while his beautiful face lay peacefully still. His eyes were closed to her, to the world, and would not open again. She would never see their blue depth or feel their warmth as he looked upon her.

"Oh, Lohkan," she whispered hoarsely, and then she gasped as the reality of his death cut through her.

The dolphin swam around them in a protective circle as she tenderly scooped Lohkan into her arms. She laid his head gently against her shoulder while her sobs echoed across the water. Her long blond hair mingled with his and created an ashen veil around them. The rain blended silently with her tears and left trails down her pale cheeks. Her blue eyes stared at the ocean around her, but saw nothing. The dolphin called out in haunting and mournful tones that matched her lament. And then, as if prompted by an invisible hand, she took hold of the dolphin's fin and he began to pull them back to shore.

Serra was not alone in her grief. Before she, Lohkan and the dolphin reached the shore, the other members of her team had gathered in the surf to meet her. Orryka, the team's oldest member, stood in the front of the group. His long golden hair lay in wet tendrils over the blue fabric of his wetsuit. He stood waist-deep in the surf and tried to keep his balance as the waves pushed over him. A beard covered his chin and accented his blue-green eyes, which were alert as he watched for Serra's presence. Orryka's kind features were now tense and guarded as they hid the pain that lay inside him. He had been the first to hear Serra's lament.

Serra's and Lohkan's race was telepathic. As the first of Serra's wails had spilled out over the ocean's surface, her painful thoughts had reached Orryka's sensitive mind. The others had soon heard her cries and had quickly gathered at the ocean's edge.

Soon they saw her.

A moan escaped Orryka's lips as he saw Lohkan's body and then Serra's face. He had never seen her in pain, and the newness of this emotion added a weight to the sorrow he felt for her, for himself, for them all. He dove under the water and quickly swam out to meet her.

Orryka carefully took Lohkan into his own arms as others helped Serra. Tears now poured down his face as he pressed Lohkan's body to his chest. He had lost a dear friend. Serra had lost her life's mate. How would they all heal from this loss? He tenderly pulled Lohkan's body back to shallower waters and then lifted Lohkan in his arms and carried him to the beach.

The beach remained silent except for their quiet cries and a few sea birds who called out in haunting tones. While their voices gave vent in hushed weeping to the pain each felt, their minds spoke deftly and sadly to one another.

Serra, do you know what happened? Orryka asked.

No! We were to meet at the rock. He did not come, and then....

Orryka heard Serra's mind as it fell silent. He knew she

could not speak or think the words that needed to come and so he said them for her.

... Something happened. Lohkan drowned.

His hands reached under Lohkan's suit and found the cord that had snapped; without it Lohkan could not breathe under water. And if he had been deep enough, he would not have been able to reach the surface in time. Orryka asked Serra the obvious question.

Serra, did Lohkan speak to you before he died?

Yes. Twice. He called my name! I wanted to believe he was contacting me to tell me he was on his way, but, I knew something was wrong! It was only seconds between his calls, and then I heard nothing.

Then he died quickly. He did not suffer, Orryka answered.

With this small comfort, he picked up Lohkan's body and gently carried him back to the ship.

We came to this planet from across the galaxy to study the life forms here. There are always risks during such adventures. Lohkan knew this! I knew this!

Serra angrily reminded herself of these facts as she tried to heal her broken heart months later. But facts contain no emotions. And her emotions were shredded into small pieces that she could not put back together. She picked a starfish out of the water and pretended to examine it as she tried to continue her studies. She steadied herself on a rock as a wave washed over her in the tidal pool where she worked. Her hands felt like someone else's, cold and foreign; her heart felt weighted and her body felt strangely detached from her head, as if she had been cleft in two with Lohkan's death.

Lohkan would not like this, this strange feeling of detachment, she thought sullenly; and then she realized she could not tell him about these feelings. With this realization, she bowed her head into her cold hands, shuddered and then began to cry.

After a few moments she slowly raised her head and looked out over the ocean through blurry eyes. It was a strangely peaceful day. The sky was a pale blue and the water's surface was glassy. The stillness of this day seemed unnatural to Serra's tormented heart.

Yet, it was a perfect day for a swim. And swimming always eased Serra's mind. As she stepped over the rocks and dove under the surface, the questions that had tormented her since Lohkan's death arose again in her mind.

Where does a soul go between lives? Where did Lohkan's soul go?

She adjusted her oxygen belt and dove deeper into the blue-green ocean. She was certain Lohkan was alive – somewhere! Each team member had agreed to reincarnate on this planet, Earth, so that they could study human lives more intimately and tangibly. Their people believed, *knew,* reincarnation existed. To reincarnate amongst a world of foreign people whom they hoped to understand would give their research team a unique and powerful point of view. The knowledge they would bring back to their planet, to their solar system, would benefit all worlds. Yet, Serra had not expected this agreement to take effect so soon ... or that she'd be separated from Lohkan.

They knew so little about what happened between this life and the next. Had Lohkan died and reincarnated immediately? Did he remember her, wherever he was? Did he miss her as painfully as she now missed him?

Where are you, Lohkan? her mind and heart cried.

Serra's grief did not heal that day or that next month. As Lohkan had died before her, she drowned that afternoon. She felt her spirit lift lightly from the weight of her body, and felt only gratitude that she would not have to go on alone in her grief. *And perhaps ...* she thought as she died ... *some of my questions will at last be answered.*

"the between ..."

At first she could see nothing. The intensity of the light blinded her, filled her with a deep sense of being loved and eased her sorrow. Then suddenly, as if someone were reading her thoughts, the light vanished and she found herself standing in a green meadow. Serra recognized this meadow from where she had once lived. To the left a large patch of purple flowers covered the field. Directly in front of her green grass ran gently up a hill; there at the top, trees stood in a thick stand across the ridge. Farther to her right was a forest, dark and deep. The branches swayed delicately, more like giant ferns than the hard twigs of Earth's trees. A cool and sweet breeze blew over the hill, across the trees and down into the meadow. On the other side of this hill lay a vast lake, clear and crystal-like in its beauty. The softly hued lavender sky caused Serra to smile as she looked at the view. She had grown up near here and this had always been her favorite place.

As she gazed longingly out over the meadow, a figure materialized several feet in front of her. The woman was slight and small when compared with Serra's tall stature. She stood just over five feet. Her figure was uniquely graceful as she walked towards Serra. A loose-fitting blue robe flowed around her as she walked, intensifying the illusion that she floated. Warm gold skin tones and her facial features indicated a race Serra recognized as originating from a region on Earth known as Asia. The woman's slanted eyes and mouth turned upward into a faint smile. She stopped in front of Serra, leaned over and patted the thick grass with her hand.

"Please sit," she said. Her voice ran across the top of the grass and into Serra's mind like the sound of wind chimes calling over a long distance. Serra sat down. The woman continued to stand near her. Her smile broadened and deepened the warmth of her dark eyes. She began to speak.

"Serra, do you understand what has happened to you?"

"Yes. I drowned," she answered dreamily. "Where am I? Where is Lohkan?"

"You are between worlds, between lifetimes. I have been sent to prepare you for your next lifetime. Lohkan is with another guide," the small woman explained.

"Who are you? I would like to know what to call you."

The guide seemed surprised by the question, but answered, "Me?" She hesitated, and then continued, "The people of the world you go to call me by many names. You may call me 'Quan Yin', the name used by the villagers whom you will soon join in your next incarnation."

Then Quan Yin continued in her soft voice to explain to Serra about the soul's journey.

"Once you reincarnate into a new life, another body, you won't remember anything. You and Lohkan will not see each other for several lifetimes. When you do see each other all of this will be forgotten," she said as she gestured to their surroundings with a graceful arch of her arm. "If you remember anything, the memories will be disjointed and nonsensical visions that will have little relevance to whatever lifetime you are experiencing."

Serra's mind felt slightly foggy with images and questions.

And yet a peace had settled over her that strengthened while it soothed. Her thoughts became quiet. Her emotions became balanced by an inner knowing that she had at last come home.

Home was this beautiful place with this comforting stranger, who explained life, death and the many choices that faced her. Home was the brilliant light that filled her with love as naturally as air entered her lungs. This loving light sheltered her heart and mind as she made her transition to this place of *between* lifetimes. Serra refocused her mind on the woman, this guide, and her compassionate words.

"Love is the essence of each soul, and the soul never dies. It changes, grows, but does not perish. Although you and Lohkan will not remember each other physically when you leave *the between*, your souls will recognize each other; the love you share will continue to grow."

"Then why did I grieve Lohkan's death? Why does part of my soul still miss him?"

"Grief itself is the celebration of life. You cannot deeply miss or mourn something unless you lived it fully or loved it completely. The depth of your grief is the symbol of how completely you loved and lived life with Lohkan. If you chose to deny these emotions you would have denied parts of your being. Only part of yourself would have lived. Only part of you would have 'felt' life. By experiencing *all* of your emotions, *all* of you lived. Eventually your grief will transform into a feeling of joy for having lived with and loved him. Neither death nor life can sever the love that is between you and Lohkan!"

Serra smiled as the meaning of Quan Yin's words passed her mind and reached into her heart. Another sense of peace washed over her. The soul existed without limit. Love was at the heart of each soul. Therefore, love was limitless in its reaches. Quan Yin returned her smile, and then Serra continued.

"This sounds so simple. Can it be true?"

"You will recognize truth by its simplicity. All else is the ego decorating truth," Quan Yin said gently.

Serra smiled at Quan Yin and her guileless answer, and this time allowed herself to accept its uncomplicated message.

"It is now time for you to go. You go to a primitive but important people, these humans. You will learn much. I shall walk beside you once you are there, though you will not remember me. What you are about to learn will not be easy, but you will need to have this knowledge in order to survive on this planet. Are you ready, Serra?"

"Yes."

"Please hold up your hands in this fashion." Serra mimicked the beautiful guide's gesture and cupped her hands together in front of herself. Quan Yin dropped one small, lustrous pearl into Serra's outstretched palms. The meadow vanished as Serra felt this pearl sink through her palm and down into her body. Serra followed the pearl as it sank through deep water and downward. Her entire focus was the pearl. The pearl became part of her. As she followed the pearl downward, all about her grew darker and darker. At last the darkness overcame her and all consciousness vanished.

Chapter 2

*D*awn brought another sharp pain which ran down Falling Petal's back. She gasped again and clenched her teeth as she bore down on the baby inside her womb. She had pushed for hours; most of the night had passed as she had struggled with the labor. Yet the baby seemed reluctant to enter this world. Falling Petal had begun to worry. Perhaps the baby knew something that she did not. After all, babies came from the other world. They carried knowledge of dead ancestors and the gods. Perhaps this baby had been warned not to come by her husband's dead mother.

Her breath came in a painful grunt as another contraction seared through her abdomen. Maybe she should send for the midwife. She called her husband's name.

"Chan!"

His worried face appeared through the window of their shack. She did not need to speak. Her expression told him everything. For a moment he hesitated, for he was afraid to leave her alone, but then he ran quickly toward the village.

An hour later he returned with the village midwife and her assistant, a young girl. They entered the small shack and stared silently at the new face before them. A girl. She was small, delicate and pale. The midwife watched as Chan realized that his wife's body no longer held life. Blood lay in a dark pool under her legs, on the earthen floor. Her exhausted body lay slumped around the baby, who was strangely quiet. The midwife shook her head slowly as she observed the scene. She pried the tiny baby from the mother's fingers, which were clutched around her child even after death. The midwife stared into two coal black eyes that stared openly back at her.

This baby was unusual. Most babies did not come into this world with their spirits attached. She had seen hundreds of births and knew that the spirit did not enter the body until a baby was several days old. When the baby's eyes saw the world around it, then the spirit entered the body. A girl baby with the spirit present at birth was very unusual. The midwife shook her head again. She would need to ask the monks what this meant. Meanwhile, the baby continued to watch her as if the little being could read her thoughts. The midwife felt the unnerving sensation of one soul reaching out to another. A mind probed her own, and a shudder spread down through her body as she again realized this baby's uniqueness.

The midwife turned to the father who had carefully covered his wife's body. His face was grave and devoid of expression, as if he wore one of the death masks for which his village was known. Upon seeing his expression, she quickly decided to say little.

"I shall care for the baby while you get Falling Petal's sister," the midwife stated.

In this village, custom dictated that the eldest sister cared for the dead body of any younger siblings. If Falling Petal's sister had been dead, her husband's older sister would have had to take this responsibility upon herself. If the husband had no older sister, then the oldest sister in a closely related family would be found to carry out the funeral preparations. Always, this responsibility fell upon an oldest sister. They came first from the spirit world, and therefore had the most knowledge of the other world. Because they were women and were able to give life, their power was doubled in strength in matters which concerned the spirit world. A woman was always in touch with the spirits, since at any time she might be called upon to conceive a life. That life, a baby, of course required a soul. All of this was common knowledge amongst Falling Petal's people. Falling Petal's oldest sister was alive. Chan's first responsibility now was to travel to his sister-in-law's home, to tell her this news.

The midwife fueled the small fire, which Falling Petal had built only a few hours ago. She filled a clay pot with water and placed it over the fire to heat. From a pouch which was tied around her neck, she took a handful of blessing herbs. They would be used for the baby. She threw them into the water and a potent fragrance filled the small hut.

The baby remained silent. She watched the midwife with her dark eyes. The midwife shuddered once more as the baby observed her movements. Quickly, the midwife turned her back to the baby and began to chant. While the prayers were completed, the water heated and infused the herbs. A gentle antiseptic had been produced. The midwife noted how carefully Falling Petal had tied off the umbilical cord with long strands of her own black hair. She must have done so with her last breath. The knife she had used lay beside her. Falling Petal had washed it carefully in another herbal solution infused for this purpose. The decoction was similar to the blessing infusion, but stronger.

Falling Petal had prepared properly for the birth. Outside the house, incense burned as an offering to placate the gods. A white cloth hung outside, over the windows, to reflect death. What had happened? What had gone wrong? Obviously the gods had needed Falling Petal, since they had taken her to their world. Sometimes the gods worked in this manner. What plans did the gods have for this strange child?

She began washing the child carefully with the blessing solution. She washed the baby's head first, beginning at the crest of the baby's skull where the spirit would enter. Yet the spirit had already entered this child. Even now her black eyes followed the midwife's hand as she was washed. Maybe, the midwife thought, she should kill the baby *now*, immediately, before the child brought bad luck to the village.

She wrapped the baby in the cloth in which Falling Petal had first placed her. Even this Falling Petal had done right. Good luck symbols had been thoughtfully sewn on the corners of the purple cloth. The midwife wondered what Falling Petal had sold to afford the silk for the delicate embroidery. She sadly shook her head.

The baby was also unusually beautiful. Her skin was soft and pale pink, like an apple blossom. The midwife stared at the little girl and again felt a mind probing hers. She started in fear. Quickly, she recited a chant that would ward off evil spirits. At that moment, she made a decision. She prayed loudly and asked for protection and strength. After telling her assistant of her plan, she picked up the baby and carried it out of the hut.

A few hours later she stood outside the monk's temple walls. Tired and dusty from her long journey, but unaware of her fatigue, she waited impatiently for someone to answer. She rang the bell again and waited. Within a few minutes, a monk who was dressed in the long robes of a novice opened the gate. The midwife bowed low to the ground before she addressed the monk.

"Please, may I speak to your most honored teacher?"

The young monk nodded his bald head and retreated to fetch his master. The midwife waited nervously and paced tiredly back and forth. Soon, an old man stepped from a side building of the temple and approached the midwife. His countenance was gentle and sympathetic. He stared first at the woman and then at the child. He nodded to the woman to speak.

"Honored one, I bring a child. I must ask for your learned wisdom about this baby, but I am unworthy."

The monk nodded solemnly toward an altar which stood nearby. The midwife carefully placed the baby on the ground beneath a tree. Then, with her head bowed, she approached the altar where a large statue of Buddha sat serenely in a garden. The midwife reached into her pouch and took out a stick of incense which she placed at the base of the alter. She whispered her gratitude to Buddha. The frightened woman declared how unworthy she was of his attention. Quickly she explained that she would not have come if it wasn't for the little being lying beneath the tree. If Buddha would keep plague and famine from her village, she explained, she would be eternally grateful. The midwife completed her prayers as she asked Buddha to cast out this evil in the form of a baby, and she promised to bring Buddha a stick of incense once a year on this date for the rest of her life. Then she stood and turned back to the monk.

The monk gestured for her to follow him to the temple, a building beautiful in the simplicity of its structure and the complexity of its decorations. Carved symbols of deities and stories of the afterlife covered the whitewashed walls in bright red, blues and yellows. The midwife picked up the baby, who had remained silent throughout her prostrations, and followed him under the carved archway and into the temple.

The old monk watched as the midwife left. She seemed greatly relieved. He observed her as she bowed respectfully toward the altar and then quickly ran the last few feet out through the gate to freedom. Once she had left, he spoke to his servant, who stood nearby awaiting instructions.

"Have the cook heat enough water to make tea and to wash this baby. Then bring the tea to me with the bowl of water and a clean cloth. Bring a warmed blanket in which to wrap this child."

He nodded graciously toward the servant, dismissing him. As the servant bowed and left, the monk turned his attention to the baby. What an unusual child she was, beautiful and delicate.

He had thought the baby dead, so still had she lain while the old midwife had prayed. Soulful black eyes stared back at him. Those eyes! They looked into his soul and saw through him.

The midwife had walked the long path up the mountainside from her village to ask for help, as she was certain that the baby was possessed by an evil spirit. She had wanted permission to kill the child, to send the evil back from where it had come. And she had demanded immediate action, before this evil cast an unlucky spell over her village. The small woman had been frightened enough not to consult the family of this child. Instead, she had stolen the child and had, thankfully, brought the baby to the temple.

The monk shook his head sadly. No family would want such a baby. If the midwife told the family what she believed, and she certainly would, the family itself would quietly kill the child. His bald and wrinkled head bent lower as he examined this newborn. His flat, even features disclosed none of his sadness. The late afternoon shadows fell across his robed and stooped figure and caused him to blend into the shadows of the stark and dimly lit room. He kneeled on the woven mat, picked up the child and rocked her soothingly in his arms. Her mouth curled up in a smile as her dark eyes watched his.

What was this?

A smile! *She smiles on the day of her birth,* the old man thought. This was impossible, was it not? This was indeed a special child. He was not sure if this child was evil. Yet he did not think that she was. Nothing about this child seemed evil, simply different. She sensed his compassion and cooed softly. *Such a beautiful child,* he mused. *Gentle and patient.*

The practical necessities of the child's care occurred to him in that moment. One of the monastery's servants had a wife who nursed a year-old son. The baby would live with this servant and his wife until she grew to an age when she might serve. The wife undoubtably would be frightened, but she must be convinced to treat the child carefully. When the girl came of age she would serve the monastery. Although the monk doubted that this baby was evil, a lifetime of servitude to the monks would cancel any possible sinister karmic bonds. Perhaps this was why the child had been brought to them. Yes, this theory explained much. The midwife, in her natural wisdom, had known this. He looked at the baby's peaceful face and immediately doubted this theory. Could this child truly be evil? No. He decided not.

When the servant returned, he sent the young man to bring the gardener's wife. The gardener and his small family lived in a hut outside the temple walls. Once the servant left, his mind again went back to the child.

The child needed a name. A name was needed that would suit an unusual baby, one that would ward off evil as well as be lucky. He sat silently and drank tea while he meditated on this. Through the window a view of the garden, with its tranquil pool and lotus blossoms, caught his eye. Lotus blossoms. Were they not the favorite of Buddha? Would a name such as this not catch Buddha's attention? Lotus Blossom. It was a lucky name.

A few minutes passed before the servant returned with the gardener's wife. She bowed low to the floor and awaited instructions.

"Buddha has sent us a child who is special. You will care for her until she is ready to serve. Treat this child with care, as if she were your own. Remember – she is not. She belongs to Buddha," the old monk carefully explained.

The woman accepted the child gratefully. This was an honor for a humble servant. She was pleased ... until she looked into the baby's eyes. She trembled. The old monk saw her fear arise and try to take hold. He touched the frightened woman's arm gently as he spoke.

"This one has been sent to cancel all the unlucky experiences of her ancestors. She is protected by the goddess of compassion herself," he said as he wisely guessed the truth. "You may take her to raise until we need her, and all bad luck will be cancelled throughout your family for many generations."

The words were an act of sympathy. This woman could not truly refuse without losing her position. She was a servant in an honored place. Her husband was a gardener for the monks. The old monk knew that this servant now wondered about the bad luck that had brought this child to her. He watched as she barely controlled her shaking, bowed again and sadly picked up the baby.

Lotus Blossom rubbed sand carefully into the bowl she held, to scrape out any stains that were there. When the bowl was sanded clean, she began on the next. The pile of evening dishes was almost clean now. A clear, rose-colored light washed over the room as the setting sun blessed the end of the day with its serene radiance.

A pink ray of sunlight fell on her black hair, which was plaited into a long, thick and shiny braid. The braid hung down her back and was dramatically attractive on her plain and unadorned figure. Her dress, which was dark and comfortable, was very worn. Her feet were bare and her hands had been roughened by years of hard work. She looked up with her large black eyes as she heard the sound of the gate bell ringing behind her and turned absentmindedly to see who had arrived.

Through the kitchen window she spotted the figure of a stooped old woman. The shrouded figure hobbled to the altar that stood in the garden. Her clothes were as threadbare as the thin wisps of gray hair that sparsely covered her scalp. She stared momentarily toward the kitchen, from an ancient face with a toothless mouth and eyes that were more gray than brown. A hint of fear touched the woman's movements.

Lotus Blossom stared back calmly. Was it really her birthday again? How had a whole year passed so quickly? No one had told her, or celebrated this day. Lotus knew by the woman's presence in the courtyard. Once a year, the old woman came to bring an offering to the altar. Once Lotus had asked the old monk, who was dead now, who this woman was. He had told her that this was the midwife who had carried Lotus to the door of the temple. She had delivered Lotus to the old monk himself.

Over the years, no one had told Lotus that the midwife arrived specifically on her birthday. Lotus had seen and known this for herself, as she was able to know so many things.

Her knowing had once been more vast, but now seemed dim in comparison. As a child she had effortlessly seen and understood the world around her. Lotus Blossom did not know how she was able to hear other people's thoughts. She heard the thoughts of the monks in their daily meditations in the same way that others heard the sound of the wind. She heard the inner ramblings of the gardener, his wife and their son as they went about their daily chores. She did not understand that the others did not have this ability. And as her ability revealed itself to those around her, their discomfort intensified. She winced as she remembered her earlier years in the monastery.

"Lotus Blossom, what are you doing? Why do you stand there like that? Have you finished sweeping the rooms?" the gardner's wife asked resentfully.

"Yes, Mother. I am done."

"Go to the monks. Perhaps they need you."

"Yes," the young girl answered obediently. Her stepmother's angry thoughts floated after her.

Only one son. I have born no other children to my honorable husband. He does not look upon me as he once did. I bring him only shame. What if he gives me away? What if he chooses another wife? Lotus' bad luck frightens away the children in my womb. Do the ancestors not hear my prayers? The Gods punish Lotus Blossom and the house she lives in! It is her bad luck that curses our home!

"Why would father give you away, Mother?"

"What? I said nothing! Go!" her stepmother had answered; and then she had uneasily watched Lotus' small figure retreat into the monastery walls.

Her stepbrother had been meaner. He had cruelly enacted the resentment her stepmother had felt. He had beaten Lotus whenever she had been slow to respond; he had treated her scornfully, and his thoughts had mercilessly reflected the physical beatings.

"Lotus! You move like the snail!"

"I am hurrying, Brother."

"Bring the water!"

"Yes, Brother," she said and bowed her head. As she rushed to carry the water to him, she tripped, knocked over the wooden bucket and spilled most of the water on the ground. Her stepbrother reacted quickly. He jumped up, grabbed a cane and began to beat the bottoms of her feet. She buried her head beneath her small arms, but was not able to hide from his thoughts.

Stupid girl! See how she cowers! What good is she to us, to the monks, to anyone?

"I am not stupid," she mumbled tearfully into her arms. For a moment the beating stopped, and then he began again with the renewed force of fear. This time his mind had been silent.

Over the years Lotus Blossom had taught herself not to listen. More and more she withdrew into herself. Inside herself she created a sanctuary where none could harm her; neither her stepmother's bitter thoughts, nor her stepbrother's harsh words reached her any more.

Only the old monk had responded to her sensitive mind, her strange abilities, with a gentleness that she had come to treasure. The old monk's face had been the only one to show genuine affection for her. And he had often, with his wide and gentle smile. The younger monks followed the old monk's example, and accepted Lotus into their world. But, they reacted to her with a reservedness she knew was born from fear.

The day had come when the old monk had called her to his bedside. His body had shrunken on his frame until his bones stood out in sharp angles beneath his flesh. His shaking fingers grasped her arm and he whispered to her.

"You will be alone now, Lotus Blossom. I have spoken to the others, and they will let you live here as long as you want. You must remember what you have been taught. Be obedient, Lotus. Ask Buddha for guidance and he will help you."

Tears spilled from her beautiful almond shaped eyes. She begged the old monk not to leave her.

"Please, take me with you. What shall I do? The others are afraid of me. Where shall I find my peace without you?"

The old monk's eyes blazed momentarily before he spoke.

"Lotus Blossom, have you learned so little? The only peace you will find is within you! I, or anyone else, cannot give you your happiness. Serve Buddha well and you will find your peace."

Lotus bowed, ashamed of her outburst. She did not know the words for what she felt, because no one had ever said the words to her. She *loved* the old monk and was already grieving her loss. She bowed humbly and asked for forgiveness. His expression softened as he stroked her hand.

"Lotus, you will not be alone. I shall pray for guidance for you as I cross over into the other world."

His hand tightened on hers. Their eyes met. Both sets of eyes were moist. A shudder passed through his body and his grip loosened and then fell. Lotus Blossom cried by his body for hours. She never again spoke of him, and from that moment an aching loneliness grew inside her. It started as a small pain that had grown into a huge void over the years. Near the doorway of her bedroom were eight marks she had notched in the plaster: one for each year since the old monk had died. Her pain was eight times as large as when it had begun.

Now, as the old midwife turned to stare at her before she began her frail descent down the mountain, Lotus felt nothing. Most of her knowing was gone. The knowing, which had been a part of her many years ago, had been replaced by her pain, her loneliness. The old woman's gaze fell away and turned inward. She sensed the change in Lotus. Her fears of Lotus had visibly lessened as Lotus' pain had grown. If Lotus Blossom had been aware, she would have known that that which had made her different existed less and less. She could not see this. Her pain was too consuming.

✳

The next day a visitor brought with him a disease that traveled quickly through the isolated monastery. Within a month, two of the older monks were dead from the influenza the visitor had brought. After another month, Lotus lay on her bed and breathed one last, rattling breath before she, too, joined them.

"the between ..."

Serra felt the intense presence of the white light around her again. A vast love filled her and for the moment eased any pain she had known as Lotus. Suddenly, the soothing beauty of the grassy meadow surrounded her. She opened her eyes to the now-familiar view. Before her sat the guide she had met earlier, Quan Yin.

Had she dreamed? How long had she been gone? Years? Months? Minutes? Already the experience as Lotus Blossom was taking on a dreamlike quality. A fog drifted over the meadow. Quan Yin, who sat nearby, smiled. Her voice tinkled across the grass to where Serra sat.

"What did you learn, Serra?"

Serra sat thoughtfully. Her mind still felt clouded and confused. Quan Yin's laughter floated across to her and washed over her in a warmth of comforting waves. Her laughter ceased and she spoke.

"Let us view this life and perhaps your mind will clear. Would you like to do this?"

"Yes," Serra answered immediately.

Near her, a dense patch of fog parted and a scene took form. Serra watched as image after image appeared quickly before her, starting with the birth of Lotus Blossom. She watched Lotus grow and learn to serve. She saw the reactions of the people to Lotus. She watched the death of the old monk, only this time she had not the deep pain, but a sense of order and rightness. Suddenly, she knew. The images vanished and Quan Yin questioned her.

"Yes? What have you learned, Serra?"

Serra answered slowly, but with assurance.

"The people on this planet are afraid of anyone who is different. I learned that they could not accept me until I became like them ... in pain. I felt how deeply connected these people are, even in these primitive states. By cutting off one of themselves from the group, in this case, Lotus, they were in essence cutting off a part of the whole. Although they don't intellectually know this yet, I can see that they will. These humans are on the verge of discovering this connection. Their growth is wondrous!" Serra exclaimed as she looked into the guide's eyes. She continued, "Also, I can see that the old monk was right. **Each individual is responsible for creating his or her own peace and happiness.** And I learned more, so much more that I know I haven't yet begun to discover!"

Quan Yin's eyes filled with a light that seemed to draw Serra into them. When she spoke, the guide's voice came from a great distance.

"Ah, Serra, you are right. There is more, but you have learned more than we had hoped!"

Chapter 3

"the between ..."

*L*ohkan felt a swirling darkness surround him, and then a great burst of light shot through him. The light muted all his senses, and then as suddenly cleared away.

He was left by a deep pond. Above the pond, a cascade of water tumbled down rocks and landed noisily in the pool at the bottom. A bank covered with spongy green moss ran along the edge of the pool to where he now stood. He could feel the velvety coolness of the moss beneath his feet. Here his senses were sharpened and all he saw seemed acutely focused and surreal. He breathed deeply, and discovered that the air contained a freshness that was intoxicating. He breathed more deeply than before, and then again. He did not recognize the scent. It was sweet, yet pungent, while at the same time subtle. This air held a strange, but appealing, mixture of aromas. He continued to breathe in the air as a drought-stricken man might gulp water. Several minutes passed before he realized he was not alone.

Near the pool where the moss took shelter under a group of slender trees stood a small man. His features were well defined and appeared large on his small head. Two tiny black eyes stared out from a cinnamon-brown face. The man's lips parted into a large white grin as Lohkan's eyes met his. He was naked, except for a light-colored wrap which was draped in folds around his waist. The garment was tied carefully with a belt made by the weaving of many colored thongs, all interlaced into a complicated pattern of braids and knots. Down one side of the belt hung a large bundle of snowy white feathers; within their midst hung one brilliant red feather. The small man opened his mouth and a breath of warm air blew forth and across Lohkan. The scent

Lohkan had been enjoying came from this man. His breath surrounded Lohkan in a warm embrace and an enormous love filled
his soul. A chuckle emitted from the brown lips, and the small
man serenely walked over to where Lohkan stood. Another
moment passed before Lohkan realized that they were looking at
each other at eye level. He did not remember sitting down.

"Where am I? Who are you?" Lohkan asked.

The brown man nodded silently and then began a communication without verbal words. He signed his message with his
hands and Lohkan heard a story in his mind simultaneously. The
mind that touched his was tranquil and loving. As Lohkan
watched the small man's gestures, he fell into a light trance state.

*You are near the Uxmahra Falls. Once, before you were
born, before your people were born, another race lived here. I
am 'Tonak', eldest of that race. When your people immigrated to
this place, my people were here. Beyond those trees are more
trees. Beyond those trees lies an ocean. If you were to follow that
ocean to where it once again meets and plays with the mountains,
and where the mountains lose their strength and lay down, you
would find a vast lake. There you would find your home. But,
that is not why you are here. You are here to rest before your next
journey. I am here to prepare you. Do you have any questions?*

The man's hands fell silent and Lohkan's mind felt strangely empty as his words ended. He sat for some time and contemplated his surroundings. Tonak seemed in no hurry and waited
patiently as Lohkan's mind adjusted to this place. Lohkan's mind
drifted aimlessly. In its wanderings a question was found.

"How did I get here?"

You thought this, Tonak answered simply, and touched
Lohkan's temple with one small brown finger.

"I thought this...?" Lohkan answered and questioned
at once.

When you were a boy, you dreamed of coming here, the
elder continued to explain. *Your desire was strong enough to be
heard. You thought this,* he repeated again.

"Is this a dream?" Lohkan asked.

No, Tonak answered.

"Is this real?" Lohkan asked next.

The small man's chuckles echoed around him. The laughter ran around the trees and washed up against the waterfall and
fell quietly into Lohkan's ears.

You might ask, "Am I real?" Tonak signed, and patted himself solidly on the chest. Then he answered Lohkan's question.

No. Not as you think of real.

"If this is not real, and it is not a dream, then what is it?" Lohkan was at a loss to describe what he did not understand. The man nodded knowingly.

This is "between."

"Between ..." Lohkan tried to comprehend. "Between what?"

The elder pulled off his belt and held it up for Lohkan to see. He pointed to the spaces between the thongs, between the braids and knots.

It is between. The between holds all worlds together!

He looked into Lohkan's eyes to see if he understood. Lohkan shook his head slowly, to indicate that he did not understand. Tonak smiled gently and nodded. He questioned Lohkan again.

Do you have any any other questions? If not, you may rest.

"No," Lohkan answered. He was tired and wanted only to sleep.

Lie down, Lohkan. Rest.

"What?" he asked drowsily.

Rest, Tonak repeated gently.

Lohkan awoke from a long dream in which he and Serra had been talking about their plans for the different incarnations they might choose on this planet. Serra wanted to try living in Asia. He had decided to live his first life on a South Pacific island. Serra's beauty and warm touch lingered in his heart, and as he came more fully awake, he wondered, *Was I dreaming? Was I really with Serra again?*

As his mind puzzled these questions, the elder appeared before him.

It is time for you to go. Do you have any questions?

"Yes. How will I go from here to...?"

The elder stopped Lohkan with a raised palm. He held up one finger, again pulled off his belt and pointed to it.

Do you see "between?"

"Yes," Lohkan answered, still puzzled.

It does not need to go anywhere. It is already there, next to this strand of leather. He pointed to one brightly colored piece of leather that ran through the belt. Its deep turquoise color suddenly seemed more vibrant than the rest. The elder continued.

It is one.

"One what?"

One lifetime. Watch how it weaves itself in and out through the belt, touching all other lifetimes. Follow it through the belt.

"I don't understand," Lohkan said.

Look. Follow it, Tonak encouraged him gently. As Lohkan stared at the belt, it grew larger. Now it was immense. He found himself walking down a turquoise path.

Follow the sound of the flute music.

"What?" Lohkan asked. An answer followed his question immediately. The sound of flutes playing was somewhere off to his left. He moved down the path and toward the sound. The flutes filled him with a kaleidoscopic symphony. Above him the purple sky had turned into night, a black sky filled with sparkling stars. The stars seemed to sparkle in tune to the music. The road turned around a curve and the night grew blacker, the music grew louder and his consciousness faded.

Lohkan felt water all around him: in his ears, in his nose, down his throat. He floated in a warm liquid which fed and nourished him. He could not see or open his eyes. He struggled to move, kicking out sporadically with his legs. What had happened? Had he somehow walked off the turquoise road and fallen into the pond? Yes. That was it. He became frantic and tried to grab onto something, anything. And then he heard the flute music again. This time the music warbled as if it were coming from a distance and through water. Tonak had told him to follow the sound of the flute. He tried to swim, but a restrictive wall was in his way. Renewed panic overcame him and he tried again to kick free and swim toward the surface. In the distance, a voice could be heard through his outburst.

"He hears and is trying to break free!"

The flute music became louder.

Lohkan wondered, *What is happening?* And then, *Where am I? If I am trapped, then why do they not help me? Can I drown here in* the between?

Lohkan's thoughts went unanswered. He decided to try to find a way out of this underwater trap. He rested for a moment and then began an even stronger attempt to get through the wall. The music stopped and an incantation could be heard, though the words were muted into indiscernible chants. Next he heard a voice yell.

"The baby kicks hard! Aagh, I think he hears!"

Another voice answered, but, again, Lohkan could not

make out the words. Suddenly, he heard the first voice groan, and then an enormous pressure squeezed his body from all sides. He gasped and drew in a large lungful of liquid. *What is going on here?* he thought furiously. He had agreed to take the body of a baby boy who was to be born to a tribes woman in the South Pacific. His mind cleared and he knew at once. He was that baby, about to be born! The pressure intensified and the woman's groans became screams. The liquid compacted and pushed him about like a lost seal.

Instinctively, Lohkan reached out with his tiny hands and tried to grasp anything he could find to hold onto, to slow his entry into the world. He did not want to leave the safe cushion of this womb. Even as he had these thoughts, he wondered at them. These instincts overrode all else. He grasped and searched in a futile attempt to stay there. The pressure intensified, and he felt himself pushed down into a tight-fitting tunnel. The liquid felt as if it were draining away, wrung from his lungs. His feet pushed forward through this warm, dark tunnel, while his head remained caught in a vise-like grip. As a strong hand grabbed onto his feet, he tried to grasp onto the sides of the tunnel one last time before he was squeezed out into an obnoxiously bright world.

He announced his displeasure with one loud cry.

For days his visible world had been a strange black and white blur. Some colors leaked through, but were diffused into a nondescriptive gray. What were clear, though, were his auditory senses. In fact, his hearing was acutely refined. The adults around him spoke in loud booming voices. Lohkan longed more then ever for the muted safety of the womb.

With each passing day, one face and voice became more distinct and familiar. The voice belonged to a breast that sated his hunger and need to be held. The voice sang songs that filled Lohkan with a deep sense of love. The voice cleaned him and told him how big and strong he was. Lohkan wondered about the appearance of the face that belonged to the voice.

Gradually, a face began to take shape. The face that belonged to the voice had an intricate tattoo that covered its mouth and wide cheeks. The voice told him that the face was to be called "Moma." Moma told him that she adored him while Lohkan traced the tattooed pattern on her cheeks with his small pudgy hands.

Lohkan learned that Moma lived with another face named "Popa", though Popa was often not allowed near him. Moma was careful whom she let near him, even to the point of monitoring Popa's visits. Lohkan did not mind. He had grown to trust this woman who wanted to be called Moma.

One day Lohkan felt the heat of the day in the middle of the night. He whimpered, and Moma awoke to check on him. When her careful hands felt this heat, she cried out in alarm. She picked him up and carried him somewhere, to another place where another tattooed woman lived.

Her face was older and her tattoos were disfigured by wrinkles folding one into the other. Lohkan thought that this might be more fascinating if he weren't quite so hot. The old woman with the wrinkled face placed large wet leaves all over his body. Although the leaves felt good, they did little to cool him, and he wondered why she did not just bathe him in a cool bath. The wrinkled face distorted into horrifying grimaces as she chanted over his small body. The heat in his body intensified and the room about him began to spin.

A split second later, Lohkan found himself floating on the ceiling above the baby, Moma and the old woman. Moma's face looked pained, and Lohkan watched as she turned to the healer for comfort.

The healer placed her hands gently on the young woman's shoulders. Her old, tattooed face filled with compassion for the young woman's loss and then slowly she began to explain about the baby's passage to the spirit world. Comprehension and then denial alternated on Moma's face. Lohkan recognized death now, and watched as the old woman soulfully began a death chant. The room began to spin again, and he found himself racing toward the white light.

"the between ..."

Tonak awaited Lohkan by the waterfall. Lohkan questioned him before he even breathed in the sweet air.

"What happened? I agreed to live that life on a South Pacific Island."

And so you did, the elder signed. *What did you learn?*

"That babies have consciousness!" Lohkan exclaimed. "I thought I would forget who I was! As this baby, I felt and heard everything around me!" he said in an excited voice. "I don't remember that from when I was born into the body that I knew as Lohkan," he ended; confusion tainted his voice.

Tonak tried to explain.

When a soul takes on a human body, it remembers the between *for a limited time. As the body grows, the soul's memory departs. By the time most individuals complete a lifetime, all memory of other lifetimes and dimensions is removed. This is necessary in order for most individuals to retain their focus on the life, the lessons, that they choose.*

Lohkan sat in amazed silence. When he spoke, it was to ask a question.

"Do all souls enter bodies at the same age?"

No, answered the elder. *Some do not wish to have this experience and enter at a later time. The closer to the birth moment that the soul enters the body, the more the soul carries with it knowledge of other dimensions. You entered in the womb, and so your memories were mostly intact. If you had lived, your memories would have faded as you grew older.*

Tonak's hands remained motionless, and then he began to speak once more.

Babies are always born with varying degrees of awareness. What else have you learned from this lifetime, Lohkan?

Lohkan answered thoughtfully.

"We were sent here to study life forms and the human race, and their environments. In my previous incarnated life during those studies, I noted that this is a superstitious people fixated on rituals and ceremonies."

Lohkan fell silent and the elder waited for him to continue.

"Just now, I experienced the value of these ceremonies and rituals as I floated above my body. I saw that Moma will find peace, knowing I have been assisted to the spirit world by her medicine woman. It does not matter whether her beliefs or views of 'the spirit world' are true. What is important is the comfort and peace she is finding in these ceremonies. While the people of this planet react superstitiously, the rituals they uphold have an important purpose."

The small man smiled. Large white teeth shone across his face in a reflective grin. He signed deftly while he spoke telepathically.

Lohkan, do you understand that your people, and others, do not have these rituals and ceremonies because they are not needed?

Lohkan nodded yes. Finally, he was beginning to understand. Tonak continued.

All that happens throughout the universe has reason, has a purpose, a source. All reason, purpose, is guided. Nothing occurs without guidance! *Do you understand this?*

Again Lohkan nodded silently. The moss beneath his hands and feet felt luxuriantly soft. The small man's hands were hypnotically calming. A newer knowledge was growing inside of Lohkan. An inner awareness of something larger than he had ever expected awaited him. He nodded to Tonak that he understood. Ceremonies, and each part of life, held a purpose! And babies ... babies were keenly aware!

He felt a deep peace wash over him as he breathed in the sweet scent of the air. The waterfall fell gracefully behind the elder. Lohkan watched it and felt a deep weariness overcome him. The elder patted the moss next to him. Lohkan felt himself lie down. And then he fell into a deep sleep wherein he had no awareness at all.

Chapter 4

*F*rom underneath all the rubble, a young voice could be heard crying out for help. The men worked faster and lifted dirt, wood and rock from the pile. One man found the broken pieces of an infant's cradle. He held them up to the mother who waited nearby. She screamed and clutched the air in a futile attempt to grab them. She could not, for the man stood several feet away, on the edge of the pile. The man placed the shards tenderly on the ground. The child's voice fell silent as he did and the crew stopped working. The mother groaned and fell to her knees in fitful pleas. Another man ordered the group to continue the work. After he did so, he stepped over to the prostrate mother.

"Gina, go to your mother's house and rest. The men may work for hours. You will exhaust yourself while you wait."

He did not say that the wait would most likely prove to be a fruitless and painful one. Chances were that the child would die long before they were able to dig him out. Throughout the village people were digging through the large piles of rubble that once, several minutes before, had been homes. Only three men could be found to try to dig out this particular child.

In a larger area of town whole families and groups had been buried. Gina's husband had been killed instantly by a rock falling from an avalanche that had been started by the earthquake. Most of the eastern side of the village, closest to the mountain, had been buried under rock, dirt and debris. Her mother's house had been left sound. Gina's home had not been so lucky. She faced the leader now and shook her head vehemently and said, "No!" She strode past him and began to lift large rocks from the pile.

Two hours passed before the boy was found. A man yelled

out and Gina pushed everyone aside as she attempted to get at her son. They had not heard even a whimper from the child for the past hour. The men stepped back reverently, knowing the child would be dead. The one who had found him had only to glimpse at him to know the sad truth; the boy lay motionless and did not breathe. This man closed his eyes in sorrow as Gina pushed him away.

Gina carefully moved the last few branches out of the way, and beneath these one large wooden beam lay across the boy. Her breath caught in her throat and a sob choked her as she froze, staring at her young son. His black curly hair was covered with a thick layer of dirt, and his soft brown eyes were closed behind lids that were hidden under dirt and death. Tears blurred her vision for a moment, until she wiped them away angrily with one harsh movement of her hand. As she did, she reached down with her other hand to lift the boy's head. She froze again when she noticed that the beam did not weigh down on the boy.

Gina cautiously felt around the beam and found that there was a half-inch space between her son and the wooden beam; dirt loosely filled in this space. She gasped and felt her son's body quickly with gentle hands. No broken bones! Yet he did not seem to breathe. Hastily, she called out to the surrounding men. The leader, Caesar, climbed over the pile to Gina's side.

"If we are careful, we may be able to dig around him and lift him out," Caesar announced after examining the boy. Quickly Caesar directed those around him.

"Move back! We must not put too much weight on this area. It could collapse! No, Gina! You, too, must wait over there," Caesar said as she tried to step closer to watch. Gina stepped back after strong, but sympathetic, hands drew her away.

Caesar stayed and carefully pulled rocks off the dirt pile, using his hands as a shovel to move the dirt which encased the rocks. Soon he and another man had dug a large hole around the boy's shoulders, middle and head. Although they could not see the boy's feet, they decided to attempt to pull him free. They could only hope that the boy's feet and legs were not trapped. Each moment that passed brought the added danger of another aftershock. They had to try to remove the boy now, while they had him, or he could be buried again. He was probably dead anyway, but they had to try. Gina would not have allowed any other option. As Caesar put his hand on the boys neck to lift him, he knew. Tears welled up into his dark eyes, and he swallowed before he called out to Gina.

"Gina?"

She answered with her eyes; they stared at him with an intense pleading. She saw his tears and began to tremble. He answered her gently and absolutely.

"He's alive."

✳

"Thank you for letting Antonio live," Gina whispered.

Antonio watched his mother's bowed head as she prayed in the morning light. The sunlight caught her beauty and reflected it out to the world in a halo of golden light which surrounded her dark hair. Her gentle features and deep brown eyes were the most beautiful sight Antonio saw each day. He reached out, clasped her hand and smiled up at her.

Black curls covered his small head. His face was long and oval, as his father's had been, and he smiled often and easily, like his mother. His nose was small and straight, also like his father's. His expressive brown eyes watched as Gina went to the stove and began to prepare breakfast.

The pastel walls of their small house filled the room with warmth and light. Herbs hung from the darkened and exposed beams of the ceiling. Rough ceramic bowls were piled on a wooden shelf on one wall. In the corner sat Grandmama's chair, with its worn red pillow on the seat. Antonio limped happily across the floor, pushed himself onto a stool and sat patiently at the old wooden table, which was pushed up against one of the gold-colored walls. As he did, his grandmother stepped into the kitchen. She greeted Antonio happily.

"Antonio! How does your foot feel today?"

"Good, Grandmama!"

"No pain?"

"No! Look!" he said cheerfully.

He jumped from the stool and limped awkwardly to his grandmother, and then back to his stool.

"Ah, your foot grows strong, Grandson!" She turned to her daughter and spoke quickly. "Gina, go to the well and get some water."

"Mama, look! There is a bucket of water there by the table," Gina protested softly.

"This is not enough water to make bread. I want to get an early start before the day grows warm. Please, daughter."

As Gina left the house, Grandmama sat in her chair. Her white hair was piled neatly on top of her head. A stained, sleeveless tunic was tied carefully over her faded blue dress. Her black eyes twinkled as she watched Antonio. She motioned for him to join her with a wave of her old plump hand, and then helped him climb up onto her lap. She rocked him gently and spoke in a hushed voice.

"Antonio, Caesar is coming today to work on the farm. I must bake my magic bread! It will enchant him and he will never want to leave us. Would you like that, Grandson?"

Antonio grinned at her while he nodded yes.

"Good! Shhh! Don't tell your mother!"

Fragrances of anise, cracked wheat and yeast floated over the house, out through the door and onto the path. Grandmama had said that the scent would draw Caesar to their door and enchant him. And so it did, or at least Antonio, a three-year-old who was ready to believe the reasoning and wisdom of adults around him, thought it did.

When Caesar followed the heady aroma to their house, a marvelous set of events occurred! Caesar entered the room, dusty and tired from the days work of tilling the fields. His strong hands held Antonio's small ones for a moment before he sat at the table. His plain and kindly face smiled shyly at Gina, and then he bowed his head formally to Grandmama. Antonio stood silently by the table. He held the table's edge with his small fingers, peered over the top, looked up at each of the adults who surrounded him ... and then held his breath with anticipation.

Caesar broke the bread in half, took one half in his hand and lifted the piece to his face. He sniffed deeply, and the magic happened. Just as Grandmama had said it would! He smiled widely, first at Grandmama, then at Antonio and lastly at Gina. To Antonio, that smile suddenly encompassed everything that was good and magnificent in the world. Caesar smiled for what seemed a long time before he spoke. When he did, he spoke in a clear and rich voice.

"Grandmama, I believe Gina and I should wed within this month, before the cold moon's climb into the mountains again."

The statement meant more than was apparent to a three-year-old's ears. What had seemed a declaration really had been a question. Caesar addressed Grandmama, because without her permission he could not marry Gina. Also, Gina could refuse if she chose not to marry him. But Grandmama's magic had swept through the house and enchanted them all. As Gina smiled back at Caesar, she silently gave her promise to him. Grandmama responded by rising out of her chair, the chair that no one else sat in, and inviting Caesar to take her place. Everyone smiled. Gina and Caesar would marry in one moon's time. From that moment they became a family. They decided to live on together in

Grandmama's house where magic happened.

"Antonio, come eat!" Gina yelled out pleasantly.

Antonio waved good-bye to his friends as other mothers in the countryside called out at that moment for their sons to come home. Soon the road that had been a noisy playground was empty, except for unsettled dust. As Antonio limped back to the house, his mother dished out two bowls of stew for herself and her son. Antonio was the eldest of their three children. The two youngest children were with Caesar in the village. Antonio entered the house with a bright smile.

"Mama, did you see me kick the ball? Further than Horatio, even!"

Gina smiled at her tall son as he enthusiastically picked up his bowl of stew and, between mouthfuls, told her of the game. Although he was still a boy, Antonio had grown taller than Gina and almost as tall as Caesar during these last several years. When he was done, he stood, bent over, kissed his mother on the cheek and ran out to begin his afternoon's work.

Antonio started at the base of the mountain and criss-crossed back and forth through the remaining forest in search of kindling and wood to burn, because the immediate area encircling their house had long been combed clean of wood debris. He limped up the hill, unaware of his disability.

The mountains lay around him like a thick green blanket, which comforted and offered safety. Antonio looked forward to each afternoon when he could escape here and sing with the birds. His mother and father wondered at his affection for this place, especially since an avalanche from the Mountain God had almost killed him here. Antonio could not explain this love himself. He did not reason that the quiet and solitude he found here was a welcome respite from the pity he found in the village.

The villagers meant well. They tried to express their kindness and compassion through well-meant acts of tenderness that more often left him feeling different and inadequate. Only in the forest did he feel competent and strong. He did not feel different here.

Antonio held out his hand, and a finch alighted on his finger. The bird cocked its head and watched through one dark eye as Antonio whistled to it. Then the bird lifted its head and answered Antonio's whistle in a beautiful song. The birds in the trees joined in, and soon the forest was filled with their melodious symphony.

When his basket was full of wood, he lifted a leather strap that was attached to it and placed the strap across his forehead. The basket settled neatly against his back. He picked up another bundle of lighter kindling in his arms and tied it with a length of grass rope. Antonio fashioned a handle by making a loop with the rope, settled the bundle comfortably in his left hand and began the long walk home.

The sun had sunk lower in the sky, and hung as a golden circle above the western hills. The meadows, trees and village were all bathed in this sunny light as Antonio climbed down through the forest. Views of the valley and hills beyond were visible through the trees, but the best view could be seen from the bald place on the mountain where the avalanche had struck. Some days Antonio hiked to this area on his way down the mountainside. Today, he quickly decided not to go home by that route, as the sun would set rapidly during spring's shorter days. By late spring and summer, the Sun God would stay up late celebrating, and he would have a longer day to enjoy. During early spring, the Sun God was still lazy and sleepy from his winter hibernation. As the gold hues turned a rosy orange, Antonio hurried home.

Caesar and Gina stood under the starry sky in front of their small house. Inside, the children were soundly asleep. A dim shaft of light fell from the window and highlighted Caesar's worried expression. His brow was wrinkled over his strong nose and his eyes were heavy lidded with sadness. Gina wrapped her shawl around her shoulders to fight off the night's coolness and Caesar's words.

"Antonio must learn a trade!" Caesar repeated to Gina. He knew that Gina was hesitant to give up their oldest son to an apprenticeship. Gina's attachment to Antonio was understandable, and he did not argue this point. Instead, he addressed her with issues that they both needed to face. He, too, would be sad to see the boy leave. He was a remarkably cheerful child.

"Gina, he cannot farm. His foot will not carry him throughout a full day of work without a great deal of pain. He cannot gather wood for the rest of his life. He would feel shame, doing a boy's work when he becomes a man. If he learns a trade, perhaps becoming a tool smith, a wood carver or a potter, then he will be able to trade for any goods he will need for his family or himself. He will be able to contribute proudly to our family when he returns to us."

"He already contributes! Have the gods ever given more

sunshine to a child?" Gina asked stubbornly. "He could work in the garden! Who says that he will return, Caesar?"

"The mountain. It has claimed the boy from the first. Do you think, Gina, he will ever be able to live far from it, or us? Please Gina, think of what you ask. Antonio needs this. I think of him only. I do not want the boy to go, either."

Gina bowed her head and burst into hopeless sobs. Antonio would go – not far, only but a few miles, to the other side of the village, where several tradesmen lived. Yet she would not see his face each day, nor hear his happy voice. And though the tradesmen lived in the same village, Antonio could not walk to his work each day and then home again at night, for his deformed foot would not carry him. Also, as an apprentice, he would be expected to live with his master.

Caesar put his arms around Gina and held her. His throat ached; this decision gave him no pleasure.

When Caesar awoke the next morning, he took the bread and meat Gina had packed for him and began his journey to the village. When he returned home, late that night, he brought news that an apprenticeship had been arranged. Antonio was going to live with Don Giovanni, the village potter.

Antonio dug his hands deep into the clay bank, pulled a large mass of clay from the ground and carried it back to the Don. He placed the clay on a large flat stone, and once the Don had nodded for him to proceed, Antonio began to knead the clay into a workable mass.

Antonio's thoughts drifted like the clouds above him, loose and free. He thought of the past six years in the Giovanni home. The Don had been a fair and kind master. He worked Antonio hard though, as was expected. Some days Antonio's arms and shoulders ached as he turned out pot after pot for the Don to sign.

Antonio's skill had more than surpassed his master's. What had been merely pots in the old man's knowledgeable hands had become art pieces in Antonio's soulful ones. Over these past four years, the Don had become quite prosperous due to Antonio's skill. Antonio carefully lifted the newest pot from his wheel. He played with the idea that he might sign this one with his own name, but rejected the wish. Instead he signed it with the Giovanni symbol and placed it on the shelf to dry.

He began another pot – he hoped the last for the morning. When this was done he could either stop for lunch or work on a piece for himself. The Don gave him this time for himself several months ago as a reward for his hard work. When this last pot was finished and signed, Antonio began working a fresh piece of clay into a bowl. When the bowl was finished, he carefully began to etch patterns of birds into the soft clay on the outside of the bowl. He had to work deftly and delicately, for if he punctured the thin clay with his stick, then the piece would be ruined and he would have to start over. Also, the clay had to be at its wettest in order for the etchings to work. As the clay dried it tended to crumble, and the fine designs of the birds turned into indiscernible scratches. He finished the bowl without mishap and smiled. If this bowl fired without breaking, it would be the sixth this week. He needed only four more to complete the set of bowls he wanted to bring to his family during the winter celebration.

Early in winter a celebration was held to honor the Sun God before he retired into his winter hibernation. The Don gave Antonio this day off each year, as it would have brought the Don's family bad luck to do otherwise. This year, for the first time, Antonio would bring his family a present of his trade.

Each bowl was etched with a different bird from the forest that Antonio knew intimately. No one else would understand, or hear, the songs that Antonio heard in his bowls as he drew the birds on them. Music filled the air around him in a silent symphony of memories of happy times. A different bowl was made for each member of his family. Though there were only six people in his family, including himself, he wanted to make four extra pieces for friends or relatives who might visit. The finest bowl was slightly larger than the rest and had an hawk's graceful form in flight covering the inside. This piece was for his father Caesar. On the inside of another bowl, slightly smaller, a grouse was drawn, with all the complicated patterns of the mother hen's feathers finely detailed. The rest of the bowls, including one for himself, had birds in flight drawn on the outside of each. He could not explain why he had etched them this way. His hands were directed by his feelings. His feelings demanded beauty in this form.

Antonio sent a prayer to the Sun God and asked that this sixth bowl would make it through his fires unscathed. He was allowed the use solely of the throw-away clay. Clay that had been unusable for the fine wares of Don Giovanni was given to him for his private work. This meant extra work in the processing of it, and even then a flaw, if he missed it, might cause the piece to burst into shards in the kiln. That none of his private pieces had yet broken in the kiln was a testament to Antonio's skill.

Antonio did not sign this latest piece with his own name. The piece would go unsigned. The bowls would have neither Antonio's signature, nor the Giovanni symbol. Once Antonio finished his apprenticeship he could sign his work, but not until then. He simply placed the bowl at the back of the drying rack as a seconds piece, and then went back to the Don's work.

On the morning of the celebration of the Sun God, Antonio began the long walk home with all ten pots carefully packed in dried straw and placed in a sack with a leather strap, which he carried across his forehead and down his back, as he had once carried firewood.

The walk home seemed shorter each year. His legs, as they lengthened, carried him more quickly, in longer clumsy strides, toward his family. As he recognized the pathways he had once regularly frequented, the mountain arose closer and larger.

As he turned down the path, his parents' house became visible in the shade of the ancient tree which stood next to it. The house rambled off at odd angles – Caesar's additions to the main structure as the family grew in size. Grandmama had died long ago, before Antonio had left for his apprenticeship, but Gina had been blessed with life seven times. Of the seven, the gods had chose to leave only three besides Antonio. These three siblings, all sons, had grown into healthy boys and young men. Two were working in the fields with their father, and one had been sent to apprentice as a carpenter just this year. The oldest, next to Antonio, stood outside the house watching for Antonio's return. Antonio was soon recognized by his lanky silhouette and pronounced limp. His brother called out, and soon the rest of the family tumbled outside to greet Antonio. Everyone bustled around Antonio and spoke at once. Finally Gina yelled loudly so that all could hear.

"Our oldest son has returned home. Please let him come inside, where he may tell us of himself and the Don. What do you have in the sack, Antonio?" she asked, her dark eyes puzzled. Her luxuriant black hair had begun to gray over these past three years, and her skin now held the first wrinkles she would know. Antonio thought she had never looked more beautiful, and he told her so. She answered his compliment with laughter mixed with tears.

"Antonio, you are avoiding my question. What have you carried back in that sack? The Don's home is a far away, and you have worked hard to carry whatever it is. Please open your sack and show us."

By then the family was inside the house, in the main room which had become the kitchen and living area combined. Antonio grinned happily; one by one he took out the bowls and presented them to his family, starting with his mother and ending with his father. As he did, the family became strangely quiet. No one had ever seen bowls such as these. Such wealth! The youngest son finally broke the spell of silence.

"Look Mama, my bowl has a finch drawn on it!"

The clamour of voices that poured forth after the little boy's exclamation left Antonio dizzy with pleasure.

"They are beautiful!" exclaimed Gina.

"How did you earn the money for the clay?" his father asked, and then he stated proudly, "These, my son, are the most beautiful bowls in the world!"

"Does the Don know you made these?" his carpenter brother wanted to know.

"A starling? Why did you pick this bird for me?" asked his loudest brother. Everyone broke into laughter. Antonio gazed over his family and smiled. He drank in their love and enthusiasm while he could. The day would end quickly, and he must walk back to the Don's very early in the morning. Now he must take in every moment, because these moments would have to last him throughout the year.

After a long and abundant dinner, Antonio and his family sat outside on mats placed under the big tree. The fields were empty after the harvest. The sky was cloudless and dark blue. Antonio's brothers sat in a happy pile around him, one a copy of the next. They were all cheerful and homely, with the protruding noses and strong foreheads of Caesar and the gentle full smiles of Gina. Antonio differed from his brothers only in his features, which were straight, clean and attractive. In their natures they were all the same, warm and big hearted. Gina happily sat in the midst of her brood and held her eldest son's hand.

"How is Don Constella? Is he fair to you?" Antonio asked with genuine concern. Many master-apprenticeship relationships were really master-slave relationships. Antonio had been lucky, and he wished the same for his brother.

"Don Constella is fair, and more than kind since Papa arranged my marriage to his daughter Rosalina."

A silence fell on the family. Antonio sat up straighter, while his mother's hand tightened on his. The oldest children in a family were almost always married first, before younger siblings were allowed to marry. Last year when Antonio had come home, his father had told him that he would look for a wife for him while he was away. That no marriage had been found for him, but was instead planned for his younger brother, was obviously painful for everyone but that brother.

Tears shone in his mother's eyes, while his father's begged for forgiveness. Antonio swallowed, and then joked. He could not bear to feel different, here in his own family.

"Ah, I see that no good women came of age this year ... only second ones for second sons. Don't worry, Papa. You have not found a woman equal to your oldest son's talents!"

Everyone laughed in relief, and then joined in the joke.

"Yes, Rosalina is the type of woman that would wear a god's patience," said his mother.

"I heard she was ignorant of the trades and thought only of food," said his youngest brother. The third brother continued the kidding. "Most likely she will be as round as a ripe plum, with an appetite like that!"

The carpenter son started to protest in behalf of his betrothed, but stopped when he saw his father's expression. He quickly changed what he had been about to say and laughed.

"You are all right, but we all know that the best must be saved for the oldest son. I must be happy with my fat wife."

Later in the evening, when the sun had fully set and the moon rose above the mountains, Caesar asked Antonio to walk with him in the fields. Caesar gently brought up the promised marriage arrangements.

"Antonio, I tried to arrange a marriage between you and Rosalina, but she would not agree. She is not as your brothers have teased, fat and stupid. She is only young and foolish. She would not marry a crippled man."

Caesar had decided not to hold the truth from his son. He did not want to hurt him, nor did he want to insult him with falsehoods. Caesar looked at the tall boy, now a man, who limped next to him. Antonio's disfigured foot dragged a trail in the soft and newly harvested earth. He knew the pain that the boy must feel, yet Antonio said nothing; he did not complain or feel sorry for himself. Somehow that made the circumstances worse. Rosalina was truly a foolish girl, and something else was true. Caesar spoke this next thought out loud.

"Antonio, something you said today held truth. Rosalina was not good enough for you. She is too ..." he struggled for a word,"... simple." Antonio began to protest, but his father stopped him. "No, Antonio. Listen to me. You have an artist's talent, which is rare. Your heart is open and large. It would have been drained uselessly on one such as Rosalina. I shall spend this next year searching for a good wife for you. Next year at this time, I shall have a bride for you. I promise you now, and the gods, that I shall do everything possible to fulfill this promise."

Antonio nodded his gratitude, but doubted that his father could fulfill such a promise. His father could not change what the gods had already set in motion. The gods had let him live many years ago, but if they had wanted him to marry, they would have left him whole instead of leaving him a partial man.

Antonio left early the next morning, filled with a rich contentment by his visit with his family, and at the same time, saddened with resignation to his fate.

The next winter solstice brought no new bride for Antonio, but another arranged marriage for the third-youngest brother. Again, Caesar promised Antonio and the gods to find Antonio a mate, but there was little enthusiasm in his words.

At least Antonio had the comfort of knowing he would return to his family soon, as his apprenticeship would end in six moons from the Sun God celebration. Then he could return home or choose to stay in the village. Already he had chosen to come home to the mountains he loved. His father had been unable to find him a wife, but he did find a clay bed, a half mile from the house by a creek in the forest. The clay was thick and buttery in hue. The promise of this abundance alleviated most of Antonio's disappointment. He returned to Don Giovanni's pottery studio jubilantly.

Don Giovanni was sorry to see the boy go. Something in Antonio's cheerful nature brought out a generosity in him that he did not normally possess. The boy was a skilled potter – he did not like to admit how skilled – and he was good company. If only he had a daughter to marry to Antonio, then indeed, he would be wealthy the rest of his days, but he had never married and he had no children. He began to ponder this scenario, and grew to like it so much that he decided to do something about it. His brother had four daughters. If he adopted one that would be willing to live with him, then he could arrange the marriage with Antonio's stepfather Caesar. As the Don laid down on his bed for the night and rested his large head upon his pillow, he decided he would go and speak to his brother in the morning.

Don Giovanni sat outside his brother's house and studied the girl as she worked. She was pretty, but not exceptionally so. The word that came to mind as the Don watched her was ... clever. Her hands were quick and her eyes were sharp. She immediately understood that something important was going on and sat up straighter. Her father broached the subject.

"Daughter, your uncle has brought a marriage proposal to me." The girl's eyes brightened and she waited excitedly. "His apprentice Antonio finishes his apprenticeship this spring and seeks a wife."

"That clumsy cripple!" the girl burst out. Her father continued as if her words had not been spoken.

"You would live in town in your uncle's big house, and become his adopted daughter. You would travel with your uncle to trade his pottery, perhaps even to Greece."

"I can't believe you would ask me to marry a cripple!" she stated coldly. "No, Papa. I won't do it!"

This time her father heard her and tried to reason with her.

"Now, Daughter, do not judge Antonio by his unfortunate foot. His face is pleasing and his nature is blithe." As he spoke, he fantasized about the wealth he could ascertain through this marriage. As the wealth grew in his imagination, so did his description of Antonio. "This is a young man gifted by the gods. Such talent! He will be famous some day, and you would be also, as his wife."

"Have you the moon's madness inside you? Did you not hear my words? I said NO, Father! Do not stand here and act like a fool in front of Uncle and me."

Her uncle glowered at her, took his brother's arm and pulled him from the room. "Your daughter speaks the truth. She is not a good match for the boy. Let us not trouble her any longer."

They went back into the house and debated the matter. In the end, Don Giovanni convinced his brother to ask his next daughter if she would consider a marriage arrangement. Perhaps this would shame her older sister into acceptance, or possibly this daughter might accept the offer.

Don Giovanni and his brother presented the arrangement to the next daughter, but were met with a similar response, only quieter in form. They tried the third daughter, but were again cooly rebuffed. The two men returned to the house, where they drank wine and discussed the problem.

In Don Giovanni's mind, Antonio was quickly slipping away. No more fine pottery ... he would have to find a new apprentice. No more laughter from the lips of a boy who had become like a son to him. His world grew grayer by the moment. His brother's thoughts were similar, but laced with avarice. He watched the wealth he had envisioned disappearing before he had had a chance to enjoy it. In desperation, the brother spoke rashly.

"I shall give you Lucinda to have as your own daughter. When she comes of age in another year, you may marry her to Antonio."

Lucinda was the youngest of his four daughters. To arrange a marriage for the youngest first, before the others, was unheard of in their village. To give away his daughter at this young age was also unusual. He called to Lucinda, who weeded the garden that lay behind the house. The girl came as bidden and bowed in front of her uncle. Don Giovanni studied her. She was small, even for her age, and her face was not rounded and heart shaped like her sisters. Instead, she was slender and petite: small hands, small lips, a small chin and nose. She was still too young to tell whether she might become pretty. Don Giovanni remembered her as a baby. She had been an exceptionally beautiful baby, with pale white skin, hence her name. But she had turned out disappointingly plain thus far. He studied her further.

She was obviously polite, and had a gentle manner. Her glance was honest, not shy or bold. There was nothing cunning or deliberate about her. In fact, she reminded him of Antonio. He decided in that moment that the girl was the perfect choice.

"Yes. It shall please me much to take Lucinda as my daughter," the Don said with genuine happiness.

The girl started and her light skin became even paler. Her father toasted his brother and both men grinned. What they now toasted was that Lucinda was too young to refuse.

For a week Lucinda cried herself to sleep while she listened to her mother fight with her father about the adoption and marriage arrangement. Finally, one night the house was quiet with the stillness that comes at the end of a long storm. In the morning Lucinda's mother had had a change of heart. Lucinda's father had convinced her mother that Lucinda would stand to inherit her uncle's wealth, as well as marry a man who was bound to become wealthy. Her mother's mind was filled with miserly dreams, and now Lucinda suffered the pain of her mother's insensitive words as she attempted to persuade Lucinda of her good fortune.

"Lucinda, little girl, why do you cry? Antonio is a talented potter."

"I do not want to marry a potter. I do not want to leave our home," Lucinda said firmly, and then she began to cry anew. She buried her small face in the blankets on the bed where she sat.

"Do not speak foolishly, Lucinda! Your father has made a good match for you. Do not embarrass your father with your tears. Wipe your nose and come to the table to eat! Your father and sisters are waiting."

Her mother stood, scowled at her daughter and then angrily left the room.

Lucinda felt betrayed, first by her father, and now her mother. Her sisters had taunted her all week, and she felt alone and abandoned. She had no choice but to go to her uncle's once word was sent for her to come. She had not wanted to leave her family, but now she almost looked forward to the peace she would find in their absence.

While Lucinda worried over her new life, Don Giovanni sent a messenger to Caesar and Gina. The messenger was to bring Caesar back with him, and one day while Antonio worked diligently in the studio, his father unexpectedly arrived. Antonio greeted Caesar briefly, and then his father went into the house to see Don Giovanni. The worried look which creased his father's face left Antonio fixedly concerned. Each pot he tried to make collapsed into a heaped mess on the wheel. Antonio gave up trying to work, placed his wheel aside and began to pace the length of the studio.

Finally he stopped his weary pacing, when his deformed leg would no longer carry him. The setting sun now filled the studio with warm red light. The smell of wet clay perfumed the air. Drying pots surrounded him on the stacks of wooden shelves. Antonio pushed some dried pots aside on a bench, sat down and awaited Caesar's return. He anxiously rubbed his throbbing leg.

Hours passed before his father came back outside. Antonio noticed immediately that his father's face was more relaxed; the creases across his forehead were gone. He approached Antonio slowly and put his arm around his son in an affectionate greeting. He bade Antonio to listen to the news he had for him. Antonio listened, and barely breathed. Gradually, his father began to explain.

"Antonio, the Don sent word to me that an important matter concerning you needed my attention. I ran most of the way here. I thought, 'Is our oldest son hurt, dying?' I arrived and saw that you were fine. Thank the gods!" He took a breath, patted the boy on the shoulder with the relief he felt earlier again surfacing and then continued. "The Don has made a very generous offer to me. It is a marriage offer of his daughter for you."

"The Don has no daughter!" Antonio burst out with confusion. His father patted him on the shoulder again.

"Yes, Antonio, he does. He has adopted his brother's daughter just for this purpose. He is fond of you and does not wish to lose you or your abilities. We have talked long. I have told him that this choice is yours to make. I have negotiated a fair marriage contract if you want to go through with this."

"What is this arrangement?" Antonio asked, more than curious by now.

"The Don went to great lengths to find you a bride because he wants you to stay here. I believe he genuinely cares for you. I explained that your mother and I were hoping you would return to our home and work there. Already your brothers and I have begun the building of your studio.

"I shall not lie to you now. The Don sees what you may not have seen yet. He knows he will grow richer if you stay here; also, he knows that this wealth would go to your own family if you leave."

His father stopped now to allow the significance of what he was saying to be absorbed by his son. Antonio was stunned. He had thought of what he might earn in trade, but never so prosperously. His father observed his son's amazement and continued.

"The Don will give you his daughter in a year's time, when she comes of age."

"Comes of age?! How many summers has she lived?"

"Eleven."

"Eleven!"

"There is more. She is the fourth daughter. Her sisters are not married."

"What?" Antonio now moved from stunned to shocked. He had known that if a marriage arrangement could ever be made, that it would most likely not be in his favor, but this was worse than he had imagined. A child. A fourth daughter. His ego was beyond bruised, and he felt beaten to a numbness he had not known before. He could not bring himself to speak, and so said nothing. His father put his arm around Antonio's shoulder, and spoke compassionately and in earnest.

"Antonio, it is not as bad as you would think. I do believe that the Don's offer is a thoughtful one. He says the girl is kind and gentle. She would be ready to marry in three years, by tradition. You could marry her in a year, when she comes of age. This is early, but not unheard of; some do marry at this age."

Antonio was able to speak for the first time.

"Not go home to you and Mama? The mountains...." His voice trailed off.

"Antonio, I have told the Don of your love for your home, the mountains and your family. He has agreed that you and your wife could live one week out of each month at our house for the first five years. He will supply the building materials for a second studio, and a servant for you. Antonio, I must tell you, I have searched for two years now; I have not been able to find a marriage arrangement for you. I believe the gods have sent you a gift through the Don."

Antonio spoke weakly. "What did you say ... about five years?"

"Ah," said his father, "the Don has agreed that you may choose to live wherever you wish after five years. He grows older and is lonely. He would like you and your wife, his adopted daughter, to live with him during these five years to ease his loneliness. This choice is yours to make, my son. After five years you could start your own studio and live with us," he added hopefully.

He meant to encourage the boy toward what was a fair and prosperous marriage, but he was struck by how much he had missed Antonio these seven years. He sat silently, awaiting Antonio's decision. The boy was pensively quiet. Minutes passed before Antonio spoke.

"Yes, Papa. I agree to this marriage."

Caesar nodded solemnly. He held the boy's gaze for a long moment. Nothing more could be said now.

Antonio anxiously watched Lucinda's young face as they were introduced. This large room, with its tall ceilings and whitewashed walls, was the main living quarter of the Don's house. It was not only spacious, but also comfortable and luxurious. Large dark beams were spaced along the ceiling. A mural of the village covered one wall in the rich earth tones and golden colors of early morning. Oversized wooden furniture surrounded the young couple, who were dwarfed by its size. The Don quietly spoke each of their names to the other, and then as quietly, he left the room. Although they were now alone, Antonio knew that servants worked nearby to spy on the young couple for the Don.

Antonio continued to stare; and Lucinda, with a child's honesty, did not try to hide her dismay. She put her face in her hands and began to weep. Antonio winced from her reaction. He knew that she would find his twisted foot repulsive, but had not expected such a strong response.

At the same time, Antonio was moved by her youth and innocence. Suddenly he felt a deep compassion for the girl's predicament. Had he not been sent away from his family when he had been young? In fact, he had been only a year younger than she was now, and hadn't he been frightened? He bent and whispered to Lucinda.

"Please let me know what I may do to end your suffering. I know the fear you feel. The gods could not have meant for someone so young and small to be separated from her family."

Lucinda was surprised by his response, and answered with the first hint of the woman she would become. "I do not cry because I miss my family. I cry because I think I cannot marry you."

"Could you please tell me why?" Antonio asked, although he knew the answer. No woman or girl would willingly marry a cripple. Her parents must not have told her before she had come to live with her uncle.

Lucinda spoke. "I cannot marry you because you are old and tall," she stated directly in her child's voice.

Antonio was delighted. She was rejecting him for normal reasons. There was no guile in her; she spoke the truth. He must seem middle-aged to her. He broke into laughter as a gaiety filled him. She did not see him as different! Just old and tall. He laughed louder. Lucinda looked up at him with annoyance behind her tear-stained eyes.

"Why do you laugh at me?"

Antonio took her small hand and continued to smile at her. She stared up at him defiantly.

"Lucinda, in a year I shall not seem so old to you. Then, if you are not ready, I shall wait for you."

"What if I don't want to marry you at all?" she asked, growing more comfortable with Antonio.

"Then we won't marry. I should not want to see you unhappy. Stay here with your uncle and me for this year. Will you try, Lucinda?"

"Yes." She nodded her head.

Antonio would always remember their first week together vividly. Lucinda carried herself with dignity, although she was obviously frightened. She held her head upright and hid her tears, until night stole over the village and she had a private place to shed them. The Don noticed her tear-swollen eyes though, and decided that Lucinda needed a woman's hand; he wisely sent for Gina instead of the girl's mother. Antonio noted how Gina took the frightened girl into her heart, and that Gina and Lucinda became friends instantly. In many ways, Lucinda reminded him of his mother.

Antonio's love and respect for Lucinda grew over the next two years, and often Gina commented on his good fortune.

"The gods have blessed you, son! Lucinda is good and wise. Many woman lack such wisdom!" she said as she straightened the kitchen in the Don's house.

"But, will she marry me?" he asked in a moment of doubt.

"Antonio! Were you not listening? Lucinda is sensible, as well as kind. Do you not see the way her eyes follow yours?" Gina said. She brushed a stray piece of her hair, which had grayed dramatically in the last year, from her face. He felt his mother's warm eyes searching his for an answer.

Antonio looked down at his disfigured leg. His foot was mishapened into a twisted club. His calf muscles had become overly devolped and his leg was as gnarled and ugly as an old tree limb. As he sighed, the image of himself crept into his mind, and their conversation.

"If she is sensible, Mama, she will marry a whole man! One whose handsomeness is not marred."

Gina's expression, which was angry as well as pained, told him he had carried his self-doubts too far. "Antonio! A good woman needs only a good man! A man's goodness is not weighed by his beauty! But his beauty is weighed by his goodness!"

Antonio swallowed his tears. He hugged his mother tightly and then let her go. She smiled mischievously and took out a large ceramic bowl, one Antonio had made. As she did, he realized that something magical was about to take place. Gina carefully began to make bread.

Soon the smell of Grandmama's bread floated out through the house and into the street. People who had been frowning that day smiled as they came upon the bewitching aroma. Lucinda drifted into the kitchen to ask about the intoxicating smell. A magic of peace and well-being settled over the Don's house. On that day Antonio could feel his grandmother's magic at work, and he knew that someday he and Lucinda would marry.

The years passed quickly after their wedding. They continued to live in the Don's house, except for the one week each month during which they lived in the countryside with Gina and Caesar. Their first child was a daughter, sweet and good-natured, like her parents. Then their son was born two years later.

Antonio's mastery of his art grew with each passing year. No other potter could match his skill, and his work grew in demand, until finally the old Don surpassed his goals. One day a representative from a far-off country arrived.

"Don! Don! A cart is coming! The cart is for you. There is a strange boy walking behind the cart!" a young village boy yelled as he ran toward the Don's house.

The Don stepped from the studio and out onto the dusty street. The afternoon sun spilled across him and cast a large shadow across the ground. His wide girth was intimidating as he yelled crossly at the young messenger. "Speak slowly, boy! Who is coming?"

"A man brings a cart for you, Don Giovanni!" He spoke more slowly as he bowed and addressed the Don. "I cannot see inside it because it is covered with a cloth. Two guards walk beside it! A boy, a strange boy, walks behind the cart. He is chained to it!" the boy said breathlessly.

Soon the cart appeared around the bend in the road, as the young messenger had described. A petite, well-dressed man rode on a seat at the front. As the cart reached the Don's house, the small man jumped down to the road.

"Hail, Don Giovanni!" he said and bowed low to the dusty earth. "I bring you tribute from my Lord! Your reputation has grown wide, as wide as a wealthy man such as yourself stands. My Lord sends these tokens as gifts!"

The odd, small man lifted the cover from the wagon and displayed the wealth that lay hidden there. Then he hastily brought forward the boy who was chained to the back of the cart.

As he did, Antonio stepped from the house to see what had caused the shouting. Before him was as strange sight. A young man, more a boy, stood naked except for a loin cloth. His nakedness was not strange, but his skin color was. From head to toe, the boy's skin was a rich dark brown. Short, black and kinky hair covered his skull. When he opened his mouth, his white teeth shone like a beacon from his frightened face.

"What do you think of this, Antonio?" the Don said, and chuckled.

"He must be tired," Antonio answered compassionately as he watched the strange child. "Why is he here?"

"A gift! A gift for the studio of Don Giovanni!" the small man answered before the Don could speak.

"Unchain this boy! Antonio, bring him into the stables, where he may rest," the Don spoke impatiently and then motioned to the ambassador to follow him. "Come! Come! We shall talk about your Lord and his gifts."

Several moons after the servant arrived from the Lord, Lucinda gave birth to their third child, a little girl. Their oldest daughter was then eight, while their young son was six. The gift of this birth, after all those years, was miraculous.

Antonio smiled as he thought of his youngest child, now a busy four-year-old. She was determined to become a potter like her grandfather and father, and followed them everywhere.

Antonio knew that Lucinda worried over a female child who displayed such unabandoned delight in a man's occupation. At first Lucinda asked Antonio to discourage her. Then, one day as she watched her youngest daughter's pure joy as she played with the sticky clay, she was given to a change in heart.

"Antonio, perhaps we should let Ninfa play in the studio as you wish? She will not continue this play for long," Lucinda said.

"Ah, this will mean more work for you, Lucinda," the Don said from his desk, where he was calculating the week's trade. "Let me hire another servant to help you wash her clothes."

"Grandpapa! Look!" Ninfa said as she held up a crude clay cup she had made. The Don laughed and picked up the cup.

"Ah, see, Lucinda! You have no need to worry. She does not have her father's talent," he said and winked at Lucinda. The Don picked up Ninfa and hugged her to his large chest. He loved the little girl and played with her more often now than he traded.

Antonio smiled at Lucinda as she threw up her arms in surrender.

"I cannot fight all of you!"

Antonio took Ninfa from her grandfather's arms and set her on the table. Secretly, Antonio had begun to teach this youngest child his trade. His son and oldest daughter showed no interest. He loved them as they were and had no desire to push them into a trade they did not want. His son was destined to be a merchant, as he was sharp and could already out-trade many of the adults around him. He reminded Antonio of the old Don. His oldest daughter wanted nothing unusual, only to cook, bear children and have her own family someday. She would be ready to marry in two seasons' time. He and Lucinda had several marriage offers for her that they were now considering.

Antonio bent and picked up a raw piece of clay. He broke off a small section and showed Ninfa how to knead it into a ball. He smiled as he thought of his happy family. He had begun peacefully to knead his larger piece when a loud crash came from behind him. A shadow passed over his work area, and his heart stopped for a split second. Ninfa's face froze into a frightened stare. He quickly stood and turned around.

The Don had collapsed on the floor.

The Don's funeral was the largest the village had ever seen. As he had predicted years ago, Antonio's talent had made him quite wealthy. That wealth was opulently displayed now in his funeral parade. Banners with symbols of the gods in gold leaf hung from poles, which were carried around the village square. Flower petals covered the dirt road on which the bier was carried. Large quantities of fresh food were laid out around the Don's body so that he could eat well in the afterworld.

Antonio and three other men carried the Don's large body, which was wrapped carefully in his death cloth, to the fire and placed it in the center. As Antonio walked away, he struggled for a moment as his leg, which had become arthritic with use, buckled. His bearded face, which had matured over the years, contorted with pain. He regained his composure and continued to where the other members of his family stood.

One by one, the villagers came forth, and each placed a stick beneath the Don's body. The larger the stick, the more honor the individual placed on the person who had died. Antonio's log, one he had dragged from the mountainside, lay in the center of the pile of faggots. He stood back and watched as others paid their respects.

Lucinda stood next to him with two of their children. Ninfa was with a servant back at the house. Tears flowed down Lucinda's face as their son picked up a small log and dragged it to the pile. Her pretty skin had a gray cast due to her grief. Her long dark hair had been carefully braided and then twisted into a tight crown on her head, to emphasize the seriousness of the occasion. She glanced up at Antonio, who also cried freely. He put his arms around her waist and held her tightly. The last person placed a stick on the pile of timber and stepped back. Antonio took a shaky breath, and then stepped forward. He ceremoniously lit the piles of dried grass that were placed in a circle around and under the funeral bier. The grass leapt into flames, the smaller sticks caught and the fire swiftly consumed the wooden tributes, and the man who was sanctified.

Later, a party was held in the Don's big house. All night people came and went, drank, ate and in the end paid their respects to Antonio and Lucinda. Some were already calling him Don Antonio. Just before dawn, when Antonio felt he could neither grieve any more, nor comfort another person, he stole out to his studio.

A peace settled over him as he hammered out a piece of clay. Expertly, he kneaded and pounded the clay, until not an air pocket remained. Antonio looked at his surroundings as if for the first time, as he had done so many years ago.

The sun rose; its slanted beams fell through the open studio door. Antonio had not slept at all that night. He yawned loudly and finished the pot upon which he had been working. The apprentice – "Bruno", as the local people called him – climbed down the ladder and addressed Antonio.

"Don, do you wish the kiln fired this day?"

He winced at the new title spoken by his apprentice. "No, Bruno, not today or tomorrow. Let the kiln rest while the Don makes his passage to the spirit world."

Bruno nodded, though he did not completely understand his master's customs. At that moment Don Antonio's youngest daughter strode into the room. Ninfa's heart-shaped face split into a large smile as she saw Bruno. Antonio watched as the little girl ran laughing to where Bruno stood next to the drying rack. Bruno was second in her heart next to her father. The relationship was an odd one, but Antonio understood it. The little girl loved clay and pots; Bruno to her, was a keeper of pots. Antonio called her to him. She squealed with delight when she saw that he, too, was there.

"Ninfa, come here."

"Papa, Papa! I did not see you!"

She embraced her father's long legs. He picked her up and pressed her soft round cheek against his bearded one. She laughed as his beard tickled her face. Lucinda walked in to the room at that moment and smiled.

"Ah, Ninfa, there you are. You have not eaten your breakfast. Come back inside."

Antonio handed Ninfa over to his wife and followed her

back inside to eat their morning meal. A servant would bring Bruno his breakfast outside.

When Ninfa asked to work in the studio full-time under her father, Lucinda almost fainted. She pleaded with Antonio not to let their daughter take this path.

"No man will marry such a woman! Please, Antonio, think of your daughter's future, and not of what will please her now. She will grow tired of this hard labor, and will want to live in a woman's home. What will she know of a woman's skills? Her hands will be dried and cracked, and a stranger to woman's work."

He knew Lucinda's arguments were legitimate, and definitely more practical than his own feelings in this matter. Yet he could not ignore the intensely passionate feelings he did have. Why could his daughter not choose her own path? Why could she not create pottery as beautiful as any man? Who made these laws? He decided in the end to let Ninfa choose for herself. Lucinda had been deeply hurt by Antonio's decision. She relented that Antonio's decision had been right only after Ninfa had worked with the clay for three years and showed no desire to quit. Rather than tire of this work, she instead lived for her creations. Lucinda would never argue this point now, after six years had passed and her daughter's interest had not waned. Yet the subject still caused her to worry in the middle of the night, for who would marry such a girl?

Lucinda did not need to worry, because a man waited for Ninfa as steadily as the night waited for the moon.

"I don't know, Antonio. He is a good young man, but he was a servant. You would have your daughter marry a man who once served?"

"He finished his apprenticeship over four years ago. He is the best potter in our studio, as good as Ninfa herself, and he was a servant for only a year before he came to us."

Antonio watched his wife's dismayed expression when he mentioned Ninfa's talent. Antonio continued to address this issue.

"He will make an honorable husband for Ninfa. Lucinda, think this over. They love each other already. No love will have to wait to bud and then blossom between these two, for already a bouquet of flowers exist! Ninfa will not marry anyone else. She has said so."

"She is willful because you allowed her her own mind."

"As I did you so many years ago. I have never criticized you for knowing what you have wanted. Do not ask me to criticize our daughter now."

Lucinda bowed her head under his argument. The match was a good one, and Antonio knew Lucinda understood this. He did not know why Lucinda fought this arrangement. Ninfa would never marry anyone but Bruno. And, more importantly, no other man would want Ninfa. Lucinda shook her head, and then reluctantly gave her consent.

"Come in," whispered Lucinda to her daughter. "I do not know how much he hears or understands."

Ninfa came in, carrying her children, twins, a boy and a girl. Both had the heart-shaped face of their mother, with dense, curly, chestnut-colored hair. Their skin was a beautiful tawny shade which reminded Antonio of the clay they used in the studio.

Antonio wanted to yell that he heard everything. He understood all that was happening to him. The stroke had left him helpless; he could not walk or speak. He could barely swallow the gruel his wife made for him. He wanted to tell his wife how much he loved her, how after all of their years together she was still beautiful to him. He wanted to tell Ninfa how proud he was of her, her talent, her husband, their children. Of all his children, Ninfa was dearest to his heart. Where were the others? Surely Lucinda had sent word of his stroke? Ninfa sat down on the bed next to him and placed a grandchild on either side of him. He wanted to smile at them. What beautiful children Ninfa's mixed marriage had produced. He tried to speak, but a grunt was all that sounded in the room. Lucinda responded to his attempt by taking his hand.

"Do not try to speak, Antonio. The healer says you must rest."

Tears fled from her beautiful eyes, and Antonio wanted to comfort her, but he could not. Even moving his chest to breathe was an effort. His grandson cuddled closer to his chest for a moment, before Lucinda removed him.

"He cannot breathe easily. Grandpapa is not well. Come with me and I shall get you each a piece of bread."

Lucinda took each grandchild's hand and led them to the kitchen to fulfill her promise. When she had gone, Ninfa took up her father's hand and held it to her cheek. She cried freely, and whispered to him.

"I want you to get better, Papa, but the healer says that if you do get better, you will not have use of your hands and legs. I cannot bear the thought that your hands will make no more beautiful pots." She cried harder now.

A single tear found escape from Antonio's eye. It would be Ninfa who would tell him the truth. The healer and Lucinda had not spoken before him of his recovery. He did not want to live the life his daughter described. Had he not lived fully, and better than most men? Could he ask for more? No. The gods had given him his life once before; they would not do so again. He wasn't sure he wanted to go on, anyway. He was tired, very tired. He thanked the gods for what he had been given – a very rich life – and fell into a sleep from which he did not awaken.

"the between ..."

Antonio felt himself moving through space and time. Images flashed past him, memories of his life. His grandmother, mother and father were there to greet him, and then they were gone. A brilliant white light exploded inside his very being, and then Serra found herself back in the meadow. The small guide sat nearby, silently awaiting her.

Serra was speechless with a humbled awe of what she had lived and experienced. What could she say about Antonio's life? She had been a man! And, Antonio's last thoughts had been true. He had lived a very rich life. There was abundant joy on this planet. She looked at the guide, who simply smiled at her. For once the guide had no questions.

Serra rested in the meadow and the sound of birds chirping drifted through her thoughts in an intricately woven song. More images of Antonio's life floated in with the songs. She found herself smiling as she thought of this life. The bird songs turned into a long-playing movie of Antonio and his life. She reviewed it joyously and laughed out loud at moments when the joy filled her and spilled out. She cried as she felt Antonio's disappointment when his father could not find him a wife. Serra saw clearly now that **the obstacle she had been given in this life, a disability, had been the very thing that had led her soul toward joy**. Because of it, Antonio had been led to Lucinda. She sat for what seemed like days, digesting who she had been.

She knew that Antonio had been wiser because of the other lifetime experiences. She saw that, as Antonio, she had used the knowledge she had gained from her other two lifetimes. Antonio knew that to find happiness in each moment was his responsibility. He had this knowledge within him from Lotus Blossom. Antonio also knew, from Lotus, that the servant he had been given needed a status of his own, and so he allowed his servant to become an apprentice, and then a family member. As a man, he helped his daughter break free of societal restrictions through the knowledge he had gained from being a woman. Antonio was a better person because of lifetimes of accumulated knowledge and experience. Finally, the guide stood, walked over to where Serra sat and placed one small hand over Serra's eyes.

A brilliantly vivid scene appeared before Serra's closed eyes. Antonio and Lucinda danced at their wedding. The joy she saw and felt in this scene was boundless. The guide spoke.

"Yes. You were sent to experience joy. Keep this memory in you always, Serra! **Joy exists on this planet.**"

The guide took her hand away and Serra felt herself falling in slow motion to the ground, where the purple flowers cushioned her body and embraced her with their fragrant scent.

Chapter 5

*B*reathe when you swing! If you hold your breath, your power cannot flow through you and into your sword."

Kazuaki picked up the sword that was almost as tall as he was. The hilt of the sword dwarfed his small hands, and the strength of both hands was required to hold it steady. His arms trembled with fatigue, but he did not complain. Instead, he focused harder on swinging his sword while breathing as the sensei had instructed. He swung the heavy sword again, and again. The sword began to dip and sway as he moved it through the air. Finally he could control the trembling no longer.

The sensei watched the small boy. All morning the boy had worked on his sword movements. *This one,* the sensei thought, *has the heart of the samurai, but no skill. See how, after four months, the boy's skill does not improve; yet he does not give up, he does not complain.*

Small muscles were developing along his little shoulders and arms. The sensei motioned to the boy to stop, and felt the boy's relief as he bowed and handed the sword back. The teacher bowed in response as he accepted the sword and motioned for the boy to follow him.

"Kazuaki, you will bathe now. Then we shall meditate."

The sensei waved to a servant who stood nearby to follow the boy and assist him. The servant bowed low, his hair brushing the floor. A small garden surrounded by beautifully sculpted trees lay behind the dojo. The trees' twisted shapes encircled a pool where steam rose in spiraling columns.

The old servant undressed Kazu on a black stone bench that sat near the pool; the boy climbed into the hot spring pool, where he closed his eyes with pleasure as the warmth of the water eased his sore muscles. A groan escaped his lips, and his eyes flew open as he checked to see if the servant had heard him. The servant was busy folding the boy's clothes and appeared not to notice. The old man turned toward him and begged permission to retrieve the young boy's kimono. Kazu nodded, yes, and watched the retreating back of the old man.

As soon as the old servant was out of sight, the boy allowed himself an expressive groan of contentment. He surveyed the scenery around himself and wished futilely that he could stay in the comforting pool for hours.

Beyond the mineral pool and trees was the remainder of the garden, serene in its simplistic beauty. The cherry trees were in full blossom and scented the air with their perfumed pink flowers. Beyond the shelter of the modest orchard, a view of a mountain, tall and intimidating, covered the horizon for as far as the boy could see.

The servant reappeared and waited silently by the bench. The boy closed his eyes and ignored the old man's presence. Five minutes passed, and the boy climbed out of the hot water and allowed the servant to dry and dress him. Though the sensei would not expect him for another half hour, he wanted to arrive early in order to impress the teacher with his commitment.

When the sensei and the boy left the temple, the sun was well past the midday mark and heading toward the hour when it would sleep. During the last half the boy's stomach had rumbled unceasingly. Kazu prayed to Buddha to allow his stomach to stop its fitful noises, but Buddha did not hear his prayers. Unbeknownst to the boy, the sensei had taken pity on him and had released him from his meditations early.

The sensei called the old servant over and told him to take a message to the cook and to the cook's servant. They were to bring rice, soup and tea to the sensei's living quarters. Kazu followed his honorable teacher into his dwelling.

The boy was more troubled in this moment than he had been earlier. Kazu was sure he had been brought here to be disciplined for his noisy stomach, as he had not heard the sensei's command. He kneeled on a mat in front of the sensei. His stomach rumbled loudly again, and the boy bent lower in an attempt to quiet it. The sensei addressed his prone figure.

"Kazuaki, did you not eat your midday meal?"

"Hai, Sensei. I ate very little. I am trying to discipline myself to do without, as my father did. I thought that, if I am very disciplined, I might become a better samurai."

The sensei nodded, but said nothing. His dark robes rustled quietly as he adjusted his position. His black eyes stared between narrowly slitted lids. His tawny skin was without wrinkles and gave no indication of his age. His wide flat nose sat above thin lips that were expressionless. His long black hair was tied at the base of his neck. When Kazu glanced up, his teacher's face told him nothing. Kazu swallowed and waited. Minutes passed, and the sensei neither moved nor spoke. A soft knock sounded at the door; finally the silence was broken.

"Come."

The cook's servant, a young woman, carried in a tray of food. She carefully bowed to the sensei and to the ancestors' altar before she served. Once that was done she lit several small lanterns and, with many small bows, gracefully left the room in the same manner in which she had entered. The sensei motioned for the boy to eat.

A gentle breeze stirred the small lanterns, which were bowls filled with fish oil and wicks. The room grew darker as the sun set lower in the sky. Outside, evening birds could be heard calling good-bye to the sun. The boy tried very hard not to eat quickly and chewed his rice longer than he normally would. He did not want to appear weak or greedy.

The sensei saw this and wondered about this boy, as he often did. *What do I do with this one?* the sensei wondered silently. *Look, he shows discipline even when I know his hunger overwhelms him. So sad that he has shown no skill.*

The sensei knew that he could not afford to be soft or compassionate in the decisions he made concerning the boys he trained. This circumstance was more difficult than normal. Never had he come across a child with determination like Kazu's that could not develop some skill. The few he had encountered with little skill also had had little desire. Even those, through diligence, were brought to an acceptable level so they could move on to become samurai. But, this boy....

The sensei had meditated last night and early this morning as he sought an answer. He had watched the boy work with the bokken. His lithe body, clad in hakama, had clumsily maneuvered the little wooden sword. The sensei had decided to move the boy past the bokken to a full metal sword, in hopes that the nature of the sword would bring out some talent in the boy. This, too, had failed. To continue when the boy had no chance would only postpone the pain and dishonor the boy and his family would feel. And still the sensei could not bring himself to send a messenger to the boy's father.

That night the sensei dreamt a vision, which decided the matter with finality. He awoke his servant before dawn and commanded the old man.

"Get Kazuaki. Bathe him, feed him and then bring him to the temple." The old man, still not fully awake, backed out of the room in a perplexed state.

Meanwhile, on his knees, the sensei waited impatiently in the temple for the boy to arrive. Twenty years of training and discipline kept him from rising and pacing. When the boy did arrive, the sensei rose to greet him with a calm he did not truly feel. He instructed the boy to pray before the altar.

A beam of sunshine shone through an open slat in the temple wall and fell before the prostate forms of the sensei and his pupil. Upon seeing this sign, the teacher signaled to the boy to finish his prayers. After respectfully bowing toward the altar, the two left the temple and went out into the garden, which was bathed in early morning light. The sensei sat on a bench and gestured for the boy to do the same.

"Kazuaki, today is your last day here. I have made a decision concerning your training. You will not become a samurai."

Kazu's shoulders dropped and he swallowed hard to fight back tears. He could not believe what the sensei had said. Not become a samurai? His family would know dishonor. His father's shame would be endless. The boy was so disappointed he felt as if he had been stabbed. The pain his failure brought to him was tangible. How would he face his father again?

The sensei watched the boy's reaction and waited for his news to finish its damage. There was nothing he could do about this part of his decision. The pain the boy suffered belonged to him alone. When enough time had passed and the boy's breathing had returned to a more even rhythm, the sensei spoke again.

"Kazuaki, I am sending you to Master Kurosawa. There you will learn jujitsu. Once you have learned all that may be learned from Master Kurosawa, you will go to the Empress and present yourself for service. I shall bring a message to your father explaining this decision. Go and ready yourself for your journey."

Kazu stood and bowed to his teacher. He no longer had to fight his tears, for he was too shocked to think of crying. Why would the sensei suddenly send him away in this manner? Although he was saddened by the thought that he was never to become a samurai, he was relieved that the dishonor that had frightened him only minutes ago had been partially taken from him. The teacher stopped him as he walked away.

"Kazuaki."

"Hai."

"You have studied very hard."

Kazu accepted the compliment and went to his quarters. The old servant met him a few minutes later. As he owned very little, Kazu was packed within a few minutes. The servant took Kazu's small box of possessions and lifted it into a cart. Next he lifted the boy onto a cushioned seat, where another servant, a young man, waited to take the boy on his journey. The old man bowed to the boy and wished him well. The driver called to the ox to move on, and the old man drifted out of sight as the cart moved around a bend in the road.

The trip, for Kazu, had been almost enjoyable – for one who had known nothing but discipline during his young life. He arrived at the door of the jujitsu master's home in a somewhat perplexed state. The servant who guided Kazu rang the bell at the entrance and spoke comforting words to him. Minutes ticked by before the bell was answered by an ancient man with a face full of wrinkles and a toothless mouth. After the servant had explained his mission, the old man waved the boy and the servant through the gate.

Two hours later, after they had eaten and rested, Kazu and his servant were brought to Master Kurosawa's chambers. They entered, bowed to the ancestors' altar and then knelt on mats on the floor. A few minutes passed before Master Kurosawa entered the room noiselessly, in ghostlike fashion.

The master was not as elderly as the servant who had answered the gate, but he was decidedly old. His skin was wrinkled around his eyes and mouth, as if he had had cause to smile often in his life. His head was bald, and his body was as muscular as a young farmer's might be. The old man moved with a grace that Kazu, in his young life, had never seen, creating the illusion that he flowed through space.

The master took no notice of the boy, but instead greeted the servant. The boy was shocked that he was not greeted, and kneeled in stunned silence.

"Iori, how is your master?" asked the old man.

"Hai. The sensei has known health these past few years since he graduated to sensei. He sends this boy to study under you, Kurosawa Akira. He asks that you watch after the boy's safety."

The old man clapped his hands and, where there had been

no one a moment ago, a servant appeared. The old man spoke to his servant.

"Bring this boy to the chamber beside your own. See that he has adequate clothes and bedding. You will serve him."

The servant bowed before the boy and then led him to the recesses of the house. When they had gone, the old man spoke to the boy's servant again.

"Iori, please speak the message your master sends me."

"Kurosawa Akira, my master had a dream several nights ago. *Buddha* visited the master and gave him directions concerning this boy. He said the boy had too much metal in his body to become samurai. He said the boy's path was destined ... that he was to become a jujitsu master. Once this is done, the boy is to offer his services to the Empress. *Buddha's* message, in this dream, was very clear. *Buddha* further told my master that the boy was to be brought to you. My master has brought *Buddha's* message to the boy's father, Hosokawa Hidetada, himself."

As the servant finished his narrative, a sadness swept over the old man's features. He thanked the servant and, oddly, told him that there would be no need for him to return to his master. Then he told the servant to go to the housekeeper and present himself for service there.

The old man went to the temple to pray to Buddha. Questions interfered with his peaceful reflections. *How odd. A Buddhist vision sent to a Shinto samurai sensei....* Buddha was known and well respected by the Shinto, but was still new when compared with a religion that was thousands of years old. He trusted the vision and its content. He knew that truth lay there, and he knew that the relatively young sensei, whom he had met a few years earlier when he had traveled to the Emperor's city, was now dead. He thoughtfully began a Shinto chant for the brave young man who had given his life in service to a god he did not recognize.

Days passed before the boy was brought to Master Kurosawa. Again he was brought to the teacher's chambers. The room was bare except for the ancestors' altar in one corner, a small table that sat in the center of the room and the floor mats that surrounded it. The teacher returned the boy's bow and then informed him of his new path.

"You now will begin the path of jujitsu. Today you will know the first lesson of your new path."

The boy bowed and begged permission to ask questions.

The old man assented to the boys wishes.

"What questions does one so young have to ask?"

"Please, Master Kurosawa, my servant said that my old sensei is dead. How did he die?"

"He was killed by your father."

The boy was shocked. For what reason would his father kill his teacher?

"Why?"

"He dishonored your family."

"How?"

"You have many questions, Kazuaki."

"Hai. Please, I wish to know."

"He brought news to your father that you have no skill with the sword."

A blush reached up over the boy's face and grabbed hold of his ears. He bowed his face to hide his shame. The master now asked him about his beliefs.

"Do you think that the only honorable path is that of the samurai?"

"Hai,"

"You find shame in the knowledge that you cannot master the sword?"

"Hai." The boy shrank lower as his body crumbled with embarrassment.

"Do you wish to return to your family?"

"No," the boy answered quickly.

"Do you wish to study jujitsu?"

"No," he answered as quickly.

If Kazu had looked up, he would have seen one of the smiles that had created the wrinkles on the old man's face. The old man nodded and was silent. Moments later, he spoke.

"Kazuaki, tell me what you know of a samurai's way."

The boy was surprised, and stuttered an incomplete response.

"The way of the sword, ahh, to serve and protect ... the way of strength." He finished more confidently than he had started. The old man nodded again and smiled. He told the boy to rise.

"Buddha was wise to send you to me. Go and eat your mid-day meal. Rest. This afternoon we will begin your training."

Kazu began to protest.

"Master, I do not need to rest. I have rested for days...." His voice trailed off as he realized his impertinence. The old man reacted with a slight lift of his eyebrow.

"Do as I say. That will be your first lesson. Obedience."

The days proceeded like the first. Kazu meditated in the morning after breakfast. Then he ate his midday meal, and finally, in the afternoon, he was active. The teacher's lessons seemed ridiculously simple and childish. Kazu had long ago forgotten that he was a child.

One day the master instructed him to do nothing that day but play with the cook's son. Kazu was insulted and horrified. What kind of sensei was this old man?

The cook's son was small for his age, but agile and quick in hands and mind. Ginbei took a small bow, a child's toy, and a miniature arrow. He placed the arrow on the sinew cord of the bow, pulled the cord back and released the arrow. The arrow struck the middle of a straw dummy, which had been set up for practise. He smiled widely, clapped his hands together and then turned to Kazu.

"Kazuaki, it is simple. Try to hit the straw man with your arrow."

Kazu growled in response and grabbed the bow from Ginbei's small hands. Ginbei's wide-set eyes winced in fear. Then he quickly regained his composure and stood silently as Kazu took his first arrow in hand. Kazuaki missed the target and growled louder.

"Grrrrrr!"

"Kazuaki, do not try to hit the target. Let the target find the arrow," Ginbei offered softly. He smiled encouragingly at Kazu and was met with an angry frown.

Kazuaki tried again and again, but soon all of the child's arrows lay on the ground surrounding the target. Only one arrow was stuck in the straw man: Ginbei's arrow.

In his annoyance, Kazuaki threw the bow on the ground.

"This is a stupid game!"

"No, Kazuaki! It is fun. You did well. It is your first time with a bow," Ginbei protested.

"You tricked me! There is something you did not tell me!"

"No, Kazuaki! There is no trick." Ginbei tried uselessly to defend himself.

"These games are for the son of a cook, not for the son of a samurai!"

"No, Kazuaki. This is a game for all warriors."

But Kazuaki ignored him. He marched off into the small orchard, where he wandered and pouted away the remainder of the afternoon.

When the cook heard about his son's failed attempts, he went to their master to express his sorrow at his son's failure. The old man answered serenely.

"Do not worry. Your son has not failed. I have watched him. He is a good and sensitive boy. You have lost no honor by his actions. He has served me well and as I have planned."

The cook left, much relieved, and returned to the kitchen, where he skillfully gutted several fish for dinner. He informed his son, when the boy returned from an errand, of their master's pleasure. Although both son and father were happy, they were also confused.

The following two weeks passed much as the first, with morning meditations, a leisurely midday meal and then simple exercises in the afternoon. At the end of the two weeks, again Kazu was instructed to play with the cook's son. Ginbei tried to teach Kazu several different games, as he hoped to find a game that Kazu would enjoy. But Kazu took no interest in anything that took him away from his path of becoming a warrior. Again, he ignored the cook's son and brooded. The master remarked not at all about this day, or the next.

This began a pattern. One day a week Kazu was expected to play the childish games that the cook's son patiently taught him. The old man praised the cook's son gently and ignored Kazu on these days. Finally Kazu could not stand this treatment any longer, and when he was instructed to play one morning, his anger escaped him and burst out from him in angry words. Everyone was there: the servants, the cook's son, the gardener and the old man.

"What kind of teacher are you?" he yelled angrily. "I waste time on these days, doing nothing, when I could be learning! You ask me to play with a servant! If my father hears of this he will have your head, old man!"

The courtyard was stunned into silence. The servant, who carried water to the house, stopped. The cook's son knelt and whispered a prayer to Buddha. The gardener stopped weeding and quickly turned his back on the scene. The master, who sat on a bench, stood slowly. He spoke to the boy, ignoring the horror in the eyes around him.

"Kazuaki. You will come with me."

He walked away and did not turn to see if the boy followed.

The boy's shame forced him to follow his sensei; but he trotted after the master with a touch of arrogance in his step. He refused to back down now that he had made so courageous a step forward. He would get the training a samurai's son deserved. He held his head high as he walked. When they had rounded the stone pathway and were hidden by a small stand of trees, the master stopped. He stood and stared at the boy until the boy finally dropped his eyes, and then his head. The master spoke quietly. Each word sounded like a round stone dropped heavily into a pond.

"You dishonor yourself and your family by your words." There was a long pause before he continued. "Kazuaki, you have only metal in your ki. You do not know the wind, the earth and, most importantly the sun." Again the old man paused. "Your life does not know balance. When you can come to me as Ginbei now is, then we will continue with your training. Until then, I shall no longer teach you."

Kazu's mouth dropped open and his eyes widened. The old man was putting a servant above him. In that moment, he hated the old man. The master looked at him with pity! Just what did the old sensei want? The old man spoke as if he heard Kazu's thoughts.

"Now go, and play as you have been instructed. When you know one game, completely, come to me and tell me about it. Until then, I do not wish to see you."

With that, the old man turned and gracefully walked down the path, away from the trees, the garden and the boy.

Kazu did not go and play as he had been told. Instead he sat down beneath the trees and contemplated his circumstances.

If he left, how would he get home? He could send word to his father. Surely his father already knew where he was. Why had his father not sent for him? Perhaps his father did not send for him because he was ashamed of him. His father had been told that he had no skill with a sword, that he would not become a samurai. That must be the reason no one had come to retrieve him.

He could leave and find another teacher, one that would help him to learn the sword. His first sensei obviously did not know that of which he spoke. He had been an unskilled teacher. Yes, that was it. His first teacher had not been able to recognize his skill, that was all.

As Kazu reasoned with himself, he knew that he lied to himself. He had respected his first sensei's abilities. Why had his first sensei sent him to this second one, who had no skill at all?

His thoughts rambled on as he sat beneath the trees and fidgeted with the material of his pants. His small hand rubbed the cloth between his fingers absentmindedly.

Where could he go? He knew he would not be allowed to escape. Maybe he should humor the old master so that he could move on with his lessons. Yes. This was it. The old man was crazy. If he humored him, he could study more until he figured out a way to escape. Kazu stood and left to find the cook's son.

That afternoon, and the next day, Kazu worked at learning the game the cook's son taught. He memorized each step his "playmate" showed him, until he was certain he knew how to hit the target with an arrow. And, with this certainty, his arrow finally found the target. Kazu smiled smugly as his arrow struck the straw dummy. He presented himself to the old master that evening after dinner.

The old master was sitting on the bench in the courtyard. He watched the sun as it set on the horizon. Kazu begged to speak and was given permission with one nod from the wrinkled bald head.

"Master Kurosawa, I have learned one game as you have instructed."

The old man nodded for the boy to proceed. Kazu carefully detailed how he had watched Ginbei and learned how to hit the target with his arrow. When he was finished, he waited for the old man's praise. The two steady brown eyes met his own and the old man spoke.

"Kazuaki, I see that you have learned nothing. Go back and *play* this game until you have learned it."

Kazu's anger rose, and he held it back with great effort. He bowed stiffly and returned to his chamber.

For the next week Kazu played this game and others, until he felt he was better than the cook's son. "Now," he said out loud to himself, "I know this game completely." Again he went before the master. And again the old man only shook his head.

"No, Kazu, you must learn to *play* the games!"

Kazu returned to his chamber again. He tossed and turned throughout most of the night. His young life was wasted under the care of a fool of a teacher! When he finally fell asleep, he slept for only a few hours.

Twice more Kazu tried to present his learning before the master. Each time, the master rebuffed Kazu's words. The old man actually told him to study Ginbei *in play*. Kazu was furious.

He could out-run, out-throw and almost out-shoot that stupid servant boy! That particular night he slept not at all.

When he joined the cook's son in the game the next day, Kazu was bleary eyed and sleepy. When his turn came and he stepped up to shoot his arrow, he slipped and fell in the mud face first. When Kazu looked up, he saw that Ginbei had come to his side in concern, but instead of helping him to stand, the servant boy began to laugh at him.

Ginbei threw his hands up in the air, pointed at Kazu's face and howled with laughter. Kazu's face puckered into a frown, which caused the cook's son to laugh harder. The servant boy's laughter made Kazu furious. He jumped up quickly and ran toward the stupid boy. As Kazu did, Ginbei ran to escape Kazu's fierce temper. He slipped in the same mud, and fell face first into it. When Ginbei looked up, Kazu saw for the first time what had caused him to laugh.

A clear cackling sound rose up over the courtyard. The birds stopped singing. The gardener looked up from his work, and a servant in the house came out to inspect this new noise. There lay the cook's son and Kazu, laughing together in the mud. The hoarse, cackling sound came from Kazu's unpracticed throat. The servant shook his head and went back to work, the birds began to sing and the gardener smiled.

Kazu and Ginbei played all afternoon in the mud. They made mud balls and threw them at each other. They built a palace and put toy stick samurai around it to protect it. They stuck their faces in the mud time and again, to make each other laugh. At the end of the day, as his servant washed him, Kazu's jaw ached from laughing. A weariness settled over him, as if he had finally put down a heavy basket that he had been carrying for years. The next morning the master called Kazu to him.

The sensei said nothing to Kazu, but ordered a servant to bring tea and food. When the tea had been served the old man gazed at Kazu with a serene smile. He asked him one question.

"Did you *play* yesterday?"

Somewhere inside himself, for the first time, Kazu understood the old master's request. The boy beamed with happy memories as he smiled and nodded yes. The old man rewarded him with a wide smile of approval. Then he asked the boy to tell him all about his play.

Now that the sun had found its way through Kazu's armor, he was allowed to return to his studies. Still, each day he played with the cook's son. Ginbei came to represent companionship and play to Kazu, and Ginbei changed in Kazu's mind from a servant into a valued friend.

One day a messenger came bearing news for Kazuaki. The news was brought directly to the sensei, as etiquette and code required. Moments later, the sensei entered the garden where the two boys played. His kind features were serious, and something else was different. Kazu suddenly realized that the old man was relieved. But, about what?

"Kazuaki, please come with me," the sensei said as he headed down the path that lead to the temple. Ginbei only shrugged when Kazu questioned him silently with a look.

A moment later the teacher and boy stood outside the temple. The afternoon sun was subdued in the early winter months. This diffused light softened the teacher's old face and cast a yellow glow over both teacher and student. Kazu watched the sensei expectantly as he waited for him to speak.

"Kazuaki, we have received news today of your family."

"Hai."

"Your father has died. The funeral was a month ago."

Kazu was stunned. He did not answer, and instead stood with his small arms folded into his sleeves; he hugged his body as he sought to brace himself against this news. Many thoughts passed through his mind. A mixture of emotions blocked his throat from speaking. The strongest of these was surprise at his own reaction as the shock of the news passed through him. He felt no grief, and instead felt a sense of exhilaration at being unburdened!

In that moment he knew that a fear had been growing inside him that he might be taken from the dojo. He had come to love the graceful movements the old master taught. He loved his friend Ginbei. He loved the courtyard and temples that had become home to him, and he did not want to leave them. And, he realized at last ... he loved the old master. The sensei seemed to sense this and gently placed his hand on Kazu's shoulder. His expression was tranquil and compassionate as he spoke.

"Come, Kazuaki. We shall pray for your father. We must give our gratitude to Buddha." Kazu did not ask for what he would express gratitude.

He had received his freedom.

The teacher continued with the simple exercises in the afternoon until Kazu had perfected the movements into an intimate grace. Kazu was ready to move to the next level.

One day Kazu entered the dojo and found Ginbei waiting in a student's position; he knelt respectfully on the floor near the front of the dojo. A moment later the sensei arrived, kneeled on the floor and returned bows to each of the boys. After the sensei had prayed to Buddha for direction for each of the boy's training, he spoke.

"Today, Kazuaki, you begin new lessons. Ginbei will be a worthy opponent for you."

Kazu looked sideways at Ginbei. His mind raced with the implications of what the sensei had said.

Worthy opponent? Ginbei? How long has he studied? A cook's son cannot study martial arts. This is forbidden! The old man had hidden Ginbei's training well. For Kazu had never heard either the sensei or Ginbei or any servant speak of it. His inner reflections were interrupted by the old man's voice.

"Kazuaki, Ginbei understands that he may not use or speak of his training away from the dojo. You will not speak of this either. Please rise and face each other," the sensei instructed.

Kazuaki and Ginbei stood, bowed to each other and fell immediately into the ready positions, with feet apart, one hand raised to ward off attack and the other hand clenched to strike if necessary. Although the boys were the same age, Kazuaki stood four inches taller then Ginbei.

"Ginbei." The sensei nodded toward the cook's son. Ginbei understood this quiet instruction and struck at Kazuaki with his closed right hand. Kazuaki's mind was still distracted by Ginbei's newly revealed skills, and his mouth fell open as Ginbei easily lifted Kazu over one shoulder and flipped him onto the floor.

"Teishi!" The sensei instructed the boys to stop.

Kazu stood, rubbed his shoulder and looked in bewilderment at Ginbei. Ginbei bowed once and then turned back to the teacher. The teacher nodded for them to try again. They faced each other, bowed, and then the sensei spoke Ginbei's name again.

This time Kazu was ready as Ginbei attacked. He dropped to one side and away from Ginbei. Kazu quickly rolled from his shoulder and jumped into the ready position. When he did, he saw that both Ginbei and the sensei were smiling at him. The sensei nodded for them to face each other. After each boy had bowed, the Sensei instructed Ginbei to attack for the third time.

Before Ginbei's hand reached its destination, Kazuaki kicked out in a circular motion at Ginbei's legs and brought him down to the floor. Kazu followed this with his hand to Ginbei's throat. Ginbei's face grimaced with unspoken pain.

"Teishi!" the sensei said firmly. Then the sensei told them firmly to sit down.

"Kazuaki, you do not learn jujitsu to fight, to inflict pain on your enemy. You learn jujitsu so you will not have to fight. You develop your ki to protect and serve others, not to harm. Ginbei, come here."

The sensei quickly inspected Ginbei's neck and shoulder.

"Go to washer woman. She will know how to heal this. Kazuaki, stay here."

Once Ginbei was gone, the sensei stared silently at Kazu. For many minutes the sensei did not speak. As the time slowly passed, Kazu's discomfort grew. When the sensei spoke his words shattered Kazuaki's previous world.

"Kazuaki, your father is dead, but he still rules your world. You must take his sword from your heart." The old man stopped and studied Kazu's face and then continued. When he spoke, his voice was hard and his expression was serious.

"The way to strength is not through aggression. There is no honor in fighting when you do not have to fight. You could have avoided Ginbei's attack. Jujitsu will teach you to control not only your own ki, but your enemy's energy, as well. You must not abuse this. To abuse this would cause disgrace to yourself and your enemy. You are bigger then Ginbei. You used this strength against him and, in doing so, only showed your own weakness."

Kazu stared back at his teacher, his face expressionless. Only the red tint which now crept across his cheeks showed his embarrassment for this scolding. The teacher spoke once more before he dismissed Kazu for the morning.

"Kazuaki, jujitsu is the 'gentle art.' From gentleness comes true strength. You may go to the temple now and pray."

Kazu bowed to his teacher and quietly left the dojo. His shoulders were weighted heavily by his shame.

The lesson Kazu learned in the dojo that day was never forgotten. And, as he moved through his lessons, he grew from a fierce boy into a strong and gentle man. His black hair was worn in a knot at the back of his neck. His square, flat face, with his wide-set eyes, was attractive in its serenity. He grew tall and carried himself with the grace and gentleness of the iris and with the certainty of the sun.

One night, a young woman, a few years older than Kazu,

was brought to his chamber. The old sensei had taught him about the balances of energy. The master explained that if all energies were not nurtured and kept in balance, an illness would result. He further explained that when a boy becomes a man, his fire must be fed or part of his ki will become weak. The young woman before him had come to instruct him in the care of this ki, this energy.

She stood with her head bowed, dressed ceremoniously in an embroidered kimono. Her silky hair was tied into a knot on the top of her head. Her skin and hands, Kazu discovered, were softer than flower petals. That night she began to introduce Kazu to his body and its needs.

Kazu's life progressed further into balance with the young woman's assistance. She became more beautiful to him as he became more intimate with her and himself. Nights became a time of sensuality and retreat. He rested and knew another kind of balance. A peace that Kazu had not before known settled into his life. And again his exercises took on a new depth and joy.

When peace had entered every part of Kazu's life, the old master, who never seemed to age, called Kazu to his chamber. The sun had risen hours before, and Kazu had just finished his morning's meditation.

"Kazuaki, you will have your midday meal with me," the old man stated. A few minutes later, the servants brought a lavishly prepared meal. They ate in companionable silence until Kazu was no longer hungry. The servant brought in fresh hot water for tea, and the old sensei himself prepared tea for Kazu. When this was done, the old master spoke.

"Kazuaki, this afternoon there will be no exercises. Today you will pack. Tomorrow you and Ginbei will leave for the Empress' palace."

The young man sat in stunned silence. This was due to happen, yet Kazu had not thought it would for another year or two. He did not want to leave, but there was no question in the sensei's eyes, no hesitancy in his voice. Tomorrow he would leave. As the young man stood to leave, the old man placed one hand on his shoulder. His old eyes brimmed with tears as he began his farewells to Kazuaki.

"Kazuaki, you have learned well. Remember the balance that has become part of you. Remember that the source of this balance is inside you. Remember that Ginbei knew this balance before you did. Remember the house you represent and the honor of this house. I am proud of you. I know you will represent this house well." The old man bowed to the young one, one master to another, and then turned away without shedding his tears.

They had lived in the palace for ten years. And there Ginbei enjoyed his servant's role to Kazu. When no one else was present, they joked with each other, and sometimes Kazu served Ginbei as part of the joke. Kazu and Ginbei understood that the old master had given Ginbei honor by choosing him to accompany Kazu to the Empress' palace.

The Empress was as delicate as a flower and yet as hard as the rock on which the palace was built. Kazu did not like her, but he understood that his job had no relation to his opinion of the Empress. He simply had to guard her.

Day after day passed into year after year. Kazu became skilled in a way that could be accomplished only by years of practice. His life was a serene one and, for the most part, uneventful. The Empress was demanding, but she had a dignity that made it tolerable.

One night as he walked down the hallway of the palace near her chambers, Kazuaki's path as a jujitsu master was finally tested. He heard a quiet sound. And then he saw a slight movement to his left, behind one of the great tapestries that lined the palace walls. Kazu fell instinctively into the ready position he had learned so long ago. He melted his body into the rock of the palace floor. He imagined himself as invisible and then drew all his ki into a wall of strength.

As the assassin left his hiding place, Kazuaki might as well have been invisible for the assassin never saw or heard Kazuaki move. Kazu spun toward the assassin in a graceful leap and kicked the sword out of his hand. As the assassin turned to fight him, Kazu's mind and heart felt this opponent's energy, and he quickly found his weakness. This time he used this weakness only to protect.

With two swift moves, Kazu saved the Empress' life. He threw the assassin over his head and onto the floor. Kazu leapt lithely over his assailant, then twisted the stranger's arm behind him while applying pressure at the elbow. If the assassin moved, his arm would break instantly. As Kazu rebalanced his breathing and his will to hold this prisoner, the sound of guards running was heard in the hallway. The assassin had been stopped in less than two minutes.

No word of Kazu's success was known outside the palace,

as the country would lose power if the people knew that the palace walls were penetrable. Fear would spread; the Emperor's reign would lose the status and importance it sought to maintain. The assassin was swiftly executed. The palace guards who had guarded that section of the palace were sentenced to death quietly, so that no questions would follow. New guards were found and Kazu was given a room directly next to the Empress' quarters.

This new status brought a quiet pleasure to Kazuaki and Ginbei. The added benefits were enjoyable, even though Kazu had less time than before this event. The Empress had always been very demanding, but she became more so after the attack.

For years Kazu guarded the Empress. Twice more assassinations were attempted, and each time Kazuaki saved the Empress' life. The Empress became so dependent on Kazu that any private fantasies he had had about leaving the palace were rapidly dismissed.

Kazu missed the quiet countryside. He missed the temple, the gardens and the dojo and his sensei. He knew that Ginbei missed his father, his mother and sisters ... and his studies. Kazu knew what Ginbei had given up by serving him. Kazu had privately hoped that they could return to the dojo so that Ginbei could continue in jujitsu, but the Empress' fears made this impossible.

When the Empress died of old age, Kazu himself was middle aged. Her continued reign had allowed peace to continue in the country. Her husband had died long before her, and she died happily, knowing that their eldest son would succeed to the throne.

The Empress' son did not possess the awareness of his father or his mother. Kazu and Ginbei were dismissed honorably from court with the excuse that a new sensei was needed to replace Master Kurosawa, who had died the year before. Although the dismissal was said to be honorable, Ginbei was hurt by this obvious slight. The new Emperor simply wanted younger guards surrounding him. Kazu finally convinced Ginbei to know joy from this decision by reminding him of the freedom they now faced. They would go home.

Kazu and Ginbei returned to the house where they had met, become friends and learned to play. Both men became instructors to young boys who were brought to the dojo. In teaching, Kazu found a tranquil pleasure that he had never known as a guard. And in this secure place of peace, Kazu passed away one night after a lifetime of discipline.

"the between ..."

Lohkan looked around at the familiar setting. The elder was there as before, kneeling by the waterfall, dipping his hand in and out of the water.

"What are you doing?" asked Lohkan as he approached the small man. The elder stopped and signed his answer with one wet hand and one dry hand.

I am washing away resistance.

"What?"

As you did, the elder continued to explain. *You needed to wash away the resistance you felt as Kazuaki.*

"I'm not sure I understand."

The answer the sensei wanted from you was there with you at all times. First you had to wash away your resistance. Sometimes resistance comes in the form of something you have been taught to believe.

Kazuaki was taught to live one way. When he gave up the idea that the sword was the only path for him and that work was the only existence, he was able to accept the fact that he needed to learn to play, to find balance. When he – you – gave up your resistance, you were opened to the answer.

This is so in all parts of life. **When you hold on tightly to one belief, your mind will not be free to pick up another.** *Your resistance acts as a wall and separates you from any truth you might find.*

Lohkan smiled in response. The elder smiled in return, and then questioned Lohkan.

What else did you learn?

Lohkan answered immediately.

"**Balance in life, in all things, is necessary for peace.** Balance creates harmony. The lack of balance creates discord. Also, I learned where to find strength. **Strength comes through acts of gentleness.**"

He stopped and thought about what he had just said. The elder questioned him again.

What did you learn from your father?

"I learned about arrogance."

What is arrogance, Lohkan?

"The inability to see beyond oneself and self concepts."

The elder nodded his head again to encourage Lohkan to continue. Lohkan breathed in the sweet air around the waterfall and resumed his dialogue.

"Arrogance creates another wall, a high one, that lets no one else in, that shuts out all others' thoughts and ideas. In that isolation you may hide from many parts of life, but mostly, I believe, from what you are really afraid of ... whatever that is."

Of what were you afraid, Lohkan?

"Failure."

Of what was your father afraid?

"His vulnerability."

The elder took Lohkan's hand in his and gently dipped it into the water.

Chapter 6

"the between ..."

Serra awoke after a long and nonsensical dream. Images moved, one after another, through her subconscious. Antonio made clay pots that Lotus Blossom scrubbed clean with sand and carried to Serra, who placed them in her work room on the ship. She rubbed her face with her hands as she sat up, and petals fell away as she did. She picked one up and examined it closely.

The background hue of the petal was a pale blue, while across the midsection a pattern of dark purple spots was densely sprinkled. At the tip of the petal, a pink splash of color gave the impression that someone had dipped it in paint. From this spot came the wonderful fragrance that now surrounded Serra.

At that moment a strong breeze filled the meadow and sent the loose petals into the air, where they swirled around Serra in a merry dance. She smiled as she watched the petals dance faster and faster. As the breeze became a gusting wind, the petals were drawn together into a tight spiral. All at once the wind stopped. In place of the mass of swirling flowers stood Quan Yin.

"How did you do that? Where did you come from?" Serra asked with astonishment. The guide said nothing and continued to smile at Serra's delight. The meadow was still and peaceful around them. Serra's sense of peace and well-being intensified in the guide's presence. At last Quan Yin spoke.

"Are you ready for your next lifetime?"

"Yes, but...."

"What do you wish to know, Serra?"

"Where am I? Is any of this real? Is this one long dream? Was I really Antonio or Lotus Blossom?"

"I promised you that I would answer your questions, and so I shall."

The guide's voice moved through the air and flowed around Serra, as if it were a wave of water settling with a gentle force over Serra's mind and body. Quan Yin continued.

"You are here on this planet – your home planet – but you are also between dimensions. If one of your kind were to walk into this place, they would not see you, but you would not cease to exist ... nor would I. We could see them if we chose to see them, although they could not see us. This 'seeing' would require an adjustment of the frequencies in this *between*. That could be done. You are not here to experience others' lives, so we do not see anyone. There is no need to."

The guide waited as Serra digested this new information. Somehow Serra understood the concepts of which the guide spoke, although she did not know how this understanding occurred. The guide continued.

"Lotus Blossom and Antonio each lived and, in them, you lived. You are they. They are you. There is no dream. You asked what was real. **Reality is that on which you focus.** If you, as Antonio, were to retain memories of these other lifetimes, then you would be unable to focus on the life of Antonio. The confusion would be too great. The reality would cease to exist."

"How do I remember these lives as I am now, as Serra?"

"You are at the core, the center."

The guide stopped, held up her hands, and made the shape of a sphere with them. As she did, a clear crystal sphere took form. She moved her small, delicate hands away, and the crystal sphere floated in the air between them. Serra watched with amazement. The guide gestured toward the sphere and continued her explanation.

"Serra, this sphere represents you. All you have learned from all your lifetimes is contained in this sphere."

She touched the sphere lightly, and a burst of blue light exploded in the center, where it continued to glow.

"The center, the blue light, is you. All around you is all that you have experienced."

Quan Yin's beautiful face glowed with pleasure as she taught Serra. Flowers were woven throughout her black hair, which was coiled delicately on top of her head. Her blue robe shimmered slightly as she raised her arm and touched a spot on the outside of the ball. A small yellow light appeared and glowed transparently.

"This is your lifetime as Lotus Blossom. This ..." she touched another spot, and a red-hued light appeared, "... is your life as Antonio," she said.

Serra watched the magical sphere with growing awareness.

The guide nodded and went on with the lesson.

"In the center of these is always you. **Your soul remains consistent. What you focus on is what changes.** If you looked out from the center toward ... here, where the yellow light is, you would see the reality of Lotus Blossom." Quan Yin drew her finger from the center blue light to the yellow glow. "Since you, Serra, are the center, you have the ability to see all of them, to know all of them. Each lifetime touches another, but they are not linear! Antonio affected Lotus Blossom as much as Lotus affected him. As long as you exist, they all exist. You are the center, and you cannot cease to exist!"

"I'm not sure that I understand."

"You will, Serra. Everything is inside you."

"Where are we on this sphere? Serra asked as she tried to sort through these new concepts. The guide pointed to a spot inside the ball, near the center, and a lavender light glowed next to the blue one, overlapping it.

"How do other souls' lifetimes touch mine?" she asked, with the senses of awe and confusion growing equally.

Quan Yin quickly formed dozens of spheres, which encircled Serra's. Many touched hers, or overlapped it. Others floated nearby. Quan Yin clapped her hands, and the air filled with hundreds, thousands, millions of spheres. They crowded the meadow, filled every space. Some overlapped others until they almost covered one another. Countless crystal spheres touched. All the spheres, each with a blue light inside, were touched by another. None, not one, was separated and off by itself. The concept was staggering. Again the guide spoke.

"We are all connected. When one life is touched...." She touched a ball, and it immediately brushed against its neighbors, which bumped up against others. The effect was a shimmering wave of crystal spheres and lights. "Then all are affected," she finished.

Quan Yin clapped her hands together, and the spheres disappeared, except for two balls. One Serra recognized as her own. The second overlapped hers in perfect balance. The two spheres almost made one. The two centers sat next to each other, and the energy between them formed a perfect figure eight. The guide spoke.

"You see yours, and this one that marries yours is Lohkan's."

A deep longing filled Serra, but she did not have time to follow it. Quan Yin pointed to a place on her sphere, and a beautiful green light glowed there.

"It is time for you to focus now on this life, Serra."

The breeze blew up and caught the spheres. They tumbled off in the wind and Serra found herself chasing after them.

If the wind had not blown that day, then perhaps the tragedy that touched countless lives would not have occurred, but luckily it did. The winds had ridden in before the storm, had come in quickly, too fast, and had surrounded the small fishing vessel in unrelenting gusts. A small child watched from beneath a tarp where he sat in the bottom of the boat, as the wind captured him and his father and pitched their boat about in uncontrolled fury. His father, who was dressed in layers of wool beneath a primitive oiled-cloth coat, rowed uselessly against this onslaught. His father had tried desperately to outrace the storm, but the storm had ridden up on this fierce wind and caught them. It pulled and tore at his father's coat like a wild animal might have attacked its prey, with sharp and deadly teeth. His father held on tightly to the oars and tried to fight this force, but the storm was more powerful.

Suddenly, the storm used its full strength and impatiently smashed itself against this dory and its passengers. The little boy ducked his head under the cloth as rain fell in heavy sheets that seemed to bruise his skin. The last image the little boy saw before he hid was his father's rain-soaked face contorted in anger as he stood and shook his fist at the storm. A moment later, a fifteen-foot wave crashed over the boat and knocked his father overboard into the unforgiving waters, which took his life guiltlessly. The wind and storm, in a mistaken fit of perversity, left the little boy inside the boat.

He had been too frightened by the fury of the sea to cry out, and lay hidden beneath the cloth, frozen by wind and cold. For the next hour the ocean tossed, smashed and drenched the dory with its anger. The boy had heard of the anger that lurked in the seas. Sometimes it was vengeful, as he now witnessed. Other times it was sinister, as when the mists crept over the water and dissolved a man and his boat in dense gray fog. As the son of a long line of fishermen, the boy had heard all the stories.

That he and his father had been caught by the storm, had not seemed odd or wrong to the boy. He knew that each day his father sailed out in his boat might be his last. His mother had prayed to Saint Nicholas, the patron saint of sailors, to protect her husband. The boy knew the prayers by heart, and repeated them now out loud to the sea. As if the sea or Saint Nicholas himself heard the prayers, the storm suddenly abated. The boy peeled off the heavy wet cloth, looked about and cried out weakly. "Da! Da! Where are ye? Please, don't leave me, Da!" He cried softly and buried his face in his hands. Because he hid his face, he did not see the large wave bearing down on him. The ocean, with dogged intent, sent one final attack upon this last victim. The wave struck with a hurtling force against the dory and split it in two.

Erin ran up to the house, yelling loudly as she did.

"Ma! Ma! Come see! There! Down by the surf, on the beach, is a boy! Ma, I think he might be alive!" she said breathlessly.

Erin's mother dressed quickly, throwing her woolen cape over her shoulders. She followed her daughter down to the beach. There, as she had been told, lay a boy.

He breathed, but barely. His small hands clasped the remaining two feet of the bow of a dory. The small fingers rigidly clenched onto the wood, and she had to fight to unclasp them. She wasn't sure of his age. He looked as if he were about eight or nine years old. His red hair was matted against his cold, blue skin, and the woman feared that, although he was not already dead, he would certainly die soon. She carried his water-soaked body back up the beach and to her cottage.

Once there, she carefully stripped him of his woolen clothes. She rubbed his blue skin until it turned pink, and then wrapped him in the comforter from her own bed. Her daughter heated water over the fire while the mother checked the boy for broken bones. Other than a large lump on the back of the boy's skull, there were miraculously no injuries. She dressed the abrasions she found near the lump, which were probably caused by a splintered piece of wood. Once this was done, she made a pot of tea for herself and her daughter, as well as for the boy.

She took a small bowl of broth from a pot of soup which simmered at the back of the fire and carefully spooned sips into the boy's mouth. He swallowed some of the hot broth, but still did not awaken. The woman left the boy then and put on her cloak again. She spoke to her daughter.

"Erin, I'm goin' to get Father McGuinnen. If the boy dies he'll be needing last rites. I'll be home soon."

Erin sat vigil over the strange boy. He was close to her in

age – a little younger, maybe. He looked oddly peaceful for someone who had almost drowned. Since she lived near the sea, Erin
often wondered, *What does it feel like to drown? Are God's angels
waiting for you under water to carry you to heaven? What happens if you do not receive last rites? Can you go to heaven anyway?* As she thought about these questions and others, the door
flew open and her father entered the cabin.

Her father was not a man whom Erin could love. He was
hard and angry. His small eyes were black, instead of green, blue
or gray, and were often squinted with suspicion. His hands were
gnarled from the long, cold work of fixing nets and fishing the
cold oceans. His back was bent from arthritis that had formed in
an old injury. He had never smiled, so far as Erin knew, and his
fist had found its way to Erin's face or her mother's too often. He
saw the boy and growled at his daughter.

"Who be this lad?"

Erin swallowed and backed away. "I don't know, Da," she
whispered. Her father pushed her out of his way and approached
the unconscious boy. He pushed the boy's head back and forth
roughly as he examined the lad.

"Erin! Where did this lad come by?"

"I found him down on the beach, Da."

The father stood over the boy and observed him. Suddenly
he reached out and slapped the boy's face again and again.

"Awaken, lad! Why do ye sleep in my house?"

Erin gasped, and then ducked behind a chair. As she
watched, the boy's eyes flew open. He stared around himself in
confusion. His eyes were a clear green that seemed unnaturally
bright. Erin's father was about to drag the boy to a sitting position when the door banged open.

His wife entered the room, followed by the local priest.
Father McGuinnen's eyes widened when he saw that the boy was
not only alive, but conscious. He stepped over to the boy and
began to examine him.

"Who are ye, lad?" the priest asked plainly, but the boy
only stared back at him with a bewildered expression. Erin's
father watched the scene and commented.

"The lad's probably daft and dumb. Can ye take him with
ye, Father? I'll no have him here. He don't belong in this house."

The priest ignored the man's words and studied the boy
further. He had a good-sized bump on the back of his head,
which could explain the boy's lack of response. The lad was obviously dazed. Father McGuinnen tried again.

"Lad, don't ye know yer name? Speak, lad, and tell us who ye are."

The boy mouthed words silently, but no sound came out. The priest prayed quietly to the saints for help for the poor lad. He stood up and addressed the husband.

"Now, Paddy. Ye know I have no room in the church for this lad. But, ye do. Ye have this roomy cottage, and I'll swear on the Bible that this lad'll no be any trouble to ye. Take care of the lad while I send word round to see if any put claim to him." The priest lowered his voice so that only the father could hear. "God has sent the lad to ye, to replace yer son that died. When he heals he'll be a good workin' lad for ye."

The man thought this over. He did need help. His back ached worse each year. His son, who he had hoped would ease his days and work alongside him in the boat, had died a year ago from pneumonia. He looked at the boy and his unusual green eyes.

"Aye, Father. We'll keep the lad until he heals. If he's daft, I'll not keep him."

The priest nodded. "Aye, aye, most likely the boy'll not live, anyhow. Call me if that happens." The priest referred to the boy's death casually, and then he left the cabin without staying for tea.

The woman ladled more broth into a bowl, and again spoon-fed the boy, who drank the broth greedily. Behind her, her husband paced and lectured. They'd keep the boy only, *only* if he could be of use. He'd have no dullard using up their space and precious food. He ranted for a half-hour, and then went to the bedroom to nap before dinner.

His wife closed the door to the bedroom and sighed. The boy watched her every movement through his strange eyes. She spoke quietly to her daughter.

"Erin, go n' get some water from the well. Be quiet. I don't want to wake yer Da."

She chopped wild onions and roots and put them into a pot which hung over the fire. She dumped in chunks of a variety of fish her husband had caught that day. She pinched a branch from a bunch of dried herbs that hung from the wall and put this, too, in the pot. There was no bread this week, because they had not had enough of a catch to trade for grains, or honey. In fact, she had not tasted anything sweet in months. The wild fruit brambles had been stripped bare by birds, before she had been able to pick even one berry. She took out a wooden bowl and carefully measured a teaspoon of salt from it into her palm. She added this to the stew. Erin dragged the heavy bucket through the door without spilling any water or making a sound. Throughout all that happened the strange boy watched them closely. He seemed fascinated by every move, as if each thing he saw was new to him.

The woman quietly removed a tin from a high shelf and pried it open. She put her finger to her lips as she looked at her daughter. Silently she drew out three biscuits. She poured tea and gave one biscuit to her daughter and one to herself. She took the third to the boy and broke it up into chewable pieces, which she placed one by one into his open mouth. He reminded her of a baby bird in the way he sat and waited for each piece.

She took her biscuit and tea and sat at the table with her daughter, who had already finished hers. The woman ate fervently. The biscuits were a rare treat that she gave her daughter and herself. Often she looked over her shoulder, toward the closed door to the room where her husband slept. She caught herself listening for his snores and hoped that he would not wake up. Not yet! She finished the last of the biscuit and relaxed. Her daughter smiled up at her. This was their secret. They both looked at the strange boy. Now someone else shared their secret.

The swelling on the boy's head went down, but he did not talk. Paddy ignored him, except to yell at him now and then. Erin encouraged him to talk and the wife spoke to him each day, but still he did not respond.

"Laddy, do - ye - know - yer - name?" Erin asked slowly.

"Erin, I don't think he understands. Leave him be now," her mother said as she watched the two children who sat on the bed by the window. Erin's brown hair was twisted into a tight braid that lay over one shoulder and bobbed up and down with her head as she spoke. The boy reached out and touched this braid with his thin fingers. His clear green eyes followed Erin's as she talked. Erin pushed his hand away from her hair and her small nose wrinkled as she disagreed with her mother.

"No, Ma. He does understand! Watch."

Erin walked briskly across the cabin floor and pretended to pick up a heavy log by the fireplace. She grunted, twisted her freckled face into a frown and then turned toward the boy.

"Laddy, can ye help me?"

The boy stood and walked slowly to Erin. He was a few inches shorter than her and very thin. He wore a pair of Erin's father's pants that had been pinned and rolled up to fit him. He pulled up his pants, carefully bent over and lifted one end of the log as Erin lifted the other end. They pushed the log onto the coals at the back of the fireplace, and then he stood back and stared into the flames that erupted.

"See, Ma!" Erin hissed.

"Aye, I do. Maybe he'll talk yet," she said doubtfully.

But the boy remained silent over the next few weeks.

The wife massaged her right shoulder with her fingers. She was tired, dreadfully so. She had been splitting logs all morning. The wood she had just split lay in a pile around her on the ground. A fine mist had begun to fall from the sky and would dampen all the wood if she did not get it stacked quickly. Paddy was out in his boat and would not be back until dark. Erin was indoors, cleaning. She sighed, stared out at the ocean for a moment, and then stooped to pick up the wood. A slight rustling of fabric announced someone's presence, and she turned to find the boy working beside her. He quickly picked up the split logs and silently stacked them on the wood pile. The wife worked with him, and soon the wood was neatly stacked.

"Thank you, Laddy," she said as she turned to thank him, but he was already gone.

A few days later, as the wife cleaned out the fireplace, again she heard the soft sound of the over-large pant legs brushing against each other. The boy dropped to her side, took the scrub brush from her wet and blackened hands and began to clean the stones for her. She looked about to see if anyone was watching, and then rose wearily to her feet. She crossed the room, sat down slowly in one of the chairs by the table and peacefully put her head on the wooden surface to rest.

An hour later, she awoke when someone shook her arm. She instinctually covered her face with her arms and cowered, fearful that her husband had found her lazily sleeping the afternoon away. Strong fingers pried her arms down, and she raised her face to two remarkable green eyes. On the table before her was a steaming cup of tea and a biscuit. She turned quickly toward the fireplace. It was spotlessly clean, with the bright flames of a new fire licking its inner walls.

The boy stood silently beside her. And then, without knowing why, she began to quietly weep. He carefully pushed the teacup toward her. Her fingers touched his small ones as she took the cup, and for a second she held his hand tightly. She looked into his young face and nodded.

"Thank you, Laddy."

But he did not respond.

"I'm taking the lad to father McGuinnen this mornin'," the husband said between mouthfuls of porridge. He wiped his rough hands across his face to wipe off some food. The wife started and dropped her teacup. Tea splashed over the table and down the front of her dress. She quickly mopped up the spill with a rag before her husband's anger arose.

"Paddy..." she began to protest.

"Don't argue with me, Mary! The lad's useless."

Suddenly, the years of loneliness and despair flashed by her. The endless hours of hard work with little reward overwhelmed her. The life that lay ahead of her without the boy's small acts of kindness was unbearable.

"No! No, Paddy! He's staying here with us! God sent him to us! Who are you, I ask, to argue with God?"

She threw down the rag and glared at her husband's startled face.

Mary's bravery so surprised her husband that he was shocked into inaction for some time. During the next few days he came to the conclusion that the boy might still be of some use, even though he was dull. This reason, more than his wife's demands, caused him to announce several days later that the boy could stay.

As the boy grew, he looked in all outer appearances to be a normal young man. His red hair was thick and bright. His back became strong and powerful from long hours of pulling nets out of the water. His legs were trim and muscular. Only his eyes belied his innocence. They stared vacantly into the distance whenever the boy was idle. The startlingly green color with which the boy had been blessed added to his already disconcerting gaze. He never learned to speak; not because he couldn't create sound through his mouth, but because he simply did not have any interest. He groaned in his sleep and infrequently called out, "Da." And yet he never spoke a sound during his waking hours. Whatever the boy had experienced so many years before at sea had shocked him into silence.

While Mary did not exactly come to love the boy, for how could she love what appeared to be an empty shell, she was quite fond of him. She depended on him for his tender acts. For with her he was his most gentle. And when no one else could call him back from his distant, empty gaze, only the woman's voice could bring a response from him.

Erin did grow to love the boy. For some reason, from the time the boy had joined their family, her father had stopped beating thcm. Neither she nor her mother discussed this strange phenomenon, but each night Erin prayed to her patron saint that this good luck would continue. One night when she prayed, a thought suddenly occurred to her. Perhaps the boy was a guardian angel sent from her patron saint. With each passing week this idea grew into a fully formed belief. The boy's gentle manner encouraged her theory, and she came to love him as she might any religious figure.

Paddy saw the boy as a valuable workhorse. The boy worked hard and did as he was told. Since the boy had a strength for drawing in nets that Paddy did not possess, his help enabled Paddy to increase his catches. Because they were able to stay out longer and bring in larger catches of fish, his life improved considerably. He was able to trade for goods that had long been needed.

In the village, Paddy's obvious change in prosperity changed the villagers' response to him. They began to respect him, and with this respect they treated him differently. His self-confidence grew and spread into his home life. He no longer desired the release of his bitterness by beating his family. Thus, Paddy, too, came to depend on the dull boy. The boy became his own personal servant or possession ... or so he thought.

People in the village responded to the boy, each in their kind. Many of the young boys taunted and teased him. Some were more cruel than others, and threw rocks. Many of the young women were taught to stay away from him and his strange gaze. And as the strange, dull boy grew into a young man who was actually fair to look upon, the parents encouraged their daughters more than ever to keep away.

Old men in the village treated him with disdain, while their wives clucked their theories back and forth, concerning the boy's problems. The favorite theory was that God had punished the boy for some sin from his life before he came to their village. The old women were sure of this, and in their later years prayed each Sunday that his soul would find redemption.

For the priest, the boy became sustenance for his work and self-esteem. Everyone else in the village called the boy "Laddy." The priest had christened the boy and named him "Christopher", after the patron saint of those who traveled. He saw the boy as a lost traveler in the world which surrounded him.

In the boy, he also saw a grand and awe-inspiring reflection of his work, for he was certain that Christopher's gentle countenance was a direct result of his own spiritual guidance. Christopher sat and gazed with rapt attention as each week he personally lectured the boy on religious doctrine. His gaze never flinched as he listened to the sermons, and the priest was certain that Christ himself had sent the boy to him for spiritual counsel. As the boy's life passively progressed, the priest's self-worth expanded with righteous success.

When the boy died one day during a boating accident, the whole town mourned, although no one had ever known him.

"the between ..."

The path that led to the top of the ridge was lined with new green grass. Serra reflectively walked this path to the top, where the guide awaited her. She nodded to the guide, but did not smile. She felt peaceful and honored to have experienced the life she had just led.

Quan Yin took Serra's large hand in her small one, and they walked along the path that now ran parallel to the top of ridge. Below them, to their left, the wide lake lay in all its splendor. To their right the forest sat, thick, lush and deep green. They came upon an outcropping of stone, and the guide sat down on one of the large rocks. Serra sat on one of the boulders next to her.

"Serra, do you wish to review this life you have experienced?"

"Yes."

She did, but she felt unusually quiet. After several minutes Serra spoke.

"You sent me to this lifetime so that I would understand what you tried to explain to me before I left." This was a statement, not a question. She took a deep breath and continued.

"Christopher's life was devastated by his father's death. His devastation affected everyone whom he met. All were eventually touched by his experience, though they were not consciously aware of this."

"Yes, Serra. Your experience on the boat eventually led to

peace and prosperity for the family who fostered you."

"Yes. This seems strange, that one person's tragedy could touch so many," replied Serra.

"Yes, Serra, but the boy was sent as a guide to this family."

"A guide?"

"Yes. Christopher was a guide to this family ... in a way, to the whole village. Is this not obvious?" Quan Yin questioned her with a smile.

"Yes." Serra nodded slowly. "Here in *the between* it is clear."

"How did you feel as Christopher?" the guide asked.

"Detached. I felt as if I were never quite in his body; as if I hovered a few feet away, but was still part of him, me. This experience was confusing and humbling."

"When a soul is sent to act specifically as a guide, it will experience some sort of soul removal, as you did. The shock of the boating accident moved you out of Christopher's body enough to allow a larger part of you – your center – to take control. This allowed Christopher to go through this life with relatively little pain, and still he accomplished the work he – you – were sent there to do.

"Before you left you decided that you wished to help a family that was troubled. You wished to experience 'service' completely. If you had gone into service as a religious figure or person of good works, your service would not have been as thorough because your ego would have required a different lesson."

Quan Yin stopped talking and waited for Serra to digest these concepts. After Quan Yin knew by Serra's radiant expression that she understood, she continued to question her.

"What else did you learn, Serra?"

Serra stared at the lake from where she sat. The sky was mirrored there in soft purples and blues. A wind blew across the water's surface and disrupted this perfect reflection. Serra reached out with her hand as the wind rose above the lake's surface and up the hillside to where she and Quan Yin sat. As the wind blew across her fingers and lifted her hair, she answered Quan Yin's question.

"I learned that most people Christopher met were not deliberately cruel. Their insensitivity was based on the fear they felt. Very few were calculatingly unkind. Most were simply afraid of me. In my research, I have noted that many races of this planet have a tendency toward cruelty in their cultures and societies. Now I would change that assessment. I would say that these people and their societies are afraid."

"What else?" The guide gently probed Serra onward.

"I learned that each life, no matter how dull-witted, intelligent, magnificent or small, is important. No life is without meaning. Christopher appeared ignorant and dimwitted to the people around him. Yet he touched every person in that village. **Everyone, each soul, is important and has a purpose!**"

The guide smiled as Serra talked. Suddenly, Serra asked a question that she had meant to ask earlier.

"Time! I was in a fishing village off the British Isles – after the time of Christ. The fishing village was a mixture of Irish-Scottish Christian followers. What happened? I was in Italy around 1400 B.C. as Antonio, and then I jumped to 1750 A.D?"

Quan Yin answered by materializing the crystal globe once more. She pointed to the blue light in the center.

"Serra, you are the center. Time is not linear, as you already know. It exists all around you. You moved into what is known as the 'future', because the lesson you wished for was there."

The guide touched the green spot on the sphere.

"You did not move 'ahead.' You went to a different place in your sphere. That is all. You changed your focus."

She took Serra's hands and placed them around the crystal sphere. Then Quan Yin drew a line from the blue glow in the center to the green spot that floated on the outside of the sphere.

"You are not living separate lives, one lined up one after another. Each life surrounds and touches the next. All are a part of you, your life, this sphere."

Quan Yin traced the sphere with her fingers, and as she did, hundreds of fine crystal lines connected many bright spots in and around the sphere. The sphere glowed as if a silvery spider web had encased it.

"Time is what holds all lifetimes together! It fills and binds space. It exists all at once! You turned your focus to here," she stopped and pointed to the green glowing light. "And went to this place in time. You and your co-researchers have used this theory to travel through space. Now you are using this same theory to experience other lifetimes and dimensions."

Serra puzzled over this new application of a theory in which she was well trained. Her people, and other races, had learned long ago to move through space with their spacecraft by applying the theory that time existed all at once. She had not applied it before to a spiritual journey. What had begun as an anthropological journey had turned into a spiritual one. She now knew that the two could not be disconnected. How could they, when she was at the center of both? Quan Yin touched her shoulder.

"I must leave you, Serra. Think about what you have learned."

The guide vanished then, while Serra watched. She left Serra sitting on the cliff with the beauty of the sky above her, the lake below and many questions inside her.

Chapter 7

*I*n the beginning she thought she might escape from the thieves, but she did not. As she ran through the forest, her footfall gave her away. The crunching of leaves beneath her feet echoed loudly through the woods and led the men to where she ran. One ran ahead and caught her while two others came from behind. In seconds she was trapped. They raped her there where they caught her, in the depth of the forest where none could hear her muffled shouts for help.

When Iduna awakened she was dreadfully cold. Her body shook and her thighs, stomach and arms throbbed from the beatings the thieves had given her. If she had not resisted, perhaps the bruises would have been less. Yet something inside her had been unable to give up. She had fought heroically and had suffered for her courage. She tried to sit up, but her head swam from the blows it had taken during her fight. She searched her scalp with trembling fingers, and felt the wetness that was blood.

Closing her eyes, she sent a silent prayer for help to the gods. Maybe one god who was not too busy with the petty doings of man might find her and help her. She managed to lean on one arm long enough to scoop up handfuls of leaves, and then she covered her body carefully in the dried, thick carpet on the forest floor. She had just finished covering her shoulders and head when she lost consciousness. Only her forearm lay visible.

Iduna retreated into a deep state of unconsciousness and fever for two days. Fortune followed her bad luck, and no rain fell during this time. Her layers of fur and leather protected her body and kept her warm enough to survive the cooling nights of autumn. Around her, birds sang uneasily as they watched the mound of leaves, which moved ever so slightly with her uneven breathing. One brave fox sniffed her arm, but found the scent human and unpleasant. The urinating the men had done after their violent deed acted as an invisible barrier and warded off other animals with its strong ammonia stench.

And so she lay, asleep, fitful and delirious, until the fever broke on the afternoon of the third day. When she awoke from this hard slumber, she at first remembered nothing. Iduna knew not where she was. She did not know how she had come to lie there on the ground, covered with leaves. Stiffly, she sat up and brushed piles of leaves from her body. As she saw the purple bruises on her arms and thighs, her memories came back to her. For a long time she could not move. She cried noiselessly.

Eventually the setting sun was what prompted her to move. To remain in the forest after dark would be dangerous. Iduna did not realize that she had spent two nights there already. She stumbled to her feet and shakily began to walk home.

Her cottage lay east of the forest in a glade which was filled with sunshine even in the winter. Her husband had gone on a hunting expedition with his brothers and was due to return in two days. Iduna's parents lived a short walk from her cottage, on the further side of the glen, in the midst of the west stand of the forest. She knew she should try to get to her parents, but she doubted she could get that far. Iduna walked through the woods in this way, in physical pain, thirsty, exhausted and yet practical in her thoughts. Survival had taken over and would not allow the horror of what she had experienced to come through until she had reached safety again.

When Iduna stepped out of the forest and into her familiar glade, she was surprised to see smoke coming from the chimney. Perhaps her mother had come to visit. She walked across the yard in a daze, squinting in the sudden brightness of dusk, which was far brighter than the now-black forest. Voices penetrated the thick walls of the cabin and fell out into the night, mens' voices.

Suddenly, she froze as her body understood the meaning before her mind did. Thorbjorn was not due home yet. The thieves were in her home!

Her legs began to shake violently as she tried to step backwards without making any noise. With each step, she grew more frightened. An overwhelming fear of being discovered overcame her. Terrified that the unspeakable would happen again, she turned and rushed toward the trees. Just before she reached the edge of the forest, the door of the house burst open and the voices within rushed out into the quiet dusk. Without looking, Iduna ran. The voices and the men followed her.

"There she is!"

"Quick."

"Iduna!"

A strong arm grabbed her by the shoulder and dragged her to a stop. She began to strike out wildly. Her screams and cries were deadened as a hand fell over her mouth. Another arm went around her waist, while someone else held her arms down. A male voice shouted a command.

"Iduna! Stop! It is me, Thorbjorn!"

Thorbjorn shook her until she opened her eyes. The shock that had been suppressed until now took hold. She sobbed hysterically and tried to pull free. Thorbjorn motioned for his brothers to help lift her, and gently they carried Iduna back to the cabin.

For days she did not talk. Her mother dressed and bathed her wounds, and she lay in a corner of the bed, curled up in a ball like a frightened animal. Thorbjorn and his brother tracked her footprints back to the site of the attack. Because four days had gone by, the footprints of the attackers were difficult to follow. They could see that at least two men, probably more, had attacked Iduna. Until she talked they would know little else. Thorbjorn returned to the cabin each night exhausted by the ineptness of his search and his inability to avenge his wife. Finally he gave up his search and focused on the preparations he needed to complete, to prepare for the onset of winter. Iduna's mother came each day to cook and clean. Autumn moved away one day and let winter take its place, and Iduna awoke after her long illness to find her mother working in her stead.

Snow howled around the cabin in piercing shrieks. The thick log-and-mud walls kept the cold at bay, but still Iduna could not get warm. She pulled a fur wrap over her head and continued with her tasks. She built up the fire with another log and an armload of kindling and went back to stirring the dough that would eventually become hardtack.

Three moons of winter had passed. Her dreams were dark and quiet ... too quiet, as if the thieves were waiting there in the darkness for her. Consequently, she slept little at night, and instead napped in the middle of the day, when the limited sunlight could protect her from the darkness. Large circles developed around her eyes, and her thick blond hair fell limply over her shoulders. She retained full memory of her experience, which, although she tried not to show it, left her jumpy and afraid.

She always had been strong and brave. Her parents had

boasted of her bravery to all their tribe members. "Iduna," they had explained, "is braver than most men." Now she felt afraid, all the time. Something had been ripped out from inside her. The strength for which she had been known now appeared to be dwindling like the flame of a candle when the wick has been trimmed too short. Some days the flame barely flickered at all, and she felt as if she could scarcely breathe. Many days she was certain that the best part of her had been extinguished.

A strangling fear of something else had grown inside her. She had been unable to resume coupling with Thorbjorn. He was gentle and patient with her torn soul and frightened body, and yet she could not bear his advances. Each time he approached her, she became frozen and dead, as if in those moments the candle truly had been blown out. Her fear was that nothing warm remained inside her. Her love for Thorbjorn existed, but she could not feel it. Her heart, in its search for peace, had temporarily closed all doors. Would those doors ever open again?

Another fear grew alongside this one. For these three moons she had not experienced a woman's ritual. She had not bled. This, she knew, was a sure sign that she was pregnant. If she and Thorbjorn had not mated these three months, then one of the thieves' spirit must have decided to stay and impregnate her. She told no one: not her mother, and especially not Thorbjorn. If she were with child from a thief's spirit, then she would have to kill the child when it was born. The three thieves had been darker of skin and hair. Surely the thief's spirit would leave traces of darkness on the child. She would know when she saw the baby. If the child was darker than she, then she would kill it. Tormented by these fears and doubts, she worked through each day, hoping the next would not be as long.

Long ago, two moon cycles, Thorbjorn had first noticed she carried a child. Five moons had passed without a woman's ritual. Thorbjorn had been quiet when he had noticed that her stomach was rounder and her breasts fuller with the mother's miracle, milk. She worked at hiding these signs, but her body, in its youth, was determined to ripen quickly, faster than some. Thorbjorn said little after his discovery. When another moon had passed, he asked if Iduna knew whose spirit occupied the child.

Part of Iduna's strength lay in her honesty; not only with others, but in herself. She could not hide the truth from Thorbjorn, and confessed that she feared the unborn child might *not* be of Thorbjorn's spirit. Iduna explained her theory that the child would be dark in coloring if it contained the thief's spirit. An event that should have brought them closer, instead saddened them, for both now carried the burden.

One day Thorbjorn told Iduna that he was going to check his traps. Instead, he trudged through two miles of snowdrifts to his parent's cabin. His tall figure was bowed under heavy winter clothes and from the one lie he had just told his wife.

He discussed his plight with his mother and father at length. In the end, his parents explained that Iduna was right. If the baby's coloring was dark, it should be killed. His parents had explained that, by clan custom, if the child was of the spirit of the thief, then it was not only the baby who would be tainted. He would have to remove Iduna from their home and end their marriage. Thorbjorn returned home empty handed from his supposed hunt, and he was obviously depressed. His blue eyes were a cloudy grey, and he could not bring himself to look into Iduna's worried ones.

Before Iduna had been raped, they had had a joyous and prosperous marriage. When Iduna had chosen him over the many suitable men in their valley, Thorbjorn had been elated. That elation had never diminished. Iduna had been a beautiful and hearty woman, an enjoyable companion, and a strong mate. His heart now ached as if from the weight of a large stone tied to it. He had little hope left because he was afraid he had lost everything.

Spring was not hopeful that year. Thorbjorn's and Iduna's parents awaited the birth anxiously. Thorbjorn prayed to the gods each morning that the child would be of his spirit. He prayed to keep his wife, and that she would heal.

Iduna grew more depressed as the pregnancy progressed. Her parents advised that she not show herself publicly. They did not want their daughter to suffer any criticism or gossip. And so the sunshine her body so badly needed was denied her. Her dreams grew darker, and though the outside world grew lush and green with spring's growth, she did not see it. Flowers poked up through the last of the snow, and she did not enjoy their fragrance. While the forest and meadow became brighter and more beautiful, her depression deepened.

The pain of the rape had not been left behind on the day when it had happened. It had crept along with her, invading every part of her life. She saw each day as a long tunnel of darkness in which she knew nothing but a numbing dread of the child within her.

At last the day came when she would finally have her answer. The pain awakened her before dawn and sent shivers up and down her body. This was the first sensation she had felt in almost nine months. The labor lasted throughout the day and into the night. Though Iduna's mother tended her with all the knowledge she had gained from many births of her own, nothing she offered Iduna was of any comfort. Her mother began to doubt that her daughter would live through this birth. A midwife was called, and the birth proceeded with the same degree of difficulty. The midwife, an old woman of great stature, towered over Iduna's twisted body. She commanded Iduna gently, but shook her head silently in answer to Iduna's mother's questioning eyes.

Hours later, almost a full day from the onset of the first contraction, the child was born. His hair was soft, wispy and white blond, like his parents'. His eyes were an unfocused blue and his pink hands reached stubbornly for a nipple. Iduna died shortly after her son was born, without ever seeing his lightness.

"the between ..."

The waterfall spilled down over the rocks noisily, but its splashing seemed to be a far distance away in Lohkan's mind. He shook his head as he tried to clear his thoughts. A deep melancholy came over him whenever he remembered Iduna's memories. Slowly ... his mind came back into the place that had now become a sanctuary for him. The waterfall's musical noise swelled, peace settled inside him again and Iduna's torment became distant and muffled.

Once he was fully conscious of the waterfall, the moss beneath his feet and the sweet air, the elder appeared before him. Tonak nodded to Lohkan with a tender look of compassion, as if he understood the intense pain that Lohkan had experienced as Iduna. The small man pointed to the ground and gestured for Lohkan to sit. He then began to speak through the graceful movements of his hands.

We shall not ask you to look at this life, Lohkan, as we have done with others. We understand that your race does not experience this kind of violence, and we do not wish you to have to observe it again.

He then placed one small hand over Lohkan's heart and spoke directly into his mind.

Lohkan, you must release the pain that you are holding from Iduna.

Before Lohkan could answer, tears streamed down his face and sobs burst forth in uncontrolled waves. As he cried, he wondered at the intensity of this release, and his inability to contain it. It was as if part of himself watched this outburst from outside his body. Objectively, he knew this expression of his sorrow to be right, and he had no desire to hamper it. He gave in completely and bent over, bowed by the weight of his grief. He cried as never before.

Finally, the sorrow was washed away from his being. He straightened and looked into the eyes of the elder, who had been waiting patiently for him. Tonak's eyes were dark brown, close to black. Their warm darkness engulfed him in a blanket of compassion that opened his heart again. The elder then spoke.

Lohkan, do you need to discuss any part of this life?

"Yes," Lohkan answered, growing stronger with each breath. "Yes. I do," he repeated with more assurance, and then began.

"We knew of this violence from our studies of the different races on this planet. To experience this was far more horrifying than anything I could have imagined...." Lohkan stopped as emotions arose and smothered him.

Yes? Tonak nodded for Lohkan to proceed. Lohkan breathed deeply and then continued.

"These men – the thieves – acted out their inner power struggles by physically raping Iduna – me. Their emotions – feelings of powerlessness and inadequacy – were out of control ... or so each man thought. Because they could not control their inner struggles, they acted them out violently."

Lohkan sat quietly and the elder stood nearby. The small man's hands were still as he observed Lohkan's reflective face. The two men could not have been more physically different, yet they both reacted from the same heart. Lohkan spoke again.

"Iduna's pain lay mostly in the shame she felt. That shame came from *feeling* the imbalances in these men. It was somewhat like the time when I fell in the wild boar manure as Lohkan on Earth. That feeling and smell of the slick excretions on my skin stayed with me for many days after I washed it off. Serra and Orryka laughed when it happened.

"Iduna's pain was like that manure. She had been forced to be intimate with something foul and unpleasant. The shame of touching something so indecent was not something she could wash off. The smell of that horror stayed with her. The physical pain of the beatings and rape could, and did, heal. The intimacy with the unbalanced souls did not."

Lohkan was quiet again. The elder's next simple question brought truth rushing to Lohkan's consciousness.

What was the true *horror of this experience, Lohkan?*

"I believe the true horror was in coming face to face with what we have inside each of us. All humans have that rage and power struggle contained within each body. To have to see that part of humanity through Iduna's experience was the most painful...."

Lohkan stopped for a moment, and then hurried on, because if he hesitated, he would not be able to speak of what he now saw, what he now realized.

"I remember thinking that the thieves' darkness was no different from what lay inside me. The rape unleashed that part of me! I fantasied killing those men, torturing them, cutting off their hands for beating me and cutting off their...." He hesitated as he realized what he had been about to say. He went on, honestly, each word bringing to light what he had not been able to face as Iduna.

"I wanted them to suffer! I wanted those men to be punished for bringing my own darkness to my consciousness. I ran from this darkness! I tried not to think about it! The darkness inside me became a monster that I could not bear to face. I wanted to kill the shame of my own darkness, as well as that of my child! I would have killed my child had I lived, because I never would have believed that he did not carry my darkness – not the thieves' darkness: mine!" He thumped his chest with one large hand and choked back a sob. "Tonak, I would have taken a life rather than face my own dark abyss. In that abyss was too much pain!"

The elder said nothing, but placed a small brown finger beneath Lohkan's eye. He took his finger away and began a delicate and soothing response.

You have learned to see, Lohkan. This is often a painful process. In being human, a soul must face all parts of itself, including what you refer to as darkness. This planet Earth is a place where souls sometimes come to confront this part of themselves.

This darkness is inside all of us. You are me. I am you. We are a whole of many energies that create and move us. In being human, you have just experienced the hardest task of all. You have met your inner demons.

Now you must befriend them.

"How?"

Forgive.

Tonak stepped back and began an elaborate explanation in the form of an intricate dance with his hands. Lohkan watched, became quiet, and a calm filled him as the elder's words flowed past his mind and filled his heart.

To heal this part of you, you must first meet it, know it. This you have done. Next you must face it.

A large black shape appeared to Lohkan's right. He started, and began to rise.

Do not run, Lohkan! By running away from it, you give it power. Face it. It is not stronger than you. **You must decide which will be stronger – your love and compassion – or your fear.**

The black shape loomed over Lohkan and appeared to grow taller. The shape became blacker and, as Lohkan's fear and doubt grew, the shape became a defined mass. An eight-foot-tall man without features, only blackness, faced him. The elder's mind penetrated Lohkan's.

Fear is darkness. You decide! You may choose love.

"How do I love something as dark as this?" he gasped.

Forgive it. Forgive yourself, Lohkan.

"How do I forgive something that causes so much pain?"

By removing the pain. See this form with compassion. Do not focus on your pain; move beyond it. You have felt its struggles. It wants to be free as much as you do!

As Lohkan focused on the pain the black figure felt, a strange feeling came over him: a sadness for the creature. His own pain began to evaporate as his compassion for the dark creature grew. The black figure lightened, becoming dark gray and opaque. The elder's voice broke through his concentration.

Forgive, Lohkan. Forgive!

Lohkan began by speaking to the dark image.

"I forgive you for hurting me ... for hurting yourself," he said softly.

"I forgive you for wanting to hurt others," Lohkan spoke more firmly. "I forgive myself for supporting you in your desire to hurt. I forgive you because I know that you truly did not want to hurt. You just wanted the pain to go away."

As Lohkan said this last phrase, his compassion grew and he became brighter within himself. The elder encouraged him gently.

Lohkan, you have forgotten to forgive one other part.

"What?"

Think, Lohkan.

Suddenly the answer was visibly clear. He spoke, almost shouted, the words as tears again spilled down his face.

"I forgive myself for running from you! For not having the courage to face you! I forgive myself for being afraid. For not loving you...."

As he said the last words, a profound feeling of love, as well as compassion, filled him; not only for this darkness, but for all life, all creatures, everything in the universe. He felt himself connected and part of everything. At that moment the image lightened, until where darkness had stood before him, his own mirror image appeared.

A rushing sound filled his ears, bursting into a crescendo of music so overwhelming he was sure it would break him apart. Suddenly, he was surrounded by a bright white light. He felt himself spinning around and around. Just as he was about to lose consciousness, a small hand touched his.

He was back by the waterfall. The elder's face was lit by a beautiful smile. His black eyes were knowing and kind. He put his small brown hand back on Lohkan's chest once again and spoke four words.

We are all one.

Lohkan awoke in a daze and looked around himself. He did not know how long he had been asleep. There was no time in this place. He stretched lazily and enjoyed his sense of well-being. His soul felt boundless. His mind felt intoxicatingly free.

After a brief moment he went to the waterfall and rinsed his face. The sun sparkled brilliantly on the water. The sky was a rich purple hue and the air around him smelled deliciously fragrant. A burst of light came from behind him. He turned happily to greet the elder, to thank him for what he had learned.

Before him stood Serra.

Part Two

300 BC - 1850 AD

Chapter 8

"the between ..."

*A*re you real?" Lohkan asked."Yes," Serra said, and laughed as she stood gazing at Lohkan. She did not want to move. She wanted just to stand and look at him forever. Physically, Lohkan's face was the same. His features were strong, attractive, and his blue eyes were as penetrating as ever. Blue eyes were common amongst their people, but Lohkan's were lighter than most. On someone else, a different personality, they would have been described as icy and cold. On Lohkan, the faint blue was clear and brilliant. She smiled again. In fact, she could not stop smiling or staring. As she stared at him a large tear rolled down his cheek.

What is it, Lohkan? You rarely cry. What has happened? she asked telepathically. There was a difference in him. Although he was physically the same, he looked – no, *felt* – different somehow. She ran to him and buried her face in his shoulder. He touched her hair, her arms, her back. Wordlessly, they dropped to the ground and made love. Their thoughts flitted around the act, caressing where fingers could not.

You've grown ... become more beautiful, she whispered softly in his mind.

Sometimes, as I fell asleep in Japan, I remembered someone ... someone I loved, but could not find, Lohkan said.

Yes. I experienced that, too, she answered. Their voices touched each other's minds and were sensual and arousing.

I ached whenever this happened, ached for what I could not describe – for you, Serra! Lohkan said with passion.

He kissed her more deeply. His hands touched all parts of her, as if he wanted to memorize her body with his fingers, to never forget her again. She reacted with a soft moan.

When I came here to the between, *this longing turned into peace. Somehow I could feel you here! I knew I would see you again,* he said telepathically while he physically sighed.

I know, Serra answered softly.

Suddenly, Serra wished that she could make love to Lohkan on the island where they had first met. A flash of light blazed around them, and they looked up. Serra laughed as she recognized their home island. Lohkan smiled as he looked into her eyes.

They abandoned themselves to the joy of their reunion and left questions to be answered later.

Lohkan and Serra spoke together for what seemed like weeks. They wandered through the orchards until Serra wished to lie in the meadow; and magically, as before, they were transported there. They continued to share what each had learned, and each was awed by the other's experiences. What little pain they still felt was soothed by the comfort of sharing it. As they talked, made love and rested, a joy grew within them that surpassed any they had known hitherto, even in their peaceful home world.

The time came when they felt their departure coming. They would part again and move into different bodies, where they would not remember each other. Lohkan spoke to this one evening as they sat watching the second moon rise over the lake. Below them the lake reflected the two moons, while hundreds of islands glittered on its surface. The night sky was mirrored in a serenity and beauty that seemed to continue endlessly across the water.

"Serra, sometimes I wish that we would not have to go back. I think, 'This is enough. Could we learn more? Do we really have to go back there? What else do we need to take back to our people?'"

Serra kissed Lohkan's eyes closed as she whispered her answer quietly in his mind.

There is always more to learn! Learning is endless. I don't want to go back at times, either, she admitted, and then continued. *We have a commitment to finish our work. Orryka and the others are counting on this information.*

He answered by brushing her neck with a soft kiss. He pulled her to the ground, and again they made love. As Serra thought about their upcoming lifetimes and drifted to sleep in Lohkan's arms, she wondered when they would make love again.

Serra awoke first. She reached for Lohkan instinctively, wanting to know that he was still there with her, that he had not reincarnated yet. As she felt his sleeping body next to her, she lay back down and listened to his dreams. He was dreaming about someone named Kazuaki. The name sounded Asian, and she questioned if this was one of his lifetimes.

Kazuaki carried a sword that turned into a small bird. The bird was delicate and entirely white, except for one small red feather. Serra wondered about this "sleep" state. As her mind reflected upon the different realities they were experiencing, a very small man materialized next to where she lay.

The man's skin was dark brown, almost black, moist and glowing, as if golden honey coated him. His features were large, protruding, and conveyed kindness. Except for a white garment that covered his lower body in graceful pleats, he was naked. From this robe hung a group of white feathers with one red feather in their midst. He caressed Serra's face with one small hand, and as he did, tears fled down her cheeks. Serra felt as if she had been reunited with an old friend, a cherished family member who she had not seen in years, millennium. But, she could not explain this deep sense of familiarity. Serra felt and heard a gentle voice in her mind.

Hello, Serra!

"Who are you?"

Tonak! he said in her mind, and then made one small gesture with his hand, which represented his name. His hand swept through the air like a bird in flight.

You had a question? he asked.

"Yes," Serra said as she sat up. She smiled as she immersed herself in Tonak's rich, dark eyes. "Do we sleep here? What state are we in? That is, what consciousness do we take when we are not awake?" She stumbled uncertainly through her question.

When you lose consciousness of this place, the between, *you go into another dimension. There is no word for this dimension in your language, or in mine. Let me show you.*

Serra nodded yes, and was quickly swept away. The waterfall vanished. The air changed and she felt herself shrinking. The elder laughed as her eyes widened at what she saw next.

Thoughts echoed around them. Hundreds, thousands of voices moved around them in a crowded, but orderly, display. As a thought was heard, it quickly took shape in a symbolic grouping of objects. Those objects collected together to form a scene that was transparent and dreamlike. Serra watched as one thought went through this process. She heard a whisper.

I do not wish to experience pain any longer.

The words floated into a symbolic image. A woman with thick blond hair walked through a forest, bent, placed a baby on a pile of leaves and then walked away. She turned and waved sadly to the infant as tears spilled down her face. As she did, she transformed into a crow which took flight. The crow flew rapidly into the forest. And as the crow's talons touched the branch of an evergreen, it transformed into a brilliant white ball of light. It suddenly exploded, and the scene disappeared.

"Whose thoughts are these?" Serra asked aloud.

They are Lohkan's. This is the place where thoughts become dreams. Although these are not his alone. Many others are here. The thoughts of others whom we meet and touch are also here.

"What is this? I don't understand."

Your thoughts have energy. Though your physical form rests, your soul continues its journey. Here your soul's knowledge takes visual form. This may happen here, in this dimension.

"Could we do this back in *the between?*" Someone asked from behind Serra. She turned and saw that Lohkan had joined them. He took her hand and held it tightly. His face was serene in its question. The elder hesitated before he answered.

Lohkan, you do experience this in the between. *This dimension is only one aspect of* the between. *Look!*

The floating images disappeared. The thousands of thoughts were silent. They were floating in a white space. All was still; only white brightness surrounded them. The elder continued his explanation. He pointed to the air, and a large, three-dimensional space cruiser materialized. It was the ship Lohkan, Serra and the others had used to travel to Earth.

Pretend this spacecraft is the universe, the elder explained. He touched the ship, and it became transparent. *Here,* he pointed to a complex series of ducts and tunnels in the ship, *is the between.*

Inside these ducts are conduits. He touched another spot, and hundreds of brightly colored lines wove throughout the ducts. *These conduits are the other dimension you just saw. They convey thought, much as a conduit conveys energy. The conduit is in the duct. The duct is in the spaceship. They are all one, all interdependent upon one another. The spaceship would not run without the duct, or the conduit. The between would not function without its other dimensions.*

The elder pointed to a large room near the center of the ship. The room was an amphitheater with a large crystal in the middle. Seats surrounded the crystal. Into this room the hundreds of ducts, with their thousands of conduits, were channeled. The room resembled an octagon with thousands of brightly lit rays bursting forth from it.

Serra and Lohkan stared silently at this beautiful display.

This is where ideas or dreams go to manifest into reality! Tonak explained. The elder was quiet while they digested this, and then he spoke again.

Do you see that each part is dependent upon the next? All the independent dimensions form a whole! He whistled softly, and the spaceship vanished.

The other dimension you just saw is in the between. The between *is here in the light. The light is* The One.

They floated in the white light. Wisps of air pushed them around in a gentle play of space and flight. Lohkan asked the elder a question as they began to move faster.

"What is, 'The One?'"

The elder's laughter raced along with them.

It's you!

"What a ridiculous theory, Anastasos! Where do you come up with such ideas?"

Euripides laughed as his best friend explained his latest philosophy. Euripides was slim, tall, with fine, handsome features and blond curly hair. His brown eyes were filled with a merriment that was contagious. His best friend conceded the point and began to laugh too. The best friend, Anastasos, was a few inches shorter than Euripides, but still taller than average. Anastasos' brown hair was dark, and his features were pronounced, yet still attractive. His gray eyes now twinkled as Euripides laughed at his theories.

"You have had some foolish ideas yourself, Euripides," he said with a chuckle.

"None, definitely none as blasphemous as yours. Perhaps that is why the teacher likes you, Anastasos. Are you coming to the lecture tonight?"

"Yes. Of course."

"I'll meet you after the baths then, unless I can get you to change your mind?" hinted Euripides.

"No. You know I do not like the baths."
"I shall see you later then."
"Until we meet, Euripides."
"Yes, my friend."

Anastasos followed the well-worn path past the buildings. The afternoon sun shone on the pastel walls. Sweat dripped down his sides under his tunic, and his sandals made a slapping sound against his feet as he padded along on the packed earthen street. Above the city, a brilliant turquoise sky accented the beauty of the pale walls. In the distance, a harbor lay in seafaring splendor. Several large boats were moored at the docks. Like a line of ants, slaves formed a narrow dark line going to and from the ships.

Anastasos was barely aware of the view – his mind was elsewhere. He excitedly wondered what the teacher would introduce them to tonight. He loved their debates. The teacher always began the class with the teachings of Aristotle and Socrates, and then moved on to an open discussion. Tonight promised to be as enjoyable as all the other classes had been. There was no reason for it to be otherwise.

For these past six years, he had studied. Now the end of his studies was nearing; though, for Anastasos, that was debatable. This was the very subject about which Euripides had just laughed. Anastasos felt that learning did not end just because you left the Academy: life was the ultimate school. Euripides had laughed and argued that school was a building with a teacher and other students. Euripides had always had a solid and earthy view of life. This was one of his qualities that Anastasos loved best.

Anastasos' mind wandered around this philosophy and others as he came to his parents' home. Inside, he dropped his tunic on a bench and went to the baths to refresh himself. He liked to bathe, just not in the public bath houses.

A male servant brought him a fresh tunic and informed him that the evening meal would be served in the courtyard, since the day was already cool. On most days, it was too hot to sit in the open courtyard. The milder afternoon promised a delightful evening of soothing breezes from the sea. Anastasos thanked the servant, and then joined his parents in the main living area of their home.

His family was wealthy, and enjoyed one of the larger houses which sat at the top of the hill, overlooking the rest of the city and the harbor. Servants moved in and out of the living area, where large cushions stuffed with goat hair made comfortable seats. The cushions were covered with a cotton-and-wool material woven with an ancient white horse pattern. Beautifully carved tables held stone vases and sculptures. A servant carried in a pitcher of water with a ladle draped against one side. The servant offered him the cool water, and Anastasos dipped the ladle into the heavy pitcher. He drank two ladles full of water, and then motioned that he was done. The servant offered the ladle to Anastasos' father, who declined. His father's large, hooked nose and wide lips were creased into a frown. The afternoon light reflected from his silver eyes. He tapped his fingers on a pillow as he addressed Anastasos.

"How are your studies, Son?"

"Fine, Papa. I am sad that they are ending." He did not bother to mention his theory to his father.

"We have indulged you long enough. It is time that you took your place in the city. I was approached today by a friend who suggested you might work for him. You have said that you have no interest in my business, which hurts me deeply. Perhaps you would like his," his father said with a touch of sarcasm in his voice.

"Not another banker, Papa?"

"No," his father answered in a grouchy tone. "He owns a ship. He is a trader and merchant. I thought you might find an interest in his business."

"Doing what?" Anastasos asked, truly puzzled.

"He has need of a young, clever mind to organize his trade."

"Papa, no!"

"Tell me! What do you plan to do? You cannot go to school forever!"

Anastasos bit his lip to keep from smiling.

"Yes. So I've been told. Do not worry, Papa. I shall find something. I do not mean to be disrespectful. Thank you for your offer. I don't think I'll eat dinner here tonight. Euripides asked me to meet him."

"Again! You spend more time in Euripides' home than your own."

"No, Papa. We'll meet somewhere else. Probably at the bath houses."

"I suppose this is the way of all young men. Watch the stars and travel safely, Anastasos! At least take one of the servants with you. You worry me, the way you travel alone."

His father clapped his hands, and one of the servants came forward: a young man, tall and dark, about eighteen years of age.

"Follow Anastasos, will you? See that no harm befalls your master."

Anastasos looked at the servant sheepishly and shrugged. The servant followed him out of the house.

Euripides was happily surprised to see his best friend. He lay in a large bath of warm water while, behind him, a young female servant massaged his shoulders. Steam rose up and around him causing his already curly hair to curl tighter. Anastasos dropped his tunic and joined him.

"Well, Tasos, what changed your mind?" Euripides teased.

"Papa is dining in tonight."

"Ahh...."

"Ah, nothing. Your father does not pressure you into trade. He is proud of your studies!"

"Yes. This is true. Lucky for me though that your father pressures you. I get to see more of you this way," he said, and then laughed.

Anastasos ignored his friend's teasing and sank lower into the hot water. A young female servant, more of a girl than a woman, came to the side of the pool. She dropped her cloak and stepped into the pool behind Anastasos. Her small breasts floated on the surface of the water as she stood awkwardly, waiting for him to speak his wishes. When Anastasos did not respond, Euripides nodded for the girl to proceed. She began to knead and massage Anastasos' tense shoulders.

"Why do you fight this?" Euripides whispered. "It is your heritage. There is no harm in these earthly pleasures."

"I have already explained how I feel about this," Anastasos said stubbornly.

"Yes. We all know of Tasos' valiant fight to free slaves and servants. Why then is *he* here tonight?" Euripides nodded toward the servant who had followed Anastasos.

"Papa sent him."

"Ah, your father was in a forceful mood today. I now understand why you are here. At least you could relax and enjoy yourself," Euripides suggested.

Anastasos merely shrugged and sank even lower into the water. A half hour later, Euripides stood while one of the bath-house servants towelled him off. He smiled at the shy girl, which caused her to blush and drop the towel. Awkwardly, she bent over, directly in front of his naked groin. She blushed even more and Euripides chuckled to himself. Anastasos shot him a warning look. When the girl left them alone, Anastasos reprimanded his friend.

"Why did you do that? You frightened her. She is just a child, and she cannot say no to you."

"I did nothing!"

"You laughed."

"You're right. I did. I should not have, but most would not agree with you. Luckily for you that I do, and that it is me who is your best friend. I shall leave her a coin to make up for my blunder. Does this satisfy you?"

"It would have been better had you not teased the girl at all."

"What has gotten into you today, Tasos? If I did not know better, I should say you are jealous!"

"Jealous! Of what?"

"Of me, of course." Euripides laughed.

"What?"

"Come now, Tasos. We have the same philosophies, but I am not burdened by mine. You are. I accept the time and heritage to which I was born. You do not. Take the bath houses as an example."

"The bath houses?"

"Yes. I can enjoy them, while you, obviously my friend, are lost to their pleasures. The servants cause your soul distress. The sexual favors make you wonder if you are invading the other person. The favors are given freely, and yet you will not take. I agree that none should be forced –"

Anastasos interrupted. "Perhaps their positions force them. There are pressures in life other than physical ones, Euripides."

"As I was saying, I agree with you. Have I not apologized enough? I have never taken one of the servants. But, I do not let their positions hurt me."

"Perhaps you do not care."

"Ah, now you wound me, Tasos. How can you say that?"

"I am sorry, Euripides. I know that you care."

"My point is that maybe you take on their pain too much, Tasos." Now he was serious. Euripides leaned forward on the bench. He touched his friend's knee lightly.

"You cannot take on the world's pain, Tasos, though I love you for trying. You can only act in your best conscience, which happens to be finer than most. I fear in the end you will only hurt yourself."

Tasos nodded, then rose and dressed. They left the bath houses and walked down to the waterfront, where several eateries lay. They bought skewered and roasted meat and wandered around the market place, which was mostly closed for the day.

113

After they ate, they walked back up the street from where they had come, and headed to the Academy.

"What took you so long to get here?" Euripides asked his friend, who was a half hour late. He watched Tasos approach and noted that Tasos' gray eyes were especially stormy this day and Tasos' strong features, his large nose and wide, full mouth, were set in an expression of concern. Euripides continued to vent his frustration at having been made to wait. "You are never late! Did the servant not tell you that my message was important? Well, answer me. Where have you been?"

"With Papa. Why are you upset? What has happened, Euripides? I came as quickly as I could. What is it?" Anastasos asked in a worried voice. His dark brown curls fell over his brow, which was wrinkled with concern. Euripides' face broke into a grin.

"You've been offered a teacher's position at the Academy!"

"What? Me? Are you sure?"

"Yes. I overheard two of the instructors talking at the bath house this morning. I don't think anyone else knows, except those on the council."

Anastasos was numb with shock. He had hoped for this, but had told no one of his ambition, except, of course, for Euripides. He rubbed his face with both hands and shook his head to clear it. The stormy look cleared from his eyes and his full lips were parted in a an expression of bewilderment. Euripides burst into laughter.

"Have you nothing to say, dear friend? I would have thought you'd burst into song at the very least."

"I am truly speechless," Anastasos responded. Euripides laughed louder.

"Ah, I never thought I should see the day when Anastasos would be speechless!"

"Be quiet."

"Ah, he finds his voice. Can you do no more with it, other than to complain?" Anastasos ran down the steps of the bath house and Euripides followed.

Anastasos spoke hurriedly. "Please, Euripides, let me think. I must come up with a way of telling Papa, a way of which he will approve."

"I should have guessed. You have just come from a meeting with Papa. What is the problem now? Your unwillingness to enter trade? A philosophical misunderstanding? Tasos, stop! I cannot run and talk."

The two men slowed their steps to a casual stroll. Anastasos answered Euripides' questions.

"He wants to know what I shall *do* now that my studies are finished at the Academy."

"This is wonderful! You have an answer!"

"How comical of you," Anastasos answered sarcastically. "You were named for the playwright. Perhaps *you* should write plays, Euripides."

"That's an excellent idea!"

"Please, can't you be serious for even a minute?"

"Of course, Tasos. Let's think. What shall we say to Papa in order to gain his approval?" His voice was serious, but his humor lay shallowly in his brown eyes. He continued.

"Can you not tell him the truth? An offer from the Academy is a great honor. Perhaps, if you could get him to understand this honor?"

Anastasos shrugged at his friend's suggestion.

"Perhaps ..." was all he said.

"Tasos, you are not trying! Would you truly accept defeat so easily? This does not seem like you."

"I have not given up!" Anastasos answered hotly.

"That is better. Now, what will you say to Papa?"

"That I am going to become a teacher at the Academy ... after they have made their offer, of course."

Euripides smiled.

As they left the Academy, they met two soldiers just outside the entrance. Euripides bowed grandly. His blond curls fell over his dark eyes and hid his expression and his flat, even features. Anastasos nudged him with his elbow. The soldiers frowned at Euripides' humorous display. They were not sure if he was serious.

"Rome has encroached into every part of Greece," Euripides muttered to his friend.

As Euripides and Anastasos walked down the street, a woman's voice was heard singing in the darkness. Her voice was rich and melodic. As they rounded the corner of one of the buildings, they bumped into the owner of the beautiful voice.

She was tall, with long black curls that fell to her waist. Behind her followed a male servant in the shadows. Her voice hesitated in its song only for a minute, when the two men bumped into her. She laughed, a sound that was almost as enchanting as her singing, and continued on her way. In her hands she carried a large basket of flowers that most likely had been given to her by a lover. The night air was filled with their fragrance and her voice. Anastasos stopped to watch her walk away. Euripides watched Anastasos' expression. Anastasos' gray eyes and full lips showed his appreciation for the woman with a discreet smile. As the woman drifted out of sight, Euripides questioned Anastasos.

"Have you decided?"

"Decided what?"

"Do I really have to ask again?"

"No," Anastasos said flatly.

"Well?"

"I cannot marry her."

Euripides tried to hide a sigh of relief. He continued to question Anastasos.

"Have you told Papa yet?"

"Yes"

"And?"

"He was not pleased. This is the third arrangement I have turned down."

"Why don't you tell him the truth?"

"Which is what?" Anastasos looked at his friend with a raised eyebrow and then continued. "That I am in love with my best friend? That before I met you I had always been besotted by women, any woman. Now, I don't know what I am interested in ..." his voice trailed off.

"I have tried to understand," Euripides began, "how you, an instructor of philosophy, can have such difficulty in accepting a homosexual relationship. Is it that you do not truly love me?"

Euripides was serious. His brown eyes looked confused and hurt. The beautiful curve of Euripides' jaw and straight line of his nose suddenly appeared plain and severe, instead of attractive, as his normally cheerful lips fell into a frown.

For the past several months they had tried to find a place for these feelings, this love. They each, Anastasos reflected, had gone through many infatuations in their youth, all involving women. Since they had met at the Academy, each had slowly stopped their involvement with women. Whether through arranged matches or accidental meetings, women had played a less and less prominent role in their lives. Each instead sought out the other's company. Several months ago Euripides had been the first to admit his feeling, his desires. He had sought to discover and understand them with the one person who would understand him. Upon his confession, Anastasos had laid out his own confused emotions. They were in love with each other, though neither had known what to do about this.

Over the passing months Euripides found an acceptance of this, his love for Anastasos. Homosexuality was a common practice in Greece. Several of their friends from the Academy were practicing homosexuals. That Euripides and Anastasos had these feelings would not seem wrong or unacceptable to many in their society. Still, Anastasos had not come to an acceptance of his feelings, their feelings. He could not yet disclose himself or consummate their relationship.

"You know that I love you."

"Then why? Why can you not experience this love? Is it your father? I cannot believe that he approves of this practice, no matter how common it is. He does not approve of anything! Tell me. What, Anastasos, prevents you?"

"I don't know. I don't believe it is because of my father. Although I know he will not approve. He wants an heir and is wounded that I have failed a son's duty," Anastasos said, and mimicked his father's gesture of clutching his heart and tilting his head backward. Then he sighed sadly.

Many men married women solely to bring their offspring into the world, while continuing a deeper relationship with a male lover. But Anastasos loved only Euripides. To hide that love behind a false marriage felt unbearable to him.

Anastasos sadly turned away. They had walked between the buildings and now stood in the shadows of an alley. Euripides put his hand on Anastasos' shoulder and turned him around.

"Please, answer me. I need to understand. I love you, Tasos. I can think of no other. Long ago I stopped seeing women. I see only your face. If there is no chance of a union, then ..." he hesitated and choked back a sob, "... I don't think I can continue in this relationship."

Euripides swallowed and waited for Anastasos to respond. The shadows hid his tears. In the increasing darkness, Euripides could not see that Anastasos also cried. The struggle was tearing them both apart. Euripides began to talk again when no answer was forthcoming.

"I have had an offer recently."

"What?" Anastasos started.

"Yes. To marry Porfirio's daughter. If I am not to take this step with you, then I must get on with my life. I have never met another for whom I feel the love I feel for you. I was once interested in women, and so a woman I shall marry. Since you will not...."

He stopped and choked again on the lump that had formed in his throat. The past several months had been agonizing. Again he put his hand on Anastasos' shoulder.

"Please, Tasos, dear friend, if you have ever loved me, try!"

Anastasos cried soundlessly. His body shook under Euripides grip. He spoke. His voice was hoarse and broken.

"Euripides, I ..." he stopped. "I have never loved anyone more than you. I just can't take this step."

Euripides' hand fell from his shoulder. The silence that now lay between them was vast and painful. Neither spoke. Each was encompassed in a cloud of confused emotions and ideals. There were no immediate social restrictions that kept them apart. Only a confused ideal and vision distanced the two. Neither Euripides nor Anastasos had ever seen himself in anything other than a heterosexual relationship. That their feelings for each other were so strong, that they existed at all, was confusing. Euripides had been able to make the leap that was necessary in order to continue. Anastasos had not been able to do so. That he was unable to caused more confusion on top of an already painfully baffling situation. He honestly did not know why he could not accept his feelings. And more frustrating than this, he did not know why he could not act on them. Anastasos turned to speak to Euripides; but, in the depth of their silence, Euripides had fled.

When Anastasos saw Euripides several nights later at a play, he was with another couple and a young woman. The couple laughed with abandon as Euripides tried to explain a concept to the young woman, who obviously could not understand. Anastasos watched from a row that was set several feet higher. Euripides did not know he was watched. Anastasos left when the play was finished. Alone.

The following week Anastasos lectured in one of the classrooms. One student, a young man, stood up and began to argue against Anastasos' view. Soon the whole class was involved in the heated debate. Euripides watched from behind a column. When the class came to an end, Euripides departed before he was discovered. Depressed, he walked the empty hallways before the students filled them.

Months passed in this way. Each watched and followed the other's progress from afar; neither knew that the other did this, and neither knew the other's torment. One day Euripides happened upon an old instructor who had known them both.

"Hail, Euripides! Where do you go?"

"To the theater, Appelles. I am working on a new play."

"Yes. I have heard of your success, though I have not been fortunate enough to see either of your plays, I am sorry to say."

"Ah, that is indeed your loss!" Euripides joked.

"Where is your friend, Anastasos? You two were inseparable. He was always a serious one, but filled with intriguing ideas. I thought that you two might...."

"Might what?" Euripides asked. His breath had become shallow. He tried to hide the seriousness of his question with a smile.

"I thought that you two might form a relationship," the old instructor said nonjudgementally. In that moment Euripides remembered that Appelles had lived with a male lover for many years. His expression betrayed him, and the old man gently put his hand on Euripides' arm.

"Why don't you come back with me to my house? Hector will be thrilled to see you. We could talk. What happened, Euripides? Your pain is evident."

Euripides nodded and followed the old man down the street, until they came to a small villa set back behind a courtyard. Olive trees filled the front yard. A grape arbor covered the walkway that led to the house. As they entered the house, Appelles yelled loudly, "Hector, come see who I have brought home as a guest!"

Another old man, bald and stooped, came into the room. He saw Euripides and his face broke into a smile.

"Euripides. How many years has it been since we last saw you? Eight? Ten? No, I believe it has been eleven years! Sit. Sit. The servants will bring us wine." The bald man snapped his fingers at a young boy who waited nearby.

"Hector, Euripides' heart needs spilling. It overflows with pain," Appelles said compassionately.

Euripides blushed at the old instructor's direct words. He tried to lighten the mood with a joke, but his voice cracked and the words were humorless. Hector nodded knowingly and waited until after the wine had been served to speak.

"Tell us, Euripides. What weighs so heavily upon your heart?" Again the old instructor began to speak, but his partner cut him off.

"Appelles, let Euripides speak for himself. Go on, Euripides. Something obviously has caused you pain."

Euripides tried to smile as he spoke, but he could not hide his affliction or his need to talk to someone. Soon he had poured forth the whole story while Appelles and Hector listened. Euripides finished his tale sadly.

"Anastasos could not bring himself to commit to a relationship. We parted several months ago."

"Perhaps," began Appelles, "Anastasos was willing to commit to a relationship, but not one of your liking."

"Can't you see his point, Appelles?" Hector took up Euripides' cause. "Euripides could not go on without a commitment! This would be too much to ask!" he argued passionately.

"Hector! The point which I am trying to make is, maybe Euripides would be happier with Anastasos in his life under different conditions than not at all. Look at him. You are not happy now, are you, Euripides?"

"No. I've been miserable these past few months."

"You see! Euripides, go to Anastasos. Begin again. Start where each of you is comfortable. Then, maybe, if the gods grant it, your relationship will grow into the one you wish for."

Hector was silent and watched Euripides' face. A slow smile had formed on the young man's countenance while he listened to Appelles. When Appelles was done, Hector took over.

"Euripides, you must remember one fact. You must love Anastasos now, as he is, not for what he will become to you. If you try to love him for a potential that does not now exist, then your heart will truly be broken once more. If you love dear Tasos for who he is and what he might bring to you right now, you will know love and, more importantly, peace of mind."

Euripides nodded and placed his head in his hands. He wept silently while Appelles patted his back. Both older men were quiet out of respect for Euripides' sorrow. When he was done crying, Euripides wiped his eyes with the back of his hands. He spoke in a shaky voice.

"I have kept this inside for so long that I had begun to think lately that I would die of a broken heart."

"Think of how Anastasos must feel right now. He, too, suffers as you do. Go to him, Euripides! He needs you as much as you need him."

Euripides agreed and thanked the two men. He departed quickly, promising that he would soon return, and that he would bring Anastasos if he could.

He found Anastasos in the lecture hall of the Academy. No one else was in the hall, as a class had ended some time ago.

Anastasos sat quietly and stared into space. In his distraction, he did not hear Euripides' approach until he stood before him. The effect was magical and disturbing. Anastasos jumped when he first noticed Euripides' presence. Euripides simply smiled.

"Are you preoccupied? I would like to speak to you," Euripides stated in a flat voice. All of his hope lay in this moment. Anastasos answered him.

"Yes. I, too, have wanted to speak with you, but not here. Let's go to the amphitheater. No one is there now. A class with one of the new instructors will be here soon," Anastasos explained.

They left, side by side, and walked to the amphitheater. They climbed until they had reached the highest level of seats, which not only commanded a view of the theater, but also of the hills, city and ocean beyond. Euripides sat and waited for Anastasos to do so, too. He was about to speak when Anastasos interrupted.

"I have missed you, Euripides. The past few months have been empty without you. I have not changed. I still am unable to...." He stopped for a moment, breathed deeply and then began again. "I cannot go on without you. This I know. I don't know how, but I shall try to meet you in this relationship. I have told my father, and he was greatly disappointed in me ... as he usually is. He will not get the heir he wants so badly from me. This is beside the point though. I love you, Euripides, and cannot live without you. I was going to try to find you tonight, to tell you this. I was planning how, when suddenly, there you were." Anastasos ended with amazement in his voice. One tear, small and silvery, fell down his cheek.

Euripides took Anastasos' hand and rubbed it. He spoke softly, almost in a whisper.

"I had come to the same conclusion. Dear Tasos, I shall not ask you to do what you cannot. Let us begin again as friends. Let us not decide now what shall develop later. I just want you back in my life. I, too, cannot go on without you."

They sat together silently for a long time. Neither spoke, for there was no need to say more. Their hearts had already decided.

Euripides held Anastasos' hand while the medic checked Anastasos again. Euripides' blond hair was shot with gray. Fine wrinkles lined his handsome face. The physician shook his head as he explained Anastasos' condition. Anastasos had aged dramatically during the past several months of his illness. His dark hair was mostly white. Deep worry lines lined his forehead. His skin constantly had a yellow cast to it now, which made him look ill even on his good days. This day was not one of his good days.

"Not long. Maybe a week. Maybe a month. Perhaps a year? Only the gods know. Your heart has been weakened by this last attack, Anastasos. You are to rest each day, most of the day. Your classes will have to have a new instructor. I'll contact the Academy myself. Euripides, he is to do nothing strenuous! Do you understand?"

"Yes. Of course. Do you think I am a fool? I'll make sure he rests."

The physician left while Euripides instructed a servant to bring water for Anastasos. The medicine the medic had left was bitter tasting. He gave Anastasos the water himself and dismissed the servant.

"You shall stay here, friend. I have already sent word to your house for your servants to bring your clothes and possessions. I shall not have us living separately where you could die alone. If we have so little time left together, I want to see you as much as possible."

Anastasos nodded weakly. He had not the strength to protest even if he had wanted to, which he didn't. He took Euripides' hand and squeezed it once before he fell asleep.

Euripides stood by the bed for a while and watched Anastasos sleep. Their years together had been wonderful and difficult. During the last two decades they had come to an understanding, an acceptance of each other and their limitations. Though they had never consummated their love physically, they had grown closer than most couples ever would. Their love had flourished without physical representation. This had been hard for Euripides, but, ironically, had been worse for Anastasos. He had been plagued by long moments of guilt and failure. Euripides stood by the bed and remembered with clarity their struggles of years ago.

"What is bothering you, dear friend?" Euripides asked. The two men walked together on the beach on a cool evening. Sea breezes blew over them. A crescent moon rose above the bay.

"Does it not bother you that our relationship will never be consummated?" Anastasos asked with passion.

"Yes. It does." Euripides spoke sadly. "Yet, I'd rather you were here walking beside me than not at all. I love you, dear Tasos. How can you doubt that after all these years?"

"I don't doubt your love for me! This I never question. I...."

"Yes?"

"I hate living with the pain I have caused you! I hate the daily guilt of keeping you from a more ... satisfying relationship!" Anastasos whispered harshly.

Euripides took his hand and spoke softly in the lingering twilight.

"No one else could bring me the satisfaction that you do. The friendship, the joy, the pain ... it is all part of you! And, it is *you* I love."

Euripides had learned to live within their limited relationship, by simply remembering how painful it had been to live without Anastasos. There had been times when his tolerance wore thin, though. And during these times, it had been Euripides whose patience was tested.

"Please, Anastasos, I do not wish to see you now!" Euripides had said painfully. Anastasos had been confused. He had stood in the hallway of Euripides' house. The morning shadows had fallen across the stone floors and had hidden Euripides' face and his expression. Anastasos had come to share breakfast, only to find Euripides in a dark and intolerant mood.

"What has happened?" Anastasos asked.

"Nothing! I am tired, that is all."

"You didn't sleep last night?"

"Not that kind of tired, Tasos. I am frustrated. I want to hold you, sleep with you! This will never happen. My heart aches! My mind does not allow me to sleep!"

Anastasos sighed and placed his hand on Euripides' arm, but Euripides pulled away. He tried again. This time Euripides did not struggle. He placed his hand over Anastasos' and smiled weakly.

"Forgive me, dear friend. I am happy. It is only a moment's struggle. It will pass. Come in and eat your morning meal with me."

Euripides walked into the main room of the house, knowing that Anastasos followed. They would always follow each other throughout whatever pain each suffered. Their friendship would endure. And in this they had a found a comfort that was deep and encompassing.

Euripides bent now and pulled a wool blanket over Anastasos' sleeping form. The white and gray of the blanket matched Anastasos' hair. A few months ago Anastasos had had his first heart attack. A month later, the second one occurred. Then another, two months later. This latest attack was the worst by far; Euripides was shocked and relieved that Anastasos had lived.

Euripides straightened, rubbed his sore lower back and decided to go to the market to buy flowers to fill his house and to cheer Anastasos.

When he stepped outdoors the day was overcast, unusually gray and moody. Euripides grimaced as he looked at the foreboding clouds. He ran his hand through his graying curly hair and yelled to one of the servants.

"Get the horses and carriage. I think I shall ride, instead of walk, to the market." As Euripides waited, a large raindrop struck his forehead. Then another. The sky seemed determined to weep for him and Anastasos. A moment later Euripides climbed into the carriage and started off down the hill to the market. Small drops were falling steadily now. Euripides opened his mouth and turned his face skyward to enjoy the rain. As he did, a group of soldiers ran onto the road ahead, spooking the horses. One horse pulled in one direction, while the other struck out in the opposite. Euripides pulled on the reins and tried to bring the horses to a halt. Instead of stopping them, this encouraged the moody horses to join. The horses suddenly jumped in the same direction, and the carriage toppled over with Euripides beneath it.

Anastasos did not die a week, or a month, or even a year later, as the medic had predicted. He died an hour after Euripides, upon hearing of Euripides' death. During his final and strongest heart attack, Anastasos had smiled. As the smile left his lips, he whispered, "I am coming, Euripides!"

"the between ..."

They entered the meadow almost simultaneously. Serra looked up into Lohkan's eyes, and she fell against him with a sigh. They held each other for a long time before either spoke. When the silence was broken, it was by Serra, who asked a question.

"Why?"

As she asked it, Quan Yin appeared before them. She floated above the purple flowers several feet from where they stood. Quan Yin looked at Lohkan and introduced herself.

"Hello, Lohkan. Serra has told me about you."

Lohkan stared openly at the beautiful woman before him. He had never seen such pure beauty and light in one person. Her black eyes twinkled with warmth and compassion. Her smile was entrancing. The sound of bells flowed from the slightest movement of her body. She floated in a sphere of white light that emanated love – a love that was as powerful and encompassing as the white light itself. He felt awed and speechless. Quan Yin spoke again and broke the enchantment.

"Do you know why, Lohkan, you were unable to consummate your relationship with Euripides?"

She motioned toward Serra, who also awaited his answer. There was no judgment in her words. She wanted to know if Lohkan understood his experience. Finally, he found his voice.

"I'm not sure. I conclude partly because of what my family believed. While my father accepted this in other people, he saw it as a weakness in his own family. I tried to deny that he had any influence over me. I can see that he did. He tried to control the whole family through guilt. There is more that I don't yet understand, though."

"Please sit." Quan Yin motioned for them to join her. They sank into the bed of flowers as two young birds might land in their nest; they were immediately comforted and nurtured. Quan Yin began to explain and question them at once.

"Lohkan, you and Serra lived as husband and wife for how long before you died?"

"Over one hundred years, by Earth's accounting of time," he answered.

"You have known each other intimately during that time, have you not?"

"Yes," Lohkan answered again, and he smiled at Serra.

"Serra, you embodied a feminine role during the marriage, while Lohkan embodied male energy. Is this not correct?"

"Yes," they each answered.

"Lohkan," she began her explanation, "you have known Serra only as a woman. When you enter a lifetime, though your memory of other lives is not intact, your essence remains the same. That essence does carry those memories, somewhat like an echo." Her last words, "like an echo", echoed around them in a playful example.

"You have had no experience relating to Serra from the viewpoint of a female. You have only related to her from a male viewpoint. Serra was able to make the leap of seeing you as her lover because she had known intimacy with you while you were a man. This change was not so great for her. You had never known Serra in a male form before you became Anastasos.

"As Anastasos, you were naturally drawn to Serra because

of your history with her. That she took a male body, Euripides, could not impede your desire to be with her, although it could block that expression of your love for her. You were not sent to this life to experience homosexuality. You were sent to know each other without a physical, sexual relationship. You were sent without the genetic and particular pleasure-seeking input which homosexuality requires. You were sent to experience two male heterosexual bodies. You were sent to experience the love that *friendship* would create.

"The depth of your knowledge of each other led your friendship into realms you might otherwise not have known. Your desire to make love to Lohkan, Serra, was a natural response that 'Serra's' essence would have to Lohkan. That you were unable to meet with Serra as Euripides, Lohkan, was understandable. You were not there to do so. You were there to *be friends.*"

Lohkan and Serra listened silently. Their minds were filled with the joy and complications they had known in their life in Greece. Lohkan asked a question that he had thought of often when he had embodied Anastasos.

"What is homosexuality?"

"A choice," the guide answered simply.

"I don't understand," Lohkan answered her.

"When a soul chooses an experience, a lesson, many factors are required to meet this choice. A soul simply chooses what form and in which style the choice will best be met."

"You said earlier that a genetic and pleasure input must be made for this choice. Could you explain this?" Serra asked now.

"Homosexuality is based upon a combination of genetic makeup and experiences. Experience dictates our pleasures. For instance, if you as Lohkan had lived many lifetimes as only a man, and suddenly you chose a female embodiment, and if that female body also had a genetic coding that was appropriate, then you would most likely have a homosexual experience."

"Are you saying that homosexuality is genetically predisposed?" asked Lohkan.

"In the physical sense, yes," the guide answered, and then continued. "In the spiritual sense, all souls are bisexual. Each soul has male and female energies. You, Serra, have both female and male energies inside you, in your essence. As do you, Lohkan."

"I'm confused," Serra said, "What happens if someone is genetically predisposed toward this choice, but not spiritually?"

"Ah, this becomes yet another choice," Quan Yin answered.

"How would this other choice manifest?" Serra asked, truly curious.

"The soul might embody an asexual person. Some of the religious figures of this world have taken this choice. Some others choose a life of isolation, because their needs are different. They have chosen to abstain as a natural course for themselves. They are naturally drawn to this decision by their choice."

They sat silently together. Serra had not thought of the numerous spiritual choices that mating might take. She and Lohkan had traveled throughout the galaxy, had met countless races. Many had different mating practices from their own. Some races embodied both male and female organs in one body. Others reproduced by cloning. The endless possibility of choices was suddenly overwhelming. Quan Yin interrupted her reflections with another question.

"What did you learn from this experience?" She directed the question to each of them. Lohkan answered first.

"That it is more than possible to love someone deeply," he said as took Serra's hand, "without physical expression. Love is not dependent upon sex. Nor is sex dependent upon love. Although I would not wish to have one without the other again." He smiled at Serra. Serra grinned, too, and then spoke.

"I learned that, in human cultures, the sexual bond is emphasized sometimes more than the emotional bond between people. Lohkan and I were forced to see beyond that. Once we did, the joy we knew together was...." She fell silent, as no words came to her to express the depth of their joy.

Lohkan answered for her. "Complete," he said, and took up Serra's line of reasoning. "I felt complete when I was with Euripides, even with the guilt I felt about our abstinence. "

Serra nodded her agreement. Quan Yin questioned them further.

"What else did you learn?"

Neither Lohkan nor Serra spoke now, as they were each lost in a reverie. After a moment, Serra continued.

"As Euripides, I was raised under a certain set of circumstances. My parents were both open minded, supportive, loving and compassionate. My father supported me in all my choices. He did not try to make me into another version of himself. He was happy in whatever I chose, as long as I did not hurt myself or another. He did not try to control me. He gave me the freedom to make my own choices, my own mistakes."

Quan Yin turned to Lohkan. "And you, Lohkan?"

"My family life was the opposite of Serra's. My father tried to control the entire family through guilt. Whenever I began down a path of which he disapproved, he said or did something to try to manipulate or control that path. Throughout my life, not only did I feel I was failing Euripides, but also my parents.

"I constantly felt trapped by failure. I failed to fulfill my father's dreams. I failed to consummate my love with Euripides. My life was filled with guilt, which kept me from experiencing a more complete joy, a more complete life. Now I can see how futile that guilt was. My feeling badly helped no one. In the end, I only hurt myself."

Quan Yin smiled thoughtfully and then responded.

"**Guilt requires the enslavement of one soul to another by emotional bondage.** It heals nothing and only hinders. Or, as you said, Lohkan, 'It traps the soul and refuses joy.' **At the core of all acts, all decisions, are the expressions of love or the lack of them.** Your father was unable to express joy and, therefore, was unable to allow you free expression."

Everyone became silent. The guide floated above them while Serra and Lohkan sat hand in hand amongst the fragrant flowers. After a while, what seemed like hours, the guide spoke.

"You will need to rest before you go on to your next life."

They each nodded, lay down in the flowers and then they fell into a deep sleep, where their love mingled into a blissful state of peace and tolerance.

Chapter 9

"the between ..."

I think that if we were to go here, to this point...."
Lohkan pointed to a place on a transparent sphere
which floated between Serra and himself. The sphere
represented a three-dimensional view of planet Earth. The spot
that Lohkan touched glowed pale blue on the northern reaches
of the western continents, near the Arctic circle. Lohkan continued, "That this area would provide us with an interesting scope
of a foreign environment, as well as give us an intimate experience with animals. What do you think, Serra?"

We might not meet in this lifetime, she answered telepathically. *I believe our experiences would be worthwhile enough to
chance this, though.*

Lohkan nodded his agreement and the sphere disappeared. They had searched for days for an experience they could
share together. Each wanted the knowledge of animal and
human interdependencies and of a foreign climate. Their own
planet was mostly tropical and temperate. The arctic was the
obvious choice.

They had debated the eastern hemisphere's colder regions,
but decided that they wanted to move to the western hemisphere
for its unique cultural environment. The southern polar regions
were too sparsely inhabited for their research. Consequently, they
were led back to the northern polar sections again.

In their search they had found several small tribes of
hunters and fishermen who lived with dog teams. These tribes
were expecting an unusual number of births. Lohkan and Serra
had studied their choices, and had come to their decision.
Lohkan would reincarnate into one tribe, while Serra would
reincarnate in another that lived two hundred miles away from
Lohkan's. Considering the primitive state of travel and the

weather conditions, it was doubtful they would ever meet.

As the sphere disappeared, the guide appeared in its place. She smiled at their surprise and her laughter rang out over the meadow in the harmonic sound of bells and wind. As the wind swirled around them in circles, Serra's hair flew about her face in untamed spirals. Quan Yin's voice cut through the wind.

"You have decided?"

"Yes," they each answered.

"Then it is time."

The wind blew harder, the bells rang louder, more resonantly, and the meadow vanished.

The wind blew from the north and west. The wind also came from the south and east. The wind came from all directions at once, making travel impossible. The gods had decided to clean the earth and, in their haste, many lives were claimed that winter.

Anyone who had chanced the harsh winds and pelting ice crystals was robbed of all senses, and eventually of his or her life. Small children had gone to meet Mother Earth after wandering only a few feet from the snow shelter. Strong men had been driven mad by the constant howling of the wind gods. Game had long ago fled south, but the tribes had not been able to travel as fast as the herds; many starved before winter relented her claim. As spring dawned, stark and naked, those who lived celebrated the earth's spring celebration ... sparingly.

Another year passed before the tribes were able to replenish their furs, foods and people. During the second summer, after the great cleansing by the winter gods, more children were born than at any other time in their remembered history. Twins were not uncommon. Families grew strong again.

The oldest of his grandchildren walked beside him, with her small mittened hand in his larger one. He smiled at her wide-eyed expression. A hood encircled her face in a wreath of white and brown fur. Ice crystals were frozen on the tips of the fur where her breath had condensed. She smiled back at her grandfather, a wide toothless smile. She had lost her front baby teeth recently when she had fallen on the ice. He smiled harder at her black smile.

The old man was dressed akin to the child. His distinctively lined face was surrounded by a gray and black furred hood. His parka was thick, warm and tanned on the inside to a water-resistant suppleness. His leggings had been tanned in a similar manner, but with the fur side turned inward. Double-thick moccasins covered his feet. Over his hands, fur mittens kept out all but the most bitter cold. The child next to him looked as if someone had stamped out a miniature model of himself. Only the designs along the sleeves and hood were different. Hers were symbols that a female child would wear. His were those of a man, an old man, who had lived long and honorably. He was very proud of this child.

Ten years ago most of his grandchildren had died. The following year after the great winter, his wife had known that her time had come to return to the gods. She had walked out onto the ice to meet her death. Alone.

The summer after his wife's passing, many children had been sent by the gods to make up for their greedy cleansing of the earth. This grandchild had been born that summer. Many grandchildren had been born since, but none were as special to him as Blackfeather.

She smiled up at him again, and his heart warmed in his body as it grew larger. He was taking his granddaughter out with him to train their dogs. This one, this child, loved working with their dogs as much as he did. She was fearless around the strong creatures. This had at first frightened him, but it had also intrigued him. Though he was concerned that some harm might befall her, he was reassured by her unusual patience and instinct around the animals. The dogs sensed this same quality and were more gentle with her than with the other children.

He had promised her that, when she reached the age of eight, he would let her have her own pup to train. She had turned eight a month ago. In another three moons, when the puppies were born, she would be allowed to pick out her own. Today he would show her the fine leather leashes and how they were woven. He barked out a command to one of the lead bitches as they drew close to the pack.

A white dog with tan markings jumped up expectantly. He commanded her to stay and ran his hands across her snowy fur. His granddaughter waited obediently like the dog, in a sitting position. The girl and the dog both greeted him with still, yet excited, faces. After the old man inspected the harness, he called his granddaughter to his side. As the dog sniffed the small girl it waved its tail back and forth. All the dogs knew Blackfeather. The old man began to explain the leather weaving their tribe used.

"Do you see how the harness fits? If the harness is too tight, the dog will not run as long or as fast. If the harness is too loose, the dog can slip out of it. The weaving allows the dog to move freely. A good team is held by a firm harness and a strong hand."

The little girl nodded. She knew this, because she had watched her grandfather work with the dogs since she could remember. He continued anyway, starting from the beginning. All that was learned had an ending as well as a beginning. The gods had made it this way so that their children would know harmony. Even though Blackfeather knew more than most her age, her training needed to proceed as the gods had taught, starting at the beginning....

Today's beginning lesson was more of a review, but a happy one. The time passed quickly, and Blackfeather was sad when her Grandfather informed her that they needed to return to their family's hut. They held hands as they walked back to the ice structure. The day's dusk was followed by a full darkness as the Arctic's limited display of daylight faded.

Blackfeather awoke smiling. She snuggled closer to her mother's back and put one small, brown arm around her young brother to draw him closer to her for warmth. She dipped her head outside the furs for a moment to listen. She heard her father's steady breathing on the other side of her mother. Everyone was asleep. She decided to wait for someone to rise and light the fire before she rose.

Outside, daylight was already brightening the barren landscape. She heard the dogs barking to the Wolf God. Grandfather had explained that the wild wolves remembered the knowledge the gods had taught them, while most dogs had forgotten much of this knowledge. Their dogs were bred with the wild wolves to ensure strength in the lines. Their tribe's pack was known for its strength and for its intelligence.

Today she would get to pick out a puppy for herself from the two litters recently born within the pack. Blackfeather wiggled excitedly as she thought about this day. Her dog day.

Next to her, her mother yawned sleepily. Blackfeather's heart raced as she realized that soon she would get to meet this day. Grandfather coughed on the other sleeping place, where he shared furs with one of her uncles. She heard her uncle rise and start the fire after he had relieved himself. *Soon,* she told herself, *I shall go with Grandfather to pick out my puppy.*

Breakfast seemed markedly slow and restrained to Blackfeather. Her meal of hot fish stew with dried smoked fish had no flavor. She chewed and swallowed her food quickly and waited for Grandfather to call her. Finally, he did.

"Granddaughter, you are quiet. Don't you want to pick out your dog?" he teased her.

She jumped up and pulled on her outside parka and mittens over her indoor tunic and thick fur leggings. Her Grandfather smiled as they joined hands once more and went outdoors.

Near the area where the dogs were tied off was an enclosed den. The den was made of sticks, mud and stones. Inside the den lay the lead bitch with her four puppies. She panted happily as her puppies nursed. Blackfeather and Grandfather squatted a few feet away on their haunches. The morning's dim light played on their features. Grandfather's face was old and weathered, while Blackfeather's young one was earnest and intent. Grandfather waited while Blackfeather stared at the pups, and did not hurry her.

Blackfeather had known which pup she would choose before this day arrived. She had known each pup since its birth. She now pretended to decide, so that she could enjoy the puppies a little longer. While the puppies were this young, three weeks old, she was not allowed to bother them or their mother, but she never tired of watching the small bodies nestled closely to their mother's side. Grandfather interrupted her admiration with a question.

"Blackfeather, perhaps you need to hold each puppy one more time, in order to decide?"

Her brown eyes widened, and she nodded yes soundlessly. She held her breath while Grandfather went to the den and picked out one pup, a white one like its mother. He placed the small puppy, who wiggled and whined its protest at being removed from the nipple, into Blackfeather's arms.

The white puppy settled down quickly as it felt the fur of Blackfeather's parka. She stroked its small head gently and murmured dog noises to it. After a few minutes, Grandfather took the little pup away and placed it back with its mother.

Next he brought her a second pup. This one was brown and gray, with longer black hair shot through the coat. She knew that as each puppy grew, its color could change dramatically. She turned this little one over and rubbed the soft underbelly against her cheek. The little male puppy whined loudly as Grandfather took it away.

The third puppy was also a male, like the two before it. His tiny blue eyes stared up at Blackfeather with a curious stare. He licked the air, and the end of Blackfeather's nose. His white and black coloring created dramatic markings in the shape of a mask around his blue eyes. She handed the puppy back to Grandfather and waited eagerly for the last pup.

This last pup was a female and, consequently, somewhat smaller than her brothers. Her clear blue eyes stared back at Blackfeather's rich, brown ones. This puppy's markings were especially appealing. A reddish brown outer coat lay over a creamy white undercoat, with black hairs shot sparsely and evenly throughout; the prettiest colors of all were the rich charcoal and golden-toned hues on her back and face. Blackfeather murmured a small whine to the puppy, and the puppy answered in kind as it wagged its petite tail.

Grandfather smiled at her as she cuddled the last pup to her neck. He ran one hand down the puppy's back and then spoke.

"Blackfeather, perhaps you have chosen one?"

She nodded and smiled.

"This one, Grandfather. This is the puppy," she said proudly. He patted the small pup once before returning it to the mother.

Blackfeather began training her puppy after two more moons had passed. She began by acquainting the puppy with the leashes and harnesses that the puppy would someday wear; she carefully tied a miniature harness onto the small body. When the puppy became agitated, Blackfeather distracted her from the leather with a game of tag. After the morning passed, she removed the harness and brought the pup back to her mother and litter mates. Each morning they did this, until the puppy associated the harness with fun.

Once the puppy sat happily while being harnessed, Blackfeather expanded the puppy's training by tying a small rock onto a long leather thong. She carefully tied the other end of the thong to the harness. The puppy tried to chew and tear at the thong and rock. Again Blackfeather's job was to distract the puppy until the rock no longer held any interest.

Some days Grandfather assisted her with the training. He watched how she handled the growing puppy and showed her how she might better guide it. When he decided the puppy was ready to train before a sled, he helped her fit the puppy for a sledding harness. They built a miniature sled together and taught the puppy to pull and to halt on command. The puppy responded and learned quickly, which, Grandfather explained, was a sign of good breeding.

The old man and child worked together side by side, until one evening when the family sat by the fire outside the summer hut. The summer hut was built of wood, dried mud, rocks and leather. During the summer their small tribe moved from place to place as it sought out favorite hunting areas. Blackfeather's uncles and father hunted together with other men in the tribe. Often the men disappeared for days, as they collected game from their trap lines or fished in their slippery kayaks.

Blackfeather, Grandfather, her mother, brother and new little sister stayed at the summer site, where they tanned hides, made new clothes and trained the young dogs. One night Grandfather spoke solemnly to Blackfeather.

"Blackfeather, your puppy is ready to try pulling a larger sled. First though, she must learn to answer to you. For her to do that she must understand that you are her older sister."

"Older sister?" asked Blackfeather in a confused voice. She chewed the end of a long piece of sinew, in order to prepare it for threading. She was helping her mother make new moccasins for herself, her younger brother and her father.

The days were very long now, and they worked into the evening to take advantage of the light. A small fire burned, infusing the camp area with smoke from the fresh herbs that had been thrown over it to keep the mosquitos at bay. Blackfeather brushed away one small insect which had made it through the dense, fragrant smoke.

"Yes, you must become her older sister. Come here, Blackfeather." He patted the ground beside him. She obediently set down the long cord of sinew and went to Grandfather's side. Her mother picked up her younger brother, who had fallen asleep near the fire, and carried him inside the hut, where the baby already lay fast asleep. Blackfeather waited for Grandfather to speak. He quietly sat and stared into the coals of the fire as if some magic lay there. The firelight and summer evening light blended into a golden glow, which reflected on the old man's face. The wrinkles around his eyes were shadowed into many fine lines, which spread outward as the winter stars burst out rays in a twinkling sincerity. His gray hair looked yellow in the firelight. The night air moistened his skin and hung in tiny drops from his gold and silver mustache. After many long minutes, in which Blackfeather had begun to fall asleep, he spoke.

"Blackfeather, you are an older sister to your younger brother and baby sister. Do you know this?"

She nodded. "Yes."

"You guide and teach your younger brother now?"

"Yes," she said as she looked up at Grandfather.

"Your puppy must see you as an older sister, as a guide," he began to explain. "She must look to you for guidance. Not me. Not her mother. You. Do you understand this, Granddaughter?"

"Yes, I do."

For months the two had been playmates. The puppy and she had wrestled, chased each other and played tug-of-war. Now she needed to change their relationship. Grandfather spoke again.

"Let me tell you a story, Blackfeather.

"Long ago, the wind blew strong and wild. The wind was the only force in the universe. It blew through the heavens without hindrance from any other creature. Nothing else existed in the sky. Nothing stood in the way of the wind.

"The wind became wild, *and* very lonely. One day, after the gods had watched the wind's reckless actions, they decided that the wind needed something to blow against, something to stop it. The gods created the stars. As the wind blew through the stars, it found it could not blow as hard or as recklessly. The wind was forced to slow down as it blew around the stars. In this way it was directed into a path of calmness.

"Many, many moons passed, and the gods watched the wind as it moved through the stars. The wind had learned discipline from the guidance the stars gave to it, but still the wind seemed sad. The gods decided that the wind needed not only guidance, but also someone to play with. And so the gods created the clouds.

"They made clouds that would weep. They made clouds that would grow dark and talk in loud voices. They made clouds that would spit mouthfuls of fire onto the earth and light up the sky. They made clouds that were fat, lazy and white, like the owl's feather. The gods wanted the wind to have many friends with which to play. The wind played in the skies with the clouds and became content with so many friends, and the gods saw that the wind was now happy. Now and then, when the wind has no friends to play with, and the Moon God hides the stars, the wind again becomes wild, and runs over the ice and land. As happened many winters ago, before you were born, Blackfeather."

He fell silent and stared into the fire. Blackfeather looked up into the dusky sky where the stars were hidden and waited for

Grandfather to speak. After a few minutes, he continued.

"Blackfeather, you must be the stars <u>and</u> the clouds to your puppy. If you do not, she will grow to be wild and blow across the land as a dark wind. An older sister is both stars and clouds."

He finished and stared into his granddaughter's black eyes. She nodded her head soundlessly. Her expression was serious and intent. He took her small hand in his roughened, aged one and gestured toward the place where the dogs slept.

"What will you call your puppy, Blackfeather?"

She smiled as she thought of the puppy. The puppy's siblings all had different colored eyes. One had dark brown, almost black eyes. Another had green and gold eyes. The third brother, who looked more and more like his mother, had blue eyes that were almost white. His were a washed-out blue that was penetrating, and disturbing. Blackfeather's puppy had eyes which were the most beautiful color she had ever seen. She had never seen another dog with this color. The puppy's eyes were a rich blue encircled in green. The effect was an arresting shade of turquoise that looked like the shadow on an iceberg when the summer sun tries to shine through its mass, but fails, and creates sparkling blue-green shadows. She answered with the obvious name.

"Blue Eyes."

"Ah, I think that this is a good name. Her eyes are unusually clear. They will see more than most."

Blackfeather did not understand what Grandfather meant, but she was warmed by his approval.

Winter arrived in vivid display of white. Snow storms hit, one right after another, until every inch of land was thickly blanketed. The tribe had begun its winter migration and was safely camped for almost a moon's cycle before winter sunk its teeth into the earth and covered the tundra in her snowy shrouds.

During the first storm, Grandfather suggested that Blue Eyes sleep with Blackfeather. This would strengthen their bond, he explained. She had been thrilled by this idea and had excitedly made a new sleeping place for herself and Blue Eyes at the back of their hut. The dogs always slept close to their campsites during the winter months. Blackfeather had grown up with dogs as an integral part of their family. Many times certain dogs were brought into their temporary shelters; sometimes during training, but more often after the dog had reached maturity and was less likely to chew up their household. Blackfeather wondered why

Grandfather was letting her keep Blue Eyes indoors when she had not yet known a full cycle of seasons.

Blue Eyes had cut her adult teeth three months ago, but she still acted like a puppy and mouthed sticks and any bones she found. Blackfeather knew that she would have to watch Blue Eyes carefully. If the puppy chewed even one moccasin, her father would put the young dog back outside with the pack.

Grandfather spent more and more time with her and the young dog. He taught her how to weave a new and differently styled harness from the one she had been using. He showed her, again and again, how to train and work with the dog. He taught her never to strike at Blue Eyes. A dog would never trust a family if it was treated violently, and trust was essential in a sled dog team, in a pack, in their tribe. "Trust," he explained,"is as necessary as thick ice. If the ice is thin, then eventually it will crack and drown whoever stands upon it." Their tribe consisted of men and dogs where trust needed to be as thick as winter ice.

As Blackfeather built a trusting relationship between herself and Blue Eyes, she also had to establish strong boundaries for the young and energetic dog. Grandfather taught her how to move and speak as a wolf. She barked her commands firmly instead of speaking or signing them. She growled deep in her throat whenever Blues Eyes disobeyed her command. She learned to handle Blue Eyes with a firm and tender touch, as the puppy's mother once had. "This," Grandfather said, "is a language your dog will understand." Blackfeather learned to lead gently without physical violence, and Grandfather watched her growth proudly.

The wind had stopped howling when Blackfeather woke to the day. She dug her hands deeper into Blue Eye's thick fur, and hugged the dog closer to herself. She stuck her face into the dog's fur to warm her nose and breathed in the heady aroma of dog fur, outdoor air and leather. Blue Eyes lived in her harness most of the time now. The dog stretched out with a long deep yawn, but did not get up. Blackfeather heard someone stirring the coals into a fire. After a few minutes she arose, dressed quickly and went outdoors to relieve herself. Blue Eyes followed.

When she came back inside her mother was unusually quiet and serious. Blackfeather helped prepare breakfast for her younger brother. She then masticated dried fish and spit the chewed mash into a bowl for her little sister. When this morning meal was ready, she repeatedly dipped one finger into the fish mush and put it into her sister's mouth.

After breakfast her mother asked her brother, Blackfeather's uncle, to take the little boy outside. The uncle nodded as if he understood something that Blackfeather could not understand. Her father had already left with a cousin to check their trap lines. Grandfather was outside with the dogs.

"Blackfeather, please come here and sit by me. I wish to speak to you," her mother said seriously. Both Blackfeather and Blue Eyes answered quickly and obediently. They sat together on their haunches in front of Blackfeather's mother.

"Your grandfather's time has come," she said openly. "Today, when the sun begins to set, he will go out on the ice to meet his last hour of sleep. Today we will make him his favorite foods and pack his favorite tools into his pack."

Her mother's words were clear and strong. Only one small tear, which glistened on the edge of her wide dark eyes, betrayed her sorrow. Blackfeather had known that this time would come. When a person reached a place in this life when the physical body became as a baby's, toothless and feeble, then the person was ready to pass on to the spirit world.

The world they lived in was physically hard, wearing and unforgiving. The old and sick suffered in the extreme cold and did not last long. In an environment where all resources and energies were needed just to keep the tribe functioning, the special care needed by the very old and ill could exhaust those precious resources quickly, devastating the other tribe members.

But, Grandfather did not seem feeble! Blackfeather had noticed, when she was not training Blue Eyes, that Grandfather's mouth grew more empty. True, his food resembled the mash they made for their little sister. Blackfeather suddenly realized that she could not remember when she had last seen Grandfather chew a piece of jerky. But, he was smart, and still very clear! She began to protest, but her mother reprimanded her sternly.

"Blackfeather, you are old enough to understand! Do not ask to take your grandfather's dignity from him for your own selfish desires! Do you respect him so little?"

Blackfeather winced at the words. She tried desperately not to cry, but tears fell down her cheeks in spite of her efforts. She swallowed over a pain in her throat that was new to her. Blue Eyes whined and licked her face nervously. Blackfeather stared up at her mother and tried to speak, but the pain in her throat had removed her voice. Instead she bent and crawled out through the small entrance of their hut. She did not know where her feet were taking her. She did not see the scenery around her.

She did not know what she sought, until she found herself in Grandfather's arms.

Neither spoke. He held her until her tears had exhausted her and left her empty. When he spoke, his voice was clear and did not belie his decay.

"Blackfeather, do you remember the story about the stars and clouds? I shall live in them; I shall become your star."

"I shall be alone."

"What? What is this?"

"After you leave ..." she sobbed once more, "I shall be alone." She could not explain what she meant. She simply knew, understood, that no one in her family would understand her as Grandfather did. He held her tightly and whispered into her black, shiny hair.

"Blackfeather, don't you know that you are never alone? Don't worry, Granddaughter. I promise that my spirit shall *always* be with you."

In the evening, when Grandfather walked out into the wilderness alone, the dogs paced nervously. When the sun set, they broke into song, with howls that echoed long and sorrowfully over the barren landscape. In their hut, Blue Eyes joined into the howl. Blackfeather, with her arms clasped tightly around the dog, tilted her tear-streaked face upward, and joined them.

Blackfeather checked the leather lead and saw that it had been chewed through.

Blue Eyes was gone.

When Blue Eyes had come into her heat cycle, Blackfeather had tied her near the wolf trail so that she could mate with one of the wild wolves. She had heard the arrival of the wolves last night, when their camp dogs had broken into a frenzy of howling. This morning the wolves were gone. Blue Eyes had gone with them. Only her small paw prints lay next to large wolf tracks in the snow. The tracks trailed into the distance, across the tundra and away from Blackfeather.

Blackfeather swallowed the fear that rose in her throat. Tears formed in her eyes and blurred her snowy world. Her breath came out in steamy clouds and distorted her world even further. Her wide dark eyes searched beyond her tears toward the horizon. But, nothing was there. The tundra was empty of all but windswept snow.

What if she never saw Blue Eyes again?

She struggled with her feelings and remembered

Grandfather's words when he had trained her years ago. At the time, Blackfeather had been trying to teach Blue Eyes to come when her name was called. She had pulled on the long leather lead attached to Blue Eyes' harness and had demanded that Blue Eyes come to her. Her anger had mounted as Blue Eyes had stubbornly sat on her haunches and had refused to move. Grandfather had scolded her gently.

"Blackfeather, don't try to force your dogs! You cannot control any creature. Though you are the stars and clouds to Blue Eyes, she is free. Let her come to you!"

The moment Blackfeather had stopped forcing her, Blues Eyes had come happily to her side.

Blackfeather stared out over the tundra now and prayed to the Wolf God to protect Blue Eyes and to bring her safely home. She prayed silently that Blue Eyes would want to come to her side again.

Weeks passed, and Blackfeather spent part of each day searching the horizon with her eyes for any sign of Blue Eyes. As each day passed, Blackfeather's hopes dwindled, until even the faintest of hopes seemed foolish to her practical nature.

One day, as she punctured fish on a stick to smoke over a fire, a cold wet nose pushed against her hand. It was Blue Eyes. Her coat was matted. Her paws were muddy and worn. Blue Eyes smiled happily at Blackfeather and wagged her tail as Blackfeather buried her face in her thick fur. Surprisingly, the same pain that Blackfeather had felt when Grandfather had died, returned this day. Her throat ached. Her hands shook. Tears ran down her brown cheeks as she silently prayed her thanks to the Wolf God for protecting Blue Eyes.

Blue Eyes' puppies were big now, six moons old. This was the third litter Blue Eyes had had during the last six years. Grandfather had taught Blackfeather that to breed a bitch too often produced a weak dog, and was cruel to the animal. As a woman who gave birth too often became waned and exhausted, so was this true of dogs. Every two years, since the first time Blue Eyes had run off, Blackfeather had taken Blue Eyes to the wolf trails and set her free. Each time, a few weeks later Blue Eyes had returned to their camp.

Blue Eyes was a magnificent dog. She was large, with a long thick auburn and gold coat. The dark gray and gold mask she had had as a puppy had turned into a light gray and yellow mask as she matured. She still had the thick creamy undercoat, and all her legs were creamy white, when they weren't muddy. And her blue eyes had remained a clear shade of iceberg blue.

Blackfeather watched the puppies play as she tried to decide what to do next. Her uncle wanted her to travel with him many days' journey to tribes in the east. There he wanted to trade some of Blue Eyes' puppies for some new dogs. Their tribe was known for the quality of the dogs they bred. Grandfather had been the leader of their tribe, and now her uncle was.

Her uncle was a humorless man who had mated late in life, just last year, and Blackfeather felt little for him. Marriages were preformed simply in the clans. A man and woman agreed verbally to mate, the tribes were informed and, then, the marriage was completed through the couple's physical joining. Blackfeather had thought her uncle was humorless because he was lonely; yet the young woman he had brought to their tribe one day had done little to enhance his disposition. Her uncle's new wife was now pregnant and due to give birth any day. Consequently, she could not travel with her husband.

Her uncle wanted to travel while the fall air was still warm. They would lead the puppies in harnesses without any sled. He, Blackfeather and three other members of their tribe would carry their few camp items on their backs.

The trip sounded enjoyable, and Blackfeather welcomed the adventure. Her reservations were based on her reluctance to give up the puppies. Though she understood this to be a wise course of action, as new dogs would strengthen the blood lines, she had difficulty relinquishing Blue Eyes' offspring to other tribes, strangers who had their own individual dog training practices. Blackfeather was so focused on her thoughts that she did not hear her mother approach.

"Blackfeather! Your uncle awaits your answer! If you do not decide soon, I shall decide for you," she said firmly. Her skin was wrinkled and windburned. The hair around her face had begun to gray. Her eyes were still attractive and large in her wide, flat face. An ache in her back had begun to bother her lately, and this made her impatient. She loved her daughter, but did not understand her willfulness.

Blackfeather faced her mother, but listened with a bowed head as a good daughter did. Her black hair was braided tightly and fell down her back, over her fall parka. She was taller than her mother, even with her head bowed, and was as pretty as her mother had been at the same age. She waited respectfully for her mother to continue.

"Blackfeather, you cannot mate with any of our tribe. The

other clans are too close to ours. You must go to another tribe to find a mate. Your uncle is the leader of our tribe. As his niece, you hold a high status. You can have almost any man you want. Why do you *not* want to mate?"

"It's not that I don't want to mate," Blackfeather said soft-ly. She looked sideways toward the puppies and then back at her mother. "It's just that I have not met a man I like as much as our dogs!" she said with passion. As she said "dogs", she signed the gesture for "love" with the movement of her closed hand across her heart and stared directly into her mother's eyes. As she said the word "man", she signed the word for "harsh" by striking one hand across the other.

"I know you love the dogs, but, this is not a good answer," her mother said with compassion. She snorted softly, chuckled and continued. "Blackfeather, I did not want to mate when I was your age. It is time you took one, though. The decision is made. You are going. I shall tell your uncle." Her mother walked stiffly toward their hut to deliver this news.

Blue Eyes led her puppies skillfully. She nipped at their muzzles and growled at any who decided to run in the lead. She pinned her oldest puppy when he decided to pick on the smallest one, a black-toned female. She quickly broke up any fights and administered to her litter efficiently and gently. By the time they reached the eastern tribes, the puppies were a half moon older, and they had had their first trail training.

The eastern tribe was camped in the dense forest that lay there. Blackfeather's tribe lived mostly on the open tundra, and she liked this new area, with its heavily scented pine forest and needle-covered ground. The needles crunched as they walked across the earth in the brisk traveling pace she had learned as a girl. Late in the day they came upon the campsite which lay in an open area of the forest.

Autumn air filled the camp area, mixing with smoke from cooking fires, tanning leathers, dog hair and human and dog excrement. All these, with the exception of the heavily scented pines, reminded Blackfeather of her family's camp. They were greeted with a quiet warmth, which was typical of the tribes in the north. Soon the host tribe had cooked a meal to celebrate their arrival. Blackfeather tied the dogs nearby, where she could watch them, and then went to the fires to offer her help.

During the meal, Blackfeather heard some news that sur-prised her. They were not the only ones coming to this tribe to trade dogs. Another tribe, from farther south and east, would arrive soon. She wondered how, and if, this would affect their trade? Maybe she could trade directly with this other tribe, if their dogs were good enough. The next day, by mutual agreement, everyone decided to postpone trades until the other tribe arrived.

For two more days she enjoyed the forest setting of this tribe. They were a gentle and peaceful people, very much like her own. Their customs differed very little, and their physical characteristics were almost identical to those of Blackfeather's tribe. On the third day after their arrival, Blackfeather decided to take Blue Eyes and the puppies for a run in the forest. The forest's dark beauty entranced her, and she traveled farther than she had meant to go. She was brought out of her reverie when Blue Eyes began to growl.

At first she heard nothing, and then she heard something coming through the woods in the distance. She stopped, stood with her head turned toward the noise and listened. The puppies were silent for once as their mother stiffened into a guarded stance. Blackfeather stood motionlessly as she decided what to do. They could most likely outrun whatever it was. If it were a black bear, once it caught scent of the dogs, it would run away. If it were one of the great red bears that fished for salmon, then it would be better if they left right now. She had heard tales of these giant bears. When they were in a foul mood they could viciously attack humans and dogs. Just at that moment, she heard a welcome sound, the happy barking of dogs on the trail. The new tribe was coming. She quietly tied up Blue Eyes and the puppies and stood to wait.

The forest lay hushed around them when, with a sudden burst of noise, two dog teams came running through the trees. Following the dogs were a dozen or so people. Blackfeather stood transfixed by the sight, for these dogs were beautiful, and unusually large ... at least a head taller than Blue Eyes. A man sighted her when one of these tall dogs turned and growled in her direction. The stranger called dogs and people to a halt with one loud cry. He turned the reins over to a small woman who stood next to him and approached Blackfeather.

"What tribe are you from?" the stout man asked politely. He was dressed in summer skins that were painted with designs she had not seen before, and were skillfully made. She answered and pointed back through the forest.

"I am from a western tribe of the north tundra. The tribe you seek is a short run through these trees," she said.

"Yes, I know," the strange man answered. He appeared to be about the age of her uncle, and almost as serious.

She awkwardly waited for the brusque man to speak and, when he did not, she offered a polite suggestion.

"If you lead, my team will follow behind yours."

He nodded and returned to his tribe to explain. Blackfeather waited a moment for their teams to get under way, and then followed reluctantly. She had loved the peace and stillness of the forest, and was not yet ready to leave. However, to not do so would be an insult to these people. In essence, she would be telling them that she did not want their company, and so she ran swiftly back to camp behind Blue Eyes and the puppies.

The trading was friendly and fierce. These new people knew dogs as well as Grandfather had, as well as Blackfeather did. Her uncle was an excellent trader, though a poor dog handler, and came to Blackfeather often to ask for her thoughts on one dog or another. One of Blue Eyes' puppies had been born with a pure white coat. This puppy alone would bring them two new dogs and a load of furs. As the trading went on, Blackfeather steeled herself to accept the fact that, when they left this place, she would be minus all but one puppy. She had decided to keep one of the males, who looked remarkably like his mother, and tied him with Blue Eyes while she examined the other dog teams for any dog she might like to have. Eventually she chose two.

One was a young dog, a female who looked as if she was close to a full season of cycles. This female could be bred to the puppy she had chosen to keep. The second dog was a male, about three seasons old and well trained. He was not a lead dog, though Blackfeather did not know why. He had all the qualities that made a good lead dog: strength, agility, endurance, intelligence and patience, without too much willfulness. A certain amount of willfulness, or independence, was necessary. A willful dog would turn away from a command if there was impending danger that the musher might not see, such as a crack in the ice. An obedient dog could lead a team and its musher to their death. This dog's spirit and intelligence was visible from twenty yards. She spoke to her uncle about her interest in this dog, and he threw her choice into the bartering.

While her uncle traded, she behaved in the manner in which her mother had taught her. She helped cook meals, assisted in making sinew and other leather products and demurely watched the young men with shy eyes. If she saw one young man she liked, she was to tell her uncle, and he would make the arrangements. She hoped furtively that one would have the same love and commitment to his dogs that she had.

Sadly, none of the young men there looked upon their dogs as anything but work animals. Most were rough in their handling of the creatures upon which they were seriously dependent for their survival. A few were even cruel. It seemed that none saw the importance of trust and union that Grandfather had taught her. She sighed unhappily and realized her uncle would be furious when she informed him of her decision.

One day, as she helped scrub out bowls, the loud clamor of dogs barking and howling arose in the camp. As she looked up, another dog team, a small one of four dogs, was driven into camp by a strange man. The camp's tribal leader went to the man and greeted him. A woman next to her informed Blackfeather that this was the leader's cousin, who lived three day's travel to the south. The young man tied off his team, and began to methodically check each dog's paws for rocks and burrs. Next he went to the lead dog and lovingly stroked the bitch's large gray head. Blackfeather recognized the wolf strain in these dogs and smiled. As she did, the young man looked across the camp that separated them and into her eyes ... as if he knew she watched him. For Blackfeather, it was love at first sight. She gasped audibly, and the woman with whom she was working looked up again to see what held Blackfeather's attention. The woman spoke bluntly.

"His name is Silverfin. He is mated. He does breed strong dogs, though."

Blackfeather felt as though all the air had been removed from her. This young man was close to her in age, maybe a few years older. He loved his dogs – that was obvious! He used wolves for breeding. Something in his eyes had stirred something inside her ... a resonant call of something she could not remember, something important. She bowed her head and refocused on her work to hide her feelings.

That evening a strange coincidence occurred. As Blackfeather sat by the fire with the other woman, her uncle came and informed her that there was a problem in the trade agreements. As he spoke, the other women fell silent and listened.

"The large male you want is also wanted by someone else."

"I thought the trade was already made?" Blackfeather asked curiously.

"It was not tied."

Her uncle referred to a custom of tying a thong of leather around the item bartered for once a trade had been completed.

"Who wants him?" she asked stubbornly. She was not easily going to give up on this animal. In her mind he had already become part of the pack.

"A tribe member. If you could choose another dog, then peace would be kept in this family," her uncle explained.

"Which family member wants him?" she asked, still unwilling to surrender the trade.

"Silverfin."

Blackfeather sucked in her breath and held still. The young woman next to Blackfeather stared curiously at her. Blackfeather's heart raced while her mind softened. She spoke in a whisper.

"Could we barter with this man?"

"Yes, I believe I can."

"Could I come with you?"

If her uncle was surprised by her request, he did not say so. He nodded, and headed back to the spot where the men had been bartering these last few days. She followed her uncle, numb with anticipation. Several of the women from the fire circle followed. Problems in the trade gatherings always caused an interesting diversion. This trade negotiation would create stories to tell by the long winter fires for many years to come.

Silverfin stood when he saw who followed her uncle. He nodded mutely and waited for her uncle to speak. While he did, Blackfeather studied the young man. Silverfin was a little taller than average. His long black hair was pulled back neatly at the back of his neck with a leather thong. His tunic and leggings were skillfully made and accented his slim body. His face was impassive and strong, an attractive face. Blackfeather had heard the other women in camp discussing Silverfin. Many thought he was handsome; all said he was kind. She held her breath when he briefly looked up into her eyes. She stood directly behind her uncle, who was seated on a log. She had not heard the trade agreements and, therefore, did not know how to respond when her uncle questioned her.

"Blackfeather, you do not answer. Speak."

She stood silently, feeling extremely foolish. Her uncle repeated his question impatiently.

"Silverfin wants the male you have picked out. He will give you a dozen beaver furs if you select another dog!"

The offer was excessively generous, and Blackfeather blushed deeper as all eyes were turned on her. Finally, she spoke in a hoarse whisper.

"This is not necessary. I shall pick another dog."

Her uncle glared at her for throwing away this unexpected bounty. But, the expression on Silverfin's face made up for her uncle's hostility. He smiled at her in a way that caused her heart to stop for a brief, yet long, second. When he spoke, she could barely hear his words over the loud beating of her heart.

"I would like you to accept the furs as a gift."

There were many murmurings around the camp.

"I've never seen trading such as this! Giving away furs? What could Silverfin be planning?" said one of the young woman who had followed Blackfeather to the trading circle.

"Ah, observe how he looks at the girl. More goes on here than the trading of furs!" said the young woman's mother.

"Silverfin no longer thinks clearly!" said one man.

"His wife will kill him!" said Silverfin's cousin as he made the sign for "grizzly bear."

In that moment an undeclared love had been demonstrated. Those who saw it were awed, and perhaps a little frightened. Those who heard about it later thought the teller exaggerated. The story passed quickly around the camp like a swarm of mosquitoes. No one was immune to its bite.

Therefore, it came as no surprise the next day when Silverfin approached the uncle with an offer for Blackfeather.

"I desire to speak to you about Blackfeather."

"Yes."

"I wish to take her as a second wife."

"A second wife? Blackfeather is the daughter of my sister," her uncle answered. For Blackfeather to go to a mating as a second wife would be an insult to her, her family and her uncle's abilities as a trader.

Silverfin pursued.

"I am already mated, or I would offer her the position of first wife. I mean no insult to you or your family."

"You do insult us! She has the knowledge of dog breeding. My father chose to pass on his knowledge, his gift, to Blackfeather. She carries his spirit. She cannot be a second wife!"

"I have heard of your father." Silverfin said. This was the ultimate compliment he could make to the uncle. The words softened him, but only slightly.

"If I could, I would let you mate Blackfeather, but I cannot. This mating would bring dishonor to our tribe. We had hoped that whoever mated her would become a member of our tribe and live with us. Our need of Blackfeather's skill is too strong to allow us to send her away for a mating."

Silverfin exhaled softly, and then tried again.

"I would be willing to come with you, join your family. I would bring my dogs, and my first wife."

Her uncle grimaced. The suggestion was tempting. Another woman would mean another set of hands. Silverfin's dogs would add to their wealth. But, what did he know of the first wife? What if she was a woman of ill temperament? One disagreeable person could make the winter long and unbearable. Also, to accept less than a first wife status for Blackfeather would lower the status of the whole tribe. Blackfeather's uncle was a stubborn man, and was careful not to show that he had begun to waver. He responded gruffly.

"We do not need more dogs."

"Then why are you here?" Silverfin sensed some advantage, and pressed on quickly. "I am a good trapper. My wife came from a tribe that knows a secret way of tanning skins until they are soft and pliable. Look."

He held out his arm. The fine leather work that Blackfeather had noticed the day before had not gone unseen by her uncle. He grunted, and then fell silent for several minutes.

"I shall give you my decision tomorrow," he said, and walked away.

※

The men who gossiped did not know that the person about whom they gossiped sat on the other side of the hut where they visited. They talked loudly, with a growing interest in their subject. One man was considerably smaller than the other, and had to keep looking up at his tall friend to get his point across. He emphasized his words with gestures from a sign language which was ancient and widely used across the continent.

"Silverfin knows the moon's madness," the short one said. "He has asked for Blackfeather as a second wife." He made the gesture for "wife." "Her uncle will not allow this match when many better ones are available."

"You forget that Blackfeather is a willful woman. If she wants to mate with Silverfin, she will. She has a sled dog's stubbornness," the tall man replied.

"Yes. I have heard that the old one, her grandfather's spirit, watches over her. Beavertail said he saw the shadow of his spirit as the old one followed her. That old one was strong when he was alive." The small man made the sign for "shaman" when he said Beavertail's name.

"The old one is more powerful now," the tall man said, and made the sign for "spirit world." "If the old one wants his granddaughter to mate Silverfin, no one will be able to stop this mat-ing, not even the uncle." As he said the word "uncle", he made the sign for "dog shit."

"There are forces more powerful than the spirits," the small man said.

"What?" his tall friend asked in disbelief.

"A first wife!" the small man answered, and both men burst into laughter. Chuckling, they walked off together toward the trading center.

Silverfin shook his head as the two men walked away. He had stooped to fix a broken lace on his moccasin when the two men had stepped from the hut with their loud gossip. Everything they had said was true, especially about a first wife's anger. He had questioned his sanity since his talk with Blackfeather's uncle earlier that morning. His wife would not understand. He did not understand himself.

His wife was a strong-minded woman, soft only when she chose to be. She carried their first child, and would not be able to travel until after the birth. *What had I been thinking of when I made an offer for a second wife?* Silverfin wondered. He had met a woman, a young woman, and suddenly he had been swept away in some kind of madness. He had one good wife. What did he need with another? Yet, he was unable to stop himself from thinking about Blackfeather.

His wife, Vole Ears, would not accept a second wife. She was not a woman who shared what she considered to be hers. In their tribe she was known for hoarding. He had married her after he had been unable to find another woman who was not too closely related. Now that choice seemed ridiculous. Vole Ears hated dogs. She tolerated them only as useful work animals which could serve her needs. *What had I been thinking,* he asked himself again, but this time added, *to mate with Vole Ears?* He unconsciously made the sign for "moon madness" as he asked himself this question.

Silverfin had begun walking toward the perimeter of the camp as he had this inner dialogue. He kept walking through the thick forest, toward a river where he could bathe. The cold water, he decided, would clear his head. He enjoyed the autumn air and woods around him as he hiked. Birds played in the branches above his head. A woodpecker pecked out a wooden drum beat in an evergreen nearby. The sound echoed through the forest in a happy resonance of life.

Silverfin wandered slowly through the woods, until he came near the river. As he approached it, he thought he heard splashing and stopped. Cautiously, he crept through the brush until the river came into view. Below him, bathing in the river, was Blackfeather and Blue Eyes. Blue Eyes?

His eyes widened at the the scene before him. Sled dogs usually hated water. Somehow Blackfeather had coaxed Blue Eyes into the water, under obvious protest. She hugged the wet dog to her naked body and laughed loudly as Blue Eyes mouthed a loud protest. The dog tried to shake the water off as it stood chest deep in the river. This caused Blackfeather to laugh even louder. She shook with merriment as Blue Eyes gave her a disgruntled look, slipped out from under her arms and waded toward the beach. Once on shore, the dog shook itself again and again and raced in circles. Blackfeather laughed hysterically, and suddenly lost her footing on a rock. In a split second she was down, immersed in icy water. Silverfin began to laugh, and then realized the dog might hear him. As he watched Blue Eyes, he would have sworn the dog was laughing, too. In the next moment, Blackfeather shot out of the water, sputtering and dripping long streams of cold water. She gasped, and then broke into laughter again. Silverfin watched from where he sat crouched in the undergrowth.

Her young body was strong and supple. Long black hair hung in ringlets down her back as she began to wade out of the river. Her stomach was small and hard, as were her breasts. Blackfeather's wide face beamed with joy. Her eyes were wide-set, large and black. The nose on her face was small and inconsequential above full lips. Silverfin sat stunned by a longing he did not expect. As a closely quartered people, the tribes saw nudity as a natural part of life. He had seen naked women and men all his life. Many of the women he had seen were easily more attractive than Blackfeather, although she was pretty. None had caused him to feel like this.

He sat, stunned by the emotions that coursed through him, and watched her lie in the sun next to her dog. She lay naked to the world, unaware, unafraid. He felt that somehow she had cast a magic over him from which he could not escape. He stood and, as if drawn by a cord which pulled him along, he began to creep to where Blackfeather lay. He had stepped a few feet when Blue Eyes sounded a warning growl. Blackfeather awoke and hurriedly sat up.

The river played a tune behind her that added to the illusion of magic in the air. Silverfin kept approaching, slowly, as if time had slowed down and his steps were directed by someone else's will. He stopped on the bank of the river a few yards in front of Blackfeather. The sand was warm in the afternoon sun. The sky rested brightly above them, with a blue that stung his eyes when he tried to look at it. Blue Eyes had ceased growling and stared beyond him at some unknown point, her ears pricked forward. Blackfeather waited quietly as Silverfin stared. Her body was covered with brown sand and her eyes were blurred by sleep. The spell was suddenly broken by the sound of her voice. Silverfin felt himself crash to the earth as if he had just awakened from a dream in which he was falling. The river gurgled and did not sing. Yet, his heart still did as he looked into Blackfeather's eyes.

"I was dreaming about you," she said. "Grandfather was there, and he brought you to see me. He told me not to worry, that you and I are true mates, spirit mates ... like the wind is to the stars." She pointed her small hand toward the sky, and made the sign for "stars." "He said that he would help us. Then I saw you walking through the brush to the river. Blue Eyes growled and I woke up."

They stood silently and stared at each other. Blue Eyes waited next to Blackfeather and continued to stare beyond Silverfin, toward the forest. Silverfin looked behind himself, toward the woods, but saw nothing. When he turned back to Blackfeather, she had begun to dress herself hastily. He went to her and put one hand over hers to stop her. The hand beneath his was trembling.

Deftly, he untied her lacings and pulled off the tunic she had just put on. He untied his tunic from his leggings and stepped out from them. Placing the soft leather on the ground, he pulled Blackfeather onto it. He rubbed her soft cheek with his rough one, and ran his hands down her back and over her breasts. Without thinking, she took his hand and placed it between her legs, and then bent over. Silverfin mounted her from the back and slowly pushed his way into her, moving very gently. They made love in the sand, as if they were in a dream. Movement became prolonged and sensual. The air around them touched their skin in a warmth of breezes which were electric and soft. Blackfeather felt a surge of sensation, pain mixed with pleasure. A bursting, deep inside, where her womanhood lay, brought her a wondrous feeling of expansion and joy. Silverfin collapsed on her back a moment later, lost in release. Protectively, he wrapped his body around hers and held her tightly to him, as if she might slip away. The forest lay still around them and the sun kept them warm. Blue Eyes lay nearby and watched the forest expectantly.

After a moment they rose, and Blackfeather went back into

the river to wash the blood from her thighs. Silverfin pulled off his tunic and joined her. The water brought reality crashing down on him. Its icy wetness grounded him to what he had done. What he now must do. He and Blackfeather were now mated according to tribal customs. He had to take her as a second wife. Her uncle would have no choice.

That had not been his motive when he had approached her and then made love to her. He had been moved to Blackfeather's side by forces greater then he understood. He could barely remember moving toward her. Something inexplicable was at work here. The entire experience had an other-worldly quality, an enchantment to it. Not that he had not experienced each part of it. That was exactly the point; he had felt every movement acutely, as if each step, each touch had been intensified. Their lovemaking had had a momentum of its own, as if someone outside them had directed it.

He ducked under the frigid water to clear his head again. When he came out, Blackfeather had gone back to the shore and begun to dress. Blue Eyes sniffed her carefully near her groin, and then stared at Silverfin, who stood shivering in the water. Again, he would have sworn that the dog was smiling.

When he came back to the beach, Blackfeather sat in the open sunshine on a rock. Blue Eyes sat next to her, and she hugged the wet dog to her chest. She silently watched Silverfin dress with just a hint of a smile playing across her features. He looked at her, and then spoke his earlier thoughts.

"We are mated. I shall tell your uncle."

"No."

"Why not?"

"He will be furious that I disobeyed him. He told me to stay away from you until he has made his decision. That is why I came here to the river. He will not understand that I did not plan this, that you did not force me. Let me tell him that I wish to be your mate."

"He'll say that I have only offered you a place as my second wife. He will tell you that this is not a high enough status for you. He will be right."

"I shall tell him that I would be honored to be your second wife."

"He will say, 'No.'"

"Then I shall tell him that I have already decided. He cannot decide for me. The choice is mine. He does not own it."

"This he will not forgive." Silverfin pointed out the obvious as he continued to dress. He shook his head, and then added one last remark.

"If at any time you do not want to tell your uncle alone, send word to me. I shall tell him." He took Blackfeather's hand and held it to his chest. She pulled his hand to her face and brushed his coarse palm against her cheek. She dropped his hand and signed that she would leave first. Silverfin watched as her small figure followed Blue Eyes and disappeared into the brush.

✳

"No!"

"No?"

"This is an impossible mating. You deserve better than a second wife status. We do not know her. We do not know if she will be worthy to join our tribe. I like Silverfin. He is worthy, but I shall accept only an offer of first wife."

Her uncle then gestured with the sign for "finished" or "ended." This sign, if gestured in a slightly different manner meant "death." Long ago, to keep peace during the long winters and harsh, exhausting conditions, certain laws, or customs, had been established. A leader had been given the authority to end disputes with this one gesture. The fact that it so closely resembled the sign for death was not an accident. On rare, very rare occasions, a tribe member could be sentenced to death by banishment, if the tribe member in question was seriously endangering the well being and existence of the tribe. The sign was made to remind whoever was being addressed that a serious decision had been made, and that an even more serious threat was involved for anyone who chose to disobey. Blackfeather started to protest to tell him it was too late, that she was already mated, but her uncle glared at her in a way that froze her tongue in her throat. She watched his retreating back despairingly.

The following morning, as the different tribes broke camp and began to ready themselves for the journey home, Silverfin went to Blackfeather's uncle to speak with him. Her uncle stood rigidly as Silverfin approached. His black mustache drooped further as he frowned and his hand tightened on the harness he held as Silverfin began to speak.

"I have come to ask for Blackfeather as my second wife," Silverfin stated plainly.

"Do not waste my time! I shall not accept an offer of second wife for Blackfeather. Bring me an offer of first wife, or none at all!" He gestured again with the hand sign for "finished" and turned his back on Silverfin.

This sign, known for its power, was recognized throughout

most of the northern tribes. Since this gesture was used rarely, to use it at all emphasized its importance. When it was used between non-family members or people from separate villages, a silent message was given that any who saw it were not to question the authority or the decision without causing dishonor and, perhaps, great discord to all who were involved. Silverfin was speechless.

He turned around rapidly and looked about the camp. Those who had watched looked away nervously. His cousin shook his head firmly: "No!" Then the older cousin signed that Silverfin should leave. Silverfin looked for Blackfeather. He saw that she was with the dogs, leashing the puppies for their new homes. Silently he went to collect his new dog, and then changed his mind. Instead, he took up the armload of beaver pelts and brought them quickly to Blackfeather, before anyone could stop him.

"Here. I keep my promises!" he said loudly, so that the whole camp could hear, and then whispered, "I promise that you will be my wife. I shall find a way." Silverfin strode back to the area where his new dog was kept. He struck up a conversation with his cousin and forced himself *not* to turn around and look at Blackfeather. An hour later, Blackfeather, her uncle, their tribe members, Blue Eyes, the puppy and four new dogs set out on the trail.

For once Silverfin did not see the passing scenery as he ran through the woods behind his dogs, a dangerous situation. His mind raced far ahead of the dogs.

He could not separate from his wife without cause. Bad temperament and lack of shared interest would not be seen as a just cause. Nor would falling in love with someone else be suitable. His tribe would just see him as foolish. As his mind dwelled on these thoughts, his dogs brought him home safely. He arrived back at his home camp three days later, early in the morning.

After he had tied up the dogs and brushed the larger knots from their coats, he walked dubiously toward his hut. He did not look forward to seeing Vole Ears. He stepped into the dark of the hut, calling out a greeting. No one responded. A moment passed before his eyes adjusted to the darkness. Once they had, he was able to see that he was indeed alone.

The fire had burned down to a few small coals. The bed furs had been pushed against one wall. A fur that Vole Ears was working on lay in a heap on the floor. Their bowls and tools were stacked haphazardly against another wall. Everything was in some kind of order, but the hut looked different ... shabby. The walls were stained with smoke, Vole Ears' tools looked uncared for and worn and the sleeping furs smelled of sweat and dust.

Silverfin stepped outside and looked about the camp. Several huts away from his lay Vole Ears' best friend's dwelling. The friend sat outside the hut now, scraping a skin that had been stretched tightly on a wooden frame. The friend did not notice Silverfin's approach until he stood beside her.

"Curly Hair, where is Vole Ears?" asked Silverfin. Wavy or curly hair was a rare physical trait amongst the northern tribes. His wife's best friend was a petite woman with a nasty disposition. Her disposition was what made her hair curl, explained the tribe's shaman half jokingly. Her curly head turned back toward Silverfin. She grimaced and shot him an angry look.

"Don't know! Perhaps if you were not gone so long with those stupid dogs you might know yourself."

"Know what?" he asked suddenly suspicious.

"Huh!" she grunted, and turned back to her work, but not before she turned and looked toward the forest on the other side of camp. Silverfin pretended not to notice and went back to his hut. He watched Curly Hair carefully. When she went inside her hut to get another tool, he ran quickly from his hut and into the forest.

Silverfin circled their village and came around to the other side of the forest. He followed a trail to the spring until he heard noises. The grunting and moaning noises came from somewhere east of the trail, and were unmistakable. He crept through the brush stealthily, until he came upon a clearing. A large round circle of grass lay mysteriously in the midst of the forest. His tribe oftentimes used this area for ceremonies. Silverfin lay down to watch the scene before him.

His wife sat on top of a man. They were in the midst of lovemaking, and oblivious to their surroundings. The scene was shocking, not because his wife made love to another man, but because she was having sex.

Silverfin's people believed it was wrong for a couple to have sex during the last three moons of a pregnancy. They believed a man's organ could block the baby's view into the world and frighten it. His wife was in the last moon of her pregnancy. That the scene before him took place in the sacred circle made it even more blasphemous.

Silverfin clenched his jaw to keep from yelling. His brow knit into angry furrows. He unconsciously made the sign for "dark spirit" as he watched his wife. He bent his head, closed his eyes and breathed deeply to calm himself. The sounds of their lovemaking seemed to grow quiet.

After a few minutes, he raised his head, watched the couple and debated the situation. The man, who was a member of the tribe, he had never liked. The man had no wife and was known for sleeping with other men's wives. Sometimes men openly shared their mates with unmated men, if the women agreed, but this was not common. Other times visiting tribes exchanged spouses as part of complicated networking to create social obligations. After a spousal exchange, the couples who had swapped would always be welcomed in each other's camps as extended family. This provided an important advantage to a nomadic people. This man's disgrace was that he took secretly without asking. This man's dog team was ill kept and often underfed. The treatment of the dogs bothered Silverfin more than the philandering. As he stared at the man, he suddenly decided he liked him, very much. He smiled resolutely as he backed away and toward the trail. He had found an answer to his problem.

✵

While he sat in front of the hut, Silverfin reworked an old harness to fit the new dog he had brought back. He hummed a song and smiled intently when Vole Ears walked up to him. She scolded his bent head accusingly.

"You are early! You said you would not return for half a moon cycle."

"I thought you would be happy to see me, Wife," he said innocently. He raised his eyebrows as he spoke. His wide-set eyes stared back at her with a coolness that belied his smile. A repressed anger that she did not see lay there. "Look. I brought home another dog. He is strong and will make our line stronger."

"Humph!" she grunted, pushed past him and ducked into their hut. A moment later a shriek erupted from within and she dashed back outside.

"What did you trade for the furs? I see nothing, Husband! What have you done now, Silverfin?!"

"I gave them to another tribe I met at the trade gathering, as a peace offering. I am hoping to trade with this tribe more often."

"What? You fool! I worked for months on those furs! You were going to trade them for a bear pelt. You idiot!"

Silverfin continued to smile, in fact he beamed at her,

157

which enraged Vole Ears further. Suddenly the smile disappeared, and Silverfin ordered Vole Ears to go inside the hut. The order was so unexpected that she obeyed. Silverfin followed her.

"I saw you at the circle this morning," he announced, once they were inside the hut. Vole Ears' face fell into a frown. Her hand trembled slightly, and she quickly tried to deny it.

"You speak foolishness. You have just returned. How could you see anybody?"

"I saw you with Elk Tooth," he said simply.

The words were powerful and broke down Vole Ears' composure. She knelt and began to shake all over. She spoke in a trembling voice.

"What will you do?"

Silverfin turned his back on her. He needed to approach this carefully. His wife had to be frightened enough to give into his wishes, because she wanted to, because she saw no other choice. Yet he did not want to purposely hurt her. He decided that speaking the truth would be the quickest and least painful course to take.

"The council will most likely banish you from our tribe for offending our sacred site and customs. Elk Tooth will be banished, too." He let the words sink in before he spoke again.

"Elk Tooth will not want you as a mate. He'll see that your banishment carries bad medicine."

He did not need to say what fate awaited a woman, pregnant, alone in the wilderness. Tears began to stream down her face and her whole body shook violently. He felt a great compassion for her in that moment, and decided he could not push her any further. She was not truly possessed by dark spirits. She had acted out of selfishness. She was more than sufficiently frightened to listen to his solution.

"I know of a solution," he said. Her expression was curious and disbelieving, as she listened without speaking. "I shall go to Elk Tooth and tell him this. I shall explain that I, as your husband, do not wish to see you punished. I shall tell him that if he takes you as a wife, I shall tell no one. You will both be safe, but you must agree to divorce me."

She nodded as she saw hope. She wiped away the tears from her cheeks quickly while Silverfin asked her another question.

"You and Elk Tooth have been mated for some time," he said first as a statement, and then followed with his question. "The child is of Elk Tooth's Spirit, isn't it?"

"It is possible. I believe it is. Only the spirits know,"

she answered meekly.

"I shall tell him it is his child. He will believe this. Wait here while I go and talk to Elk Tooth." He used the sign for "finished", the first time he had, and left the hut.

When he returned two hours later, the hut had been cleaned, the fire built up, and a pot of caribou stew sat bubbling over the fire. Silverfin spoke immediately, for he did not wish to prolong his wife's pain. And he wanted to get away from her as quickly as possible. Her presence had become like a bad taste in his mouth.

"Tomorrow, Elk Tooth will bring three dogs in exchange for you. You will then move into his hut."

Vole Ears began to protest. "You have traded me for dogs!" Finally Silverfin expressed his anger.

"You were lucky that I was able to trade you for such a high price! You are not worth any trade!"

"Yes, of course." She bowed her head, frightened that Silverfin might change his mind and tell the council. She tried to placate him, "I shall begin packing. What do you wish me to leave you? Would you like the furs?"

"Take whatever you need, but leave all the harnesses, and enough sinew to repair them." Silverfin said, and then left quickly.

The following afternoon, Silverfin packed all of his belongings onto a sled and harnessed up the dogs. The traveling would be difficult without the ice or snow on which the runners would normally slide. The trip would be hard on the dogs, but with three extra dogs in the team, the burden would be somewhat lightened. He called out to the dogs to go. His tribe members shook their heads, thinking that he had fallen into some kind of madness because Vole Ears had left him.

The journey to Blackfeather's village was long and arduous. Day after backbreaking day left Silverfin and the dogs exhausted. When they finally reached Blackfeather's camp, the first winter snow storm hit, with soft, large flakes that belied winter's fierceness. Blackfeather's uncle greeted Silverfin sternly as he and the dogs strode proudly, but wearily, into the small village.

"I cannot believe you would be so foolish, to travel this distance without an honorable offer."

"I ask that Blackfeather be my first, and only, wife."

"What of your first wife?"

"I traded her. We are no longer mated."

The uncle nodded his consent. Blackfeather moved quickly to Silverfin's sled to help him with the dogs. She looked down to hide her tears of joy and relief. The tears fell to the ground in drops, which froze on the way down in the frigid air and landed with a faint tinkling sound, like miniature crystals falling to the earth. The rest of the tribe gathered around them to help the worn traveler, now a member of the tribe. They would celebrate later, after he had rested.

The wind blew over the shelter while Blackfeather worked on a new harness for her grandson to use as a training leash. Tomorrow their youngest grandson, Whale Tongue, would pick out his first puppy. Blackfeather smiled toothlessly as her old hands tried to tie a knot that eluded her fingers.

Across from her, Silverfin smiled also in their shared excitement. Silverfin carved a bone whistle for Whale Tongue as a present for his "dog day", as Blackfeather called it. His back was bent with age, and his hands shook as he carved the whistle. Although all three of their children were talented dog handlers, none had the enthusiasm of their youngest grandson.

The latest litter had been sired by Blue Eyes' great-great-great-grandson. Blue Eyes had died almost thirty full seasons ago. Blackfeather had mourned her passing for years, until another dog had given birth to an almost identical version of Blue Eyes. The family had decided to name her Blue Eyes, in honor of the old dog. The litter outside had been sired by the second Blue Eyes' great-grandson.

The knot came together, and Blackfeather put her work down to take a break. She had hoped to live one more winter in order to train this grandson, but this was not to be so. She and Silverfin had agreed to go out on the ice together. Her sight was mostly gone and she saw only shadows now. Still, they felt a profound peace in the life they had created together. Their oldest son, the boy's uncle, would take over his training. Their time was at an end. She stood awkwardly and went to their sleeping furs, where she lay down and gave herself up to sleep.

The next morning she was awakened by her grandson. Small brown hands shook her awake.

"Wake up, Grandmother! Today is my dog day!"

"Ah, so it is," she smiled at him. She dressed slowly, and then joined Silverfin, who waited outside. Her breath cast small clouds in the morning dawn as she followed them toward the whelping den. The three watched excitedly as the puppies played in the den. After awhile, Blackfeather suggested that Whale Tongue hold each puppy, in order to help him choose. She and Silverfin smiled at each other over the boy's hooded head as he held each pup. After he had chosen, they returned to the hut, where Silverfin gave his grandson the whistle he had made. They celebrated by playing games until dusk came again and sleep called them all to bed.

A week later, Blackfeather took her young grandson in her lap and told him the story about the wind and the stars and the clouds. Then she told him that she and Silverfin would return that day to the sky, where they would become stars. "You will see us," she explained, "because we shall shine brightly in the night sky." Whale Tongue had cried sadly on her lap, as she had on Grandfather's lap so many years ago. Her heart ached as she held him tightly. Tears ran from her dark eyes. She repeated Grandfather's words to her grandson.

"Do not be afraid. You will never be alone."

That evening she and Silverfin crept out across the snowy tundra, where spring had just begun to show itself in small slivers of grass which poked through the shallow places in the snow. They walked until they had traveled a few miles out onto the ice flows. In the moon light, Silverfin and Blackfeather picked their way across the great expanse of ice that was already beginning to creak and moan as it prepared to break up in the first thaw. They found there an iceberg that lay blue and surreal in the moonlight. They held hands and walked out onto the ice. And then they held onto each other one last time, rubbed their cheeks and noses together and fell into a final sleep. As Blackfeather drifted off into the quiet cold night, a warmth and peace filled her old body.

"the between ..."

Blackfeather and Silverfin came to consciousness together

in the light. White fog surrounded them and bounced them along in a peaceful buoyancy of floating particles. A shape began to take form in the fog, and Grandfather stepped forward. His dark eyes twinkled with pleasure. His gray moustache lifted as he smiled widely and reached out his short arms to Blackfeather. She instinctively ran forward and into his arms. As she did, a burst of white light exploded around them, and Serra found herself held by Orryka. Lohkan seemed dazed for a moment, and then his confusion turned into merriment as Orryka spoke.

"Serra, Lohkan, welcome back."

Orryka's tall and imposing figure seemed to fill the air. His long blond hair fell across his shoulders gracefully. The white robe he wore shimmered in a display of pastel colors as he moved. His bearded face broke into a large grin, and he embraced both Lohkan and Serra in his wide reach.

"When did you get here?" Serra asked around her smile.

"Serra, you forget that over two thousand Earth years have passed. While you and Lohkan have been experiencing other lifetimes, other realities, I left my physical body hundreds of years ago."

"You were Grandfather," she said, and shook her head as she smiled. "Now I understand why I was so comfortable with you. I felt as if I had always known you."

"Was it you who watched after us – after you died?" Lohkan asked curiously.

"Yes. I had a difficult job in trying to get you together."

"You did that?" Serra asked, stunned by yet another piece of information.

"Did you think you did that alone? You two lived a hundred miles apart. You needed help. Lohkan, you weren't planning to go to the trades, were you?"

"No," Lohkan answered. "I had this constant nagging feeling that would not leave me alone. That feeling told me I had to go to the trades!"

"I was that *nagging feeling*," Orryka said, and then laughed. "I brought Silverfin to the trades, and then to the river that day. You could not see me, Serra, but Blue Eyes saw me. I had agreed to watch over you."

"When?" Serra asked in a bewildered voice.

"When I held you in my lap; when you were a little girl as Blackfeather. I promised *always* to watch over you. I did not know how seriously those promises are taken here...." He opened his arms expansively and gestured to the waterfall, forest ... to *the between*. "I was happy to keep this promise," he said warmly.

The air around them filled with the sound of hundreds of flutes. The sound was piercing and beautiful; its resonance filled Serra and Lohkan with an intense serenity and wonder. The air glittered briefly in front of them, and the elder appeared.

Welcome, Orryka. Serra and Lohkan, you are back.

He smiled up at Serra, and then whistled softly. The waterfall vanished, and they were on a spacecraft. Serra recognized the ship on which they had flown to Earth thousands of years ago. They were seated in the chairs she had known so well, before a metallic screen. On the screen, the life of Grandfather, then Blackfeather, and finally Silverfin, played out. When Silverfin and Blackfeather had died in their sleep from exposure to sub-zero temperatures, the screen went blank. After everyone had sat silently for a time, the elder addressed them.

Orryka and I have already discussed his life. Would you like to discuss yours?

"I would," Lohkan said as he looked at Serra.

Yes, she agreed telepathically.

What did you learn? The elder asked as he sat in the silver-colored chair. His small legs dangled over the edge of the chair and did not touch the floor. He seemed to enjoy this latest illusion. If it was an illusion? Panels blinked on and off behind him. A view of Earth from space was displayed on a monitor on one of the panels. Lohkan answered his question.

"The frigid conditions we lived in led our tribes to an interdependent, nomadic lifestyle with dogs." Lohkan continued, "The dogs became our link to survival. They were more than animals. They were respected members of our extended family."

"Though not everyone saw these creatures in this way," Serra reminded Lohkan as she gently touched his arm.

Why would they not? the elder asked.

"Their egos would not allow them to see the dogs as independent, intelligent creatures. Perhaps those who felt differently from us needed to see the dogs as inferior in order to make themselves feel more important or superior. They could feel superior by dominating another species, rather than seeing the dogs or animals as an important part of their world. I can see that to believe this way, or not, was each individual's choice of lesson. One choice over another did not make the individual bad or good. Each person was experiencing what he or she needed to learn," Lohkan said compassionately.

The elder swiveled in his chair toward Serra. He looked at her expectantly.

"I learned about the responsibilities of being involved with another creature," Serra began. "I could not 'control' or 'own' the dogs by the care I gave them. **No creature owns another, whether that creature is human or in another form, such as a dog.**" Then she added gratefully, "Blue Eyes became a valuable teacher and friend."

"What did she teach you?" Orryka asked.

"Boundaries."

"How?"

"Dogs and wolves live in packs, where boundaries are clearly established. In caring for this puppy, I was forced to set boundaries," Serra said as warm memories filled her mind. The image of Blue Eyes stealing a moccasin caused her to laugh before she continued.

What do you think would have happened if you had not set clear boundaries? asked Tonak.

"She would have run all over us and our lives. She would have created chaos, and we would have been the ones to allow this," Serra said decisively.

When adults, whether wolves or humans, are not clear with their offspring, in essence they are telling the child to decide, to be in charge. If you were a child, and the adults around you asked you to make the decisions, what would happen? How would you feel? Tonak asked slowly.

"I think I'd feel insecure and frightened, and then I think I would become wild, like the wind without the stars to guide it," Serra said thoughtfully. She smiled at Orryka, who sat in a chair next to hers. He tenderly put his arm around her shoulder.

Living closely with animals had been a challenging experience. Serra tried to imagine what their dogs would have been like without the attention, boundaries and love they had given to them. Serra knew that this situation would have been, at worst, disastrous and potentially harmful; and, at best, unpleasant. She shuddered to think of any animal or creature growing up without proper care. Orryka spoke as if he had trailed her thoughts.

"Yes. You and Blue Eyes gave a lot to each other."

They sat silently together, each lost in their own revelations, their own inspirations. Serra thought about the sacredness of life: how each animal in the their tribes' spiritual belief had significance and was a teacher. A question suddenly occurred to her.

"Do animals reincarnate?"

Yes, the elder answered simply. *Sometimes a soul will chose to take an animal reincarnation repeatedly. Sometimes that soul, in animal form, will chose to reincarnate with someone who has chosen a human reincarnation. These two souls may chose to go through several reincarnations together.*

"Can a soul who has reincarnated as an animal reincarnate as a human?" Lohkan asked.

There are countless life forms. To say one has more importance than another is inaccurate and an illusion. *A soul who has chosen the experiences of a human embodiment may choose that of another life form. Whether it is a dog, a reptilian being from another galaxy or a subterranean life form, does not change the equation. The options of life forms throughout the universe are limitless, Lohkan! Some choose to cross over from human to animal to extraterrestrial to astral to ... the possibilities are endless. Yet many do not choose this. Many require a more homogeneous experience.* **All lives are connected. Each life affects the next, and all lives are perfect. We are all one. The more you try to separate and categorize the essence of life, the more you limit yourself.** *Some, are able to expand their consciousness to a multitude of forms. Some are not,* Tonak ended simply.

"I was a researcher. I have spent my life, my first life, categorizing life forms. I have categorized them to keep this information clear in my mind," Serra said.

Yes. When your mind has expanded, you will not need these categorizations. You will simply be able to accept the limitless possibilities that exist in the universe, around you, in you, that are part of you! Tonak said with excitement.

"I understand," she said. Lohkan nodded, lost deep in thoughts and theories. Orryka smiled sympathetically as they began to understand these new concepts.

Chapter 10

"the between ..."

*T*he Inter-galactic spacecraft surrounded them with
its vividly displayed panels. Serra asked the question
that had been on her mind earlier.
"Is this real?"

Yes, Tonak answered, and then continued. *Would you like
to see your companions again? They will not be able to see you,
though some will sense your presence.*

"Yes!" Lohkan and Serra answered enthusiastically.
Orryka smiled and the room changed slightly. They sat in the
same places, but around them the room buzzed with activity.
The silver-gray walls of the space ship curved inward and downward. The arrays of lights on the monitors blinked. A view of the
planet Earth from space filled the screen before them and
focused on a village.

Several petite creatures, as small as the elder himself,
moved about in fast motion. Large dark eyes wrapped around
their faces like masks, and simultaneously took in the multitude
of display monitors and instrument panels with little effort.
Noseless faces with tiny mouths created blank expressions, which
hid intelligent and sensitive minds. In one wall, where there had
been no indication of a door, one opened and two tall men
walked into the room. A smaller being followed them.

Serra recognized the two tall men as members of her,
Lohkan's and Orryka's race. Orryka narrated the scene before
them.

"These twins are continuing the research their parents
began. You knew their grandparents, Yerraba and Sumkan,"
Orryka said as he referred to two of the team's members with
whom they had traveled to Earth millennia ago. Orryka gestured to a third being who stood beside them. "Yon is instruct-

ing them in their studies."

This slender being stopped abruptly. He had a domed, bald head with ridges that ran down the back of his skull. His skin was white and delicate. Large dark, green eyes looked around the room for what he sensed but could not see. Each of his movements seemed to flow like water.

"Ah, Yon senses us," Orryka said. "The twins look like Sumkan, do they not?"

Serra smiled as she watched the scene before her. Sumkan had had an unusual nose, very long and straight, and pale gray-blue eyes that were hooded and mysterious. Serra remember Sumkan's life partner and her best friend, Yerraba.

Yerraba had been delightfully funny. Behind that humor had lain a keen intelligence and a great curiosity. The boys had both the eyes and the longish noses of their grandfather. By their serious expressions, Serra doubted that they had inherited any of Yerraba's humor. She watched Yon work. He was as beautiful as she remembered. As she thought this, Yon stopped and stared at the space where they stood.

Serra, is that you?

The words rang loudly about them, as though an intercom system had been turned up too loudly. Serra looked at the elder.

"Can he hear me? Can Yon understand my thoughts?"

Some of what you think is heard by your friend Yon. All of what you feel now is felt by him. You may answer him if you wish. If you choose to answer, you must accompany your thought transmission with an emotional sense of what you are trying to communicate. Feel whatever you are thinking, and Yon will get the entire message.

Serra smiled at Lohkan, and then sent a message. *We are here, Yon. It is I, Serra, with Orryka and Lohkan!* With her words, she sent a warmth of images and the feelings she had toward Lohkan and Orryka. Their days on the star cruiser, the ideas and knowledge that had been warmly shared, the excitement of discovering new life forms on this planet, filled her mind. Yon's words came back to them as loudly as before; his tones expressed his pleasure.

I hear you. Where are you? What are you doing, Serra? How is your research going?

They all laughed. Serra instantly became confused and did not know how to respond. She smiled in her confusion and decided to send the message.

Too much at once....

Yon's laughter rang out over the group. The twins had

stopped to watch their instructor. Yon began again.

Where are you?

I don't know, Serra answered.

Lohkan tried to answer this for them all.

Between dimensions, he sent, and added an array of images and emotions he had experienced while in the light and in *the between.* Images of the elder ... as he showed them wisdom, came through. Quan Yin's beauty and compassion filled his heart with warmth and love. The countless images they had been shown in *the between* caused Yon's head to bow under an onslaught of weighty thoughts and emotions. He answered quickly.

I understand! Orryka has kept in contact with us, though we have not heard from him in years.

I was busy. Orryka joked, and Yon's laughter rang out over them again. The elder smiled and spoke to Serra and Lohkan.

Now you can see how Orryka has guided you. Although you could not see him or hear him as directly as you do here, you were able to sense the words and feelings he sent to you. Do you understand?

Yes. Yes I do! Serra said excitedly. *This is another form of telepathy.*

That is a simple explanation, the elder said patiently. *For now this explanation will help you. Later, when you are ready, we shall discuss this further.* Yon's voice interrupted their discussion.

Who is that?

A friend, the elder explained. *Serra, Lohkan, the time has come for you to go. Do you have anything else that you wish to communicate to Yon?*

Serra looked at Lohkan. Time felt elusive and watery in this place. She knew that in the few moments she and Lohkan had talked, first with Orryka, then with the elder and Yon, weeks, months, perhaps years had passed on Earth. She sent a warmth of love to Yon, followed by the words,

We must go now. I love you.

Yes. I love you ... Yon answered.

The ship and the elder vanished. Orryka took each of their hands and drew them back into the light. The fog swallowed them. And as it did, Serra wondered what they would learn next.

A mountain peak hailed the sky in a voice that could not be denied. Its call was feminine and proud. The call commanded the clouds to rain or the sun to burn brightly. Whatever the mountain decided was based upon the desire it felt moment to moment. The people had learned to live with the mountain and its diverging moods.

These native people had come to have an understanding of the mountain and the power it contained. They incorporated this power in their daily lives and, not surprisingly, enjoyed a harmonious existence. They did not fight the mountain. They did not place her in a position of worship. They saw her simply as she was: a great friend, a benefactor, a tyrant and terrible advocate, their host.

The village lay twelve thousand feet above sea level and was built in a circular design of stone, mud and straw. The inhabitants had hidden themselves in the skirts of the mountain as a safety precaution against warring tribes from the north and south. The mountain hid their presence successfully and for this, as well as other magic, the natives were grateful.

Today the mountain stared fully into the sun and cast shadows over the village, making it invisible to outsiders. A small boy played in the deeper shadows of one of the buildings, outside the temple. The temple was empty, as at this time neither holidays were being celebrated nor were disputes being brought before the council. Therefore, the temple was remarkably still and quiet. The thin mountain air around the temple was cool and the shadows were more distinct when contrasted with the bright sunshine only yards away. Winter Moon picked wild herbs that grew in the shadows and fed some llamas that grazed there. He chewed some of the pungent herb himself, grew chilly and decided to move to a hillside where the sun shone warmly.

The llamas followed Winter Moon as he drifted idly to a sunny spot outside the village. Winter Moon stopped where a great outcropping of massive rocks encircled a grassy knoll, and climbed onto one of the rocks. He fell asleep in the heat of the sun.

When the boy awakened, evening had taken the sun away. The llamas had dutifully stayed nearby, chewing their cuds as they lay folded into furry lumps. Winter Moon whistled to the llamas, and they all rose and started down the knoll for the village.

His mother awaited him. Morning Dew smiled, but then grimaced as she saw him walking along the dirt path that led to their shelter. He had not picked any greens to go with their dinner, as she had asked. He bowed his head and said nothing, awaiting her reprimand.

She shook her head, with its long, straight black hair, which had been interwoven into two long braids with a variety of colorfully dyed cloths. Morning Dew did not bother to reprimand him, for she had grown tired of hearing her own voice. She swatted him lightly on the side of the head, sent him indoors to eat and then she put the llamas in the stone and mud stall next to the house.

The next day Morning Dew sent her son to a neighbor with a loaf of flat hard bread she had made. The bread was filled with a paste of herbs and cheese. She skeptically watched Winter Moon run into the village and hoped he would actually deliver the bread.

When evening fell and her son walked absent-mindedly back to their hut she knew by Winter Moon's expression that he had forgotten to deliver the bread. He had most likely eaten it. She sighed heavily and sent him again to his supper after slapping his cheek softly. The gesture was not painful, as their people were a passive race. She rebuffed him physically to let him know she was upset, that was all.

That night, by the coals of a small fire, Morning Dew mused about her son, who had been born without any sense in his small head. She sat on a thickly woven woolen mat on the floor in front of the small cooking area, a square indentation where a hole had been scooped out in the wall. The coals gave off little heat, but little was needed on this mild summer night.

That Morning Dew loved her son was not in question. She was completely devoted to him. That she worried about his lack of interest in taking care of himself was evident. She wondered, as she had many times before, if the boy would have been different had his father lived. Soon Winter Moon would know a man's passage of life. Who would mate with such a monotonous man? She could not imagine such a person.

As she contemplated this, she wove a belt of fine soft alpaca wool. Her hands were practiced and nimble. Morning Dew did not look at her work, for she did not need to see the beautifully colored yarns to follow their patterns. She had woven for many years, ever since she could remember. Her first memories were of the soft wool her mother had placed in her small hands. Eventually she gave up wondering about the future of her son and let her mind settle on to more physical realities, about which she could do *something*.

She planned to weave another basket of wool into a beautiful cape, which she would trade for grains and more wool. The four llamas they kept would not provide her with enough wool for her weaving. She was a prolific weaver because she had countless moments of loneliness to fill.

Her mother and father had died years ago. Her aunts and uncles had invited her to live in their larger dwellings, but she had declined. She had not been able to face the daily comparisons between Winter Moon and his bright and happy cousins. Many times Morning Dew had seen her aunts shake their heads when their eyes fell upon him. Each look had brought her a dull pain. Morning Dew knew that she and her son were loved, but she had not been able to look beyond the disappointments she had in herself and in him. She carefully placed her weaving in a basket, then wrapped herself in a blanket and, lost in doubts, fell asleep before the coals.

The sun festival had come and gone again. The mountain this day had decided to hide its face in a veil of damp mist and clouds. A steady drizzle fell over the mountainside and the village as Morning Dew arrived at her neighbor's house.

The neighbor spotted Morning Dew through a partially open window and called for her to enter. During extremely cold or wet days, woven mats were hung over the windows and entrances. Today the mat over the window was partially rolled up, to give a clear view of the road and the village. The two women had been friends since childhood. Morning Dew felt she could entrust this friend with her dreams and disappointments. As her friend's name depicted, Silent Fog was good at hiding information and keeping secrets.

Silent Fog made tea from a mountain herb for them both and, while the tea brewed, each woman set up to weave. Quickly, Silent Fog's small hands performed the task. Her black hair was braided traditionally with the many colorful strips of cloth throughout it. Her face, though unappealing, was thoughtful and kind. Silent Fog's craft made up for her homeliness, because her weavings were extraordinarily beautiful and brought a high trade price. Morning Dew's envy of her friend's talent was the one subject Morning Dew did not share with her. While they worked and drank tea, Silent Fog's three children came and went without interruption.

They were all well-behaved children, kind like their mother and attractive like their father. The oldest, a boy of the same age as her son, was as bright and talented as her son was dull.

The second and third children, both girls, were smart, pretty and cheerful. They helped their grandmother spin and card the yarns that Silent Fog would make into her beautiful weavings. Both girls were next door in their grandparents' home, a larger dwelling that was attached to this hut. Again, Morning Dew sighed as she watched the youngest little girl drop an armload of wood onto the hearth for her mother to use as needed.

Morning Dew had felt alone these past several years. Alone in her work. Alone in her responsibilities. Alone in her disappointments. Alone, even in the company of her good friend, Silent Fog.

Silent Fog leaned over and complimented Morning Dew on the fineness of her weaving. Morning Dew said nothing, but continued with her weaving. She misunderstood Silent Fog's attempt at kindness and thought that her friend compared Morning Dew's work to her own. She felt a tightening in her chest as the disappointment in her work, in herself, rose and tried to choke her. She made a mistake in her weaving and had to pick out the yarn and begin again. Unfortunately, Silent Fog next made the mistake of asking Morning Dew about her son. Morning Dew blushed and stuttered that he tended the llamas. She bent to her work, bitter resentment causing her to believe that Silent Fog had the need to point out all the mistakes in her life. Her pain was especially acute, because it seemed Silent Fog's life was obviously so much better.

Silent Fog has a good and handsome husband. Silent Fog has three healthy and smart children. Silent Fog's parents are alive to support and help her with raising those children. Silent Fog is the best weaver in the village. Morning Dew's thoughts played on in a twisted view of the world. She did not see that she misjudged her friend or that her thoughts were based on jealousy. She was too entrapped in her own web of pessimism.

That night she cooked dinner distractedly, not aware of what she was doing. Inadvertently, she placed a handful of the wrong herbs in the pot of stew. The ones she used were meant to kill the lice and fleas that found their way into the llamas' fleece. She thought as she tasted the stew that even Silent Fog's food was not as bitter as hers. During the night she and her son quietly died from the poison. Alone.

"the between ..."

When Serra awoke in the meadow, Lohkan sat by her side. He looked at her and grinned sheepishly.

"Oops. Wrong herbs," he said.

She shook her head to clear it and looked about herself. The meadow was especially soothing just then. But, it was not more beautiful than where she had just been, high in the Andes. The views had been breathtaking, but she had been unable to see them. She looked at Lohkan and questioned him.

"Were you able to see the beauty of the mountains?"

"No."

"Nor I. I wonder why?"

The air shimmered. The meadow became more vivid. Lohkan recognized the shift that took place just before one of the guides appeared. As if on cue, Quan Yin appeared before them.

"Would you like to review the life you just experienced?"

"Yes," they answered together.

A cool breeze stirred Serra's hair, and she found herself back on the mountain. Lohkan and the guide stood next to her.

Before her the mountain stood, tall and fierce. The village was just as she remembered. They watched as their lives in the village played out again. Serra watched as Morning Dew's parents instilled the disappointment of whom *they were* into their little girl. She saw Lohkan's face sadden as he watched himself as Morning Dew. Then Serra watched as the little girl grew up and repeated this same sad pattern with her own son. Serra realized for the first time that she had not failed her mother when she had been Winter Moon. Morning Dew's disappointment lay in herself, *not* in her child. Morning Dew had projected all the self doubt and loathing she had been taught, on to Winter Moon. Like a genetic disease, Morning Dew's parents had passed on to her, a poor self-image and negative ideas. Then, Morning Dew passed on these patterns to her son. Serra could see clearly that had she, as Winter Moon, grown into manhood and married, most likely he would have passed these patterns on to his children. Unless something, somehow, brought awareness to him. Then he might have been able to change. Lohkan heard her thoughts and nodded his agreement.

He took her hand and sent her the message.

I love you, Serra.

She smiled, and the mountain, with its vibrant air and spectacular views, vanished. They were back in the meadow again. Quan Yin spoke.

"What did you learn?"

Lohkan answered, "I had been taught to see myself as a failure, a disappointment to my parents and the world. I can see now that that wasn't true. My parents' disappointment was really in themselves. As a child, I was too young to understand this. By the time I became an adult, I was convinced that what they said and felt about me was true. I, in turn, repeated these same actions with my son, Winter Moon." He placed his hand on Serra's knee and continued.

"I also learned that jealousy is based upon the absence of self-worth, self-love. The emotion of jealousy distorted my perceptions of the world until I was no longer able to see clearly. I could not see the beauty that surrounded me, because I could not see the beauty inside myself."

Quan Yin smiled, nodded and looked at Serra.

"Serra, what did you learn?"

"I learned how powerful words are. As I watched that little boy, I was surprised to see that he was cute, gentle and actually clever. As I was told, both verbally and silently by Morning Dew's actions, that I was dull, I eventually came to live that role.

"Also, I learned the pain of comparison. I learned the pain of feeling average. Worse. Below average. Morning Dew saw her family as dull and average because this is what her parents taught her to see. What she and I could not see, is that there is no such state as average. **Every soul, each human is truly unique! That uniqueness marks each person as special. In that specialness, no one is average.**

"I can see that I had a unique talent for training and calming the llamas, probably a trait I carried over from my other lifetime as Blackfeather; yet I never recognized it. My mother, Morning Dew, believed herself to be plain, so I saw her as plain. When we reviewed our lives, I was again surprised to see that Morning Dew was attractive, and that her weavings were beautiful."

"Yes." Quan Yin agreed. "**What we think inside, believe about ourselves and the world, is reflected back to us in the people around us.** If you believe you are talented, attractive or intelligent, then the world around you will also believe this and let you know. If you believe the opposite, that you are without talent, ugly and stupid, then the world around you will also believe this and respond in a way that supports your beliefs, your self concepts.

"An unattractive person can be beautiful if he believes himself to be so. An attractive person can be ugly if the individual believes this. Any example of this truth works. A young individual may be old. An old individual may be young."

"A wise person may be foolish?" Lohkan said.

"Yes," the guide agreed. **"Do you understand that, as your self image changes, it is impossible for the world around you not to change?** It has to, because it is a reflection of yourself. As each soul sees itself through loving eyes, *The One* becomes more beautiful."

Serra smiled widely as she looked at the guide.

"I have just begun to understand what your inner world must be like."

"Yes," said Quan Yin with gratitude. "It is wondrous!"

Chapter 11

"the between ..."

*L*ohkan and Serra asked to come back once more to the mountain top in the Andes before they went on to their new lives. They now enjoyed the dramatic views that surrounded them while Quan Yin serenely waited nearby. As they watched, a familiar event took place.

The mountain peaks, white with snow, stood brilliantly against a clear blue sky. Over the peaks, three small spacecrafts flew into view in a triangular formation. The ships came to a stop behind one of the peaks, hiding their presence from the village below. From where they stood, Serra, Lohkan and the guide had a full view of what next took place. One of the spaceships hovered near the other two, and then took off toward the sun in a perpendicular direction from the mountain where they were hidden. Any view of the ship's flight was hidden by its speed and by the sun's blinding rays.

Next, one of the remaining two ships rose into the sky, over the mountain peak and headed toward the village. As the ship came closer to the village, it disappeared. Outside the village, a translucent image of the ship came back into view momentarily as two beings floated down from the ship. Lohkan recognized a man and woman of his race. As soon as the two stood on Earth's soil, the ship disappeared.

The man and woman walked down a path that would eventually lead to the village where Serra and Lohkan had reincarnated. As they drew closer to the village, the two tall beings appeared to change form: they became two villagers. Lohkan recognized the illusionary effect of telepathic hypnosis that his people used. As he made this observation, the two small indigenous people resumed the forms of a tall, blond man and woman. He knew that any villagers who came upon this couple would see them as fellow tribe members.

His and Serra's race, as well as other races, used this form of hypnosis when they thought their natural state might frighten whomever they contacted. The couple before them would be able to study the village in close contact without causing fear or disrupting the customs which they had come to observe. He and Serra had used these skills on many occasions. Eventually the spaceship and its inhabitants would make themselves visible to the races who peopled these mountains. This process would be a slow and methodical introduction over a period of hundreds of years. Lohkan knew that their progress would be painstaking, as his people would work at a pace which matched the tolerance of the slowest person in each village. To hurry this process would only cause alarm.

Quan Yin spoke, interrupting Lohkan's thoughts.

"They began to study this village after you left. Some of the others on the ship thought that one of you, Lohkan or Serra, might possibly recognize them. Humans have varying degrees of telepathic abilities. For most, this skill has not been developed, as you have already discovered. Your team researchers decided to exercise caution, in case any latent abilities lay in either Morning Dew or her son."

Lohkan nodded. This made sense to him and seemed a conscientious decision. Had the two researchers before him been Serra and himself, most likely they would have made the same choice.

"When will the team make contact with us?" Serra asked.

"The team does not wish to interrupt your human anthropological studies during their courses through reincarnation," the guide answered. "Soon, as you know, this will eventually become necessary."

Lohkan listened and wondered when, in which life, he and Serra would again be contacted by their companions. How would that contact take place? Would he remember anything of his former life, the life of Lohkan, when his companions did make contact? Quan Yin interrupted his reflections.

"Are you ready to leave?"

"Yes," they answered. Lohkan followed his consent with one more question.

"What Earth timeline is this?" He pointed to the scene before them.

"The answer to your question, Lohkan, would depend upon which race's time reference you would chose to use. You are about to enter the period of the Sung Dynasty. A predominate method of measuring time – based on when a teacher, a descendant of Semites, was born and lived – marks the period you just left as 400 AD. The time period you are about to enter is 1100 AD."

"Thank you," Lohkan said. He wondered at his need to continue to quantify time. Was this not another form of categorizing space and matter? The mountains vanished. They floated peacefully in the thick fog of white light. He forgot about time, forgot everything as his soul drifted deeper into this place of peace.

The giants whispered in his ear, and Sees Far awoke instantly. His long gray hair fell forward as he shook his head to clear the sleep from his brain. He looked down at his hands and stared at his dark brown skin tones, which differed so dramatically from those of the tall blond men and women who surrounded him. He ran a weathered and aged hand across his chest, where intricate tattoos announced his position in the tribe as shaman. Why had the giants, these Messengers of the Gods, brought him here? What did they have to tell him?

The messengers greeted him respectfully and waited while he came fully awake. Pale hair, like the color of the straw, pale eyes, like the color of the sky or water in a clear stream, stared patiently back at him. They were taller than any beings on Earth, tall enough to touch the stars. And that was what they did. They carried messages from the stars to his people. These were the *Star People*.

The Star People stood around him in a room unlike anything he knew, except that it was made in the sacred shape, a circle. The walls were made of a smooth and hard material that was the color of his gray hair and shiny like the raven's wing. The bench he now sat on was made of the same material. He yawned once, and then nodded that he was awake.

We wish to show you something, a voice said in his head. Somehow he knew that the voice belonged to a man to his left. The pale man pointed to a screen on the silver wall.

When the sun has risen and set seven times, there will be an earthquake. Sees Far's mind translated earthquake into "Earth God's rage" as he watched the violent scene. He again nodded mutely that he understood.

You must move your people to the mesa tops, the starman continued to explain. *There you will be safe. Stay there through ten risings of the sun. After that, you can move your people back into their homes in the cliffs. Do you understand, Sees Far?*

As he nodded yes once more, his eyes closed, the room vanished and he fell deeply asleep. In the morning, his mind remembered only the warning and that the Star People had delivered it.

Seven days later, the tribe were relocated to the mesa tops. That afternoon as most people were tending the corn, beans and squash, the Earth God shook for the first time in her anger. People were knocked off their feet. Children were frightened. Ravens and crows screeched their annoyance. But, none were hurt, mortally or otherwise.

Sees Far stretched and felt the oldness of his bones. His small round chamber, which was made of stone, was shadowed, because the thick rock walls let in little daylight. He ducked and stepped through a low doorway and out into the bright day. Brilliant blue sky met his eyes as he looked out over the cliff where his village lay.

The city was built of stone, deep in a cavern within a cliff which sat hundreds of feet above a canyon. Square, rectangular and circular buildings in adobe colors met Sees Far's gaze. The walls were built of intricately stacked rocks of varying sizes. The red, tan and sand-colored masonry accented the natural brilliance of the turquoise sky high above the cliff face, and blended with the dusty, dark greens of junipers and pinons that grew along and in the walls of the canyon.

A small road, barely more than a foot path, ran past his home. He now took this road as he went to find his niece. Children ran on the roads. Adult men and women moved about, carrying clay pots and baskets in their arms, on their backs and on their heads. The pottery was beautifully decorated with the black geometric designs of their village. In the summer, on a mild day such as today, the tribe wore few clothes in this hot and arid climate. Short leather tunics or woven grass skirts were seen on many of the women around him. Sees Far now wore a leather loin cloth, as most of the men in his village did.

He spotted his niece Juniper Berry behind a building. Juniper had been asked to lead her clan after her mother had died last winter in an accident, and Sees Far watched as she again proved her leadership abilities.

Juniper's small figure stood in the center of a circle of children as she held two boys apart with her arms. Her black eyes were set above high cheek bones. An unusual birth mark on her left cheek looked as if someone had crushed some juniper berries against her face. It was for this birth mark she had been named. Her dark, wide face was now serious and reflective and her black hair was coiled back into two buns at the back of her head. The woven grass skirt she wore rustled as she pushed the boys farther apart.

"Why do you fight, Raven's Wing and Stands Tall?" Juniper asked firmly.

"Stands Tall won't give me my knife," Raven's Wing said with anger. He tried to push past Juniper Berry to grab at the other boy, who was as tall as his name indicated.

"Raven, stop!" she commanded. She pushed him back and turned toward Stands Tall.

"Stands Tall, did you take his knife?" Juniper asked directly.

"Yes. He told me I could have it."

"Is this true, Raven?" Juniper Berry said over her shoulder.

"Yes ..." the smaller boy confessed sadly.

"Then why do you disturb the peace of the tribe on this day?" Juniper said as she turned back to Raven's Wing. He looked down and mumbled his answer to the dusty earth.

"I have use for it. I need it to clean a rabbit for the ceremony."

Juniper stared at his bent head, and then spoke decisively.

"Stands Tall, do you need the knife this day?"

"No," he admitted reluctantly.

"Give Raven the knife. He will borrow it from you until his work is done." Raven's head bobbed up when he heard her words, but the smile left his face quickly as he saw Juniper's somber expression.

"Raven Wing's, do not again offer a gift you cannot give. You may use the knife only to finish this task. Once you give something away it is no longer yours. Remember this!" she said as she stared at Raven's face, which blushed red under his brown skin.

The circle of children broke up and moved away. Juniper called after Raven, who held his work knife tightly in his hand.

"Raven, come to our house tomorrow morning! I have an extra knife for which I have no use." His smile returned, and Juniper smiled widely in spite of her attempt to remain serious. As she did, Sees Far stepped forward and greeted his niece.

"Juniper, are you ready for the ceremony tomorrow?"

"Yes, Uncle," she responded respectfully.

"Come. Walk with me then," Sees Far said.

They walked toward the end of the village, to a place where the foot path narrowed between large boulders and climbed steeply up toward the cliff. From here, the cliff was lined with footholds and handholds that had been carved in the face of the rock. The handholds had been keyed precisely to protect the village from outside trespassers and invaders. Each hand and foot had to be placed consecutively, or whoever climbed the carved handholds would reach a point where they would not be able to climb any farther. Sees Far and Juniper now began the one-hundred-foot climb. Halfway up the wall, the handholds changed direction, and they moved like spiders, horizontally to the right. Soon the handholds moved upward again, and they continued their ascent. A moment later, they stood at the top of the canyon and surveyed the view that met their eyes.

Clear mountain air did little to screen the sun's rays, and everything about them was touched by its warmth. The mesa tops were covered with short evergreens trees and patches of tilled soil, which were ready for the spring planting. The sky was brilliant blue and clear except for a few thunderheads on the western horizon. Ravens and hawks circled lazily above them.

Across the canyon, another village lay in the cliff, much like their own, only smaller. People climbed to and from the villages below in a dark line across the gold-colored rock face. From this high place, the people looked like insects. A member of a tribe from the North had once come upon the cliff dwelling tribe; upon watching a procession of their people as they climbed back and forth across the walls, he had named them the Spider People. Some other tribes to the East called them the ant people. They simply called themselves *the people*.

Sees Far and Juniper walked several feet to a juniper tree, and then rested from their climb in its shade. The tree grew on an outcropping of the cliff in a limited amount of soil. Because of this harsh environment, the tree had grown into a twisted and beautiful shape. Their people had decided that the tree's spirit must be very special to have survived with so little nurturance, so they called this particular juniper "The Strong One." As they rested, Sees Far questioned Juniper quietly.

"Juniper Berry, do you remember the story of *He who walks first in the snow?*"

"No," she said as she shook her head.

"I did not think so. You were very small when I first told you this tale. I shall tell you again." He settled himself more comfortably against The Strong One.

He stopped for a moment and took a deep breath, as if he drew strength from the Great Spirit to tell his story. He was old in spirit and in body. The climb had been hard for.him. His weathered face showed, in deeply etched wrinkles, the many years of wisdom he had learned. He turned to study Juniper's young face, and noticed that Juniper also breathed deeply beside him. Sweat dripped down her smooth, round cheeks as she waited for him to continue.

The role Juniper was about to accept was a respected one. That Juniper's people recognized her skill to lead was an honor by which Juniper would always be touched. This was also an honor that Sees Far knew frightened her. Leadership was based upon the ability to bring peace and prosperity to *the people* and the ability to keep this peace and prosperity strong. Sees Far understood, from his own experiences that as the ceremony drew closer, Juniper would wonder if she truly had these peace-keeping talents. He saw these fears in her dark eyes and took her hand in his as he began his story.

"Tomorrow, Juniper, you will take your place as one of the female leaders of *the people.* You are young in seasons for this, but not in spirit.

"Every so many moons...." He stopped and drew several lines in the dirt with a stick. "Snow falls upon the land, almost as deep as a child is tall. When it does, whoever walks first must break a path for those who follow. He who walks first works harder than those who follow him. Breaking a path in the snow is exhausting and, at times, dangerous. This requires the stamina of the elk, the strength of the wolf, the clear-sightedness of the hawk and the patience of the mouse teaching its young. This is work that few want to do, because it is wearying.

"He who breaks this path also has the first view of what lies ahead. This view is clear and beautiful, like untouched snow. This view is the reward for the work of leading. Do you understand, Juniper?"

She nodded her head and waited for Sees Far to continue. He was silent and stared across the sky at the building thunderheads. A few minutes passed, and then he continued.

"Because someone, this leader, goes first, he often finds the holes under the snow that cannot be seen. Many times he will fall into these holes. Those who follow can then avoid the danger that lies there. Sometimes, as he breaks a path, he comes upon a clear area with a patch of ice, where he may slide for a few feet or fall down. Again he finds a danger that his people may avoid.

"A leader experiences all of the dangers first. A leader is not someone who makes no mistakes and behaves like the Gods. A leader is the one who makes the mistakes first, so that his people can learn from him and go safely through life. A leader is someone who has the strength to face the daily challenges of falling down and sliding out of place, so that his people may walk the path of beauty."

Sees Far felt Juniper's hand trembling in his. He looked at her and saw that tears made paths through the dust on her brown cheeks. He squeezed her hand tightly and finished his story.

"The tribe members who follow may sometimes criticize the leader for these falls, when truly what they criticize is their own lack of courage to face the falls themselves. The tribe members who follow may wonder why the leader slides, when what they truly wonder is why they could not see the ice for themselves.

"A strong leader is one who has the bravery to face not only that which lies ahead, but also that which follows.

"Do you understand, Juniper, that you were picked to follow your mother in leadership because you have this courage? You are a strong path breaker. We have watched you," he said, referring to himself as shaman, and to the council.

"Do not be afraid, Juniper. You have an elk's stamina, a wolf's courage, a hawk's clear sight; you have the patience of a mother mouse teaching its young. You are protected. The Gods will guide you. Do not be afraid."

Juniper Berry wept silently and said nothing. Sees Far knew that Juniper understood from his story that he had once walked the path she now would, and that in essence he had been a pathbreaker for her. He nudged her to look up at the sky.

"Juniper, look! The rains come! It is a blessing from the Gods for your ceremony."

Juniper smiled as she wiped the tears from her cheeks with the back of her hand. Then she gave her gratitude to him by embracing him tightly before they returned to the village.

Sees Far awoke with the sensation that someone was with him in his circular stone house, where he sometimes doctored the sick, counseled the weak and held private spiritual ceremonies. He recognized the feeling as distinctly individual and directed. Sees Far sat up, set some sage upon a few small coals left in the fire and waited for the spirit to make contact.

A rose-colored glow filled the room and accented the red

walls, with their intricately painted symbols. Sees Far closed his eyes and breathed deeply. He felt himself being lifted, and then he lost consciousness.

When he awoke, he felt a hard bed beneath his back. He recognized where he was as he opened his eyes and sat up. He was back in the circular room that was used frequently during his meetings with these messengers of the Gods, the Star People.

Sees Far wondered, as he looked around the room, how much of this contact would be remembered. The large screen, which he knew the giants used for visions, as he used the kivas, was now blank. The panels around him blinked on and off in a bright display of colors and symbols. Many of the symbols were familiar; he had brought them to his people to use in their ceremonies. A door opened, and one of the giants entered the room.

The being spoke to Sees Far without words or hand signs. Sees Far responded respectfully and with familiarity. Long before his visions of the giants and their sun disks first had come to him as a young man, he had known that he could hear his people's thoughts. This ability was not unusual or unknown amongst his people. His skills, though, surpassed any in the history of the tribe. Several other living members of the tribe also had these skills. Juniper Berry and her father were among them. The giant interrupted his thoughts.

Greetings, Sees Far, the tall man said. *Do you remember anything else?*

Yes. Sees far answered in his mind. *I had a vision of a world with a sky the color of spring flowers. Other giants lived there, other men and women of your tribe. This world had two Moon Gods.*

The tall man nodded as he listened.

What else? the giant asked. His blue eyes searched Sees Far's brown ones thoughtfully.

Your people were about to begin a great journey, a journey that would take your people many miles from your home. I was with your people. I was going to fly on your sun disc.

Do you remember your name or what you looked like? The giant prompted him to remember more. But, this confused Sees Far. Why did the giant ask him a fool's question? Of course he knew his name.

I am called "Sees Far Across The Mountains Where The Sun Discs Fly."

The giant smiled for the first time. The starman placed one of his large hands over Sees Far's eyes and the room was hidden from his view. Sees Far fell asleep quite suddenly, and awoke several hours later in his own bed.

Many summers had passed since the Earth God had shaken *the people's* homes with her anger and since Juniper had taken her place as a leader amongst her people. Buildings that had fallen long ago had been rebuilt. Juniper had fulfilled her role as leader with grace and wisdom. And Sees Far continued to have contact with the Star People who delivered messages for the Great Spirit.

Over the last winter, Sees Far had developed a constant cough that rattled in his chest and throat. The pain in his chest had spread to his bones, and his joints ached tenaciously throughout the winter and spring moons. Even the summer moons offered him little comfort. Many in the tribe were infected by the same symptoms. The "black spirit plague" had come to *the people.* The giants had offered Sees Far a cure for his ailment, but he had refused the aid. He knew the sickness that spread though his body was the Great Spirit's endeavor to reclaim his weakening spirit, so it would once again grow strong. To cheat the Great Spirit would only bring ill favor to his people. Also, he did not fear death. His people believed that death was an open doorway through which one would find a new life.

One evening, as the sun began its descent over the western canyon walls, he heard Juniper Berry's fears echoing in his mind once more. He sent the young woman who tended him to find Juniper. His chamber darkened quickly as the sun set. The fire that had burned constantly these past few months cast golden light and shadows over his shrunken body. His gnarled hands clasped at his chest as another coughing fit overcame him. Within a short time, Juniper arrived.

She had grown into a mature woman. Little had changed in her physical appearance, except that she carried herself with a confidence which made the old man proud. Her wide and serious face showed concern as she knelt beside him.

"You are frightened by what will happen to our people?" he said over a rattling exhale of breath.

"Yes," she admitted, and then quickly changed the subject as she pulled a fur over him to offer him comfort. "How are you, Uncle? Your sickness sounds worse. Let me get the healer for you."

"No," he said as he grabbed her hand. "It is my time to die, Niece.

"You need not know fear. Many guide and protect you. Others will be here to help you in this world, though I shall not.

You are a strong pathfinder, and I am proud of you. Do not give in to the whispering of weak spirits. Know that you are strong and that good spirits lead you still."

Juniper Berry ducked her head to hide her tears, which had begun to slide down her cheeks. She spoke hoarsely.

"I shall sing loudly then, so that your spirit hears me in the other worlds. I shall sing of your wisdom and truth. The spirits who come to greet you will know of your strength and power. They will know that many mourn you here in the world you chose to leave."

He gently held her hand as she wept.

And then, suddenly, Sees Far heard an owl call out across the canyon. Sees Far felt his spirit slip out of his body to follow it. He turned and watched Juniper's prone body from the ceiling, where his spirit floated. His earthly body looked ancient and shriveled on its frame. Then, Sees Far watched as Juniper realized his spirit had departed. She tilted her head upward and began a mourning chant that he recognized.

Juniper, I am still here! his soul called out to comfort her.

She stopped. A shiver ran down her back and arms. She looked around the room.

Uncle? Sees Far?

Yes! Juniper, I am here! he said, and floated down next to her. He reached out his hand to stroke her cheek, but it passed through her solid flesh. She started.

"Uncle?" Juniper said out loud.

An owl hooted, answering her call. Its voice echoed into the room and into Sees Far's soul. Juniper also heard it, stood and went to the door. Outside, the full moon had risen and lighted the village and canyon beyond. Sees Far followed Juniper and slipped easily through her and out the door.

Never had he seen a moon such as this! It was brighter and warmer than the sun! The Moon's rays called to him and begged him to chase Her. The owl hooted again in a haunting voice and flew directly toward the moon. Sees Far stared lovingly at Juniper one last time, and then followed.

The moon rose and cast a pale yellow light over the canyon walls. For the past two years since Sees Far's death, Juniper had had weekly visitations from the Star People. She had heard of them through stories from Sees Far and from her parents. She accepted their existence and place in her life. She had even come to look forward to the contact between herself and the giants.

Something about these tall blond men and women was remarkably familiar, yet she could not say what....

That they were benevolent beings was without question. That they were messengers of the Great Spirit was also not disputed. What other purpose did they have in the lives of *the people,* she wondered, as a concerned leader would. She knew that they would not arrive this night, and wanted to enjoy the quiet splendor of the canyon, so she sat silently watching as the Moon God looked out over Her world.

Night, and its illusion of isolation, had become a retreat for her. She did not have to make decisions for *the people* here. She did not have to answer questions. She did not have to settle disputes. Here, she rested. The nightfall hid her presence, except where the moon caught a piece of her shoulder and the top of her head and reflected its brilliance there.

Juniper Berry's face showed few signs of aging. Only worry lines across her forehead and gray circles under her eyes indicated that she had seen thirty-one seasons of life and twelve years of responsibility as one of the leaders. Her body was still muscular and agile, although her breasts had sagged from several winters of little to eat and the nursing of her three children. And Juniper's plain features still held their look of compassion and intelligence whenever they looked upon a member of *the people*. None of the inner turmoil she now felt showed in her countenance.

Juniper Berry reflected upon the latest problem of the tribe, which had been brought to her by the Star People. It was time to share this knowledge with *the people*. Yet, how would they accept this news? Would they work to stay together? Many of the younger members of the tribe did not believe in the Star People. How would the young ones react?

As she massaged her temples to alleviate a headache that had begun, she put her questions aside, leaned against the cold stone wall of her house and rested before night brought sleep and daylight brought its many interruptions with the tribe's needs.

The next day Juniper called a council meeting. Quietly, tribal leaders entered the main ceremonial hall, or the "Great Kiva." The Great Kiva, which was a large building framed in the shape of a circle of large timber and covered with stone, mud and straw walls, was buried partly underground. Small windows circled the above ground section of the kiva, and most of the remaining tribal members sat where they could outside the circular building, where windows would let the words of the council reach them. Juniper began by addressing the issue the Star People had presented to her.

"Aunts, Uncles, brothers, sisters, nieces, nephews and cousins, hear my words. The Star People, messengers of the Great Spirit, have sent us a vision. The Earth God will once again show its anger. This time the Earth God's anger will be unrelenting and will change our home forever. The big rivers that feed the river at the bottom of our canyon will be diverted. The spring at the back of the cavern will cease to run. *The people* will have to move.

"A journey, such as has been proposed, will take many moons. The children will not be able to walk far. The old ones will not be able to carry much. We must provide for all. We must decide as a tribe what we shall do. This journey may take as long as three summers, as we may have to stop during the cold moons to wait for the Winter God to pass over the lands. I ask you now to speak. What do you want? What shall we do?"

"Why should we leave? We can live up on the mesas for many years before we run out of water," said one of the woman leaders. Her round, brown face stared earnestly at each of the other tribal leaders.

"We do not know for how long the water will last," answered Sits Away, Juniper's aunt. She had joined the council two years ago in place of a member who had died during the Black Spirit's plague. Sits Away continued.

"There is a chance that the water will last for months or years. We do know that, in less than thirty summers, the water will be gone. Although this does not affect many of the older tribal members, such as myself, we must think of our children and grandchildren. We must see like the eagle, and not like the shortsighted hen."

"Yes. I want to know that my children, and the child that has not yet met this world, will have a safe and plentiful home," a large, round-faced woman said. Sunflower had miraculously conceived a baby at her late age. She had known almost thirty summer cycles, and now she bloomed heavily with child. Many around her nodded their heads in agreement. Juniper supported Sunflower's words.

"We must think of future generations, and not only of the ones we see before us. This will not be an easy journey, but the messengers have agreed to guide us. They have brought us trustworthy guidance before this time. I believe we may trust them now."

"We have not received messages like you speak of in many years. How do we know that these are not spirits guided by dark winds? I say we go to the Sun City. There, at least we shall know our friends and allies. What do we know of this place in the south?" a young man yelled through one of the windows.

"Too many people live in the Sun City," Juniper answered loudly. "I cannot lie to you. I have never been to this new canyon, but I have seen visions of it. Nut trees grow in abundance there, and the water runs clear and strong. I do not think that it shows wisdom to believe only part of the Star People's message. If they say that there will be no water in the Sun City, we must listen to this. Their words hold truth. I had another vision recently."

Everyone became still as they waited for Juniper to speak. As she did, the silence in and outside the Kiva intensified.

"Sees Far came to me. He said that the Star People speak the truth, that we need to listen to them. He said that, should we choose to move our people to this canyon, help will be sent to us. A child will be born that will lead our people. He, personally, will bring the child's spirit to our people. He said that I must help our people."

As she fell silent, one by one the tribes' members began to speak.

"We should listen to Juniper!" said one middle-aged woman.

"Sees Far was wise and powerful. He would not come if our need was not great!" her husband agreed.

"Many of us are too old for such a journey!" one old woman said.

"What about this child? How will we know which child is born with the helping spirit? When will this child be born?" said a pregnant woman.

"If we choose to go, when should we leave? Spring is gone. Summer is almost past. We cannot travel in the cold months," said one of the leaders of a mens' Kiva.

The voices rose, until the clamor grew deafening. Juniper's head began to throb with the intensity of emotions that surrounded her. Suddenly, she could stand it no longer. Her voice rose above the crowd.

"Silence brings peace!"

The tribe obeyed her words and quiet fell over the Kiva. A mature man, one of the tribal elders, now stood. His square, brown hands rose in a gesture for all to listen. His deep voice echoed out over the crowd.

"No decisions will be made without every tribal members' consent. For now, each member shall return to their home to think upon what has been said. Tomorrow, when the sun is in the center of the sky, let us rejoin to talk about our plans. Whatever each tribal member chooses, each of us must remember to respect that choice."

Juniper gestured with her hand that she wished to speak. The elder bowed his consent.

"I would hope that our people may stay together. If we must split up, and journey different paths, let each send the other on their journey with peace. Whatever the tribe decides, I now give you my promise that I will do everything I can to bring our people safely to their new home."

As she finished, the elder shook a large dried gourd several times. Its rattling sounded throughout the Great Kiva. The meeting was ended.

That evening, as she lay in her bed with yet another headache, her tribal members' many questions echoed around in her throbbing head. She wondered how *the people* would vote tomorrow. They would have many years before the Earth God's anger would strike, but exactly how many? She questioned herself relentlessly.

Would they leave as a people, as one? Had she clearly remembered the message from the giants? What if she had misheard their message? Had Sees Far really come to her, or had she made up this vision to comfort herself in a time of stress? Could she trust the Star People? More importantly, *Could she trust herself?*

Suddenly the pain in her head intensified, and her head felt as if it were about to explode from some inner pressure. When the pain ended, so did her life. A brain tumor halted the years of leadership and her toil of responsibility.

"the between ..."

When Serra entered the light, Lohkan and Tonak awaited her. Something about Lohkan's attitude alerted her to a change.

"What is it?" she asked curiously.

"You need to go back, Serra. *The people* need your help. I'll stay here and act as your guide. If *the people* do not move within the next fifteen years of their timeline, then most of the tribe will perish in an earthquake. The remaining members will journey to the city they call 'Sun City' and die there from starvation and dehydration."

She nodded. She had promised only hours before she died, that she would lead her people to safety. Somehow. She had been told by Sees Far that a child would be born. Suddenly, she knew that child was her.

"The child Sees Far spoke of in a dream; it's me, isn't it?"

Yes, the elder signed. His expression was serious. *You are needed, Serra. This is your lesson. You have made a promise to these people.*

Lohkan has made a promise to guide you. You will see him in your dreams and in visions. He will come to you in a form that you will accept, as Sees Far. As Sees Far, he accepted a commitment to act as your spirit guardian. He will complete that commitment as you guide these people in another embodiment. Do you understand?

She did, but her mind seemed to be swirling with questions she knew would not be answered at that moment. She nodded, "Yes." As she did, the white light surrounded and filled her. Lohkan and the elder disappeared and her conscious memories of that dimension vanished.

Sits Away awoke sharply in the dark. Her long, gray hair spilled down her back. Her wrinkled hands passed over her face as she listened to the silence that now replaced the intense dream she had just had. The beating of her heart filled her ears. The Star People had come to her.

Giants! Men and women taller than anything she had imagined when she had listened to her brother, Juniper's father, speak of them. They had called her outside – so tall were they that they could not fit in her low-ceilinged house. They stood as tall as a pinion tree, at least eight feet!

Their message had been clear. Their people must move or perish. The first of the Earth God's anger would be seen sometime between five to eight summer cycles, counting from the summer that had already passed. At first the Earth God's anger would be mild. Then, over the following summer cycles, the frequency of the anger would increase. The last of the God's anger would be spent between the tenth and fifteenth years. This would be the period of devastation ... the time when the water would be taken from *the people.*

Sits Away shook her head as she tried to rid herself of the horror she had seen. No water. No crops. Starvation. Child-barren women. Sick men. In the end, their people were gone. A few lived, but these eventually died in isolation and loneliness. She trembled violently as she remembered the dream.

The giants had gone on to tell her that on this very night the child who would lead their people would be born. Impulsively, she decided to wake Juniper and tell her about the dream.

She crept silently into the other room, where Juniper slept with her husband, and bent over her. She touched her arm and shook her gently, but there was no response. *Juniper sleeps soundly. Perhaps I had better not disturb her,* Sits away thought. She changed her mind quickly, and shook Juniper again while she whispered.

"Juniper. Wake up. We must speak!"

Still, Juniper did not respond. She lay peaceful, with her head resting in a nest of furs, her arms by her sides.

Sits Away felt an urgent need arise in her to speak with Juniper. Her heart pounded loudly again. This inner sound cast an eerie spell over the darkened room. Suddenly, as Sits Away realized that something was wrong, the urgency was replaced with panic. When the truth came to her a moment later, she awakened Juniper's husband.

"Wake up. Crow Call, wake up! Juniper no longer walks in this world."

"What? When? How can this be? Not now!" he said as he sought to deny the truth. Crow Call searched for Juniper blindly in the dark. His hands found her still form, and he cradled her to his chest.

Sits Away's old hands shook as she wept. She spoke softly to Crow Call as he held Juniper's body.

"Go, Crow, and get Silent Thunder. I shall need help preparing her body. Tell her to tell no one. Not yet! A dark wind shall strike our people once Juniper's death is known. Let our people know peace until morning."

Few slept well that night.

When the morning's light touched the opposite canyon wall and turned its yellow rocks a deep rosy gold, the first cry of morning in the village was heard from the new child that was born.

Sunflower, who had struggled throughout the night with her difficult labor, lay painfully staring at this large new baby, a boy. Blood seeped from a wound where she had been torn badly during the baby's passage into the world. As Sunflower reached for her son, she cried out in alarm.

"Ah!"

You can see me, Sunflower! Juniper said as she floated into the room and next to her friend. The image of Juniper wavered in and out of view to Sunflower's tired eyes.

"This is impossible! Juniper, you cannot be here!" Sunflower argued with the vision. She had not yet learned of Juniper's death.

No. It's not, Sunflower. I've come to lead our people. I'll live in your son. Juniper said, but only Sunflower could hear her. The healer, Silent Thunder, looked about the room in a perplexed state.

"My son, he is the one?" Sunflower asked. Her voice was hoarse with tears.

"Please, you must rest!" said Silent Thunder. She tried to push Sunflower back onto the bed, but Sunflower pushed her away with the last of her strength.

Yes. He is. Juniper said tenderly. *He is a child of the Star People. He has the ability to hear and see. He will be a shaman and lead our people to their new home.*

Sunflower shook with tears. Her body finally gave in to its exhaustion and lay back. Before she closed her eyes for the last time, she reached for Juniper.

"Thank you," she whispered. Sunflower's hand fell to her side, and she died peacefully. A smile lay quietly upon her lips.

The village learned of the news of Sunflower's vision as quickly as it heard about her death. Wails of mourning for Sunflower and Juniper Berry echoed against the cliff's walls. Two tribe members had been lost, while one had been gained. Stifled, awe-struck murmurings drifted from house to house. Two women discussed the nights events outside on the foot path. They were both small, dark and round, as many women of *the people* were.

"Big! Sunflower's baby is larger then any child ever born to our tribe! I saw him with my own eyes!" whispered one of the women earnestly. "No woman could survive such a birth!"

"How sad for Sunflower," the other woman answered compassionately. As she spoke, her open mouth showed that she

193

was toothless from an old accident.

"He has a birthmark like Juniper did! You heard Juniper came to Sunflower as she died?"

"Yes," the toothless woman answered her friend.

"Did you hear that the birthmark was in the shape of a frog?" said the first woman, as her small hands pulled closer a fur that she wore around her shoulders and chest.

"No!" the toothless woman answered, and did not hide her shock. Amongst their people the frog was considered sacred for its ability to live on the earth and underwater. "What did Silent Thunder say?"

"She said that powerful forces are at work." The small woman leaned toward her toothless friend. "Silent Thunder looked frightened. She said, 'This baby walks in two worlds!'"

Yet, these women could not have imagined the two worlds from which this child had come.

After the customary three days of silence required for the spirit of the dead to make a safe passage to the land of spirits, a council meeting was called for only the leaders of the tribe. Seven men and six women, leaders of varying ages sat in a circle within the Great Kiva. Each leader represented a branch of a clan within *the people.* Three shamans, two men and one women, sat within this circle of leaders. As the youngest of the shamans and the newest member on the council, Silent Thunder held the lowest position. She had been asked to join the council because she had witnessed Sunflower's vision. Silent Thunder had begun her training only four years before, after she had finished her woman's initiation.

A small fire burned in the center in a fire pit and gave light to the otherwise darkly lit room. Sage smoke drifted up from the fire and out through a hole in the ceiling of the kiva. For hours, interpretations of the visions were debated. To the best of her ability, Silent Thunder explained the visions, but she did not have the power of the old one, Sees Far, to understand the gods. And she was still intimidated by this group of elders. She spoke slowly, trying to draw confidence from a heart that did not feel strong.

"Juniper has returned to our tribe in Sunflower's son. He will lead our people, but I cannot say how. If all agree, Sits Away will take over Juniper's duties for now. I believe Sits Away's vision was clear. We have maybe five summers during which we may live here safely."

"Five years! How can a five-year-old boy lead our people?"

an elder of the Antelope Clan asked practically.

"I don't know," answered Silent Thunder. "I believe we may have to wait until he is older. If we wait, we will face the problems of traveling while the Earth God's anger sweeps over the land. Who knows what dangers this may bring to our tribe?"

"Let *the people* hear our words. Then let's discuss this for one moon's cycle before we decide. A moon's cycle will begin the healing for the families who mourn those they have lost," a woman from the Wolf Clan suggested.

"Yes. *The people* need time to heal," agreed an old man, the leader of the Fox Clan.

"Silent Thunder, can you watch the boy during this time? Maybe you can learn something of his nature?" suggested Sits Away.

"He is with Sweet Sage, who nurses him. I can visit him each day."

Sits Away nodded that she had heard. The tribal leaders spoke quietly for a few more minutes, and then the council ended their meeting.

They met again a few hours later, with the entire tribe. Again people filled the Great Kiva and surrounded the building. Many wept while they listened to the elders, but no one now argued for another course. In the wakes of the death of Juniper and Sunflower, *the people* had reunited and settled their differences. All wished to remain together. The Great Spirit had heard Juniper's prayers.

Sweet Sage held the large baby in her lap as she nursed him. Already this baby weighed what a child of four seasons would weigh. Her slim and muscular arms cradled him tenderly. A crooked nose sat above modest lips on her young and earnest face. After Sweet Sage shifted the baby into a more comfortable position, she looked up again at the council members who surrounded her in the Great Kiva. Sits Away began the meeting by addressing the young woman.

"Silent Thunder tells us that you care for the boy as the corn is tended. We, the council, believe that you are the boy's spirit mother. If you wish, you may take him as your son. There is no pressure on you, Sweet Sage. Another will be found if this responsibility is too much for you."

Sits Away referred to the fact that Sweet Sage's husband had died two years earlier, during the black spirit plague. Her mother, father and aunts had all died at the same time. No other in the village had lost as many family members. She was the last still alive of her clan, though she was not alone. No member of *the people* was ever alone. All were brothers and sisters. Still she did not have the immediate support of family members with whom she shared living space.

Sweet Sage smiled gently as she looked down at the baby, who now nursed. Perhaps she could start her own family. Maybe she could find another husband. The whole village would help her raise this child.

"Yes. I shall adopt this boy. Shall I name him?" She instinctively knew that, since this child was different, he would naturally live under a different set of customs. Silent Thunder answered for the group.

"He has been named already. His name came to Sits Away in a dream. He is *He Who Hears The Frogs Sing*. His shortened name will be Frog Song. He will lead our people to our new home. We are happy the Great Spirit has chosen you as his mother."

Sits Away now spoke.

"We wish to offer you the support you will need with two small children. If you wish, Crow Call and our family would like to offer our home as yours. We would adopt you into our family. We have spoken to Sunflower's husband; he has agreed. He wants his son to be raised by the village. He accepts you as the spirit mother."

Sweet Sage was moved. An adoption of one family member into another family was common, but done only with sincere intent. She nodded her consent as she blinked back tears. She thought, as she looked over the serious faces of the council, that the village's and Crow Call's losses had brought her wealth. She hoped sincerely that her wealth would spill back over onto her people's lives.

Frog Song, at the age of two, was as tall as a child of six summers. As he reached four summers, he was now as tall as a twelve year old. He was as dexterous as a twelve year old, too. His growth was legendary amongst his people. Not only was he exceedingly tall, his coloring also differed from that of his people. Instead of jet-black hair, his was a warm medium brown, like the color of nutshells. And Frog Song's skin was fairer and turned bright pink during the first spring days when he ran naked in the sun. As Silent Thunder watched the boy grow, she finally understood how he would be able to lead their people at a young age.

Silent Thunder took another handful of herbs and placed

them in a hole in the large boulder where she sat. Then she took a smaller stone to grind the herbs into a powder that she would make into a medicine. The sun warmed her back as she worked and her plain features squinted at its brightness as she hummed a chant to herself. As she methodically worked, her mind wandered over the past few years.

Four years ago, at a council meeting, *the people* had voted to stay in their homes for eight summers. Most voted this way out of concern for the very old and the very young. At that time the youngest members of the tribe would be old enough to walk the great distance. The half-dozen oldest members of the tribe would most likely die in their homeland before this period was completed. Although the decision was a difficult one, the tribal members decided that no children would be conceived during these eight years. Silent Thunder had supplied each woman with an herbal contraceptive to insure this decision. The contraceptive was made of the herb she now ground.

As Silent Thunder reflected over this and the upcoming changes for *the people,* a voice interrupted her thoughts, and she saw Sweet Sage approaching her. Sweet Sage and Crow Call were now mated. Two years ago he had decided to leave his dark world of mourning. When he had, he had discovered that, while he mourned, he had fallen in love with Sweet Sage. Sweet Sage had prospered under this mating. Her thin, young body had blossomed into an attractive woman. *She has the brightness of dawn in her spirit,* thought Silent Thunder.

"Sits Away wishes to meet with you tonight. Will you eat with us this evening?" asked Sweet Sage.

"Yes. We shall be there. When?"

"Whenever you arrive, we shall eat." Sweet Sage gave the customary polite response.

"Then we shall see you at sunset," Silent Thunder answered. Her husband had died during the black plague, but her three-year-old daughter lived, and she was naturally invited.

As the sun turned the front of Sit Away's house from yellow to orange, Silent Thunder and her daughter arrived to share an evening meal. After a dinner of rabbit stew and cornmush, Sweet Sage took the children outside to play. Crow Call, Sits Away and Silent Thunder remained by the coals of the fire to talk. Silent Thunder had understood that the invitation included more than dinner. She waited for Sits Away to speak.

"Another vision was brought to me last night." Sits Away stopped and stared into the coals. Her old face was shadowed. Only bright pinpoints of light reflected from her almond-shaped, black eyes. She continued.

"The boy's training must begin. He is to study under you each day."

"What? What shall I teach him?" asked Silent Thunder. She was not a leader or teacher. She was a healer.

"Teach him your methods of healing and tell him the stories that Sees Far told you. Frog Song will remember his knowledge of Juniper's life as you awaken him with your knowledge."

"When do I begin?"

"Tomorrow," answered Crow Call. "I shall send him to you after dawn. He will train with you every day.

"The Star People said that you would need to train him very little. They said that Frog Song will learn very quickly."

Silent Thunder nodded. She understood what the messengers meant. The boy was unusually quick. She debated whether to discuss the boy's parentage here, now, with Sits Away and Crow Call. Before she had finished her internal debate, the words found exit and she expressed her beliefs.

"Have you noticed how Frog Song looks like none of our people? Sits Away, you have seen the Giants? Does Frog Song look like the Star People?"

Sits Away looked quickly at Crow Call, who had looked toward her at the same moment. He nodded, and Sits Away spoke.

"Two weeks after Frog Song was born, the Messengers came and took me to their home. They live in flying stars. Inside of the stars are vision pools. They showed me a story.

"They went to Sunflower while she slept, and asked to speak with her. She was frightened, but did not wish to anger the Messengers of Gods, so she agreed to go with them. They brought her to their home and showed her their vision pools. Then they showed her the Earth God's anger, as well as Juniper's death. They explained that a child who could hear as Juniper and Sees Far had been able to, without signs or words, would be needed to lead his people. No other tribe members have had Juniper's skill since her father and Sees Far died."

In her confusion, Silent Thunder interrupted the older woman.

"No, this is not true, Sits Away. You can hear as Juniper did."

"No. Not as well. I will not live much longer," the old woman explained without self-pity. Her black eyes stared kindly at the younger woman, and then Sits Away continued.

"The Star People also explained that the child must grow

quickly. They offered their seed to Sunflower so that she might conceive this child. She was frightened and did not answer. They took her back to her home, and told her she needed only to act as her spirit wished.

"Three nights later, they visited her again, and Sunflower agreed. They explained that she need not lie with any of the gods, as this would frighten her. They also explained to Sunflower that she most likely would die if she chose this path. Sunflower saw this as an honorable way to die, and agreed. Then the giants explained that they must remove this memory from her spirit, or her daily life would not know peace from then on; and still she agreed. She did not remember this promise until the moment of her death, when she died peacefully, knowing that she had helped her people.

"Frog Song is the son of one of the messengers. He has their knowledge and will grow faster than our people, so that he may guide us. Now you must help him complete this work. We ask that you tell no one this tale, though many may already have guessed."

Silent Thunder left Sits Away's home quietly. She was awed by what she had learned. And, the next morning, she began Frog Song's training.

Frog Song had known that he was different by the reaction of his people. Although he had never seen a reflection of his face, he heard the hundreds of voices of his people clearly in his mind. He knew that he did not look like them; but, they loved him and he was accepted as one of *the people.* He knew that his people counted on him; he felt at ease with this responsibility, and that seemed a natural response to him. He could hear the young medicine woman's thoughts; he knew that she did not think his reaction was normal, but he had memories that the medicine woman did not have. He had his father's memories and knew that countless other worlds, peoples and customs existed. He belonged with *the people,* but his customs belonged to his father's race.

Because he had his father's memories, he knew he could not talk about his father's race to *the people.* They were not yet ready to accept the presence and knowledge of the vastly different worlds that existed. When they were ready, in a few hundred years, they would be told. Right now, the closest relationship *the people* could have to his father's race was to see them as messengers to the spirit world. In a strange way, this philosophy was correct. His father's people were here to bring the knowledge that all life was connected, as well as to study this planet and its people. That all races, all souls, came from the same source, were the same source, was an ancient knowledge amongst his father's race. This race, *the people,* held similar beliefs. It was due to these similarities that the two races worked together, albeit under the cover of dreams and at night.

Eventually, the other races of this planet would be brought to this awareness. His father's people were scientists, philosophers, and extraordinarily patient and gentle. They would work for centuries to help awaken the human races of this planet. The existence of humans depended on this knowledge; without it, they would eventually destroy themselves, as they had once done. Frog Song kept this knowledge silent, as he knew he must. He had not been conceived to disrupt his father's work.

He quickly learned all that the medicine woman had to teach about anatomy and healing, and began to study the spiritual customs of *the people.* One day, while he practiced one of the chants to heal spirit sickness, he had his first vision.

He saw an old man with long gray hair and multiple tattoos upon his mostly naked body. The old man pointed to the ground, and it began to shake violently. The old man clapped his hands and spoke four words.

Move our people now!

He awoke from the trance in surprise and confusion. His father's people had no customs or experiences such as these. Without thinking, he jumped up and ran to Silent Thunder's house, where she was preparing a decoction for Frog Song's aching limbs. A side-effect of his rapid growth and maturity had been leg and arm joint pain. She stopped when she saw his expression. She had never seen the boy, who now stood a head taller than she, upset, except when Sits Away had died. He did not seem to have the natural acceptance of the spirit world that *the people* contained in their very beings. She immediately assumed that someone was hurt or dying.

"What has happened, Frog Song?" she asked anxiously.

"I have had a vision!"

"Tell me what you have seen."

He quickly described his vision, and as he finished, Silent Thunder drew him inside her house; she told him to sit. She deftly placed sage upon a small fire, picked up a rattle made from a gourd and took a carved bone, with an eagle's feather tied onto it, in her other hand. As the sage smoke filled the room, she began to circle Frog Song. She gave him instructions.

"It has begun. The visions. Close your eyes. Let the smoke

fill your body and cleanse you. Breathe! Let your soul wander back to that meeting. Call to Sees Far and ask him for guidance. Ask the Gods for protection!"

While she shook the rattle, she circled him and began to chant. He did as she instructed, and found himself floating in a dark cave. In the distance, a fire burned brightly. He walked toward the fire and found an old man there, Sees Far. Sees Far spoke quickly and firmly.

You have come. The people *must move now. Tomorrow! Take only food supplies and what you can carry. The Earth God has lost patience and will show her temper in one moon's time. The village will be destroyed. They cannot wait, because the Earth God will not wait! You must lead. I shall show you which paths to follow. Begin by following the path that leads to the Sun City. You must leave now to reach a place of safety before the first earth shaking begins. Go! Now! There are no sun cycles to waste!*

The old man raised his hand; and as he pointed it at Frog Song's chest, Frog Song was sent hurtling back to his body. He collapsed on the floor. Silent Thunder shook him awake.

"What happened? Speak if you can, Frog Song!"

"*The people* must leave now. Tomorrow. The time has come for us to journey to our new home. The Earth God has no more patience and will strike early." He shook as he repeated the message.

Five minutes later, a messenger called the council and tribe together for an emergency meeting. Within an hour, *the people* had voted unanimously to leave at dawn the next morning and, for the rest of the day, *the people* hurriedly packed what few belongings they could realistically carry. That night, each person prayed silently to the gods for a safe journey.

In a valley Southeast of the great mesas where their old homes lay, *the people* stopped to rest for the night. The children ran about the temporary camp situated in a dwarfed juniper forest surrounded by red rocks. Many of the adults worked to set up the traveling huts, while others prepared fires and the evening meal. Silent Thunder sang a chant to the setting sun, which spread warm colors over her short, sparsely clad body. From head to toe, eyes to skin, buckskin tunic to leather sandals, she glowed in rich shades of earthy browns. She took a handful of corn meal from a leather sack she wore over her shoulder and cast it into the evening winds as a blessing on this day and on this site. The corn grains caught the last of the golden rays of the sunset and sparkled briefly in the air in a yellow curtain.

Frog Song stood by her side a moment later, and began to tell Silent Thunder of his latest prophetic experience. Silent Thunder tilted her head upward to look at the tall boy with the sun-touched hair. His hair, which was waist-length and pulled back with a leather tie, had turned gold on the top layers from a month of walking in the sun. His skin had turned bright pink over his tanned body, on his shoulders and arms and on his nose and cheeks. He had begun to peel like a lizard in these places.

"It is still," he said as he looked around. "Sees Far came to me again. He said it will not be long now."

"Did he say when the Earth God will release its anger?" Silent Thunder asked.

"No," Frog Song explained. "Only that it will be soon. He said it was good that we stopped for the night."

As he said the last of these words, the earth beneath their feet began to tremble. A woman screamed. *The people* began to run in many directions to take shelter. Silent Thunder's daughter ran to her and hid her face in the folds of her mother's tunic while Silent Thunder closed her eyes to the violence she saw around her. Her stomach rolled with waves of nausea as the Earth rolled beneath her feet. Suddenly, Silent Thunder felt Frog Song's large embrace as he put his arms protectively around her and her daughter. While the Earth God shook in its anger, she clung tightly to him.

Violent minutes passed, which seemed like hours, and then everything was still. They each looked up from their huddled pack and saw that the camp was intact. As Frog Song released his hold on her, Silent Thunder moved quickly toward her people to insure that none were hurt. A half hour later, *the people* resumed their evening activities. Thankfully, no one had been harmed. And, as the first stars appeared in the sky, Silent Thunder prepared a ceremony to give thanks for her people's safety.

Hello, Frog Song! a voice said loudly in his head. Frog Song rolled over and stretched on the ground where he had been sleeping.

Sees Far, is it you? the boy, who was quickly becoming a young man, asked telepathically.

Yes, answered the voice. *Today, as the people journey, you will come to a tall rock that looks like a finger pointing at the stars. Turn west at the rock. Follow the sun's path as it travels across the sky. I will return when it is time for the* people *to change this path.*

I understand, Frog Song answered, and then his mind was suddenly empty. Sees Far had gone.

Another moon cycle passed before Frog Song heard from Sees Far again. The season of the hottest moons was upon them. And on one of these warm evenings, Frog Song sat down to rest. As he fell into a peaceful sleep, he found himself back in the cave with Sees Far. The old man greeted him from his place by the fire. The firelight reflected off the mass of wrinkles that lined his face and became sharply accented as the old man grinned.

Hello, Frog Song! In three days, the Rain Gods will send a storm that will flood this area. In a day's travel, you will come to a hill with caves that will offer protection. You won't see the caves at first, because they face out from the western slope of this hill. There, you can wait out the storm. You will recognize this hill by a tall tree that stands on its ridge. This tree was touched by the fire of the Thunder Gods and is black and bare.

As the storm passes over the land, animals will be swallowed in the flood waters. Make as many nets as you can to catch this game.

Frog Song nodded that he understood, and then, suddenly, he was awake. He ran through the camp with a renewed sense of urgency, to Silent Thunder's shelter to tell her of this news.

At the end of the following day's journey they came to a small hill with the ghostly silhouette of a dead tree, and there on the west side of the hill, as Sees Far had foretold, was a large cave. Hastily, *the people* worked as one to weave nets and baskets from grasses, sticks and anything else they could find. A day later, black clouds rolled over the land and spit fire to the Earth.

Frog Song stood by the flood waters and helped another man pull a deer, recently drowned, from the rising waters. Lightening lit the sky in violent bursts while the Thunder Gods bellowed over the land. Rain poured down on *the people* as men and women stood as close to the waters as was safe and threw their nets into the rushing waters. The children stayed safely up on the hill and awaited orders from the adults.

One group of women caught several rabbits and two fattened grouse in their nets. One of these women, who was unrecognizable because her black hair was wetly matted across her face, yelled to some of the children to come and gather the catch. Another group of men found two freshly drowned yearlings floating in the churning water. A woman yelled as she spotted an elk's body bobbing up and down in the water's current. People yelled back and forth above the loud storm. The noise of the thunder and the haste of *the people* themselves turned into a dark and dramatic dance of survival. And, in the end, enough game was gathered to feed *the people* for at least half a moon.

✳

A fourth month of long and arduous days passed. And as *the people* traveled west, the landscape began to change. The trees thinned and sagebrush grew more thickly. The food supplies they had carried had been used up long ago. Some of the leaders grew fearful. How would *the people* be fed? Finally, one night after camp had been set up, a council was held.

"We have no beans or corn left. There is not enough game to feed our people. What shall we do?" asked one of the leaders.

"Our children grow thin. They need more to eat. We all need to rest. Our moccasins need repair. We cannot go on without restoring ourselves and our supplies," said a woman who had taken Sits Away's place on the council.

The remaining leaders agreed. Silent Thunder spoke when the many voices had quieted.

"Why don't we ask for help? Perhaps Sees Far may have advice for us. Could you contact him, Frog Song?"

"Yes. I think so."

"Tonight, then. At dawn tomorrow, we shall hold council to decide upon Sees Far's words."

The meeting ended and the council members returned to their tasks. Frog Song walked away silently. He went to a place in the sagebrush, where, in a small hollow, nothing grew, and sat down to wait for Sees Far to come to him. He quietly began the chant Silent Thunder had taught him. As he chanted, he fell into a state that was neither waking nor sleeping, and found himself in the cave once more.

Sees Far sat by the fire and poked the coals with a long stick. When Frog Song did not speak, he encouraged the boy.

What is it that you wish to ask, Frog Song?

Our people are tired and hungry. The time when the thunder sleeps is only two moons away. Winter will pass over the land. We need to hunt for food and skins. What shall we do?

Sees Far nodded and passed his hand through the air. As he did, a scene came into view, another hill with caves and a wide river nearby. Rabbits and birds ran through the sagebrush. In the distance, Frog Song recognized a herd of deer which drank at the river's edge. Grass grew along the riverbank, which was flanked by willows and cottonwoods. Sees Far held up seven fingers.

This place is seven days' journey from where you camp.

You may build homes in these caves and live there through the season when the thunder sleeps. Stay here on this hill. Do not follow the river north, as the tribe that lives there will not offer peace. Do not cross the river and follow the land west, as a desert that cannot feed the people *reaches for miles. When winter has passed, I shall guide you toward your new home again. Follow the sun's trail as it goes west. The sun will lead you to this river.*

And, with those words, Sees Far, the scene, the cave and fire all disappeared. *The people* left the next morning, and wearily continued west on their journey. On the afternoon of the seventh day, Frog Song heard a loud noise, which he at first did not recognize. The throaty sound of hundreds of small creatures became more distinct as he drew closer. When *the people* crested the hill, they saw below them a wide and winding river. From the banks of the river, hundreds of frogs croaked out a water song.

As *the people* migrated toward their new home, an enormous change took place in Frog Song. All signs of boyhood left him and he became a wise and respected member of the council. Another change began to show itself in Frog Song, a maturity of his heart.

The People had stopped for another winter's season and they were camped in a small valley. Rock outcroppings offered shelter, under which they had decided to build temporary houses from stone, mud and straw. As three women worked on assembling a stone wall, they gossiped.

"Look, Frog Song and Silent Thunder work together again," said a young woman who was called White Feet, because of a strange mutation of skin pigment that spread across her feet and ankles.

"They are always together! Silent Thunder's daughter thinks that Frog Song is her father!" said her sister, a small and homely girl with a pleasing nature.

"It is a good match," said their mother. "They are both shamans. They will understand each others hearts. White Feet, the wall is tipping! Pay attention, daughter!"

"Silent Thunder is old enough to be his mother!" said White Feet as she began to dismantle and rebuild the section of wall her mother had pointed out.

"Yes. But, Frog Song is wise enough to be Silent Thunder's grandfather. It is a good match," she repeated.

Frog Song did not know what to do. He loved Silent Thunder. And because he could hear her thoughts, he knew she loved him too. But, mixed in with her love for him were many doubts. Silent Thunder felt she was too old and too plain to win Frog Song's heart. He did not know how to bridge those doubts, to make Silent Thunder understand that age meant nothing to him, that her beauty glowed from deep inside her, transforming her plainness into a prettiness that made her interesting to him in every way. As he carried large rocks back and forth to a place where Silent Thunder was building a ceremonial area, Sees Far entered the privacy of his mind and answered his questions.

Frog Song, tell her about your feelings! This will build the bridge to her heart. Stop thinking! Act! he said, and then chuckled as he disappeared.

Frog Song dropped the rock and bent to his knees to kneel beside Silent Thunder. He had grown to a height that was at least a foot taller than the tallest member of the tribe. He blushed under his deeply tanned skin as he stuttered out his feelings.

"Silent Thunder, I wish to - to - mate with you! Please do not be afraid!" he said quickly as she hid her face and turned away from him. Her black hair had come undone from its buns and fell in waves down her back. Frog Song stroked her thick hair.

"If you could see yourself as I do, as others do! I hear their thoughts. They see the beauty that has grown in you since you came to love me. Please, do not turn away! I love you, Silent Thunder."

She turned toward him, and he saw that tears ran down her cheeks as floods ran through the lands after a heavy rain. Her black eyes searched his and with trembling fingers, she touched his face.

"I am too old, Frog Song. If you were older, and I was younger, then perhaps...."

"No," he whispered. "You are wrong. You are young, here." He placed his hand tenderly on her chest. "I am old, here." He took her hand and placed it on the side of his head.

"You should have children someday. You are young enough that you can. I am too old," she said sadly.

"Then we won't have children. I would not want to lose you in birth as Sunflower died!" he said with passion. "Please, Silent Thunder, mate with me. *The people* approve. I have already heard their voices of consent."

Silent Thunder leaned toward him and, for the first time, kissed him gently on the lips.

Two weeks later, when the building of their temporary village was complete, *the people* gave two celebrations. One was for the gods, to give gratitude. The second was to celebrate Silent Thunder's and Frog Song's mating.

The journey of hope to their new home took four summers' cycles, instead of the two or three they had planned. In the autumn of the fourth year, they came to their new home. Water, wildlife and building materials were abundant within and about the canyon. One day at twilight, in the beginning of the season when thunder sleeps, the tribe expressed its gratitude with a celebration that lasted for four days, one day for every year of their journey. They, as a people, had seen much; they had experienced difficulties and wonders, lived through sometimes impossible conditions and they had come through this together.

When the celebration ended, the building began. Throughout the season and into the spring and summer, *the people* carved out homes and walkways throughout the canyon.

One morning, as Frog Song lifted a large tree limb from the canyon floor and began his ascent to the dwellings many yards above, a small tremor ran through the ground. This tremor, though small there in the canyon, had come from a huge release of the Earth God's anger in their old home lands, traversing the many miles over which *the people* had traveled. Frog Song understood this, and smiled as he dragged the limb back up to his people.

Years passed and *the people* prospered. They developed new dyes with which to paint their beautiful pottery. A new pattern of weaving was created, which displayed the symbol of the frog, in honor of Frog Song. Many new children ran and played along the pathways of the cliff dwellings. The raven and the hawk called out companionable greetings to the village below, and in the stillness of night, Silent Thunder passed away from old age.

Frog Song continued for years without her companionship, until he, too, had become old. One night, as he lay sleeping on his bed, Sees Far came to him one last time.

"You may leave now if you wish. Your work is done."

"I am ready."

"Do you remember how?"

"Yes. This time, when I follow you to your cave, I will not return to my body."

"Yes." The old man smiled.

Hand in hand, the tall half-breed shaman and the ancient man of *the people* walked toward the fire, which grew larger and brighter as they approached it. As Frog Song stepped into the fire, his heart opened to a peace that was vast and encompassing.

"the between ..."

Serra stepped onto the grass with her hand in Lohkan's. They smiled together as they crossed to the waterfall where the elder stood. She sank down onto the soft, thick moss and breathed in the enchanting sweetness of this place. Lohkan sat next to her and waited for the elder to speak.

How are you feeling, Serra? he signed.

"Peaceful."

Would you like to rest before we review the work you and Lohkan have just done?

"No. I feel fine. I have many questions."

The elder nodded and the waterfall parted. Again they watched, as two lifetimes, which were singularly connected, played before them. She watched in awe as Lohkan's guidance became clear and real: not an illusionary game, but a vitally important reality. When the viewing ended, she leaned back in the moss and felt the moist greenery compress under her hands. Lohkan spoke first.

"You never remembered your first lifetime with *the people* after you reincarnated the second time?"

"No. It's strange. I had my father's memories, as we did when we lived before, Lohkan, as you and me. I'm not sure who that is any more!" she said suddenly.

"I understand," Lohkan replied. "When we lived on our home planet, we had our parent's and grandparent's memories in our waking consciousness. Humans on this world most often don't experience this. The scientists of our world developed this trait in our people centuries before we were born into our first lifetime, to enhance our ability to learn and to increase our working knowledge."

"Yes. I can remember my grandmother's experience of learning a new language when she was a girl on the home planet as vividly as I can remember my own experiences. Although I had my father's memories of the space ship and other worlds in my life as Frog Song, I had no memories of *the between* or of my other lifetimes. Yet, I had an overwhelming feeling of familiarity. When I saw you as Sees Far, sometimes I would begin to remember something, but that something always seemed just out of reach."

She stopped, and remained quiet until the elder questioned them again.

What did you learn from these people?

"Community," Serra said. Lohkan explained this further.

"These people, *the people,* held community above everything else. Each person was allowed free choice and their own individualism; yet the whole of the community was most important over all."

What purpose did this serve? the elder asked. Serra answered this time.

"When many share a task or an experience, the whole is made greater by the contribution of the many individuals. The individual, in turn, is made greater by the experience of the whole.

"Through the communion these people shared, great advances could be made. Not technologically speaking, but spiritually and emotionally. They were able to cross a great distance, go through amazing adversity and rebuild a life, a home. As *the people* acted as one, we found great strength, support and peace together. Through that peace, spirituality prospered. These people had skills I have just begun to learn since I chose to experience these lives!"

Tonak smiled at Serra as she continued.

"Our race is technologically advanced. We are strong and have a solid spiritual core, yet we do not pursue this in the way that *the people* do. We have a lot to learn from them.

"They saw what we see, that life exists in every form. Rocks, trees, the earth, the sun, the wind, everything that surrounds them is filled with life and energy! Our people believe this, and have studied it extensively; yet we see it from a scientific view. I know the rock has life, but I immediately break that life down into chemicals, matter and energy currents. *The people* see beyond this. They see what holds all of that together!" she finished in an excited voice. Lohkan nodded his agreement.

"As Sees Far, I learned much in the same way that I learned when I was here, in *the between.* The sacredness of life was lived daily. That made every day, every moment, rich and unique. I never once remember thinking that a day or an event was boring. Everything in and around me was filled with richness. This life, of all the lives I have experienced thus far, was most like here, but more tangible or solid," he said for lack of better words.

The elder smiled, and then signed another question.

How did you each feel in the leadership positions you enacted?

"The responsibility was often exhausting," said Serra. "The rewards were numerous, but so were the demands."

"On the ship," Lohkan continued the subject, "We shared leadership. No one person was held responsible. We were all equally responsible. As *the people's* shaman, I was responsible for the soul of every one of our people. Sometimes the weight of that responsibility was burdensome and overwhelming. As I grew older, this became easier, though it never became easy."

"Yes. In my second lifetime as Frog Song," Serra began, "this became easier for me, because I had my father's memories. This gave me the knowledge that each person was really responsible for himself, which made leadership more enjoyable. I knew that everyone played a part and was responsible for his own role. I had simply to focus on my responsibilities, and this I did. Although my part was tiring at times, I was able to find comfort in this knowledge."

Tonak nodded and waved a hand across the waterfall. The water continued its fall over the rocks and landed happily in the pool. He signed again and spoke in their minds at the same time.

How did you feel, Lohkan, as you guided Frog Song, Serra, toward a union with Silent Thunder?

He sat reflectively for a moment. His pale blues eyes looked at Serra and a slow smile spread across his face as he answered.

"Whenever I observed Frog Song, I saw a man, a different entity than the one I know as Serra. Whenever I *felt* Frog Song, I felt Serra. I love Serra. She needed the companionship that Silent Thunder brought to her as Frog Song. In this dimension, this was easy to see, to understand and to give."

Serra swallowed a lump that had grown in her throat as he answered. She reached out her hand and traced his cheek with her fingers. *You are so beautiful,* she whispered in his mind. He heard her thoughts, and answered her by taking her hand to his lips and kissing it.

Rest now, Tonak said as he smiled at their display of affection.

Suddenly, the weariness that Lohkan had spoken of earlier

overcame them. They fell asleep on the moss, with their arms around each other in a tender embrace, and without a single worry awaiting them.

Chapter 12

"the between ..."

Serra woke up before Lohkan, and stretched luxuri-
ously where she lay on the thick green moss. As
Lohkan slept, she wondered where the elder disappeared to whenever they lost consciousness of this place. Tonak
appeared before her, and motioned silently for her to join him by
the trees.

She followed the small man to the forest, and sat down on
the forest floor beneath the canopy of green. Tonak signed to her
and simultaneously spoke in her mind.

You have questions. This was a statement rather than a
question.

"Yes. Why did our people, Lohkan's and mine, decide to
intervene with these tribesmen, *the people?* I know that throughout the history of this planet we have intervened at various times
with the humans who have lived here. Yet that intervention has
always had a defined and purposeful reasoning behind it. Why
did they begin contact with this group, and then assist these people in a time of need?

Tonak smiled as if he knew more than Serra had asked. He
signed his answer while he explained telepathically in greater
detail.

*Serra, do you remember what you learned: that all souls
touch one another?* As he asked this question, the image of thousands of crystal spheres touching and overlapping one another
appeared in her mind.

"Yes. I do. What does this have to do with our intervention?"

Everything! The elder made a wide and encompassing gesture. *Because your people come from a planet millions of miles
from earth, and are physically different from* the people, *does not*

212

mean that your lives don't touch one another. The truth is, you are each interdependently connected and part of the whole, The One.

As you have already realized, the people have a lot to share with and teach your people. You are not so far apart as it may seem. **When one soul asks for help, prays or sends a silent plea for assistance, the whole or The One hears that plea. When many souls pray as one, then The One hears a greater voice. Many voices are not more important than one. Simply, many voices are louder and, in many cases, more powerful.** The people asked for help in one loud and clear call. Lohkan, as Sees Far, was able to see into the future and know of upcoming obstacles. As the people's shaman, he led his people to call out in one clear voice. The One directed your people to them to help. Your people have the wisdom of thousands of years of contact and know how and when to help.

If your people had sent one of their crew members to earth to lead the people to safety, or if they had tried to physically trans-port the people to safety, the development of the people and their culture would have been dramatically altered, and, in many ways, not for the better. Do you understand this?

"Yes," she said, and nodded. Serra watched Tonak, as she sat below the trees, as if she were hypnotized. The lavender-colored sky was above them. And Tonak's large features were thoughtful and focused as he signed his answer.

The compromise that your people made was to genetically mix the talents of each race in one body. This body required a soul who had experiences with both races: you. This compromise had risks, but seemed the least altering course to the people. Also, the half-breed that Frog Song became brought the people's future generations to a trusting and peaceful relationship between your race and themselves.

Not all races on this planet are ready, nor will they be ready for centuries, for an open relationship. For some races, who have developed their identities upon the knowledge that they are the one and only center of the universe, the meeting of other beings - especially extraterrestrial beings - would be too threatening, as it would destroy their world as they know it. This section of this planet, on these western continents, has a more inclusive belief system and will develop sooner than other parts of this planet. The people have an expansive knowledge of the universe, and therefore will be some of the first brought to this awareness. Do you understand?

"Yes. I do," she answered again. "How did Lohkan, as 'Sees Far', guide me?"

Ah, this is something you are about to find out! the elder said.

As Tonak signed the words that she heard in her mind, the trees, meadow and waterfall vanished, and she found herself spinning around in the white light. As she tried to focus, she momentarily saw Lohkan, Tonak, Orryka and Quan Yin. The spinning became faster, they disappeared from view and she lost all consciousness.

The small island was inhabited by one people, with one faith, centered about one god, in the year 1501 A.D. Sailors from across the seas had brought this one faith to the people, along with disease, war and strange animals, large dogs that were ridden, and were able to pull wagons and carts. The native people, who were not killed by pestilence or war, killed the sailors; but they kept the large dogs for a while, until they traded them to distantly related tribe members who lived on the main lands. They had found the large dogs were unmanageable and dirty, so they happily traded the animals for tools, cloth, pots and seeds.

The faith that developed was a mixture of ancient tribal customs and the god referred to as "Christos" by the sailors. The natives had abandoned the pious teachings of the strange men, who wore heavy dark clothes, even in the warm, humid climate of the island, but had kept the decorative statues of the one god, Christos. His nailed body and crown of thorns appealed to the tribal chief. That this god, Christos, had come back from the dead, impressed the chief enough to make Christos their head god. As they were a practical people, the chief reasoned, why should they hold ceremonies to lesser gods, when they could go right to the top? Therefore, he decreed that all ceremonies should be held in tribute to the number one god, Christos. Pagan rituals and ceremonies continued, but now they were in honor of Christos.

Other customs of the sailors were quickly abolished as disease struck the island. Obviously these strange men, who traveled across the seas in large clumsy boats, did not understand what pleased their god or other men. The gods always sent disease when they were displeased. The stench of these men was enough to make even the lesser gods angry. Also, their foul body odors offended the island people. The women ran from the sailors, who had not bathed in months, and who put into their bodies rotten food. The chief wondered if the men on this big boat had been sent away by the women of their far-away lands. No woman with any sense would lie with such a foul-smelling man and purposely contaminate her body. He quickly forbade any woman to even serve these dirty men.

In the end, a war broke out when some of the sailors tried violently to take some of the tribe's women as mates. Before the strange men had come on their large boats, this form of violence had been nonexistent on the island. The chief saw no other course than to eliminate the cause of the disease and violence. War became the only alternative when the sailors and their strange medicine men in their long black robes refused to leave the island.

A dozen or so islanders lost their lives, but the sailors and their medicine men were all either killed in battle or sacrificed as offerings to the new god, Christos. The ship was stripped of any emblem of their new god, and all corpses were loaded onto the boat and the boat set a fire. As the burning vessel drifted out to sea, the chief held a ceremony to the new god Christos, thanking him for removing this evil presence from their island.

The little boy rinsed a large platter of shellfish in the brackish water of the lagoon, then carried the platter back to his mother. His mother, with her thick, wavy black hair, bent over the fire and stirred the stew in the solid metal pot.

Steam rose from the bubbling stew and curled the wispy hair around her face. The woman's breasts hung heavily above the pot and dripped sweat onto the coals of the fire. Orchid dropped the shellfish one by one, after examining them, into the stew. The little boy, Orchid's son, asked if he could stir the stew with the large wooden paddle. She gave her consent with an absent-minded nod of her head.

A baby cried in a straw hut several feet back from the fire, and Orchid went to nurse her youngest son. The little boy followed his mother and sat by her side as she fed his little brother.

The sound of waves crashing on the beach became a rhythmic pounding that caused the little boy to fall asleep as he lay against his mother's thigh. The woman got up carefully, so as not to wake her son, and put the baby back in its protective bedding, a carved-out log with a finely woven net over it to keep biting insects away. She then lifted her oldest son and placed him on a mat next to the baby's bed. They would sleep the afternoon away, until the sun set and their father returned. She went back to the fire to watch the stew and to work on a basket she wove.

As Orchid wove the basket, she stopped now and then to watch the ocean for any sign of her husband. The Gods were temperamental, and she always worried whenever her husband went out to fish.

A huge orange sun sat above the horizon when her husband's boat, along with two other boats, finally came into view. Her husband and his brothers dragged their catches onto the beach. After the men had divided the fish equally among themselves, each man dragged his share back to his hut and family. Orchid smiled in relief and ran to help her husband drag the heavy load of fish and nets up to their hut on the beach near the edge of the jungle.

The head god Christos had directed the lesser gods who claimed the seas to deliver an abundance of fish to her husband and his brothers. Orchid smiled as she began to clean and de-bone the fish. She added large chunks to the stew, and set several larger fish aside to smoke over the fire. Others Orchid placed in a large basket and, placing the basket on her head, she brought the fish to her husband's parents, who lived several yards away in another straw hut. She stayed to chat for only a few minutes, because she still had work to complete, and then walked back to the fire, where the stew bubbled happily.

That night, as Orchid slept next to her husband on the mats they used for bedding, she fell into a deep sleep. In this sleep, a strange dream occurred. An older man, who looked somewhat like her people, appeared to her. His features were different – larger and more pronounced. Also, his dress was different from her people's. He wore a white cloth wrapped around his waist, over which was tied a multicolored belt from which white feathers hung in a grouping. There was one red feather in the midst of this snowy plumage. In her dreamy state, the man seemed familiar, and she stared at him.

Who are you?

Don't you remember, Serra?

That's not my name.

The man smiled gently and ignored her remark.

Serra, it is time for you to begin your work. Your time here has come to an end. Are you ready to leave?

No. Go where? My name is Orchid, not what you call me.

Why do you not want to leave?

I have to take care of my children.

That is exactly why you must leave. Tomorrow someone shall come to you again and guide you.

He disappeared, and Orchid awoke to her youngest son's demands to eat. He was old enough to be weaned, but she had been reluctant to stop nursing. Their people had small families as a tradition. If Orchid was fortunate, she would give birth one more time. Most likely this would not occur. And, most likely, this would be the last child she nursed. The typical wife gave birth once or twice. Often a man took two or three wives, if he wanted a large family. No one in their tribe knew the reason for this phenomenon.

Orchid nursed her son happily and fell back to sleep. The next morning when she awoke, she forgot about her dream. Orchid checked the fish which had smoked over the coals all night. She decided to add some green brush to the hot coals to make more smoke. Then, she picked up her youngest son and headed to her mother-in-law's hut. The old woman took her youngest grandson joyously. That her son's wife had already given them two grandsons was one of the old woman's prides.

"Where is my oldest grandson?" the old woman asked toothlessly.

"Fishing with his father and uncles," Orchid answered. She turned and stared for a moment at the sea. The ocean was strangely calm, with a few black clouds hovering above its placid surface in the distance. She shuddered, but did not know why.

"I need to go into the jungle to dig up fresh roots. I shall gather enough for each of us. Will you watch this one for me? I could carry more without him."

"Ahh, of course! You need not ask this. Come to your grandmother, little one."

Orchid's little two-year-old boy, who had tottered back to her, now stumbled over to his grandmother again. Orchid smiled and tied cloth bags over her shoulders. A few minutes later, as she climbed through the dense jungle, she heard her son wail out his protest that his mother had left him.

Soon Orchid was preoccupied with a large patch of roots she had found approximately two miles from their homes. The patch was dense and healthy. She filled two of the cloth bags and had started on a third when the storm hit. The trees bent and shook under the onslaught of the hurricane. Strange. There had been little warning. When she had left that morning, no winds had blown. Only the dark clouds she had seen far across the seas had offered any hint of a storm. But, those clouds had been far away. She wondered what evil spirit had brought the squall upon them so quickly and this unexpectedly. She decided not to fill the third bag and quickly tied up the two full bags. As she bent to lift the heavy sacks, a large limb fell from the tree that towered over her and crushed her skull.

Serra floated in the white light for a moment before she realized what had happened. Orryka floated next to her. As her mind cleared, he came sharply into view.

"Are you ready?" he asked as he smiled.

"For what?" she asked, still confused. Just a moment ago she had gathered roots in a jungle.

"It is time for you to guide Lohkan. You wanted to understand this process. We must go!"

The white fog swirled away, and Serra found herself above the stormy ocean. Orryka floated next to her. Below them, two of the long dugout canoes that the islanders used were tossing back and forth in the choppy waters. She wanted to look more closely, and moved directly above the boats. She recognized Orchid's son and husband in one boat. In the other were two of her brothers-in-law. Both boats threatened to capsize as the waves became more restless and violent.

"What can we do? How can I help them?" She looked tenderly at the little boy.

"If they ask for help, we may help them," Orryka said. As if the men in the boats had heard Orryka, they began an appeasing chant to the sea gods. Above their chants Serra suddenly heard Orchid's son's voice calling loudly. He did not use words. His soul called for help.

Mommy! I'm afraid! Please help me!

Her heart felt as if it were being torn open, and she looked to Orryka for help. Orryka hastily gave her instructions.

"They are near the beach, but cannot see it. They are afraid to pass the reefs, because if they do not time this exactly right, the waves will crush them upon the coral. If they can get through the reefs, they will reach the beach safely. Lohkan must hear or see you," he said, and pointed to the little boy. "You must not think of yourself as Serra right now. Imagine yourself as his mother. Then send this image, with whatever message you wish to give him"

"Can I lead them back to the beach?" Serra asked.

"Yes. Follow me."

Quickly Serra visualized herself as the little boy's mother.

She imagined the full body of a nursing woman. She imagined long black hair and almond-shaped eyes. She felt herself reaching out to the little boy and called his name earnestly. He heard.

Mommy?

Here! I am here! Follow me, and I shall lead you to the shore. Hurry! Tell your father!

The little boy quickly convinced his father, who was desperate for guidance. As Serra followed Orryka, she repeatedly sent her image to the little boy and told him to follow her. Slowly, with painstaking effort, the men paddled toward the spot where the little boy pointed. A half hour later, the boats pushed up onto the sandy beach. The little boy jumped from the canoe and ran up the beach to his grandmother's hut as he followed the vision of Orchid. His father and uncles followed with confusion masking their tired faces. When Serra arrived at the hut, her youngest son also saw the vision of his mother. As Serra disappeared the youngest son cried out for the second time that day.

"Mommy! Don't leave!"

"the between ..."

Serra had sat by the waterfall for what seemed like just a few minutes when Lohkan joined her. She looked up in surprise. Lohkan's long blond hair fell forward and for a moment covered his clear eyes and attractive face as he looked down at her. He pushed his hair aside and reached down with large, strong hands to lift Serra to her feet. As she stood, she questioned him.

"What are you doing here? You returned safely to the beach. I saw...."

Serra stopped because she was perplexed by this turn in events. She touched Lohkan's cheek with her hand. Her blue-gray eyes and clean features now showed the confusion she felt. A furrowed brow and slightly turned down mouth marked astonishment on her pretty face.

"A year has passed since we were lost in the storm. My little brother and I died due to a fever, which was brought to the island by another boat of conquerors."

"Time here is immeasurable," she said in amazement. Tonak materialized between them. He nodded at them and began to sign.

You were not sent to save Lohkan, Serra. You and Lohkan were there to guide those boats to shore. Your husband will be needed over these next several years. He eventually will become chief. During the upcoming passage, he will prevent the people of this island from being slaughtered into extinction. Your husband will take another mate. Through this woman, another son will be born. This son eventually will bring peace to the islanders, as they learn to integrate with the sailors who will settle this coastline.

That son will have a great, great grandson, who will represent the natives in an important political act that will give them their freedom. Do you see how one life touches another? The connection is unending!

She nodded yes, and then looked at Lohkan. "How did I appear to you? Did you see me as your mother?"

"Yes! You did great for your first try! When I was first sending images of Sees Far to you, when you were Frog's Song, I kept blending my own identity into the imaging. I tried several times before I got through to you that first time."

"Orryka helped me," Serra said. "I could feel his mind next to mine, as if he held me up through my attempt. I'd like to try this again sometime."

You will, each of you, work extensively in this manner during another passage of time, the elder said quietly in their minds. He then continued.

Rest. In a moment you will continue on to your next choice in lessons. I shall return when it is time for you to go.

As he vanished, Serra again wondered to where he disappeared.

Chapter 13

"the between ..."

*L*ohkan and Serra sat by the waterfall and talked about the lives they had just led. The warm tropical climate of those lives, with a culture that was based upon the oceans that surrounded the island on which they had lived, reminded them of their homeland. Their race lived on islands, also, and Lohkan felt a sudden nostalgia for that life.

"We shall never have that life again."

"No. Not as we have known it. I can see now how unique each lifetime is and that the gifts and problems of the individual lifetime are something to be cherished and experienced fully, because they will never be repeated in the same way. Perhaps, when our work is done, we could go back to our home planet and reincarnate there. Our experiences would be new, but we could bring what we have learned to those experiences." Serra said. She, too, felt a strong desire to experience their home world in a physical state once more. Although they were contented and peaceful in the dimension of *the between,* their home world had been a wondrous place. She had not known how much so until they had begun this journey.

A white light flared momentarily. In its wake stood Tonak. He smiled benevolently.

Do you have any questions before you go? Tonak asked.

"Yes," said Serra. "Will we ever return to our home world in a physical form?"

That depends on what you choose, he answered simply.

"What we choose?" mimicked Lohkan.

Yes. You choose each lifetime, every experience. If you choose to, you may go back to your home planet.

Lohkan looked into Serra's eyes and took her hands in his

while he spoke quietly inside her mind.

Promise me, Serra! Promise we'll go back together some-day.

I promise, she answered. And as she said these words, *the between* vanished and they felt themselves moving swiftly through the white light again.

What began as a white lie turned into a misdeed of such size and strength that even the person with the most foresight in the township would not have foreseen its occurrence. That person was Goody Bishop, who, as her name dictated, was married to the reverend of "The First Church" of pilgrims to the new world. Goody Bishop had legendary foresight that was mixed, blessedly so, with legendary nosiness. Whether she ever saw the two as separate qualities was doubtful. She saw her place in the world, under God's care, as a watchdog of wavering souls or as a guardian of the weak and wayward person. She was an interfering matriarch, and deeply proud of these attributes.

Due to Goody Bishop's virtuous intentions, Mistress Lydia Butterfield and Mister John Carpenter were married. Goody Bishop had introduced Lydia and John at a Sunday social, after lengthy and careful observation of all the eligible bachelors in the township. She had been deeply bothered by Lydia's single status. The closing of any possible open avenues, which the devil might walk through and work upon, kept the Goody awake late into the night. For everyone knew that a single woman was the devil's playground. Especially one as attractive as Lydia Butterfield.

Lydia's availability had been due to illnesses that had plagued the township shortly after the immigrants had settled there. Her fiance, an intelligent and pious man, had died six weeks after he had sent a message to Lydia in England, asking her to join him. Lydia had arrived to no home, no fiance, no money and no family. She had left her brothers and sisters back in Kent. Her parents had been quite old. Lydia was their youngest child, and they had most likely died before she set foot on the new soil of America. Her would-be husband had foolish-ly left his home claim and small wooden house to the new church. No woman was allowed ownership in her own name. A woman had to marry into ownership through her husband, which, as Lydia saw, she did not have. Goody Bishop had been determined to rectify this situation before Lydia got into trouble. Since Lydia was beautiful, Goody Bishop had reasoned that she should have an equally handsome husband. Therefore, John Carpenter had been the obvious choice.

Goody Bishop and the Reverend, her husband, did not wish to give up this extra property which had been bequeathed to the church. In this new world, many of the old laws were being rewritten. Goody Bishop had wondered if the kind-hearted townspeople might decide to instate a new law, which might give Lydia her dead fiance's property. Since the Goody enjoyed power, which involved ownership of land, she was determined to hold onto the newly acquired five hundred acre parcel left to the church. This pleasing motivation, of keeping power and land, as well as saving another soul, had pushed Goody Bishop to work harder than she ever had. Within a month after Lydia and John had met, they had been wed before the townspeople and under the laws of The New Church of New England.

The white lie was first birthed by John Carpenter, on a blustery day in late October. The brilliant colors of autumn in this new world had passed. The leaves had turned from scarlet and orange to rusty brown and dull gold. The few leaves that still clung to the tree limbs were fragile and dry. On this day the wind blew with a force that caused the remaining leaves to join their brethren on the ground.

John was in his workshop, carving a mantelpiece for the church. The wind blew in through the door of his shop and blew his long, curly, brown hair in circles around his head. A thick brown beard and mustache covered most of his lower face and hid his lips and their expressions of his moods. When John did smile, which was not often, handsome white teeth shone through his beard and increased his rugged beauty. His steel-colored eyes, which were cool in their gaze, watched as shapes of oak leaves took shape from the grainy surface of the oak. He leaned back for a moment and stretched the strong muscles of his back.

The workshop, which was a large drafty room placed against one end of the house, close to the barn, had a view of the road. The dirt road which passed by John's and Lydia's house was the main road that led through town and out toward another township, some ten miles away. The length of road that wound past their house was clear and treeless. Eventually, the road traveled through a thick, dark forest of hardwood trees and thick bramble, and was shadowed from all light. Neither the sun, the moon nor the stars could penetrate this darkness. On this clear stretch of road in front of his house, John was able to observe from his workshop the seed of his lie.

A small band of Native American Indians passed on their way to town. Two of the men, dressed in leather and furs, carried a travois behind them. Loaded on the v-shaped structure were piles of tanned furs. John watched the strangely attired natives, with their long dark hair and elaborately decorated clothing. Feathers hung in their hair and throughout their clothes. One of the men had shaved his head, except for a topknot that was wound with leather strips. Another man had a strange black symbol painted on his face and right arm. John shuddered as he watched the band of traders pass. These Native Americans were a barbaric and godless group of people. It was no wonder that God had sent the British to America to develop this vast wasteland. These natives were too primitive to realize what they had. All around them was rich soil, ample game and enough lumber to build ships, houses and furniture for all of Europe. Obviously, the Indians were stupid. More obviously, God wanted good men to settle these lands. The Indians unobtrusively went on their way to town.

Two days later, Lydia was in the general store shopping for muslin for curtains and a new pot, when by chance she overheard two men talking. As she peered from behind the tall shelf of pots and pans, where she was hidden from view, the lamplight floated across her face and accented the gold highlights of her hair and turned her hazel eyes a vivid green. Even the dull brown of her woolen dress looked rich in this light. Quickly, Lydia ducked back as one of the men turned toward her. The man was too slow, and missed a view of her young and comely countenance. Pushing the goods on the shelf to the side, she peeped through a crack at the men as they continued to talk.

One, a tall, grim-looking man with long yellow teeth, was purchasing gunpowder, while another younger and plainer man chewed on a piece of candy, waiting to do the same. They stood by the counter, which was piled high with dry goods. Teas, gunpowder, flour, molasses, material and jars of expensive candies were displayed.

"Did ye hear about Miss Constant? Mistress and Master Blackthorn's daughter?" the grim man asked.

"No."

"Some man has taken her virtue as well as her soul."

"What say ye? Is this true?" the young man asked in disbelief.

"So my wife tells me. She was at the Bishops', bringing the Goody's new dress to her, when Master Blackthorn arrived and asked to speak to the Bishop."

Lydia remembered where she had seen this grim man. He was the husband of the town seamstress. This stern, unattractive-looking man continued with his wife's story.

"The bishop's voice was loud enough for my wife to hear as she fitted Goody Bishop." The seamstress' husband discreetly explained about his wife's eavesdropping. "The Bishop thinks that Miss Constant's soul may yet be saved if the man, who seduced and spoiled this young girl, marries her."

The young man nodded and spoke with a quiet passion. "Constant is a tempting young flower. Who could blame the man who picked her? However, she ought to be whipped for such wanton behavior." The seamstress' husband agreed, and said so out loud.

"Aye. We are not the only ones to think thusly. The bishop recommended a stout whipping, and then said to send the girl directly to him."

"Why does not Master Blackthorn have the young man marry his daughter, before anyone else hears of her evil ways?"

"That is just what the good Reverend recommended, but the girl has lost her senses. She refuses to tell who the man is."

"No! Is she with...?"

An involuntary gasp escaped from Lydia, and she quickly covered her mouth with both hands. She ducked farther behind the shelf to better hide herself. But, when the conversation continued without hesitation, Lydia quickly resumed her place by the crack in the shelf

"Is she with child? No!" the seamstress' husband answered.

"How did her parents learn of her ... indiscretion?"

"Aye, now, this is a tale. When the blacksmith suggested to the girl's father that he wished to marry Miss Constant, she refused. There are not many eligible men, as ye know. This would have been an ideal chance for the girl. When her parents pressed the marriage, the girl defied them, and said that she loved another."

"Who is the fellow?"

"Nobody knows, except, of course, the girl."

The storekeeper returned at that moment, and quickly filled both men's orders. After Lydia paid for the muslin and new pot, she walked through the town on the main road that led to her home. She wondered with whom Miss Constant had fallen in love.

Many days passed, and Lydia had forgotten the gossip about Miss Constant. She was bent over a large wooden wash tub in front of their rough planked house, when their neighbor to the east passed by. She was a round, pale woman, with ash blond hair and washed-out blue eyes. Her husband was a farmer, and had planted a large crop of oats on his one-hundred-acre plot. Lydia waved to the woman. Like Lydia and John, these neighbors were newly wed and still childless.

"Mercy! Have ye finished thy new frock?"

Mercy had come by many afternoons to chat while she worked on a new winter dress. Lydia still saw her covered with the lush, gray, tweed fabric, piled around and on top of her. Mercy and her husband were too poor to afford the seamstress' fine work.

"Aye. I shall be warm as well as comfortable. Thank ye for the lace for my new petticoat."

"I'm pleased that ye like it. Do ye have time for tea?"

Mercy accepted, and then helped Lydia wring out the cumbersome, wet cloth. After they had draped it over a heavy line of rope which hung between a tree and the porch, they went indoors for tea. While Lydia set out a plate of bread and butter and prepared the tea, Mercy gossiped.

"Have ye heard about Miss Constant?"

"Aye," Lydia admitted reluctantly; she did not truly desire to gossip.

"Then ye know she was raped?"

"What? No. I had not heard of this."

"I am surprised, since thy husband John discovered the culprit."

Lydia sat down with a thud.

"No?"

"Ye really don't know, do ye?" Mercy patted her hand. "John was probably trying to protect ye. Here, let me pour the tea. Are ye all right? Perhaps ye might lie down."

"No. Really I am quite all right. Please, Mercy. Tell me what has happened?"

"Miss Constant has been, well her womanhood has been opened. Ye do understand?"

"Yes. Go on...."

"She cannot remember who did this. She says she could not see the face of the man. Luckily, your husband saw a group of Indians pass, about ten days ago, when the deed happened."

226

Lydia bit into a piece of bread without tasting it. Her small nose was wrinkled with concentration. She finally sipped her tea, which was growing lukewarm as she ignored it, and then asked Mercy a question.

"How can anyone know if the deed was done by these men?"

"Who else would do this? Ye are not suggesting that one of our town's men would violate Miss Constant?" Mercy said with disgust.

"No. I thought ye said Miss Constant remembered but 'one' man?"

"Aye, she does. John suggested that one of the Indians committed this act. Ye really are quite lucky to have a clever husband, Lydia."

"Where is this man? How will Miss Constant recognize the right one, in order to convict him?"

"The barbarians are away. They traded their goods. One took Constant's virtue, and now they are gone."

Lydia's head swam. Last week she had heard two men discussing this same story, but from an importantly different viewpoint. She continued to question Mercy.

"What will become of Miss Constant?"

"The Bishop says that her soul will be prayed for, and that she may be saved if she marries quickly. She will wed the blacksmith next month, before the winter feast." Mercy lowered her voice and looked around the empty room. "I heard that Miss Constant's father *and* the Bishop beat her to cleanse her soul. The town council is thinking of banning all trades with the natives. I think this a wise and Christian path. Who can trust these barbarians? I don't feel safe when I see them on our roads."

Lydia closed her mouth for fear that she would insult her neighbor. Making enemies of people they were closely dependent upon was unwise. The colonies were newly staked out, and unknown. The people who immigrated together and built up the new towns needed each other in ways that the people in the mother countries could not know. Without Mercy's companionship, the past winter would have been unbearable. Also, John and Mercy's husband cut firewood together, and shared numerous other tasks. Sharing work made the hard physical labor easier. Although Lydia now questioned her neighbor's story, she would not openly disagree and chance destroying their necessary bond. They finished the tea quietly and discussed the new curtains Lydia was making.

That night, when John returned from a job building an

addition onto the storekeeper's house, Lydia questioned him. They had finished supper and sat by the fireplace in the kitchen. Lydia sewed fine, tiny finishing stitches to the hems on one of the curtains while John whittled a new handle for his axe.

"Mercy visited today," she began.

"How is she?"

"Quite well. She told me about Constant Blackthorn and her unfortunate tragedy."

"That is inappropriate tea conversation, don't ye think, Liddy?"

"Well, ye can't blame her for telling me. News like this is hard to keep at bay. She told me that ye have accused some Indians."

"Really Liddy! Ye speak foolishly. This is not an appropriate conversation anytime. Especially for a woman!"

"I should think there would be no one more advisable to speak on the subject of rape than a woman!" she answered hotly. Lydia's pretty face turned red with anger.

"Lydia! Ye try a man's patience! I pointed out the obvious, that the heathens might be involved, since they were in our area. Now speak no more of this subject!" He stood and picked up his leather apron and shook the shavings into the fire. He scowled at his wife and then stormed out the door.

Lydia watched John as he angrily left their home. With his curly brown hair and gray eyes, he was handsome man. But, he was decidedly less attractive in this moment and others, whenever he was in one of his his dark moods. John was not a patient man, but he was a good provider. In fact, he was gone most every day for a good part of the day, at one job or another. A growing town such as theirs needed a good carpenter and builder. John seemed to be in constant demand. Each morning he worked for a few hours on their homestead before leaving, so Lydia could not complain that he did not keep up with his chores. Lydia wondered, as she had many times, if his impatient and sometimes surly disposition was due to the long hours he worked. She put aside her sewing and banked the fire so that some coals would be ready in the morning to start the fire anew. When John came in, he ignored her and went to their bedroom. A few minutes later, she shyly joined him.

Winter had blown over their homestead for almost three months when Lydia awoke one morning feeling ill. As she tried to move, the room swam around her, and she fell back onto the tick mattress in a sweaty collapse. She tried to call to John, but her throat ached with a fiery soreness that made speech impossible. An hour later, John found her in a delirious state, still in bed.

He ran through the soft, deep snow as fast as he could to get Mercy, and carried the short woman most of the way back to the house. When Mercy arrived, Lydia was soaked in a feverish sweat. She seemed not to know where or who she was. As Lydia moaned on in her confused state, Mercy sent John to town to get a physician. She mopped Lydia's damp forehead with a cold cloth, in an attempt to soothe her sick friend.

"Liddy, shh. Ye will be well again. John has gone to fetch the physician."

"Where is Lohkan? I haven't found him yet. He was to meet me here."

"Shh. Liddy, ye are ill. Ye do not know what ye say."

"I want to go home. Where is Lohkan? We were making plans to go back to our home. I miss the island. Have you seen Yerraba? I miss her."

"Liddy, hush. Ye are sick, dear. The physician will be here soon."

"Physician? I don't want a physician. I want to find Lohkan."

Their conversation continued on in this way until Lydia fell asleep. While she slept, Mercy picked up the house, built up the fires and began the midday meal. As she finished putting a tray of biscuits into the oven, the door blew open with a light swirling of snow, and John and the physician entered.

John directed the physician toward the bedroom before he had time to take off his coat. As the two men entered the bedroom, followed by Mercy, Lydia started her incoherent ravings again. She thrashed about in her sleep as she called out.

"Lohkan! Where are you?" Suddenly Lydia switched to another language, which was unrecognizable and definitely not English. Mercy whispered.

"She's been like this since ye left, John. I believe it's the fever. She has been calling out that name over and over. Do ye think it could be one of her family? I did not know that Lydia's family was not of English blood."

John stared at his wife in a confused silence as the doctor began his examination. As the doctor looked back up at him with a questioning expression, he answered.

"Lydia told me she was from Kent. Maybe this person is from another branch of her family. Aye, a cousin. Might ye recognize the language she is speaking, Dr. Kayne?" John asked.

The physician turned to Lydia and took her hand; he patiently examined her face, her skin and her mouth. As he began to pull back her eyelid to examine her eyes, she awakened. She looked into his eyes for a long quiet moment, and then spoke with a sigh.

"There you are. I've been looking for you, Lohkan. Can we go home soon? I'm tired, very tired. It's been so cold here." Then she switched to the foreign language that none of them recognized, except for the doctor. As he had held the sick woman's hand and listened to her speak, within a split second a series of images had fled across his eyes.

Tall men and women, dressed in strange clothes that were somehow familiar, and yet not. Strange images of a watery world with a purple-hued sky, swam before him. The visions departed as quickly as they had come. As he listened to this delirious woman mumble in her foreign tongue, something about her and her strange language felt painfully familiar to him. For a moment he forgot why he had come, and he stared blankly toward the wall. John interrupted the man, as he mistook the physician's quiet for bad news.

"Is my mistress going to our Lord?"

"Excuse me. No, do not give up on her yet! Please, Mistress Mercy, could ye be so kind as to bring me a pot of boiling water, and another of snow."

Mercy ran from the room. John paced nervously until Dr. Kayne suggested he continue with his chores. There was nothing he could do then and there. John left in an agitated state, while the doctor, with Mercy's help, began to bring Lydia's fever down by washing her entire body with the icy snow. As the snow melted, Mercy ran out to get more to replace it. With the boiled water the doctor made a dark infusion that filled the bedroom with a clear woody scent. After a few hours had passed, he suggested that Mercy rest. His suggestion that Mercy leave Lydia alone with him would not have been acceptable if he weren't a physician. Mercy hesitated for only a moment before she went to the kitchen to sit by the fire and have a well-earned cup of tea.

Dr. Kayne sat next to Lydia and slowly began to drip the heady infusion into her mouth, which Lydia swallowed automatically. He was a tall, thin and lanky man, and this height forced him to bend awkwardly as he cared for her. His cheekbones seemed to poke out of his face at odd angles. Dr. Kayne's eyes, which were large and very expressive, were a clear and vivid blue. Dense, curly black hair made him look foreign, though he was Welsh. No one, not even the kindest of people, would have thought him handsome. Yet his manner was gentle. And he displayed this as he tenderly wiped drips from Lydia's lips and chin. He continued to ease the healing potion into Lydia's feverish body as John returned to check on Lydia's progress for a brief moment, and then was gone again. When the doctor felt that he was finally and truly alone with Lydia, he spoke to her in a low voice.

"Mistress, I do not know who ye are, but I feel certain we have met somewhere. I feel foolish speaking this out loud, and I would not if I were not sure that ye would not remember my words.

"Ye are the most beautiful woman I have ever seen. I do not know why, but I love ye. I love ye, a stranger. God, help my soul for these strange yearnings. I promise I shall not hurt ye in any way. If God is willing, I shall deliver ye from the clutches of this illness. Don't die, sweet woman. I cannot bear the thought of never looking into thy eyes again...." His voice had fallen into a hoarse whisper. He kissed the sick woman's hand lightly, and once again her eyes flew open.

"Lohkan, don't be sad. I promise, I'll never leave you. I love you." With those stunning words, she fell back asleep.

Lydia stood in a circle of lady's slippers in a small patch of sunshine in the forest. John had left an hour before to go to a building site where he currently worked. She sat down on the damp forest floor, aware that she was probably staining her muslin dress. Spring this year had been magnificent. The countryside had been thick with fruit blossoms and wildflowers. Since early spring Lydia had been picking flowers each day, as part of her recuperative therapies. Dr. Kayne had recommended a daily walk through the forests surrounding her house, as a way to rebuild her strength after her winter illness. Lydia had become addicted to her morning walks, and had claimed their necessity long after she had recovered.

Sunshine poured down upon her and filled her with its warmth. Her golden hair was highlighted beautifully by the sunlight, and as she turned her comely face to catch the sun's rays, her face glowed with an inner and outer radiance.

Lydia shut her eyes and drank in the peace and well being she found in the forest. Birds called to each other in non-threatening voices, because they had become accustomed to Lydia's quiet presence. Behind closed eyes, her thoughts wandered to happy moments. Immediately, the physician's homely face arose in her mind.

The doctor and she had become good friends over the period of her long recovery, as close as a man and woman could be in their world of strict and limited social codes between opposite sexes. He was a gentle and gracious man who listened patiently to her thoughts and ideas. He never ridiculed her or told her that her words were inappropriate for a woman. Instead, he encouraged her desire to learn, and even loaned her a few of his precious books.

John had not noticed the physician's lingering visits, because he considered the man a dedicated practitioner. Also, he was relieved that he did not have to care for Lydia himself or ask for a neighbor's valuable time. Twice a week Dr. Kayne walked the four miles to their home and visited with Lydia for two hours. He started each visit with a brief examination of Lydia's weakened condition. Eventually, as she grew healthier, he bypassed the exam, and came simply to see her. That John did not notice this change was not due to a lack of observation, but more to a lack of caring and an insensitivity to his wife's needs. He was gone so much that he didn't see or care about the friendship that developed.

After a time, the doctor could not come more than once every two weeks without causing a scandal. That the people of the town had not recognized the attraction between the two was due to a simple lack of imagination. No one, not even Goody Bishop, would have imagined an attraction between Dr. Kayne's homely countenance and Lydia's beautiful one. Lydia filled the time between his visits with her walks and chores.

She thought of Dr. Kayne's kind smile, which caused her to glow with an inner warmth that she had come to cherish. Here, in this circle of flowers, Lydia allowed her thoughts to move into dreams, fantasies. In this circle she dreamed of marrying Dr. Kayne. She envisioned the children they would have together and the long hours of companionable family life. She dreamed of sometimes helping him with his medical cases, of studying medicine and learning from the doctor ... and of breaching that impossible avenue of the physical. Lydia dreamed of touching the doctor as he had touched her. He had had to know her body, nakedly, wholly, in his treatment of her illness. She wanted to know him as intimately. When Lydia stood to leave the circle, she left feeling replenished and satisfied. Her fantasies were enough for her. When she left the circle, the fantasies stayed secretly and securely there.

And even though she picked flowers often, as they grew in

abundance in the forest, she never cut any from this perfect circle. The flowers had come to remind Lydia of Dr. Kayne. Somehow, this circle represented her relationship to him: something perfect that must never be picked, without causing a disruption in its completion, its perfection.

That day, as Lydia walked back to the house, she felt a strong sensation of having been watched. When she turned to see who had intruded into her solitude in the forest, she saw no other person. She shook the feeling away and went back to her home.

For the next week Lydia continued her walks. Each time the feeling of being watched was there. She felt no threat, and so convinced herself that she was safe. She could not bear to give up these quiet, healing times. Even on the Sabbath, she broke God's laws and walked to the circle just before sunset, while John was distracted with tending the livestock and settling their homestead before dark. He never seemed to notice or care that she was gone for approximately a half hour. The circle of flowers had become Lydia's church, and on this day more than the other six, she felt a strong need to sit amidst their quiet splendor.

On this particular Sunday, she discovered who watched her.

As she stood and turned to leave the circle, an Indian stood before her. His long black hair was pulled back from the sides of his face with leather ties. Wrapped in these ties were feathers that hung down on either side of his face. The feathers were black like ink. Across his cheekbones was black paint in straight narrow lines. White dots had been painted just above the top line, below his eyes. He wore leather from shoulders to feet. The garments were loose fitting, supple and looked to be quite comfortable. More black feathers were sewn down the arms, between the leather fringe. Across one shoulder was a bow. On his back was a quiver of arrows. Around his waist was a leather belt where a sheathed knife hung. His tall figure was dignified and imposing.

For the first time, Lydia wondered if Constant's story of rape had been true. She began to tremble, but stood straight and tried desperately not to show her fear. As she stood there, the silent native approached her slowly. When he came to the edge of the circle of flowers, he began to speak in a guttural language. While he spoke, he signed and pointed toward the flowers. Something about his signed language was familiar to Lydia, and for the moment she forgot to be afraid. She seemed to understand his signed messages, and knew that he spoke about the sacredness of the circle. Suddenly he stopped and reached inside his shirt. He took out a single white and brown feather and held it out to her. She shook as she accepted his gift. Without another sound or sign, he turned and left her alone.

When she returned home, John was not there. She did not stop to wonder about where he had gone, but instead sunk to her knees to thank the Lord that he was not there to see her late return. She hurriedly prepared a cold supper and set the table. John returned a half hour after sunset and gave no explanation of where he had been.

Lydia could hardly wait for Dr. Kayne's visit that Wednesday, when she could tell him about her experience with the Indian. Soon she saw Dr. Kayne's lanky and clumsy gait coming down the road. The pleasure he received when he saw Lydia waiting for him on the porch was openly reflected in his eyes. The slender and graceful form of her body in its muslin dress looked out of place with her rustic house standing plainly behind her. She looked as if she belonged more at court or in another place where graceful ladies resided. Lydia was unaware of this or her effect upon the doctor. Questions about the natives and her story were foremost in her mind. Quickly, Lydia invited him in for tea. As the tea brewed and was poured, she told him in an excited voice the story of meeting the Indian. Dr. Kayne questioned her in his quiet and gentle way. Only his blue eyes continued to give any hint of excitement for Lydia and her story.

"Ye are sure about the markings, Mistress Lydia?"

"Yes, quite."

"I have traveled through Europe and to Asia in my study of medicine. I have met many races in those travels. I have also visited amongst the natives of these forests. While they are different from any race I have encountered, they are an intelligent, tolerant and mysteriously spiritual people. The man ye describe is known as 'Blackbird.' He is a scout for a tribe north of here. Do ye have the feather he gave ye?"

"Yes. I hid it in my sewing box." Lydia quickly stooped to a square box with a lid and opened it. She dug out the feather from beneath her yarns and needles, and held it out to the doctor. He surprised her by refusing to touch it.

"No, Mistress Lydia. Put it back. I only wanted to see the type of feather this man gave ye." He waited for Lydia to sit before he continued. "He has given ye a very powerful gift. The feather ye showed me is a hawk's feather and is sacred to his people."

"What does this mean?"

"I believe he was honoring ye. Ye said that he watched

ye for a week?"

"Yes. Well, I believe he did," Lydia said, unsure of herself.

"He must have found ye worthy in some way that is important to his people. The feather is a great honor. Keep it hidden and tell no one of this. I'm afraid our Christian brethren would not understand. I shall try to travel to his tribe in a few weeks to find an answer for ye."

They finished their tea in a perplexed silence. For the first time Lydia thought of something other than the doctor's warm smile as she sat with him.

Almost two weeks later, Lydia heard the tragic news. The news of the hanging was once again brought to her by her neighbor Mercy. An Indian had been captured and hung for the rape of Mistress Constant. When and how a trial had been held, Lydia had not heard. She and John lived four miles out from town, and she often did not visit town for a few weeks at a time. She worried in an almost feverish state that Blackbird was the one who had been hung. Mercy explained that John had been at the hanging, and had told her husband. That John had again kept important news from Lydia was no surprise. Lydia awaited the doctor's visit with more anticipation than normal. Two days later, he arrived to find Lydia in a state of nervous exhaustion.

"Doctor Kayne, please tell me, was it Blackbird who was hung?"

He immediately understood her fears and held her hand tightly.

"Yes. I am afraid it was. One of our courageous town men spotted him 'lurking' in the forests." His voice was tight with sarcasm and sorrow. "Mistress Constant identified him as the rapist. He was hung last week. I'm sorry, dear Lydia." He lapsed into informal references. "I can see that ye do not believe he was guilty. Nor do I. Blackbird was known amongst his people for his tolerance, strength and clear mind. Rape is considered a sign of great weakness amongst the local tribes. He would not have raped any woman, especially a white woman. White women are seen as ghosts and are considered ugly to the natives. I am sorry, dear Lydia, to be the one to tell ye this sad news of his demise."

Suddenly Lydia's nervousness expressed itself through the sorrow she now felt. She began to sob uncontrollably. Before he thought of what he did, Dr. Kayne put his arms gently around her, and kissed her tear-streaked face. He continued to hold her and whispered his sorrow to her. Then, as suddenly as they had started, Lydia's tears stopped. She looked up into his kind face and realized how they now stood together. She backed up quickly and tripped against a chair leg. He reached to steady her, and then thought better of it. Quickly, he apologized.

"Mistress Lydia, please accept my sincere apology for my indiscretion. I – I don't know what to say. Please forgive me." He stammered as he blushed brilliantly red. She sought to reassure him in her own awkwardness.

"No. Ye did nothing wrong. Ye were comforting a friend. I am ashamed only of my behavior. A grown woman crying as a child might. Please forgive me."

"Perhaps I should leave."

"No," she said a little too forcefully, and then blushed. "Please stay. I need to understand what this shall mean for Blackbird's tribe and our township."

Dr. Kayne sat down in his chair again and sipped on the lukewarm tea. He hesitated before he spoke.

"Blackbird's people are a gentle people, unless they need not to be." He hesitated, and then continued, "They will see this as a time to *not* be gentle."

"What will they do?" Lydia felt as if she could not breathe.

"They will have to settle this somehow, by their people's customs. I am less familiar with this tribe than some others. My guess is that a life will be taken from our village, in exchange for the one that we took."

"Whose?"

"I don't know."

Lydia worried about the doctor's explanation for days, until finally she decided that worrying would not help. She decided to begin a new summer dress to distract herself, as her light blue muslin was well worn. She decided impulsively one morning to walk to town to buy the material. John had left a half hour before, or she would have asked to walk with him. She smiled at the beautiful blue sky and warm breezes of the early summer season. Soon the humid heat would spill across the land, and these mild days would be gone. She hummed to herself as she walked, and then fell silent as she listened to the song birds sing.

A beautiful song played out loudly to her left, and Lydia stopped to listen. As the bird finished its song, Lydia heard another sound coming from the forest. She crept toward the sound, unsure of what she heard. As she neared the place from where the sound emitted, she recognized that which she heard. Below her in the forest someone coupled. She blushed as she realized how clumsily she had intruded upon the hidden lovers. As she turned to leave, the man spoke, and she froze as she recognized the voice.

She moved forward soundlessly through the brush and trees, as if an invisible cord pulled her onward. She found a giant oak tree behind which to hide and squatted down. Below her, approximately twenty yards away, John lay with another woman. He laughed as he rubbed his bearded face across the woman's breasts. From this angle Lydia could not see who the woman was. She leaned against the tree for strength and tried to get up the courage to look again. When she found the strength, the view shocked her to the core of her being.

John and the woman had begun to couple again. He had mounted her from behind and her face came into full view as she kneeled uphill toward the tree, eyes closed in pleasure. The woman was Mistress Constant.

Lydia shook from head to toe as she sank back behind the tree. The implications of what she saw rang through her mind like loud clanging bells. She felt as if she might scream, and bit into her lip until blood ran down her chin. John, the liar, had caused the death of an innocent man. John, the liar, had ignored her all these months for the desire of another woman. John, the liar, had hurt numerous people he had never known, and had robbed a tribe of a valued scout and leader. *John, the liar!* The words shouted themselves through her head until she covered her ears. When the dizzying effects of her thoughts stilled enough for her to move, she crept back out of the forest and went home.

Ironically, she did not see John for days after this painful revelation. He arose before she did in the morning and returned late at night, after she had gone to bed. In a way, she was thankful for the reprieve. She needed time to reorganize her thoughts and emotions.

During one of these troubling days, Dr. Kayne visited early and unexpectedly. He brought unusual and disturbing news.

"I have gone to see Blackbird's tribe, hoping to forestall any violence. They were willing to hear me, but not to stop their plans."

"Which might be?" Lydia asked as she folded linens she had recently ironed. She was afraid to hear his answer. Dr. Kayne ignored her question and continued.

"Lydia, Blackbird's people had more distressing news than this. Their doctor, a medicine man, told me that ye know the truth about what has happened to Mistress Constant. Is this true?"

His puzzled eyes searched hers lovingly. Lydia met his eyes momentarily, the room begin to spin and then she fainted.

The worn fabric of the sheets touched Lydia's arm as she rolled over onto her back. She moaned softly and opened her eyes. Dr. Kayne sat next to the bed in a chair, and quickly grasped her hand in his. He abandoned pretense and kissed her hand, then her eyes and cheek. She blinked sleepily, and then squeezed his hand as she began to wake up. She tried to speak, but he laid one of his long, ugly fingers across her mouth.

"Let me get ye some water."

He returned with a tin cup of water, and held her against his shoulder as he tilted the cup to her lips. When she was more awake, he pulled away and propped her up with pillows. He continued to hold her hand and spoke to her in gentle, commanding tones.

"Lydia, what has happened? What do ye know that is troubling ye? When I arrived I saw from thy expression that something has happened. What?"

She poured forth the whole story of finding John with Constant, three days earlier. The words tumbled from her mouth as she began to explain aloud the implications were of what she had seen. Tears poured down her cheeks as she spoke.

"John has done no less than put a rope around that poor man's neck with his own soiled hands! My God, how could I have been so daft! John has not approached me for relations since long before I became ill last winter. I thought he was tired from his work!" The awkwardness of her confession did not occur to her as she continued to talk. Dr. Kayne held her hand. His face was filled with concern and a seriousness that was intense even for him.

"I have not known what to do. Do I charge John before the town council? Who would believe me? The town's folks are happy. They have caught and convicted their rapist. Oh my God, they have killed an innocent man, a good man!" She began to cry anew.

Dr. Kayne took her in his arms and rocked her until her grief was spent. Lydia clung to him until a knock sounded on the door. She shook her head for Dr. Kayne to ignore it, but he relieved himself of her arms and opened the door. Mercy entered the house.

"Mistress Mercy, I am pleased to see ye. I was just going to fetch ye. Mistress Lydia has had a small relapse. Could you sit with her this afternoon? I have a patient I must go to."

He led Mercy to Lydia's bedside. Lydia did not need to pretend, as she looked terrible. Her face was ravaged and tear streaked. Mercy sat next to her on the bed and took her hand.

"Dear friend, what has happened to ye?"

Lydia stuttered, but could not come up with a story on such short notice. Dr. Kayne answered for her.

"She has had a shock. A dear friend of hers was killed and she has just recently learned of his death."

"Oh, from that strange country ... that family member ye spoke of last winter?" Mercy said, referring to Lydia's delusional rantings.

"Pardon me?" Lydia asked, confusedly. No one had told her about her lapse from reality during her illness. Again, Dr. Kayne answered.

"No, Mercy, not that relation, but another friend. She will be fine with a good day's rest," he said firmly as he looked into Lydia's green eyes. "Here, Mercy, give her this powder mixed in a cup of water if her grief overwhelms her again, but I doubt she'll need it. Mistress Lydia, I must go to see the man I spoke of earlier. I have to give him this sad news. Do ye understand? I must tell him the truth. His family also needs to know. I don't think ye need to do anything. This is out of thy hands. Do ye understand?"

She closed her eyes, nodded yes and squeezed his hand briefly. Before he left the room, the doctor took Mercy with him and explained what he had just said.

"Mistress Lydia has wished to offer her charitable services toward some of my patients. I had come to see if she still wished to do this work, when I found her in this collapsed state. She will soon be fine, I believe. Thank ye for thy kindness, Mistress Mercy."

Mercy watched the doctor walk away with determined and strong strides before she returned to Lydia's side. They spent the afternoon idly drinking tea and discussing Lydia's new dress. By evening, Lydia was still nervous, but much improved. After gratefully thanking her friend, she convinced Mercy to return to her own household.

For the next forty eight hours, Lydia went through each chore with nervous anticipation. Her hands shook as she tried to sew and she burned the bread and had to start her baking all over again. Fretfully, she watched as John set out to work each day.

Her conscience weighed heavily upon her. And anger at John, his lies and what the lies had caused sat uncomfortably inside her heart. Should she tell John that the Indians would soon know the truth? How could she, without revealing the whole sordid mess? John would run from this danger, deserting her. Yet, either in her admission or through her silence, unquestionably John would soon leave. She found, in the midst of a deep sadness for all the lies, the death of Blackbird and the possible death of her husband, that she felt little grief at the thought of John's loss. And this in itself caused a deeper sadness.

Two nights later, John did not come home at all. Two days following that, Constant's husband the blacksmith ironically gave Lydia the news that her husband had been found dead in the forest. He had been attacked, but by whom, no one knew.

Months passed, and Lydia thought that the bitterness in her soul resulting from John's actions had passed also, until the undertaker again accosted her as she stepped from the general store.

"Widow Carpenter, forgive my intrusion, but ye still have not picked out a gravestone for thy dead husband. I understand that grief is a strong intrusion upon thy life, but the people in town have begun to talk. Won't ye come with me right now and alleviate thyself of this task and worry?"

"Aye," she agreed reluctantly. She had struggled with what to have written on the tombstone. Perhaps she would just have his name, as well as birth and death dates, carved into the slate. Still, it was the custom of the town's people to inscribe a message regarding the departed person.

She followed the undertaker to his building on the outskirts of town. As she did, she passed Dr. Kayne's office. A month after John's death, he had expressed his love for her and had asked her to marry him. She had quickly assented. Then he had asked her to wait six months before they began an open courtship. The townspeople needed to see that she acted properly. She had agreed. She did not want their wagging tongues to detract from their precious relationship. As Lydia and the undertaker passed Dr. Kayne's building, she purposely held her head high and ignored it, as if she did not know him.

They reached the undertaker's building, and he showed her a variety of headstone designs. She chose one with willows across the top and contemplated the inscription once more. Suddenly, she knew what she wanted put on the stone. She gave the somewhat unusual words to the puzzled undertaker, who eventually decided the odd words came from Lydia's loss and grief.

That Sunday, the stone was placed on John's grave. It read:

𝕵𝖔𝖍𝖓 𝕮𝖆𝖗𝖕𝖊𝖓𝖙𝖊𝖗
𝖇𝖔𝖗𝖓, 1638 – 𝖉𝖎𝖊𝖉, 1663
𝖑𝖊𝖆𝖛𝖊𝖘 𝖇𝖊𝖍𝖎𝖓𝖉 𝖍𝖎𝖘 𝖆𝖌𝖌𝖗𝖎𝖊𝖛𝖊𝖉 𝖜𝖎𝖉𝖔𝖜
𝕷𝖞𝖉𝖎𝖆 𝕭𝖚𝖙𝖙𝖊𝖗𝖋𝖎𝖊𝖑𝖉 𝕮𝖆𝖗𝖕𝖊𝖓𝖙𝖊𝖗

... and below this read:

"𝕳𝖊𝖗𝖊, 𝖍𝖊 𝖑𝖎𝖊𝖘, 𝖑𝖎𝖊𝖘, 𝖑𝖎𝖊𝖘...!"

Several days later, when Lydia walked to town in the predawn grayness, she decided to visit the grave site once more. Standing near the grave, but several feet away, were Dr. Kayne and a tall Indian. The Indian's features so closely resembled Blackbird's that Lydia started for a moment, until she realized that this must be his brother. She ignored the men and went to the grave, where she stood for a moment. Dr. Kayne walked over to her, followed by the Indian. They ignored Lydia for a moment as Dr. Kayne translated the tombstone for Blackbird's brother. The Indian nodded his approval, and then signed quickly. Dr. Kayne translated the signing for Lydia.

"He said that his brother honored ye. Blackbird told his people about a white woman with a red man's customs. He saw ye in the forest and thought ye practiced a custom his people have, vision quests. He thought that since ye were white, ye probably needed help, and so he gave ye the hawk feather to help thy spirit fly. Blackbird's brother offers his appreciation to ye for speaking the truth so that Blackbird's spirit may now rest. He also appreciates the inscription ye chose. He said ye are honest for a white woman."

Dr. Kayne's eyes crinkled as he smiled at the Indian's adept understanding of Lydia's choice of words on the stone. The Indian pulled a feather from his hair and handed it to Lydia. Dr. Kayne translated the next words.

"He says ye are a member of the tribe through thy words

and actions." Lydia took the feather and asked Dr. Kayne to thank Blackbird's brother. Dr. Kayne explained.

"They have no words like our 'thank-ye.' They express gratitude mostly through their actions. I shall tell him that ye are honored by his gift."

As the doctor translated these words, Lydia nodded and met the tall Indian's gaze firmly. He nodded back, then turned and walked away with Dr. Kayne. She stood silently, alone before her husband's grave. For the first time in months, she smiled.

"the between ..."

Lohkan came into the meadow first. He viewed his surroundings, and then walked across the grass and lay down in the middle of the fragrant purple flowers, where he soon fell asleep. While he slept, Serra appeared next to him. Rather than wake him, she lay beside him, and joined him in his peaceful state of sleep. Later, the sound of chimes delicately rang through their dreams. As they followed the sound, Serra and Lohkan simultaneously came into a waking state. Quan Yin smiled at them as she floated above where they lay.

"Do you wish to review the lives from which you have recently returned?" she asked in her enchanting voice.

Lohkan answered, "Yes," while Serra nodded and stretched awake. The meadow faded away, and Serra finished her stretch in the light. Once again they were surrounded by the thick, healing white fog. Quan Yin floated nearby with her blue dress flowing delicately about her. She pointed toward a place in the fog; the white clouds quietly parted and their lives in colonial America replayed.

This overview, from this serene place, removed any of the pain of again experiencing their lessons. Serra noted, as she did whenever she returned to *the between* or *the light,* that she felt remarkably safe and secure. Although the review brought up a diverse array of emotions, those emotions did not overwhelm them as they often did on the earthly dimension. Also, within the overview of this place, everything – each joy, each pain – seemed perfect and never out of place. The viewing ended and Quan Yin spoke for the first time since it had begun.

"What have you learned from these lives?"

Serra spoke first.

"As a woman during this time, my life was sheltered. I was not allowed the knowledge or freedom a man could have. I had no legal rights. In a sense, I was treated like property, a possession."

"This taught you what?" Quan Yin prompted her.

"Isolation. As Lydia I felt confined, as if I were suffocating. The strict social codes of the period were extremely limiting. I was a second class person, without freedoms and rights. The social standards that were placed on women were ignored or modified for men.

"My father protected me, my older brothers also did, and then I married a man who continued this pattern. In essence, I was kept in isolation and ignorance, until I met Dr. Kayne. The few times I tried to break out from this isolation, society in some form, usually through John, punished me. Because of this isolation, I was extremely unaware of most of what occurred around me. The feeling of separation and loneliness that this created inside me was at times overpowering."

Serra stopped for a minute before she continued. Her face was pretty in its thoughtful repose. When she continued, her blue eyes burned with an intensity of thoughts and ideas.

"I can see that this imposed isolation was not meant to be malicious. The men in my life, including John, were acting out patterns they had learned. They honestly believed they were giving me what I should have, rather than what I wanted or needed."

"What purpose would this serve for these people, Serra?" Quan Yin questioned her gently.

"For men ... this gave them a sense of empowerment which was needed. This period was a time of exploring and reaching out into unknown worlds. Men saw themselves as conquerors and explorers. Facing the unknown was frightening, oftentimes terrifying. By dominating and controlling women, men created the illusion of power, which gave them the security to go forth into the world. I can see how frightened these generations of men must have been. No one would have said they were afraid. Their way of stating it was to dominate their wives and their households. Women were also affected by this period of exploring. Not all, but many, accepted the shelter and security of ignorance," she said with compassion.

Serra looked about herself, at the white fog that surrounded and buffeted them. She felt soothed and peaceful in this place.

Understanding came easily here. Lohkan added his views to what she had just said.

"Yes," he agreed. "The restricted roles of this period, as well as others, are foreign to Serra and myself. Now, in this place, *the between,* it is difficult for me to imagine limiting any being, whether by gender or race or anything else. We have never lived a life based on fear on our home world. Our race teaches love and compassion. We support each other and grow in a strong, secure foundation of family and friends. Yet, I understand what Serra has observed.

"As a man in this time, I saw it as my duty to protect and shelter women. I did *not* agree that women should not learn or contribute or have rights. My manhood was based upon my ability to lead and assist women, as well as other men. That concept would be foreign to our people. Now that need seems odd and primitive. I can see that **for this planet, with certain races, the growth they experience sometimes requires customs and ideologies that may seem primitive, but which are actually purposeful.** As the need for these ideologies fades, then so will the customs."

Quan Yin continued to lightly float nearby as she listened to their conjectures on what they had experienced. Her dark eyes watched them as they spoke. A look of peace and certainty lay on her lovely features. She encouraged them to continue.

"Please go on. What else of value did you find in these lives?"

Serra began again with one word.

"Truth.

"We on our planet do not and cannot lie. This is a near impossibility in a race of telepaths. In this life, I saw that the outcome of even one lie was far-reaching."

Serra shuddered for a second as she remembered the consequences of John's and Constant's lies.

"I can see that John suffered from guilt throughout our short marriage," she continued. "He never lied directly to me by explaining where he had been when he returned home late. Reviewing this life allowed me to see that he convinced himself that he did not lie to me. He told himself that he never spoke a lie to me, his wife. Yet he was plagued with guilt about his deceptions. Deception is another form of lying. Deception is manipulating events or thoughts until they no longer hold the truth. The effects of John's deception were devastating. John's lies touched not only my life, but the whole township and a tribe of Indians. That one person could negatively affect so many was truly frightening.

"The need to lie is based upon fears and insecurities our people don't have. I felt a compassion for Constant, who also lied out of fear. If she had told the truth, she would have been shunned by the townspeople, or possibly even hung as a witch."

Lohkan put his arm around Serra's shoulders, and then continued her train of thoughts.

"In a way, the whole town lied to themselves. Some of them knew or guessed that Constant had lied. The townspeople were afraid of the new world, afraid of the strange customs of the natives and afraid simply of the unknown. They could not see clearly because their eyes were tainted by this fear. It was so much easier for them to blame an unknown, foreign person: Blackbird. They could not look beyond their fear to see the truth. I think you instinctively knew this, Serra, as Lydia, when you struggled with what you should do after you learned that John and Constant had lied."

Serra nodded her agreement. She and Lohkan became quiet as each reflected on what they had learned. Quan Yin spoke into their silence.

"Lies are based on fear. A secure person will not lie. Only when one is afraid does the need to lie arise. This is not right or wrong. **Whenever fear causes a desire to lie, a soul is then given a chance to grow beyond the insecurity, the fear. The choice, of whether to lie or not, belongs completely to each individual and is his or her responsibility alone.**

"As each soul touches another, the action of each soul affects all others. A lie affects not only the individual, but the universe. When a soul is unable to act truthfully, then all feel the effects of this act. This does not mean that the individual should be despised or punished. The opposite is true. When a soul acts out a deception, or lies, it is acting from a wounded place, a place of fear. What is truly needed in this circumstance is love and compassion, not punishment. Punishment will only feed the fear. Each act touches another. An act of kindness is as far-reaching as an act of punishment...."

As Quan Yin said this, she reached forward and touched Lohkan and Serra on their arms. As she moved her hands away, a tingling began; a warmth spread through them and moved into their hearts. Smiles of comprehension spread across their faces.

"Love does not punish. Love is the element needed to heal someone who is acting out of fear or, in this case, someone who is lying."

They all remained silent for some time. Serra thought of everything the guide had said. She wondered about the countless ways in which people of this world punished each other. She thought about the scriptures of the Bible she had learned as Lydia. She questioned Quan Yin about some of those passages.

"As Lydia, I was raised a Christian. The Bible was the only book my family read for many years. Much of that book was based on a punishing God. Many of the teachings were based on fear. Often I felt worse after reading the Bible. There was a teacher mentioned, named Jesus. He taught of love. Was this why He was sent to this planet? He spoke of unconditional love, which seems impossible in a fear-based world. Who is this God that is terrible and punishing?"

The guide was quiet for such a long time that Serra began to wonder if Quan Yin had heard her. Quan Yin's eyes were closed, her head bowed and small flowers decorated her coiled, black hair. When she finally answered, the white light grew more intense, brighter. It filled their minds and souls with a profound peace.

"God, Serra, is *The One.* You, Lohkan, John, Goody Bishop, Blackbird and myself are also *The One.* **God is the combined energy of all things. We are all one. We are all God.**

"Jesus was a soul who enacted an awakening for this world. He brought the knowledge and power of love to this planet. Each soul has this knowledge inside it. His work was to awaken those memories.

"The teachings of fear and punishment are based on men's fears. God, *The One,* does not punish; yet mankind, as part of *The One,* may choose to punish. Remember that punishment is also based on fear. As a whole world is based on fear, then a natural choice would be to worship the punishment this teacher, Jesus, received, rather than the teachings. Although His teachings may appear to be wasted on this world, they are not. A seed has been planted. Eventually, this world will awaken to those teachings. As a seed needs time to germinate beneath the soil before a seedling appears, so it is with this world. The people here will remember. This germination may take thousands of Earth years, and there may be many other awakenings throughout this time, but this will happen. He was not the only planter of this knowledge, this seed. Many before Him and since have continued this work. He was one of many teachers.

"What about unconditional love?" Serra questioned.

Tears glistened on the edges of Serra's eyes as she asked. Realizations focused her mind intently upon Quan Yin's words. In her heart, hope was growing for this world as she listened to the guide's explanations. She looked up into Lohkan's face and saw that her hope was mirrored there. They had come to love this planet, the people of this world. Could Earth become a place of love and peace? She listened to Quan Yin's answer.

"Unconditional love exists everywhere, Serra! Not only here in *the between,* but on Earth. Sometimes it takes a form that is not immediately recognizable. Countless small acts of kindness display this love every day! However, the people of this planet often confuse unconditional love with unconditional condoning of behavior."

"What is the difference?" Lohkan asked.

"When someone unconditionally accepts or condones a person's actions, in many cases this is not an act of unconditional love. For instance, unconditional love does not mean that you, Serra, would simply accept Lohkan's choice to harm you. This is *not* unconditional love. If you were to accept his harmful treatment of your person or soul, this would be unconditional acceptance of his behavior, which would *not* be loving to you or him. Do you understand?"

"Yes. I believe I do," Serra said, and choked back a sob. When had this world come to mean so much to her? A tear ran down her cheek. Lohkan squeezed her shoulder in understanding, and then asked the guide another question.

"Are you saying **unconditional love does not condone unconditional behavior**? "

"Yes, Lohkan! You do understand!" the guide said, and then smiled brilliantly. As she smiled, she grew more beautiful. "It is time for you to return to the meadow, where you may rest if you choose. Do you have any other questions?"

"No," they answered. Serra's mind was brimming with what they had just heard. From what she could now feel from Lohkan, he was experiencing the same abundance of thoughts and wonder. As she looked into his blue eyes, his attractive face broke into a smile, and then he began to laugh from the joy of all they had discovered. His laughter filled her with renewed happiness, and the light and their surroundings disappeared.

Chapter 14

"the between ..."

Serra and Lohkan sat by the cliff edge and looked out over the lake. Lohkan rested his back against a large rock and Serra leaned against his chest as they watched the second moon rise in the growing twilight. Lavender tones in the sky began to turn into darker purple. This second moon was in its crescent stage with the bowl facing upward, like a silvery smile in the sky. The sky reflected off Serra's and Lohkan's blue eyes and turned them to violet. Serra continued the subject they were discussing.

"This is inconceivable to me!" she said quietly, but with passion. "How can beauty be determined solely by 'outer' appearances?"

"I don't know," Lohkan said, and then kissed the top of her head.

"If they couldn't see Doctor Kayne's beauty, what would they think of Yon, with his hairless scalp and large eyes, or of Senton, with his blue skin and gilled face ... or of the innumerable races that exist?"

The question was not truly rhetorical, and Lohkan did not answer. Instead he pulled Serra closer to him and thought about the lives they had just lived.

In the town, few had suspected that Lydia had fallen in love with Dr. Kayne. When they had announced their intentions to marry, almost a year after John's death, many of the townspeople had been shocked. Countless had questioned why Lydia would marry such a homely man, when many handsome ones would have her.

Both of these friends Serra had mentioned were quite beautiful. The various life forms of the universe would shock many of the humans of this planet. And he was sure that numerous of these life forms would be seen as ugly. During travels throughout this galaxy and others, they had made friends from a myriad of races. That any of these friends might not be seen as beautiful on this world seemed shocking to Lohkan. Serra was obviously unsettled by this knowledge, too. They had debated this subject, and still had not found answers. Just as Lohkan was about to change the subject, Quan Yin appeared.

"You have questions," she stated simply.

"Yes," Lohkan said. "We are trying to understand the human response to beauty. Some of the townspeople could not understand that Lydia could love an ugly man. Serra and I don't understand this way of thinking. Can so many humans really not see that beauty comes from inside a person's soul? This seems impossible."

Quan Yin smiled gently, and then spoke. Her black eyes returned the moons' light as if they were two stars shining distantly in the sky.

"Part of the human experience is based on reflection."

"What type of reflection?" Serra asked.

Near them a pool suddenly appeared. It shimmered faintly, as if a light came from inside it. Quan Yin pointed to the pool.

"Look in the water."

Serra and Lohkan arose and, side by side, stepped to the edge of the pool. In the still water were perfect imitations of their puzzled faces. Quan Yin smiled at them as they looked back at her from the watery mirror. She spoke quietly and lovingly.

"One of the ways in which humans learn is through reflections. Each person they meet mirrors some part of themselves back to them. It is easy for them to accept the *beauty* that a physically beautiful person resonates toward them. It is more difficult to accept the homeliness that a physically ugly person personifies. As you know, no person is ever truly homely unless they believe they are. As Dr. Kayne, Lohkan, did you believe you were unattractive?"

"Yes, I had heard all my life that God had decided to punish me by making me unattractive. My parents did not believe this, nor did they ever say it, and so I was able to learn to like myself in spite of my physical attributes, or lack of them. Most of this negative conditioning came from other relatives, neighbors and members of the church."

"It was this part of yourself, that was wounded and believed it was unlovable, that was reflected on your face. People saw imitated on your face their own private wounds. Just as when they looked at Lydia's face they saw mirrored their own private

joys. It's not that they could not imagine Lydia loving your homeliness, it's that they could not imagine themselves loving their
own ugliness, their wounds.

**"Beauty is dependent upon a soul's ability to see and
feel beauty inside itself.** If a soul cannot see its own beauty, it
will have a difficult time discovering beauty around it. For most
souls in human bodies, the need to see external beauty is thus
explained. They are wounded in some way that requires them to
see beauty outside themselves, since they cannot see it inside.
They look for a reflection that will fill and heal their wounds."

She waited while Lohkan and Serra thought about her
words. Lohkan gazed at the reflection of himself in the pool.
Suddenly the image changed, and the countenance of Dr. Kayne
stared back at him. As Lohkan viewed Dr. Kayne's face from this
place of healing, the face changed magically before his eyes. The
face was not homely, but instead it was interesting and unique.
The face had character and strength that was extraordinary.
Serra's reflection smiled next to his.

"Now you know what I saw as Lydia. Lydia thought you
were beautiful. I do, too," she said, and smiled more widely.

"True beauty begins within and spreads outward. Every
soul seeks this because of what it represents," Quan Yin said.

"Which is what?" asked Lohkan.

"Self-love."

They sat silently and stared into the pool while Quan Yin
floated nearby. As they stared at their reflections, face after face
looked back at them. Lohkan saw reflected first a South Pacific
baby, then a Japanese warrior, Iduna, Anastasos, SilverFin,
Morning Dew, Sees Far and on until his own face stared back at
him. Serra watched the multitude of faces which reflected back
at her, from Lotus Blossom, to Antonio, to Christopher and on
through her many incarnations, until she reached Lydia. Lohkan
looked up at her as he heard her thoughts.

"All. All are equally beautiful!" He said Serra's thoughts
out loud.

"Yes," Quan Yin agreed. "Come! You are now to find out
about another form of beauty."

The pool, cliffs and lake vanished again. As they did, Serra
and Lohkan were left with a lingering sense of the unspeakable
beauty they had seen inside as well as around themselves.

250

A gaunt-looking man with black hair, pale skin, the emaci-
ated body of a zealot and yet with the expression of a saint, stood
in the doorway and watched his son paint. The young man studied his subject matter with intensity and did not know he was
watched. Francois observed as his son painted the farmyard in all
its rustic beauty. On Jean's canvas the run-down barn became a
display of impressions of earth tones that were artfully revealed.
Gone were the cobwebs, the stench of manure and the thick,
cloying mud. Out from Jean's canvas came beauty in its purest
form.

The son looked much like his father, only a softening of his
features, especially around the eyes, was different. These small
details belonged to his mother and her graceful face. Francois
called to his son.

"Jean, will you bring this one to your exhibit next week?"

"Oui, Papa!"

"Would you bring it home again?" Francois asked hesitantly.

Jean turned to face him. A smile played across his lips.

"Oui. This is possible. You like this?"

"Oui," Francois answered simply.

Francois' reply was quiet, as his thoughts and manners
were. No large demonstrations for his son's talents would be
shown. No boasting or exclamations would be heard in the small
village where they lived. This quiet request was the strongest support Francois could make. He was sincerely proud of his son and
showed it in this moment. Jean looked back at his father for a
minute, rewarded Francois with a large smile and then continued
on with his work. Francois continued to watch in silence.

Jean's exhibit was held in a small gallery on the outskirts of
Paris. Each day he listened to the remarks of the people who
strolled through, and answered questions as they were asked.
Many were shocked by his subject matter, the farms, the French
countryside and the peasants he represented. As he answered the
questions of a wealthy merchant, a group of young women arrived.

Two of the girls broke off from the group and walked from
painting to painting as two hens might have followed a trail of
seeds. Jean watched, hypnotised by their fresh faces, their intense
interest in his work. They were obviously sisters, as he could
hardly tell them apart from a distance. One was slightly taller,
older, and had her arm around the younger girl's waist. Both girls
had thick, curly brown hair that was piled loosely on their heads.

Lacy, pastel-colored dresses showed that they were out for a day of fun. Jean found himself walking toward them, although he had no idea what he intended to say. The older of the girls turned and faced him with a brilliant smile.

"Are you the painter?" she asked delightedly.

"Oui. I am Jean De LaMer."

"Your paintings are magnificent! Are they not, Pauline?"

"Oui," the younger girl said, and shyly looked down.

"I am Justine and this is my sister Pauline." The older sister introduced them with a flourish of her hand.

Jean watched Pauline with an artist's eyes. She was pretty in her youthfulness, with luxurious hair, clear, pink skin and pale gray eyes. Pauline's plump body was curved nicely and in a way that was stylish. Her gray eyes watched each of his movements as he pointed out details in his paintings or as he brushed his long, black hair away from his face. He questioned her directly.

"What are you staring at?"

"Your hands – they are beautiful, like a woman's," Pauline answered honestly. As she realized what she had said, she blushed a deep rose.

Jean simply smiled and continued the conversation as if nothing impolite had been said.

Hours passed, and the other girls had left long ago to attend another exhibit in a neighboring building, but Pauline stood next to Jean and listened to his stories of the land and people who inspired him. Justine returned, stood inside the door of the gallery and called to her sister.

"Pauline, allons! We must leave. The others are waiting!"

As Pauline started to leave, Jean reached forward and grasped her young hand with one of his long, sensual hands.

"Will you come back?"

She looked away, toward the door where her sister motioned impatiently for her to come. And then she whispered her reply.

"Oui. I will return," and with this, she ran out the door.

Pauline returned to the gallery to visit him often. Eventually, Jean began formal visits to her home, and during the next year called upon her often, until it was clear to Pauline's parents that Jean would not easily go away. Pauline's father was concerned, but reluctantly gave his permission for their courtship.

One evening Jean unexpectedly arrived for a visit. As the sun set on the vineyards which surrounded the house, Jean entered their spacious and comfortable home. Gold light filtered in and warmed the walls of the sitting room where Pauline's parents sat together. Pauline's father sipped a dark, red wine and her mother repaired a hole in a delicate piece of lace. Her parents looked up as Jean entered carrying an air of excitement and pride. Pauline quietly followed and stood behind Jean as he sat in a chair across from her father.

"Monsieur, I have sold three paintings today! This patron has pledged his money and support. He has offered a small farm to me, in exchange for a fourth of my life's work. The farm is near mon pere's village near the sea. I wish to marry Pauline. May I have your permission?"

"My daughter was not meant to be a artist's wife," her father said dubiously. "What kind of life can you provide for her?" He snorted and continued, "Talent does not put bread on the table!"

"A good one, Monsieur, if you will let me. I will continue to paint and sell my work. I grew up on a farm. I will farm as well as paint. I know this place. It is beautiful, with a view of the ocean and rich soil for planting. Your daughter will live well. My family lives in the next village. She will not be alone."

As Jean innocently described this hard life, Pauline's father scowled.

"Pauline, do want this marriage?"

"Oui, Pere. Very much," she said.

"It will not be easy. Farming is hard work! The days are long. Your mother and I had hoped for better for our daughters!" he said, as he referred to his six daughters.

"S'il vous plait, Pere ..." she begged with words and with her gray eyes.

"Ah, bien, you may marry my daughter," he assented sadly.

As the young couple joyously left the room, he turned to his wife with a frown.

"She will regret this match! You will see!"

Pauline gasped as she stood in the doorway of their new home. The small timber-and-thatch farmhouse needed plastering and a whitewash throughout the interior. The outer walls were filthy, and its original bright color was faded and covered with dirt and mold. She turned and viewed the farmyard. The storage barn had begun to crumble and one of the major beams that supported the main structure of the barn had rotted. The fields lay barren under a stark blue sky and the ocean's pounding in the distance sounded hard and painful instead of soothing. She swallowed and wondered if perhaps her father had been right after all.

As she turned to speak to Jean, his expression froze her. Tears sat on the edge of his dark eyes and he would not look at her. He kicked at a broken wooden bucket by his feet and swore. A courage Pauline did not know she had crept into her heart and slowly came out in placating words.

"We can restore the farm, mon cher," she began. She tried to take his hand, but he angrily pulled away.

"Pauline, you do not know how much work this is!"

"Mon pere owes a vineyard. Of course I know!" she replied hotly, and then calmed herself. "Jean, we can do this. I will work beside you. Tell the patron that you cannot paint for a year! We will work during that year to fix this place. He must understand."

"No! I will go to him and see if I can break my contract! He has mislead me. I cannot ask you to live like this!"

"Then my father will be right ..." she said slowly.

Jean jerked up his head and stared at her. Pauline reached for his hand again, and this time he accepted her touch.

"Please, mon amour. We can make this farm work! I know we can," she said softly.

Jean swallowed past his tears and pulled Pauline into a tight embrace.

"Oui. We can," he said with finality.

The following week Jean's father sent one of Jean's younger brothers to help restore the farm. The young man, barely fourteen, was an enormous help, but with so many problems facing them, one person was not enough aid.

Together they began endless hours of plastering, sanding, painting, building, hoeing, digging, planting and weeding. And while they restored the farm, another worry stalked their lives.

Money.

Money had become an issue almost immediately after they had begun. Timber was not cheap. What little furniture there was, was in a state of decay. Lumber to build furniture was also expensive. Buying furniture was out of the question. They barely had money left to purchase milk, cheese and flour for bread. Wine had become a luxury, as well as coffee and tea. New clothes were soon forgotten. Paints, oils, brushes and canvas became unobtainable during those first several months.

Eventually, Jean was forced to beg a loan from Pauline's parents. She remembered seeing his stoic countenance the day he left to go see her father as one of the worst moments in their marriage. And the following morning, when Jean returned to their farm, his troubled face said more than words could speak. Pauline plied him with questions. She had to know the truth.

"Jean, what did mon pere say?"

"He was unwilling to give us a loan," Jean said quietly.

"What? Why?" Pauline said, unwilling to believe the truth.

"Is it not enough that you heard he said 'no?' Do you need to know 'why' too?" Jean asked with bitterness. His pride was profoundly wounded.

"Yes, I do!" Pauline angrily insisted. "Tell me, Jean!"

"He is teaching us a lesson! He said if I agreed to give up painting and went to work for him, he would help us. If not, then he said we deserved the unhappiness we have found."

"No!" Pauline struggled with the truth.

"Oui. It is true," Jean ended sadly.

A burst of colorful curses erupted from Pauline's pretty mouth. She spat on the ground and shook her fist at the sky. Jean looked up in surprise.

"Pauline! Your father is right! I should not have brought you to this life."

"No! He is wrong! He is a pig-headed fool who cannot see! Did you agree to his offer?" she asked furiously.

"No! Do you want me to give up my painting?"

"No! We do not need his help! We will succeed without him," Pauline announced decisively. Jean began to laugh. Pauline glared at him.

"What, Jean De LeMar, makes you laugh?"

"You," he said, and affectionately placed his arms around her waist. He kissed her neck, and then murmured "We will make the farm work because of you."

A rooster crowed loudly, announcing to the farm that the sun was about to rise. Again and again, the rooster proclaimed to the world that the day had begun. After he had completed his rousing summons, the rooster promptly began to pick insects out of the dirt for his breakfast. His rusty red comb and dark red feathers caught the first of the sunlight and reflected crimson back to the world.

Pauline rolled over on the straw mattress and reveled in the morning's beauty. The view that met her eyes through the window by the bed was breathtakingly peaceful. A large haystack glowed golden and pink in the morning light. Teal ducks and white geese floated serenely on the dark pond, where tall grasses and lilies grew in profusion. Black chickens ran from the rooster's aggressive attentions. White sheep chewed the grass of the green hillside with purposeful intent. Far in the distance, the blue-green ocean sent a slight haze into the morning air. The distant sound of waves crashing against the rocky shore broke the morning's silence.

She climbed out of bed and pulled on a fresh chemise. Over this, Pauline pulled on an unbleached petticoat. She drew on a dark gray woolen skirt, and buttoned on a bleached, white blouse with full darts and multiple pleats across her large bosom. She then pulled down yesterday's apron, pinned it over her shirt and tied the strings around her waist.

She tidied the bed and went to the kitchen to begin breakfast. As she passed the kitchen door she sighted Jean at the back of the house, at work at his easel. She smiled and wondered how long he had been at work.

She poured flour into a bowl with several cups of starter from a sponge that sat in a crock in the pantry. Next she added a spoonful of lard and some salt, and began to knead the mass into the day's bread. A yeasty smell filled the kitchen as she finished the dough and set it in a bowl to rise at the back of the counter where she worked. She made a dark, strong coffee in a pot, which she poured into a mug and took out to Jean. He kissed her round cheek, but kept on working.

This morning he painted the countryside in its rosy splendor. His oils filled the air and mixed with the ocean breeze and barnyard scents in an earthy aroma. He worked quickly to capture the light, which, with nature's haste, sought to change the world before him. Already the rosy colors fled and were replaced by softer yellow tones. Soon he would have to work by memory. Pauline did not bother with conversation, because Jean would not have heard her while he painted. She returned to the kitchen and made a porridge for their two children, who would awaken any moment.

Their little girl, Angelique, a nine-year-old beauty who had her father's dark coloring and her mother's rounded feminine features, awoke first. She sat sleepily at the table in her night clothes. Pauline poured a small amount of the dark coffee into a cup and added warm milk to fill it. She sprinkled dark sugar across the top and handed it to her daughter. Next, she placed a bowl of porridge, which swam in yellowy cream, before the girl. A moment later, their little boy, Louis, who was as fair as his sister was dark, joined them, and Pauline repeated the steps she had just taken a moment ago.

While the children ate, she punched down the bread and deftly kneaded the warm dough into round loaves. As she set these to rise, she stoked the fires and added more wood, to bring the brick ovens up to a heat that would bake the bread into crusty brown loaves. Jean entered the room and leaned his easel against the wall. The painting sat outside on a shelf against the house, where it would dry. He stuck a handful of well-worn brushes into a pot filled with brush cleaner and went to the sink to wash. Pauline automatically took the dipper from the bucket, and poured water over his hands as he scrubbed them with salt, in a futile attempt to get the oily paint stains off his skin. She looked at his blue, green, red and gold stained fingers, and smiled. Only once had she seen Jean's hands clean of paint stains, during those first hard years, and she did not want to see them clean again. He sat with the children and dug into the steaming bowl of porridge that she set before him.

After breakfast was finished, the children went outside to the barn to do chores and Pauline started to clean the table. Jean put his arm around her plump waist and pulled her onto his lap.

"Mon chere, today is a beautiful day! Let's take the children to the ocean for a picnic."

"Jean, I was going to wash the linens today!" she said, and then laughed as she tried to wrestle free from his thin, wiry arms.

"Pauline, what kind of parents would we be if we did not teach our children about beauty? The sheets are not so dirty that they cannot wait until tomorrow." He nuzzled her neck and squeezed her ample bottom as he talked.

"Tomorrow I must iron and sew. Who will wash the sheets then, I ask?" She smiled as he kissed her on the tip of the nose.

"Mon chere, don't wash the sheets at all! They can wait until next week. Look at this day! Can you deny that a day such as this should be celebrated?"

"No," she said as she started to relent as Jean pushed his hands up under her skirt.

"The painting is finished; we shall be able to buy that cow that you've wanted, once I collect from Monsieur. Say yes, mon amour."

"Oui."

His kissed her passionately, and then pushed her off his lap. "I'll go tell the children!" he said as he rushed out of the room.

The day was truly one to be celebrated. White, wispy clouds blown about by gentle breezes floated gayly above a peaceful sea. The sky was vividly blue and reflected across the ocean as a slate blue-gray. The grassy hillside that tumbled down to the beach, where large rocks lay in the surf, was strikingly green with spring growth.

The children ran on the sandy shore while their parents lay on a large blanket that had been spread over the grass. Pauline laid her head in Jean's lap and listened to the seagulls calling raucously overhead. The sound of their daughter's squeal sounded amazingly like one of the birds as the little girl chased after a piece of seaweed that drifted in the surf.

Pauline glowed with a beauty that was spiritual rather than physical, for she was pretty in a healthy, cheerful sense which was enhanced as she aged. The wrinkles which had started to develop and her work-roughened hands could not distract from the natural glow she carried. She knew that her beauty was what most people would have called healthy and voluptuous, not classic or charming. Fine clothes and glamour had left her life years ago and her figure had grown into a full, rounded body which was ideally made for childbearing. Yet Jean still found her as beautiful as she found him.

She looked up at his expressive face as he studied the sky. His long, narrow face was surrounded by a mass of dark, wavy hair. His full beard and mustache managed to disguise how thin he was. No matter how much Jean ate, he stayed excessively thin, like his father and brothers. His brown eyes twinkled when he was happy and turned stormy when he was angry. She watched his eyes and guessed that he probably memorized every detail of the thin clouds above them for future use in his paintings. She decided that this was the right moment to tell him her news.

"Jean?"

"Oui, Pauline?"

"I am with child," she said simply, and laughed at his astonished expression. He kissed her mouth tenderly as he smiled. When he leaned back up, he announced, "I shall have to paint you again!"

Pauline sat up abruptly.

"No, Jean."

"Why not, mon amour?" he teased.

"We have too many paintings of me. Really, it is absurd! You cannot paint me now that I am pregnant!"

"Ah, chere, for a while, this was all the fashion with the rich...."

He continued to smile at her discomfort. Pauline was an impatient model at best. Their busy farm did not allow for the long hours of inactivity that modeling required. She had posed a dozen times, and had been impatient and bossy through each session. Even when Jean had coaxed her with lovemaking, she had not changed her attitude. The last session, some two years ago, had been her last, or so she swore. She countered his argument.

"Ah, if it is the rich you wish to paint, then paint Justine. She enjoys modeling. And Henre is your best customer!" Pauline teased as she referred to Justine and her sister's wealthy husband.

"Mon amour, I do not love Justine as I love you."

He patted her round stomach and then kissed her neck. She pushed him away firmly, stood up and called to the children.

"No, Jean! I shall not argue about this any longer." Although she tried to sound harsh, her mouth threatened to curve into a smile, and Jean saw her mirth.

"Oui, Pauline," he said obediently, though neither believed him.

Four months had passed, and Pauline's full body had grown more firm and voluptuous as the child within her grew. She stretched lazily and massaged her naked body that was beginning to grow cold.

"Jean, could you please put more wood on the fire?"

He put his paintbrush down and then went to the woodpile stacked next to the fireplace. Absentmindedly, as he placed another log on the fire, he pushed his black hair away from his face. As he did so, he managed to smear red paint across his brow. When he stood to face his painting and Pauline, she burst into laughter.

"Oh, Jean, come here!" She laughed heartily as he stood before her. She used a rag that had been thrown on the floor and wiped the smudge off his face. After this she dropped back into the position in which he was painting her, and adjusted her pose. He pushed her back to get her into the correct position, and then began to fondle one of her large breasts. She laughed and pushed him away again.

"Jean, at this pace, the baby will be born before the painting is finished!"

She let him push his face between her breasts, and then

sank into the pillows of the bed as he joined her.

Veronique was born with more difficulty than Pauline's first two births. She was dark, like her older sister, but more petite, as Jean's sisters were. This new baby increased Pauline's responsibilities to the point where a maid became necessary, though where they would find the money to pay for this help was a mystery.

Pauline held the baby against her stomach in a carrier made from a shawl as she planted the spring kitchen garden. The earth was still cool and damp after an early rain. Her hands became black with the rich earth as she created holes in which to put seeds. The baby nursed quietly and peered up at the world in undisguised wonder. Pauline murmured nonsense to the baby as she crawled on her hands and knees across the garden space.

Her skirts had been tied up between her legs to keep them out of the dirt. She wore an oatmeal-colored scarf around her head to keep her hair from getting dirty. A hoe leaned up against the back of the house next to a wheelbarrow, which was piled high with sheep dung. She would put a layer of manure over the earth after all the seeds had been planted. Good, earthy smells accosted her senses, and she felt an overwhelming sense of well-being, there in the sunshine.

She had finished the planting and was attempting to scrub the dirt from her hands when she first sensed that something was wrong. The baby had fallen asleep as she suckled milk and had snored softly against Pauline's breast. Eventually, Veronique had fallen into a more quiet sleep. Pauline had moved gently, so as not to disturb the baby's peace. As she washed, she wondered why the baby did not awaken to nurse. She quickly untied the shawl and gently laid the baby on the kitchen table.

Veronique did not breathe. Pauline shook the little body in an attempt to get her baby to breathe. The baby did not respond, but instead lay peacefully still. Pauline's cry of anguish swept over the farm and hillsides, to where it at last was heard by Jean, who painted some distance away. He raced home where he found his wife in a state of collapse and his new daughter dead upon the table.

During the night, a storm had assaulted the shore, the hills and, lastly, the farm. Pauline snuggled closer to Jean, reluctant to crawl from the warm, safe shelter of thick comforters on their bed. Finally, she made a hasty retreat from their bedroom, pulling on clothes as she went. She quickly fed wood into the fire-place, building a hearty fire, and pushed the heavy cast iron ket-tle over the flames to heat water with which to wash. Warm water would feel wonderful to Jean after the bone-chilling damp-ness of this storm.

Jean joined her a moment later, half dressed and still sleepy. He hugged his wife to his side for a moment; then he pulled on boots and an oilskin before he went out to meet the storm. Pauline started a fire in the cook's woodstove, one Jean had traded a painting for five years ago, and began breakfast.

She sliced large pieces of bread, covered them with butter and set them on a plate on the table. Next she made coffee in a pot on the woodstove. She cut large slices of ham and placed them on the skillet which heated on the stove. As the ham sizzled and filled the kitchen with spicy aromas, Pauline quickly washed her face from a bowl of water on the counter. Then, as she fin-ished preparing breakfast, she daydreamed about the past thirty years.

After Veronique's death there had been a period of mourn-ing. Veronique had lived only three months, yet she had left a clear and visible mark on their lives. Jean had held her night after night during those years, before she had begun to heal, and had listened to her tears. He had encouraged her to grieve and, more often than not, joined her grieving. Through this tragedy, they had been brought closer together in ways neither could have anticipated.

The births of more children, a boy, and then a girl, did not fill the void that Veronique's absence had left. After her last child's birth, a little girl, whom they had named after her sister Justine, Pauline realized that each child was unique. One could not replace another. No matter how many children a mother had, each was precious and special. When she realized this, the healing began. She prayed for Veronique's soul to find rest and a place with God in Heaven. She prayed for the safety of her four other children and for Jean, and as she found a place in her soul for the loss of her baby, she began to feel better.

As they healed, their joy of life became visible and real again. The two oldest children, Angelique and Louis, supported their parents gently, with a compassion that spoke to their fragile hearts. The two newest children, Justine and Pierre, brought renewed life to their opening souls. The family was made whole and happiness once again reigned in the house and on the farm.

That had been many years ago, and now the children were all grown, married and with children of their own. Pauline smiled as she thought about her four children and ten grandchildren. She stopped, looked out the door into the stormy morning and wondered where Jean was.

As Pauline stepped back, she bumped one of Jean's paintings on the wall, stopped to straighten it and dusted it absentmindedly as she did. A dramatic scene of a peasant working in a field in browns, reds and golds looked back at her. She remembered Jean's career with clarity.

Throughout the years, his paintings had sold well until they were cruelly criticized by an art critic in Paris. For three years, Jean fell into unpopularity, until his work recovered. During that time, Jean become more like his father, and developed a spiritual and emotional richness in all that he was and did. His paintings reflected this growth and took on a luminescent quality that became his trademark. Although he never did acquire the fame and income of the more popular artists of his day, his work was respected. Many came to admire him simply for the courage it took to paint an unpopular subject. He continued throughout the years to paint the farms, scenery and peasants he loved most. And Pauline was as proud of him after all these years as she had been the first day they had met, so long ago. She pushed a strand of hair, which now matched the color of her gray eyes, out of her face. Unknowingly, she smiled as she thought of Jean. Their relationship had become a sensual exhibit of their love of life. Their lovemaking grew more passionate, though more gentle, as they aged. And any who saw them could not doubt the love that existed between them. Pauline smiled more widely at her happy reflections. Jean was her best friend, the person she most admired and her lover.

She looked out through the kitchen door again, when he still did not return. A dim light glowed from the open barn door and through the pelting rain. She wondered if one of the cows was in trouble, and decided to go to the barn to offer her help. When she entered the barn, she saw Jean leaning against the side of a cow, a bucket beneath her udder and his hand on her flank. The other hand fell loosely to the floor.

She smiled to herself that he had fallen asleep in this manner. This particular cow was so gentle she would have stood quietly for hours and let Jean sleep. Pauline went to Jean and shook him to wake him. He fell to the side, and she knew in that moment he was not asleep. He was dead.

Two months later, Pauline died quietly in her sleep. As the doctor could find no cause of death, he surmised that she had died of a broken heart. He explained to Jean and Pauline's children that this was not uncommon. Couples who were as closely connected as Jean and Pauline often could not live without each other. God, in his kindness, chose to take Pauline's spirit to Heaven, where she would be reunited with her dead husband, the doctor explained. The doctor did not know just how right he was.

"the between ..."

Wind blew across the water and flowed harmlessly over the dome-shaped house. Lohkan looked at Yerraba's pleased face and began to laugh. He recognized this pod as Yerraba's house on one of the islands of their home planet, before she had joined the research team and begun space travel. It was typical of the homes their people lived in, with its inverted-bowl shape and gray, metal walls. Yerraba had shared this pod with Sumkan, her husband, for many years; he and Serra had visited here often. The wind blew over the pod and them and rustled Lohkan's blond hair. Yerraba continued to smile as Lohkan looked around. Views of the vast lake, almost as large as the ocean, met his eyes from all points. Lohkan turned and smiled again at Yerraba.

"How long have you been here?" Lohkan asked, after he had embraced her hello.

Not long. I died after I fell from the carriage. I was on my way to visit the children when the accident happened, she spoke in Lohkan's mind.

He smiled in spite of the bizarre situation they were now in, that of discussing their human bodies and lives. He had become accustomed to the detachment he felt here in *the between,* but his awe never lessened, no matter how often he experienced this. Yerraba seemed newer to this, and acted with the wonder and delight of a child with a new toy.

"I wanted to see our old house, and then, here I was!" she said, and then laughed. "What are you doing here?"

"I don't know," Lohkan answered honestly.

He envisioned the meadow and the waterfall where he and Serra normally returned, and the surroundings changed magically. Yerraba's large and spacious pod was replaced by the waterfall. As the falls appeared, Yerraba's wonder grew. She laughed loudly and her voice echoed around them in an enchanting and harmonious melody. She teased Lohkan.

"How do I envision French pastries? Can I eat here? As Justine, I definitely enjoyed life!"

As her laughter echoed around them again, Serra burst into the mossy area near the waterfall in a display of white and gold light. As she sighted Yerraba, Serra smiled with pure joy, and then ran to meet her best friend. Yerraba looked as she had when they had worked together. She was wearing one of the silver uniforms that they had worn on the ship, her long blond hair was pulled back with a matching silver cord and her large blue-green eyes were as expressive as ever. Yerraba's smile was crooked due to a defect in a jaw muscle, and right now Serra thought that it was the most beautiful smile she had seen in years. Serra hugged her tightly while Lohkan watched and smiled. When she left Yerraba's embrace to greet Lohkan, Yerraba spoke.

"This was my first experience going into a human body and then returning here. I've many questions. I was told, before my incarnation as Justine, that someone would greet me when I returned. I did not imagine that the someone would be Lohkan!" She smiled widely.

"I did not know I would be the one, either, but I am glad it was me, and now Serra," he answered.

An illumination appeared near the waterfall in a brilliant burst of white and blue light, obliterating all else. For a split second, the waterfall, the trees, the soft grass ... all were hidden by this brightness. When the light faded, Sumkan, Yerraba's husband, appeared before them. Three sets of startled blue eyes mirrored his own confused ones. He looked about himself, and then at his three friends.

"Where am I? Are you real?" Sumkan asked. His hooded eyes squinted in confusion and disbelief.

Their combined laughter filled the land around them and their minds, too large for speech alone. The laughter moved from one to the next in a telepathic play of joy and wonder. Each looked at the other, waiting for someone to explain. As Lohkan opened his mouth to speak, the elder appeared in the center of the circle of friends.

They talked for days, if days existed there in *the between*. Sumkan and Yerraba had each experienced their "first" human lifetimes. Sumkan had been Henre, while Yerraba had embodied Justine, Pauline's sister. Serra and Lohkan had listened patiently these past few days, as Yerraba and Sumkan talked with and questioned Tonak extensively. The elder's calm and patience seemed to be contagious; as neither Serra nor Lohkan felt any need to speak right away, as they normally did when entering this dimension. They sat, cushioned by the moss which surrounded the waterfall, and listen to the dialogue between Tonak, Yerraba and Sumkan.

Yerraba's wonder at this place seemed to have no bounds. Sumkan's was more restrained and cautious. Serra smiled as she watched them. Sumkan often listened contemplatively to Yerraba or to the elder, with his eyes squinted above his long nose. Yerraba's crooked smile lay on her pretty, oval face during most of their talks. Their essence remained the same here, in this dimension, as it had in their bodies on the spaceship.

Yerraba had always been full of life and enthusiastic in her studies. As she watched Yerraba's enthusiasm, Serra realized that *the between,* where learning and experiences were limitless, was the perfect environment for someone like Yerraba. The longer Yerraba remained in *the between,* the more her enthusiasm grew. Serra suddenly knew that Yerraba would not return to a human body, with all its varied limitations. She smiled at her friend and knew this was *right.* Sumkan, on the other hand, was genuinely interested in human psychological development and in humanity's cultural displays of spirituality. The art world had intrigued him. As Serra observed this, Sumkan spoke her thoughts out loud.

"I'd like to go to the Earth plane next as an artist. Is this possible?"

Yerraba became quiet, the smile left her lips and she stared at her partner. In that moment, Yerraba understood all that Serra had already observed. She spoke softly to Sumkan in a voice that was assured, yet winsome.

"I cannot go with you. Do you understand, Sumkan?"

He took her hand and smiled gently. Theirs had always been a relationship of opposites. As adventurous and lively as Yerraba was, Sumkan was quiet, reflective and methodical.

"I know you can't go with me," Sumkan began painfully. "I don't want to live without you, Yerraba, but I need to go back. There is so much to learn on Earth!"

She smiled lopsidedly and tried to speak, but for the moment the words would not come. A tear ran down her cheek. Sumkan spoke for her.

"It's right for you to be here. This –" he stopped and motioned to *the between,* " – is where you belong. Going back to

Earth would only be entrenched with pain and frustration for you. I have the patience to go, but you...."

"I do not," she finished simply. They smiled gently at each other as each understood. Lohkan spoke an idea that might comfort his friends. He and Serra had experienced the pain of separation enough times for him to understand what Yerraba and Sumkan now faced. He looked at Tonak as he spoke.

"Perhaps Yerraba could guide Sumkan, as Serra and I have done for each other?"

This is her choice, as well as Sumkan's, the elder said. He gazed up at the two and awaited their decision. They nodded together and, with a blaze of light, they vanished. Serra smiled as she looked about the empty area near the waterfall. Only Lohkan's face met hers. They smiled at each other peacefully.

"Let's go to the meadow," Serra suggested, and they were there. They lay down on a thick patch of grass in the center of the meadow and held each other quietly; the next lives they had chosen would come soon enough, and in those lives they knew there was a good chance that they would not meet. This would be the last life together on Earth for each of them. Each knew they could change their minds afterward, but each doubted they would. They recognized the importance of knowing when something was completed. This study was almost finished, and they were ready to move on. Serra pulled Lohkan's arm tighter around her waist.

"Years seem like minutes or hours here in *the between.* Ten hours here could be ten decades on Earth. The ten years difference in our ages in this next life will make our reuniting on Earth more difficult," Lohkan said, as he rested his head on the grass and looked up at the sky. His blue eyes were surrounded by light, brown lashes. He ran his hand through his blond hair and then continued to talk.

"I can't experience the lessons I want if I wait ten years. Do you understand, Serra?"

"Yes," she said as she rolled over onto her stomach and looked into his face. After several lifetimes and numerous lessons, his attractive expression still caused her to forget all else whenever she looked at him. She kissed him softly and then continued.

"Tonak warned us. We'll encounter cultural differences, age differences and we'll be three thousand miles a part."

There was little optimism in Serra's voice, because she felt little hope in that moment. Each had agreed, though, that they wanted to complete the study and move on to whatever lay ahead. Lohkan spoke quietly now in Serra's mind.

I do not look forward to our separation. We'll have to hope that somehow we will be brought together. If not, at least we have the comfort of knowing that we will be reunited here.

Yes, was all she could answer.

She understood, now, all that had happened to them held a purpose and was perfect. Still, some lessons required more fortitude and patience than others. Serra knew that being separated from Lohkan would require a lot of each quality; and now she understood that theses qualities came from many souls, from the universe itself. She was not a separate, isolated being, floating through time and space. Countless lives touched hers. She was truly grateful to *The One* for all the love, support and strength that had been given to her.

As she completed this thought, the sound of ringing chimes filled the meadow. They both sat up and watched in wonder as Quan Yin appeared.

"Would you like to review the lives you have recently experienced?" she asked quietly, as she smiled at them.

"Yes," they answered.

The meadow began to fill with a white, rolling fog. Within seconds they were surrounded by its cool moistness. Dew drops clung to Serra's hair and skin. She looked up and noticed that Lohkan appeared to glow with a thousand tiny dewdrops of light. He looked so beautiful that she felt as if she could not breathe. She just sat and stared in wonder. He smiled at her, and she realized that he also saw her with the same breathtaking illusional effects. Quan Yin's voice brought them back.

"Look." She pointed to a place in the fog that had cleared; their lives replayed there. As the review came to an end, the fog began to lift, and soon the meadow was brilliantly lit by a midday sunlight. The purple sky above was rich and almost rosy in color. The air felt as if it had been washed and seemed to sparkle with a sharp cleanliness. Quan Yin spoke again.

"What did you learn?" she asked, and waited patiently for them to respond. Lohkan spoke first.

"We were given the chance to heal and use many of the lessons from other lifetimes," he began. "As Pauline, I experienced motherhood in all its emotions. I knew pain, joy, wonder, anxiety, peace and countless other feelings. I felt how unique it was to be a woman. I was loved and cherished by Jean. Any horrors of my life as Iduna, of being raped, that weren't healed, were healed by knowing Jean. He was always a gentle, loving and attentive husband.

"I experienced the wonder of creation through my children. Each child was uniquely precious and individual. Any remaining doubts I had about the individualistic quality of each soul were removed by this experience. Each of our children was wondrously different from the next. Being pregnant and bearing children was the single most wonderful experience of all my lifetimes. I shall never forget it," he said solemnly. He was quiet for a moment, as the emotions of which he spoke threatened to overcome him. Serra took his hand in hers. He continued.

"Our life was one that was rich in sensual joys. From nursing, to gardening, to lovemaking, to raising children, to living, our life was richer than anything I would have understood had I not experienced it. From the outside, I am sure it looked poor and simplistic. We had very little money. Yet, I never felt poor. Even at the beginning of our marriage, when we were truly financially poor, I felt wealthy. This life was remarkably rich in every way, except financially."

"What did this teach you?" Quan Yin asked Lohkan.

"I learned that being 'rich' is not a financial state. Money does not make someone rich. **The love that is inside a soul and the love that is shared between souls is what makes us rich.**"

Quan Yin smiled gently and looked at Serra. "You experienced this differently, did you not?"

"Yes." Serra nodded her head for emphasis. "I felt that our life was rich with love and beauty; but, I also was in a constant state of anxiety during the first years of our marriage. I was responsible for providing for our family, as Jean. Pauline's burdens were different and more immediate. Should she let Angelique visit Justine? Should she have Pierre work with her on the farm or go to school? How would she get her work on the farm done and care for our children? I respected her greatly for managing our home as gracefully as she did." Serra smiled at Lohkan and continued. "Many decisions for our family and home were made together, but the burden of financial responsibility was mine alone and rested on my shoulders. At times during the first ten years of our marriage, I felt I had failed Pauline and our children because of my choice of occupation. Yet, through my paintings, I could express and experience the richness of that life. I agree completely with Lohkan that this life was remarkably rich and beautiful. Our days were filled with quiet joys. Still, it took me many years to learn to release the guilt I felt about our financial station in life.

"I had been raised a farmer's son, and knew farming as an honest and honorable occupation. My father was sensitive and wise enough to help me toward my true calling, painting. He was never anything but supportive of my talents. He did not cause me to feel bad about any part of my life. The decision to feel bad about our state of poverty was truly my own. I wanted 'more' for Pauline and for our children. I did not see all that I did give them." Serra held Lohkan's hand more tightly. "Eventually I was healed, simply through the existence I lived. How could I feel sad when I was surrounded by five happy faces? The children grew and knew joy. Pauline prospered in this life, and at last I was able to see that my own joy had grown large and bountiful. One day, I realized it was simply ridiculous and impossible to continue feeling bad in the face of so much joy. From that moment on, I began to truly feel rich."

Quan Yin smiled and raised one slender hand in the air as a gesture for Serra to continue. Serra rubbed her cheek thoughtfully and resumed.

"My father was a quiet, but intently religious, man. As a Catholic, he had a strong faith in his family and his religion. I saw for the first time that religion is really a tool. What for, and how, each person uses it or indoctrinates religious teachings, is the responsibility of the individual. It would not have mattered if my father were a Moslem, a Buddhist or a Jew; he still would have embraced whichever religion he chose, in a loving, compassionate manner, for that was what he was, a loving and compassionate man. He did not grasp the fear-based teachings of man, but instead took to heart the love and wonder of God. He was not even particularly impressed by Christ, but he was enamored of his teachings. He taught me to love the miracle of life and God. My father helped me to heal the lifetimes I had lead; the intolerance I had known as an island woman who was conquered by priests, and my life as Lydia, under puritanical rule, were soothed. I learned that it was not religion itself, but the men who taught or dictated religions, who created love or pain."

Serra hesitated and smiled reflectively. She looked up into Lohkan's face, and her smile grew wider. The afternoon light played on her features and softened her expression into a mystical beauty. When she spoke again, her voice sounded distant, as if it floated, like her memories, away from the meadow and back in the French countryside where they had just lived.

"Religion is like a house that is empty. What an individual puts into that house will make it into one type of home or another. The home may be warm, cozy, loving and supportive to the individual. The home may be cool, sterile and only a place to retreat from the world, to hide

**from fears. Religion is a structure that allows individuals
to build their faith in whatever way they choose."**

"What about those who do not choose religion's structuring?" Quan Yin prompted her to think.

"On Earth, someone who does not follow religious doctrines is called an agnostic or, in some circles, a heathen, or an atheist, depending on the depth and expression of their choice. Now I can see that the choice to *not* experience religions would be because someone did not necessarily need this structuring. Perhaps a non-religious person is someone who does not need the structuring or illusional support of a church. This does not mean the individual or individuals are *not* part of *The One*, or God-like; it means only that they have chosen to experience their spirituality in a different form, in a way that is correct for them. I can see now that no one is ever separated from *The One*. This is a physical impossibility! How each experiences their *oneness* with the whole may take countless forms, and yet it is all the same!"

Quan Yin's smile broadened until she appeared to glow with a soft gold light.

"Yes, Serra. **We are all one. I am you. You are me. None are separate.** The style in which we represent our individualism may appear to be separate, but this, too, is an illusion."

The meadow filled with thousands of the transparent crystal spheres. All around them, the faint tinkling sound of glass brushing up against glass sounded like a soft melody of bells. The spheres began to spiral, and in the center a brilliant white light emerged. As the spheres circled faster, the light grew brighter. The rays spread out and through each individual sphere. The effect was breathtaking. Quan Yin pointed toward the spheres.

"See *The One*. All are part of the whole. You. Me. Every soul!"

The spheres disappeared, and Serra and Lohkan stood transfixed by what they had seen. After a time, Quan Yin spoke again.

"If you have no further questions, then it is time for Lohkan to leave. Are you ready?"

"Yes." He turned and embraced Serra one last time. Their eyes met. A single tear hung on the edge of Lohkan's eye as he whispered, "I love you."

Then he was gone.

Serra was left in the meadow by herself. She reflected on what she had learned. Here, in *the between,* all seemed right.

Accidents were not accidents, but awakenings for the souls who needed them. Pain existed only where it was necessary. Joy was possible in limitless forms. And love ... love was as endless and mystifying in this place as time was! She lay down in the purple flowers and fell asleep as she thought about her love for Lohkan, for *The One* and for herself.

❋

Quan Yin awakened her with a gentle touch of her hand. The place on Serra's cheek where Quan Yin's hand had been a second before felt static with electricity, and somehow soothed. She looked up into Quan Yin's beautiful dark eyes and yawned sleepily.

"Serra, we need to speak together before you go to the next life you've chosen. Soon you must leave."

Serra sat up and blinked at the purple flowers and lush green grass that surrounded her. She felt as if she had slept for just a few minutes. Quan Yin placed one of her small, delicate hands over Serra's large hand.

"Serra," she began gently and seriously. "This life you have chosen will be a difficult one in many ways. We have decided to send you back with the skills you have gathered intact. You will experience empathy, telepathy and many other skills that you have not *fully* known while human. These skills will be awkward to experience on this plane, but they will also give you what you need to survive. Ultimately, these skills will ensure the healing of all that you do experience. They will allow you to bring a healing to those around you, to this planet. However, this won't be easy." She looked compassionately into Serra's blue eyes. "These gifts will also carry pain. To go to this dimension with this kind of sensitivity and *not* experience pain would be impossible. There will be a purpose in all that you experience, the despair as well as the gifts."

"Eventually, you will be lead to experience the joys and wonders that you know here ... on Earth." She gestured to the meadow, to *the between*. "Your empathy will lead you to *The One*. Do you understand?"

"Yes," she said meekly. For the first time, Serra felt apprehensive.

"Serra, when this life is finished, if you have completed all that you have set out to do, you may go wherever you wish. Remember, you are never alone, and, Serra, remember that whenever your life reaches its lowest points you must not give up!" Quan Yin's voice held an earnestness that caused Serra to shudder.

Serra nodded again and wondered if she had the strength to face this life. To go to a life where she would feel each person's emotions and often hear others' thoughts, and to do so on a world where hate and fear were fostered, frightened her. Quan Yin suddenly leaned forward and embraced her. A charge of light, love and warmth filled her. The meadow vanished and the white light flowed around her. The last sound Serra heard was Quan Yin's musical voice.

"Serra, remember, you are never alone! I shall be with you!"

Part Three

1980 AD - 1994 AD

Chapter 15

*O*rryka floated in the busy cafe, invisible to the people who sipped wine, ate their meals, and spoke animatedly at their tables beneath him. A shimmering rainbow of colors surrounded him in a pastel cocoon. The white robe he wore moved gracefully with him, as if it were skin instead of cloth. His golden hair lay on his shoulders in thick waves. The smile that played across his lips and that lay in his blue-green eyes was for the young woman below him, a bus girl.

Most of the tables were filled with customers, and Sarah quickly cleared the few empty tables of their dirty dishes, and then carried the full bus-tray to the sink. Casual outfits of jeans and light, peach-colored shirts with the cafe's logo on the pocket were the standard uniform. Sarah's attire matched that of the waitresses, who moved around her, except that she wore an oversized apron. A cook yelled from the kitchen that an order was ready. Smells of garlic, bread, herbs and wine floated deliciously in the small California restaurant. Orryka hovered near the ceiling and watched Sarah work, as she meticulously stacked dirty dishes in the dishwasher.

Sarah's long, chestnut-colored hair was piled on top of her head, but a stray piece had fallen down her darkly tanned cheek. She patiently tucked it behind her ear and kept working. Wearily, she stopped for a moment and wiped her hands on her already soiled-apron. As she did, Orryka shook his blond head and spoke to her.

Sarah, you don't have to be that *careful. The dishes will get clean even without your precise stacking,* he teased. Although she could not hear his message completely, Sarah *did hear* enough of the message to suddenly become self-conscious. As she smiled quietly to herself, her long-fingered hands deftly rearranged the dishes into a less-than orderly display. Orryka chuckled softly and moved down next to her.

Sarah, you heard me! You're not crazy. I'm right here – next to you! Sarah, Look!

Orryka tried to make himself visible to Sarah as he stepped in front her, but Sarah walked through him and to the sink. He chuckled again and floated back up to the ceiling.

Almost! he said, and then went back to watching the scene below him and the door. Suddenly, the incident he had waited for, had planned so carefully, occurred.

The restaurant door opened, and a medium-sized man in his early-thirties with with shoulder-length, dark-blond hair, a reddish-brown mustache, wide-set blue eyes and a strong nose entered the busy cafe. He wore a denim shirt, and had his arm around a tall woman, also in her thirties, with long, red hair, blue eyes and dressed in the style of the early eighties, in a loose-fitting, flowered dress. The man pointed to a table, and then sat down after holding the chair for her.

Orryka quickly glided down next to the man's side and whispered in his ear.

Lohkan! Serra's here! Wouldn't you like to get some fresh air? The night is beautiful! Through that door is a hall that leads to an alley.

"Excuse me, Joan, but I think I'd like to use the men's room before we eat," the man said suddenly. His red-headed girl-friend looked puzzled, and then shrugged. "Okay, Thomas," she answered simply.

Thomas stood, looked about the bustling restaurant, saw a door marked with the restroom sign and headed toward it. Orryka sighed, as half his job was done. He quickly disappeared, and then reappeared next to Sarah. This time all subtleties were put aside as he tried to reach her. He shouted as he stood next to the her slim figure.

SARAH! Look up! No! Toward the side door! Serra, you must remember! It's Lohkan! He's here!

Sarah began to gather up a wet rag for washing tables, the bus tray and some clean silverware. As she turned toward the wall where the clean silverware was stored in shelves, a man walked by the open door in the side hallway and she dropped the bus-tray with a resounding crash.

Sarah's head swam, her heart began to pound loudly and small pinpoints of light flickered off to the left side of her body, as she saw this strange man walk by. He was so attractive to her that he took her breath away. An urgent need filled her, and she felt as if someone, something, was pushing her toward the doorway. She had to meet this man, to find out his name, to talk to him, to hold him....

This last thought caught her up abruptly. Sarah took a deep breath, and began to resume her work duties, but something would not let her go. Swiftly, she made a decision. She threw her bussing tray in the sink, grabbed a full bag of trash and dragged it out into the hallway. The darkness of the hall cooled her thoughts and wild emotions.

I must be crazy, Sarah silently thought as she stood in the hall. *I'm following a strange man who is older than myself into a dark alleyway. This is not good!*

No, Sarah! You're not crazy! Go! Hurry! He'll leave soon, a voice answered her. Sarah looked about herself, but no one was there. Only the dark passageway, with a dimly-lit, open doorway at one end, surrounded her. As she hesitated, a strong physical pressure began pushing her from behind, and she found herself rapidly moving toward the open door. She burst through the doorway and into the alley with a gasp of surprise.

The light bulb in the lamp by the door chose at that moment to burn out, and Sarah had only a second to glimpse Thomas' startled face up close. Something about his eyes caught and unbalanced her deep in her soul. She looked around herself awkwardly, desperate to make some sense of the situation.

Stars covered the night sky in a shroud of enigmatic beauty. Smells of fresh air mixed with stale fumes from the nearby dumpster contrasted this beauty with a more tangible reality. A dog barked somewhere in the distance and the buzzing of voices drifted out from the restaurant.

"Hi. Nice night, isn't it?" his voice said from the darkness.

"Yes. It is," Sarah answered in a quivery voice. *God! What a lame thing to say!* Sarah berated herself inside.

"That looks heavy. Do you need help with it?" the man asked thoughtfully.

"Huh?" Sarah answered.

"The trash. You had to drag it out here. It must be heavy," the man explained as if he were talking to a child. Then, without waiting for her response, he lifted the bag into the dumpster.

"Thank you," Sarah said hoarsely. *What is wrong with me? Why can't I talk?*

"I love to look at the stars," Sarah heard herself murmuring. This was not what she had intended to say.

"I do, too!" A lift in the man's voice spoke of his excitement.

"I wanted to be an astronaut when I was a girl," Sarah said before she could stop herself. *Oh my God! I can't believe I just said that!*

"Really? I can imagine that. What a life that would be – racing through the stars ..." he answered wistfully. "I'd better get back inside. My girlfriend and I won't make it to the movies, if I hold us up much longer. I'll walk back with you."

They turned together in unison and silently walked through the darkened corridor. Sarah turned toward the kitchen. A lump formed in her throat and again left her speechless. The man didn't seem to notice that she did not answer as he casually said goodbye. As he walked through the door that led into the brightly lit restaurant, Sarah ran back toward the ladies room, ducked inside and promptly burst into tears.

Thomas ordered the house specialty, handed his menu back to the waitress and then restlessly tapped his fingers on the table. Joan talked about her day, but he did not hear her or look into her pretty blue eyes as he normally did. Instead, he found himself watching the swinging door and the large open window that looked into the kitchen. Where was she? Had she been an apparition? Joan tugged on his elbow and brought him back to his circumstances.

"Thomas! Where are you? You haven't heard a word I said!"

"What?"

"I said, 'Do you want to go to Marin this weekend?' The Salivators invited us to go boating."

"I don't know," he answered distractedly.

Joan shook his arm roughly and swore under her breath.

"Damn it, Thomas! What's wrong with you?"

Her words were lost on Thomas, because at that moment Sarah emerged from the kitchen with her bus-tray. Her large, brown eyes met his, and then quickly and purposely looked away. She looked upset, and yet peaceful at the same time. A golden glow of light surrounded her. A customer spoke to her and a smile lit her graceful face as she responded and, as she smiled, Thomas felt the world around him slip away. The many voices in the cafe drifted into a quiet hum. Joan's touch on his sleeve became distant. His mind became profoundly still. The young woman looked up again and stared directly at him. The smile lingered on her full lips and Thomas found himself unconsciously smiling in return.

Suddenly, their exchange ended with a thud. With a cold shock, ice-water poured across the table and into Thomas' lap, and he was brought abruptly back to his realty. Joan's hand lay suspiciously near his glass. As Thomas mopped up the spill on his pants and the table, Joan whispered fiercely in his ear.

"I don't know who she is, Thomas, but you had better have a very good explanation!"

"She's a bus-girl. 'Girl', Joan. She can't be much over twenty-two, if she's that old. I have no idea who she is!" Thomas looked up into two intensely jealous eyes. Joan hissed out her answer.

"Don't give me a line of bull, Tom. You obviously know each other," Joan said, and threw her napkin down on the table. "Let's go!"

"We haven't eaten or...."

Her icy stare ended all debate. Carefully, Joan smoothed down her dress as she stood. She looked back over her shoulder at Sarah and stared hatefully in her direction. Joan bent, her long red curls falling forward, and whispered to Thomas.

"You either come with me now, or our relationship is over and you can stay with Miss-what's-her-name-bus-girl."

Thomas' face blanched at this challenge. A frown crossed his lips as he stared back at her. After four years, he understood her insecurities, but he was furious with her for making such a threat. He knew Joan understood that he would not throw their four-year relationship away for a strange girl. His hands shook slightly in his anger. Then, he stiffly stood.

As he rose, something knocked him back into his seat. Joan eyed him impatiently, but Thomas was too stunned to worry about her reaction. Someone had pushed him. He scanned the area around the table, but nobody stood close to them; the closest waitress was several yards away.

"Did you push me?" Thomas questioned Joan doubtfully.

"No! Of course not!" Joan said incredulously. "Let's go!"

Thomas! Lohkan, don't go! Serra's leaving tomorrow. This is her last day in California. Summer is over and she's going back to New England. If she does, you will not see her for years, maybe never! She'll get together with another man and she won't be happy. You won't be happy. Lohkan, hear me! Remember! Orryka tried earnestly to reach Thomas.

A wave of dizziness passed over Thomas, and he leaned against the table for a minute.

"Thomas, are you all right?" Joan asked. Her anger turned quickly to concern.

"Yes. I'm just a little dizzy," he replied from behind his hands. "Maybe you're right. We should leave."

Thomas stood slowly and began to walk toward the door. He did not look back at the bus-girl, because he knew in that moment, if he did, he would not leave at all. Silently, he turned, threw some money on the table as a tip and followed Joan out the door.

As Thomas walked out the door, Orryka sighed and shook his head. A split second later, a beautiful apparition floated down through the ceiling and to Orryka's side. Gently, Quan Yin put her delicate hand on Orryka's arm.

You have to accept it. They weren't ready.

No, they were ready. They simply didn't know it and ... we couldn't reach them, Orryka ended sadly.

Chapter 16

*T*homas paddled a green canoe down a deep river, which was mud-colored from the heavy winter rains. Hard rains had hit Northern California in a great sweeping wash, as if nature had become impatient with the thick layers of dust that many years of drought had created.

His only other companion was a fawn-colored dog that had long thick hair and large dark eyes. The dog barked happily at some ducks that swam by the shoreline, and the small flock rose into the air in a display of black, teal, white and brown feathers. Thomas halfheartedly scolded the dog, but his smile belied his reprimand and the dog chose to ignore him.

As Thomas raised his face toward the sky, a shadow from the flying ducks crossed his sunburnt face, and they circled once before landing farther upstream. His long, dark-blond hair was sun-streaked from countless days of sunshine during the previous summer. His beard, likewise, had been bleached by the sun into a golden auburn tone. The lines around his eyes, which burst sideways in a fan of fine wrinkles, were the only aspect of his countenance that gave away his age. His fortieth birthday was exactly nine months away.

Thomas did not feel old. Little had changed in his physical appearance over the past fifteen years since he had first moved to California from his native home in Texas.

He stayed the canoe by paddling backwards for a few minutes, so that he could watch a blue heron who stood serenely at the edge of the river. The heron swooped down gracefully and caught a fish. Less than a minute had passed, and the heron stood back in its watchful position, as stationary as if it were a carved statue. Thomas paddled on before the dog could decide to bark commands at this stately bird. Ahead, the river curved to the left, and a large, sandy beach lay at the base of that curve for fifty yards. He decided to set up camp on this beach for the night.

✳

That night, a star-filled sky hovered over Thomas from horizon to horizon. The small fire he had built burned encouragingly, as he stared into the flames in lost concentration. The dog had circled the camp many times, marking his territory, and then lay down to sleep while the man was still awake. Later, as Thomas slept, he would pace and guard camp.

Thomas was deep in reflection about his life, especially the last several years. He noticed the starry sky, the warmth of the fire and his dog's gentle snores, but with only part of himself. The greater part of him was submerged in reverie. He needed to find some answers.

He continued to stare into the flames as memories drifted into his consciousness. Before Thomas had arrived in California, and after, he had lived in unhappy and agitated relationships for years. He wondered now, as he had many times, why he had stayed in the tumultuous relationships as long as he had.

When Thomas had returned from Vietnam, he had married his high school sweetheart. Four years later, in his mid-twenties, his marriage had gone sour. The pain of his divorce and the disquieting knowledge that he had been part of an unjust war had left him distant and angry for years. And then Joan had appeared in his life, with her tall, red-headed beauty and fiery temper. After an up-and-down eight-year relationship, during which each of them had avoided any lasting commitments, they had mutually agreed to stop seeing each other. That had been two years ago. During the last two years, Thomas had decided to date only on a casual basis until he got his life together, until he discovered what he wanted and truly needed in a companion. The answers were coming to him slowly.

He added more wood to the fire, and warmed his hands in the burst of heat that resulted. The dog awoke, stretched, yawned loudly and then went off to relieve himself. When the dog returned, Thomas spoke out loud to him, as he did sometimes.

"Well, Rusty, what do you think I should do?"

The dog leaned up against him and whined in response.

"Yeah, me too, buddy. Maybe it's time we moved. Our lease is up next month. How would you like a new home?"

The dog did not answer, and instead curled up to sleep on the sandy beach near Thomas. Thomas stretched out next to the fire on his sleeping bag and bed roll. He stared up at the stars and spoke out loud to himself.

"I know what I want," he began. "I want a woman with whom I can be myself. I want her to understand and know me better than I know myself. I want her to love life, to have a wisdom that is natural and unaffected. She should be someone who is as interested in finding answers as I am. Yes. That's it! I'd like a woman with a thirst for spiritual knowledge. I want someone who's honest and doesn't play games. God, I'm tired of women who try to play games!"

Thomas yawned loudly and closed his eyes as he began to fall asleep.

"She should love the outdoors and wildlife. Maybe she could go camping with us, Rusty," he murmured softly. "Ice cream. I hope she likes ice cream."

Rusty's eyes opened at the mention of his favorite treat. He stretched slowly, and then went back to sleep. Thomas continued with his monologue, unaware.

"She should love the mystery of this universe and ..." he opened his eyes for a moment and stared at the night sky "... the stars. She has to love the stars."

This stirred a memory in Thomas that he could not quite catch. His arm fell to the ground as sleep finally caught him in her fragile nets. As he allowed sleep to drag him into her deep waters, a tune echoed in his mind. The song was "The Impossible Dream."

Days later, Thomas drove home to his rental on the coast. A thick fog had cloaked the beaches, ocean and town with a chilling moisture. He inched his way toward the street where his house was masked by dense whiteness. Something about the fog was comforting on this night. Thomas found the driveway by the small beachwood sculpture that stood at the end of it and, after he had parked the car, entered the house and started a fire in one of the fireplaces, Thomas went to the living room window, where he watched the fog drift through the night's blackness. Then, as Thomas turned back toward the fire, the room around him disappeared and he found himself stepping out onto a strange deck.

To his left were two large picture windows. Through the windows, Thomas saw a black woodstove in a stone hearth. On his right was a second-growth fir and redwood forest. He shook his head and the scene evaporated. Again Thomas was back at his house by the sea. As he climbed into bed that night, his tired mind wondered what he had seen.

Thomas forgot the vision until three days later, when he decided to visit a friend in the eastern mountains above Sonoma valley. As he drove away from the plaza and into the hills, he wondered what the vision had meant. He drove his truck up the steep, winding roads, lost in his mind's inner wanderings. Sunshine lighted the road infrequently, due to the heavy growth of trees on the hills, and the shadows offered a coolness and comfort that he did not completely understand. He reached his friend's road and drove down the dirt street until it dead-ended at his friend's cabin.

Thomas breathed in the cool mountain air as he stepped from his truck. He expected to find his friend there, but instead was met with a note tacked to the door.

Hey, Tom!
I was called to away to a fire in Mendicino County. I probably won't be back for days. Make yourself at home. There's a bottle of cabernet waiting for you on the counter. The hot tub is cranked up and ready. Don't touch my stash of chocolate!
 - Steve

Thomas sat down on the deck and crunched the note in his hands with a loud grunt. There was no reason for this to bother him as much as it did; he was tangibly angry and frustrated. He threw the wad of paper at the trash barrels that were lined up against the house and missed. He walked over, picked up the paper and tossed it into one of the large plastic bins. Then Thomas kicked the can violently with one strike and dented the side.

"Damn!" he muttered to himself. A voice startled him from behind as he swore.

"Can I ask what you're doing here?"

He turned to meet a young man who was dressed in a t-shirt, jeans and sneakers. The young man's jeans hung on his lanky body, and the sunglasses he wore slid down his small nose. His brown hair was cut short, except for one long tendril of hair, at the base of his neck. Thomas explained himself.

"I came to visit Steve, but he's not here. We were going to go hiking back up in the canyon." Thomas waved his hand absent-mindedly in that direction. The young man took off his sunglasses, folded them and hooked them on his t-shirt pocket.

"I look after Steve's place for him when he stays at the fire-house. My name is Cliff Perkins. I live in the cabin up there." He pointed back up the driveway, and then put his hand out to shake Thomas'.

"This is a beautiful place to live," Thomas said, as he shook the young man's hand. Thomas breathed deeply of the earthy aromas of the forest. The tall redwoods which surrounded Steve's deck shaded them and offered a peaceful setting. He was tired of the cloying stickiness of the coastal climate. This air here was dry and invigorating. An idea came swiftly to Thomas.

"Do you know anyone who has a cabin for rent in the area?" Thomas asked.

"Sure do! If you don't mind sharing – my place is available. My roommate left last month and I haven't replaced him yet."

A few minutes later, Thomas toured the three-bedroom cabin that this young man rented. Cliff was talking about about sports, the neighbors and cost of living, when the vision Thomas had had became real.

He stepped out onto the deck, and there, before him, was his vision. Two large picture windows looked back into the living room, where a black woodstove sat in a stone hearth. A thick sec-ond-growth forest stood to his right. A red-tailed hawk flew over the forest and screamed out in a haunting voice.

Time slowed and Thomas' heart beat loudly in his ears. He knew that Cliff was talking, but he could not hear him. A rush-ing sound filled his ears, and then everything stopped at once. His heart became a faint echo, the rushing sound dimmed, and Cliff's voice became loud and clear. He interrupted Cliff's mono-logue with a sudden movement of his hand.

"I'll take it."

"Well, I'm not sure. I still have to decide. If my best friend comes back from...."

"Here," Thomas handed him one of his business cards with his telephone number on it. "Call me when you decide. I can move in in three weeks. I'll pay two months' rent in advance."

As he drove down the mountain, Thomas wondered what the vision meant and what he had gotten himself into, by taking on a twenty-one-year-old roommate.

When Thomas arrived home from work, young men and women sat on the deck, while Cliff barbequed fish and chicken. Delicious aromas of dinner drifted out to Thomas as he stepped from his truck. The last of sunset had turned the walls of the wooden cabin from worn browns to rich amber tones. Large fir trees surrounded the small house. Laughter floated off the deck and Cliff yelled a friendly greeting. The scene was a familiar one.

"Hey, Tom. Get a glass of wine and pull up a lawn chair!"

"Okay. I'll be back in a minute," Thomas answered, and then yawned.

Inside, the party continued, as young men and women danced in the small living room. The walls shook with rock-n-roll and gyrating bodies. Thomas threw his Thermos and lunch pail on the cluttered and dirty counter. Open kitchen cabinets showed that there wasn't a clean glass in the house. Thomas left the kitchen in disgust and headed for the privacy of his bedroom.

The quiet of his room was a welcomed respite, and Thomas began to change out of his work clothes. He brushed sawdust from his woodshop off his jeans and was walking toward the closet when he heard a giggle. He stopped, and then cautiously approached the closet, as if it held a captive animal inside.

"Hello? Who's in there?"

More giggles.

"Okay. Come out!"

The door burst open and a young couple stumbled out. A youth with dark hair and dark eyes stared at Thomas. Thomas had met him, but could not remember the kid's name. His arm was around the waist of a tiny blond girl with too much makeup on her young face. She screwed up her pretty face as she tried to be serious. The boy drunkenly slurred his words as he addressed Thomas.

"Tomish! You're home."

The girl broke into a fit of laughter.

"This room is off limits," Thomas said as he looked around and noticed the crumpled bedding.

"Out! Both of you!" Thomas said angrily.

The young couple giggled and supported each other out the door. Thomas sat on his bed, put his face in his hands and swore softly to himself. Then he asked himself an important question.

"What am I doing?"

The party broke up early that night, at 1:00 a.m. and, as the guests climbed into their cars, Thomas checked to make sure each of the cars was manned by a sober driver. A young woman with soft brown hair, green eyes and soft round cheeks approached him with a sleepy smile.

"Thomas, you sure you wouldn't like some company tonight?" she said as she hooked her fingers into Thomas' belt. He peeled her hand away and directed her toward a car that was not quite full.

"Not tonight, Janine. Thanks for the offer."

"Awww ..." she moaned as he buckled her into the back seat.

With the last of the guests gone, the lights turned off and Cliff absorbed in a deep conversation about music with his latest girlfriend, Thomas climbed into bed. As exhaustion took over and his mind drifted immediately to sleep, he fell into the quiet world of dreams. Soon one dream – a vivid one – dominated his sleep.

In the dream, a woman walked up the dirt road toward the cabin where Thomas lived. Sunlight hit her from behind, hid her features and sharply outlined her slender body. She put out her hand as she approached, and Cliff, who stood closer, shook it first. Next Thomas reached out to take her hand and, as they touched, a blaze of white light exploded between them. Thomas felt as if he finally had come home. When the woman let go of his hand, a deep longing filled him. As she turned to go, Thomas realized that he had not seen her face. He watched her, and saw waist-length, chestnut-colored hair and a slender figure. The dress she wore seemed to float around her legs and her sandals kicked up mud. He tried to call after her, but could not hear the name, even as he said it.

He awoke from this dream late at night, restless and frustrated. He tiredly dressed in jeans and a t-shirt, stepped out onto the deck and whistled for Rusty. They strolled up the dusty road and came to a view that looked out over an expanse of mountains climbing away toward the north under a brilliantly starlit sky. Night's blackness lay around him as it could do only before dawn, absolute and still. Thomas stood silently watching this beauty when a question escaped his throat and hurtled out into the night sky.

"Where is she?"

He left the beautiful view, puzzled by his question, the passion he had felt and wondering who "she" was.

Several days later he dreamt about this woman again. He stood at the base of a grassy knoll in a rainstorm. Suddenly, the rain stopped, the clouds opened and several small shafts of sunlight lit the hill. As they did, a figure appeared. A woman with long, dark hair stood looking out over a valley. Her dress, which was wet from the rain, clung to her body. A strong wind came up and blew the woman's hair around her face. Once again Thomas was unable to see her features.

Thomas awoke feeling tired, lonely and frustrated. As he got ready for work, the phone rang and he answered it.

"Tom?"

"Yeah, it's me. What do you need, Steve?" he asked his neighbor.

"How's the party house?"

"Funny."

"When are you going to kick Cliff and his friends out? Does that irresponsible joker still owe back rent?"

"He's moving to Washington with his girlfriend next month. What do you want? I have to leave for the job site in a few minutes," Thomas said as he poured hot water over the tea bags in his Thermos.

"My cousin is coming to visit a friend out here. She asked if she could visit me for a few days, but I'll be at the station when she's here."

"Yes?"

Thomas was growing impatient. The dream had left him moody and tense.

"Well, I figure that since you live with a bunch of kids, you must like them...." Steve paused as he waited for Thomas to get his point. He continued a few seconds later when Thomas refused to respond. "Tom, can't you show her around? Take her wine tasting, or something?"

"Wait a minute, I thought you said she was a kid? How young are we talking about? Besides, I'm working this week."

"So, take time off. I thought that's what being independent was all about. I haven't seen my cousin in years. I think she's in her mid-twenties or something. You've dated younger than that since you moved into that party house. Come on, Tom, be a bud."

"Okay," he relented. "What's her name?"

"Sarah."

Chapter 17

Wind howled around the cabin and caused a loose shutter to bang loudly against the cabin wall. Tree branches scratched at the windows and a cat, who sat huddled in a corner, meowed loudly with fear. With a brilliant flash, a bolt of lightning momentarily revealed the world around the cabin that a moment ago had been hidden in the night's blackness.

The cabin was surrounded by a hardwood and evergreen forest, which stretched on for hundreds of acres. A few tall evergreens poked their heads majestically above the back of the cabin as if they stood guard, like sentinels at a gate. The branches of the evergreens were those that scratched mercilessly at the windows. The cat hissed as an especially loud screeching from the scraping boughs echoed through the cabin.

A river ran through the forest and formed a waterfall several yards north of the cabin. As the lightning illuminated the outdoors, a tumultuous view of the waterfall and river was displayed. The river roared frantically over large rocks and dived with abandon to the base of the waterfall, where it hurried onward, through the small canyon and farther into the forest. The canyon walls were high, so no danger of flooding presented itself, though eight inches of rain had fallen in the last twenty-four hours.

Again thunder echoed across the small canyon and shook the walls of the cabin. The occupant of this cabin lay in her bed and slept through the worst of the storm in a fevered state, until her cat jumped onto her back. The cat's cry mixed with the storm's howling and woke Sarah into a surreal world where nightmares and reality mixed.

She pushed herself up and looked about in a sweaty haze

of illness and confused lethargy. The lightning struck somewhere in the forest. It hit a tree, causing a loud trumpeting noise which sounded through the forest and cabin.

Sarah tried to get up to go to the sink to get another glass of water, but could not move. Her body was racked with fever and pain from some unknown illness. She drank the last couple of mouthfuls of water from the glass on her bedside table, and then she popped a thermometer into her mouth. While Sarah waited, she fell asleep, and woke up fifteen minutes later when a loud clap of thunder rolled over the small valley. When she read the thermometer in the light of a flashlight by the bed, she saw that her temperature was 104 degrees. Deliriously, Sarah thought that the number sounded good, and fell back to sleep.

Dreams followed and, in her fevered state, became stranger than usual. Sarah dreamt of tall men and women who were light-skinned and fair-haired. One of the beings spoke to her and asked if she remembered them. This man mispronounced her name and told her about other planets and about her work here on this planet. She eventually fell into a sleep where she did not dream at all and where she peacefully rested. When Sarah awoke the next day, she remembered nothing of her dreams, and only the storm.

Sarah sat in front of the cabin in her old Mission Oak rocking chair in the sunshine. She had made a cup of tea, wrapped herself in a blanket and then stared for hours at the beauty of the waterfall. The storm had blown the rest of the leaves to the ground, and the forest floor glittered coppery gold from the reflection of sunlight on this autumn splendor. Days passed, and she did little else. The cool autumn air acted as a refreshing tonic that soothed her worn soul. This time of solitude and reflection was necessary. Sarah needed to be alone with this abundance of quiet to find answers, and serenely she accepted her ailment as a gift.

For years she had sought to ignore her feelings through work. She earned very little as a chef and had used that as a reason to take a second job. Sarah knew, as she stared at the waterfall, that the second job was just an excuse to avoid the pain she felt in and around her.

As Sarah sat there, the convalescence forced her to face that which she had fought so hard to escape. Her life was a mess. A seven-year relationship had ended months ago. The job she had as a pastry chef had no real prospects. Inside herself a chasm of loneliness and isolation had grown and strengthened over the years. She had to get help somewhere, had to get her life togeth- er. Sarah did not know how she would accomplish this; she sim- ply decided she would. Having made this decision, a wonderfully intoxicating peace settled over her.

A friend recommended a local meditation group, from which, at first, Sarah shied away. Eventually Sarah joined, although she doubted that it would do any good at all. Each week she sat amongst strangers and wondered why she was there. What answers could she possibly find through meditation? The other members were kind to her, but their companionship did lit- tle to bridge the gulf of isolation she felt. Then, during one of the meetings, a curious event took place.

In a room at the local college, where they gathered, the group sat together in a circle. The different members sat in cross- legged positions on mats on the floor. The lights were dimmed and the instructor rang a Tibetan bell to announce the start of their meditation. Sarah had been meditating quietly for a few minutes, when she felt herself lift effortlessly out of her body.

The room became acutely clear. A school clock showed that it was well past seven in the evening. The heating system moaned and creaked as the heat came on. Sarah watched the people in the room as they meditated. Most everyone was in some relaxed pose. One woman had even fallen asleep and sat hunched over on her mat. The instructor stood out with her bright auburn tresses as Sarah viewed her from the ceiling.

Sarah looked down and saw herself, her body, sitting on the mat. Her dark-brown hair was braided into a loose braid that hung down her back and which came to rest on the mat. Her dark lashes formed two crescents over her high cheekbones and slender face. The thick green-colored sweater she wore was pushed up over her elbows. Worn places on the knees of her jeans looked thinner than she remembered. She hadn't realized how much weight she had lost due to the illness she had suffered two months ago. An odd detached feeling crept over Sarah, as if she watched from a distant place, as if she were viewing someone else and not herself. Just as Sarah was beginning to accept her bizarre state, she floated up and through the ceiling of the old brick building.

A black night sky with a quarter moon met her eyes as she looked up. Below her, cars pulled into and out of the campus parking lot. A group of young men stood around a new car, a

1985 Volvo, with the hood up. One youth lit a cigarette, and Sarah watched as the smoke drifted up and past her in the night's moist air. Somehow none of this seemed uncomfortable, and Sarah stayed there in the night sky. She watched as a friend drove into the parking lot and took a spot by the door. As Sarah's friend stepped from her car, Sarah wondered if she was visible. With that thought, Sarah felt herself falling rapidly through the building and into her body. Just as she landed solidly in her own flesh, the teacher rang the bell to announce that their meditation time was over.

Quickly, Sarah gathered up her coat and purse and ran from the classroom and into the hallway. The school doors opened, and in walked her friend. In the parking lot, the Volvo started up and drove off into the night.

An early winter chill had settled over the small New England valley when Sarah arrived for her meditation group. For the past week her mind had sought to understand the events of the last class, but she had found no answers. As she stepped into the shelter of the old building, warm air hit her face and the oversized clock in the hall told her that she was fifteen minutes early. She opened the door to the classroom, switched on the lights and sat to wait for the other members of her group.

One by one, people drifted into the room. Sarah breathed deeply, as the instructor had taught her, but this time it was to calm her apprehensions. Finally, all class members had arrived and the teacher rang the bell. Sarah closed her eyes and drew in a quivery breath. Would it happen again?

Before Sarah had time to wonder, she felt herself leave her body. She observed the room for only a few seconds, and then floated up into the sky. This time she let herself move forward without limiting her actions. She flew soundlessly over darkened hills, forests and towns. Motion became faster and everything about her blurred into nondescript shadows. Suddenly, she came to a stop in some distance place.

Where am I? Sarah wondered.

An answer came immediately, as a cabin with tall fir trees came vividly into view. The sky in this distant place was stark blue, because the sun had not set. A mountain jay flew through Sarah and into one of the trees, and Sarah smiled at the strange tickling sensation this caused. Another question arose in Sarah's mind.

Why am I here?

As if in answer to her question, a man stepped from the cabin and onto the deck that surrounded the house. The man looked out into the forest, and Sarah knew, without question, that he could not see her, did not know she was there. Something about him was familiar, but she could not say what. His attractive features were intimate and made her feel as if she were viewing an old friend. The set of his eyes and their unusual color of faint blue caused a hunger in her ... for what she could not say.

The man whistled loudly, and the sound of something running through the underbrush came from the forest. In a streak of reddish-gold, a dog burst onto the deck and ran up to the man. Before the man could pet this large dog, the dog turned and stared at Sarah. Sarah was stunned.

You can see me! she said with excitement.

"Woof – woof!" he answered and wagged his tail.

"What is it, Rusty?" the man said, and looked up and then through Sarah toward the tree. "It's only a bird. Come on, Rusty. It's time for dinner."

Rusty pushed the man with his nose, and then assumed a pointing position. When the man did not respond, Rusty barked loudly, turned in circles and looked up at Sarah again. The man laughed, shook his head and walked back into the house. As he did, Sarah head the sound of a bell tinkling softly in the distance. The cabin vanished, the sky turned into blackness and Sarah felt herself hurtling through space. A moment later, she landed back in her body. Class was over and the other members were leaving the room.

Months had passed, and Sarah's out-of-body experiences continued. Winter had taken a firm hold of the land and, one night, when the temperatures had dropped well below zero and the waterfall had turned into a magnificent, giant ice sculpture, the phone rang. When Sarah picked it up, she heard a strong, bright voice filling the line.

"Sarah! It's me, Zoie!"

"Where are you?" Sarah asked in surprise. Zoie was an old friend who lived in Northern California in the Sonoma Valley. Sarah had not physically seen Zoie since the summer she had traveled out to the West Coast, almost six years ago. Her friend's voice broke into loud laughter as she informed Sarah that she was in New England.

"You're here?" Sarah could hardly believe it. "When can you come by? When can I see you?" she asked excitedly.

A few nights later, Zoie stood on her doorstep with a large grin across her expressive face.

"I heard you calling," Zoie informed her seriously.

"What did you you mean when you said 'I heard you calling?'" Sarah asked, once both friends had settled by the woodstove with a couple of glasses of wine. Zoie went on to explain that she had had a dream weeks ago, in which Sarah had called to her for help. She finished by informing Sarah, "I've come to take you back to California. That's where you need to be."

"You're nuts!"

"I'm nuts? Okay. Stay here and freeze your butt off!" Zoie pointed to the two-foot icicles that hung from the eaves.

A week later, Zoie returned to her home in Sonoma County, and the next day Sarah bought a round-trip plane ticket for San Francisco. Sarah wondered about this impulsive decision, but set it aside in the rush of work that faced her before her trip.

As Sarah prepared for the trip, a strange event took place. One day, as she stopped at the local post office to pick up her mail, she sighted a wanted poster on the advertisement board. A convicted rapist had escaped and committed several more rapes in the rural county in which she lived. She shuddered uneasily as she read about the man, and then fearfully realized that she had to go home to an empty cabin in a secluded forest. She swallowed and steeled herself to face the isolation that surrounded her home.

For the next few nights, she hardly slept. When she did sleep, nightmares about the rapist plagued her much-needed rest. The night before Sarah was to leave for California, she arrived home to find that her cat Megan was again stuck up in one of the tall trees which surrounded her cabin. Sarah tried for hours to coax the little calico cat down from the high boughs of the old evergreen, but her efforts were to no avail. Twilight deepened, the shadows of the forest grew darker, and Sarah's fears grew as dark and deep. When the first stars hovered in the inky sky, Sarah cursed Megan under her breath, and then ran to the safety and warmth of her cabin.

Later that night, as Sarah checked her luggage one last time, she debated whether to try again to get Megan down from the tree. Megan had treed herself countless times, and would come down when she was ready. Yet Sarah could not bear to leave until she knew the animal was safely on the ground.

Sarah wrestled with her conscience as she stared out the window and toward the tree were Megan huddled in the darkness. Her own worried expression stared back at her from the window glass. Large brown eyes stared at Sarah and dared her to go out into the cold. *Coward!* they taunted.

Finally, she pulled on her coat and stepped out into the frigid night air. At first all was quiet except for the sound of snow crunching under her shoes. Abruptly, the sound of wind came up and blew through the tall pines. A ghostly wail sounded, and Sarah froze midway between the tree and the cabin. Her heart began to race, and instinctively she turned, ran back inside and swiftly bolted the door.

By the time Sarah's heart had stopped pounding and she realized that the wind had created the sound, she had been crying on her bed for nearly a half hour. More than anything, she was frustrated and irate that a woman could not safely venture out alone after dark. She turned off the lights, disappointed with herself that she could not find the strength to face her fears, and try one last time to get the cat down from the tree. As she lay there crying, a voice spoke from behind her.

Serra? Can you hear me?

She started and turned around. Before her stood a giant of a man. His blond hair was shoulder-length, and his blue eyes twinkled as he looked down at her. Sarah knew, as she lay there, that she should have been afraid, but something about the man was very familiar. He was surrounded by a golden-white light that shimmered faintly. His long white robe flowed in a rainbow of colors as he moved. He smiled at Sarah and spoke gently. He did not speak verbally, yet she heard him clearly, as if he had.

Serra, you can hear me! he said, and then added more gently, *Why are you crying?*

At first she did not answer him. She closed her eyes and willed him away. When she opened her eyes a moment later the apparition was still there. She answered his question.

"I am afraid."

You do not have to be afraid, Serra. You are not alone. I am with you.

"Who are you?" she asked.

Don't you recognize me? the man asked, and his laughter rang throughout the cabin. His laughter and his smile were infectious. Sarah found herself smiling in return, but then she again closed her eyes to make the vision go away. When she opened them a moment later, the man still remained.

"What are you doing here?" she asked stubbornly. She felt strangely comfortable with this apparition.

I am here to help you, Serra.

"My name is 'Sarah.'"

Yes. That is correct – Sarah. I am here to act as your guide.

"How do I know I can trust you?" Sarah asked.

He chuckled and Sarah smiled. Unwanted tears began to fall more freely. He stopped and questioned her.

What is wrong, Sarah?

"I am tired and afraid. My cat is stuck up a tree. My life is a mess, and now I am having hallucinations. I've really gone round the bend this time." She sobbed into her pillow. The man spoke gently inside her head. She could not escape him.

Sarah, watch. If I get your cat down, will you believe that I mean you no harm?

"Yes," she answered tentatively.

Then, look! he said. She sat up and watched as the wall of her cabin evaporated before her eyes. The man strode through it and walked up to the tree, where Megan sat twenty feet above the ground. Suddenly, he floated in the air, up twenty feet, and spoke to the cat. Megan stretched stiffly, and then began to climb slowly down the tree trunk. Sarah watched in amazement as Megan jumped the last four feet to the snowy ground and ran toward the cabin. As one velvety paw touched the door, the wall and door became solid. Sarah heard a soft meow, and she jumped up to open the door. As an icy blast of air hit Sarah in the face, the cat ran in through the open doorway. Sarah stood with her mouth hanging open, the icy air searing her bare feet and hands. There was no sign of the man. She hurriedly closed the door.

As she turned back toward her bed, he appeared again. His smile held a warmth that reached down deep inside her and touched something she could not name. She stood and shivered in the middle of the room, trying to decide what to do. The man stood between her and the bed, which was next to the woodstove. Finally, cold overcame her fear, and she ran to the warmth of her sheets and blankets. Once she was tucked in, she peered out to see if he was still there. He stood as he had before, benevolently smiling at her. She questioned him.

"Why are you still here?"

I am here to protect and guide you, Sarah. Sleep now. I shall guard your cabin and you.

She started to protest, but felt oddly safe and comforted. She yawned loudly and nestled more deeply into the pillows. She told herself silently that she had created this hallucination to get herself through a stressful period in her life. She explained away the apparition by telling herself that the whole experience was a dream from which she would awake in the morning. As she drifted off into sleep, she heard his voice once more.

You are not hallucinating, Serra. I am real. Sleep now. Do not worry any more. You are not alone.

"My name is Sarah," she mumbled, and fell asleep.

The next morning when Sarah awoke, the cabin was bitterly cold. She did not relish getting up in the icy air, and snuggled deeper under the thick comforter. Her strange dream came back to her. She had eaten little last night – perhaps that had caused the hallucination. At least she had slept well and had had no nightmares! At that moment, she remembered that Megan still needed to be coaxed from the tree. With this thought, she convinced herself that she must get up and face the cold. As she rolled over, her face touched a soft fur ball that began to loudly purr. Sarah sat straight up in bed and looked about her. Megan stood, stretched and then lazily climbed onto her lap. It had not been a dream after all.

Chapter 18

*A*irplane engines vibrated the book that Sarah held in her hand. She put it away in a handbag under the seat, leaned back and closed her eyes. She was still tired, even after last night's deep sleep. She tried not to think about the apparition she had seen and thought instead about her life in general.

She had no idea in which direction to go next. She did not know what she wanted to do with her life. Cooking bored her slightly, but not completely, and she knew she could go on for a couple more years as a chef. What would she do after that? Where would she live, and how would she make a living? Living in the same town as her ex-boyfriend was becoming increasingly difficult. She could not avoid him or the stories she heard about him. She needed a change on a much larger scale than she had ever intended. She needed to move to another part of the country and begin over completely. She rubbed the sides of her head as a headache began. She wished fervently for a sign, any sign, that her thoughts were taking her in the right direction. Was it smart to pick up and move away from her home, family and friends on an emotional whim? Was it a whim? Should she go back to school and get her degree, and with which to do what? She decided to stop trying to organize her life, and all in five minutes. She was, after all, supposed to be on vacation.

Sarah stretched and opened the shade of the window where she sat. The sight that met her eyes shocked her, and she felt herself pale. She jumped and immediately closed the shade.

The plane flew thousands of feet above the earth, and a few hundred feet above a high ceiling of white clouds. The clouds glowed golden in the early-morning, winter sunlight. Out on the wing of the plane stood a man drenched in this same golden light. His long white robe fluttered in the wind, and his longish blond hair streamed behind him. His blue eyes twinkled, and he smiled generously when Sarah saw him. It was the same man who had visited her last night. A man? This was no man, but a hallucination!

She cursed to herself, and then got up the courage to open the window shade again. As she peered out at the beautiful expanse of sky and the airplane wing, she was markedly relieved to see a normal sight. No one was there. She sighed and worried about these strange hallucinations. Was she losing her mind? Why was this happening? Hadn't she been through enough this past year, and in her life? Was this a sign that she was breaking down emotionally and should seek help?

She began to go through a list, step by step, of qualities she could check to see if she was going crazy. Was she lucidly aware of herself and her surroundings? Yes. What was her name? Sarah Abigail Clark. How old was she? Twenty-eight. Where did she live? North Hampton, Massachusetts. How tall was she? Five feet and seven inches. How many brothers and sisters did she have? Two of each. What were their names? Charlene, Bruce, Pauline and Wayne. She listed them from oldest to youngest. She was next to youngest, between Pauline and Wayne. What was her favorite pastimes? Reading. Canoeing. Hiking in the New England forest that surrounded her home. Where was she going? To Sonoma, California to visit her friend and cousin. What would she do when she returned?

Sarah could not answer this last question, and sank further into the seat on the airplane. Maybe this is where the problem lay. She was suffering from some unusual neurosis due to an identity crisis of sorts. Maybe she suffered from the side affects of sleep deprivation. She closed the window shade and muttered to herself.

"I guess I am crazy."

You're not crazy, Sarah.

A kind male voice spoke next to her. No one had taken the seat beside hers since Sarah had boarded, and her eyes flew open as he spoke. The man who had been on the wing of the airplane a moment ago sat contentedly next to her in the adjoining seat. He smiled at her and continued to speak. Sarah looked around, but no one else seemed to see or notice this strange man. He literally glowed as he sat there; a warm golden color filled the space where he sat. His presence immediately caused a strong sense of love and longing in Sarah, somewhere deep inside, that she could not yet touch. She trembled slightly as he spoke to her in his soft, rich voice.

Don't worry, Sarah. You are not going crazy. You are waking up! You can see and hear things others cannot. This does not make you crazy.

"That's what you think! Who are you?" she whispered and looked around again to see if anyone heard. A businessman across the aisle, in the center row, ignored her and scribbled notes on a pad of paper in his briefcase. A couple in front of her chatted about their trip to Boston. A very large man sat behind her with his head on his chest; deep rumbling snores poured through his lips as he slept. She looked back at her peaceful companion, expecting him to be gone, but he sat there as before and smiled at her.

I am an old friend, Sarah. I was sent to help you – right now, to bring you to California, he said.

"Why? I don't understand."

Sarah, sleep. You need rest. Don't worry about anything. I'll be with you.

With these words, he disappeared, and a faint glow hovered where he had just been. Sarah stared sleepily at the haze he had left. Her eyes began to feel unbearably heavy and, though she had many questions, her mind could not stay awake to try to answer them. She yawned once and fell asleep.

A loud speaker overhead blared out that Sarah's flight had landed. Sarah dragged her overnight bag, a suitcase and her purse through the busy airport. She did not see her cousin at first, and wondered if he had been called out to a fire. A voice caught her attention, and she turned to see her cousin Steve. All six feet and four inches of him was as trim and muscular as Sarah remembered. The freckles across his nose spoke of a youthfulness that belied the lines that had begun to appear around his forty-year-old eyes and mouth. His carefully shaved face broke into a lopsided grin as he saw her. Sarah laughed as he boyishly picked up her slim body in a big bear hug.

"Hey, cous! Glad you could come for a visit!"

She wrestled free of his muscular grip and smiled up at him. "Here, put those muscles to use," she said, and pushed her heavy suitcase toward him. He lifted it as if it were a balloon, and took her overnight bag, too.

"Come on, cous. I don't have much time. My shift is in three hours. If we hit traffic and I'm late, then I'll be one sad puppy."

They drove the two-hour route through San Francisco, across the Golden Gate Bridge and into Marin County. Tiburon and Marin passed by in a blur of shopping centers, car dealerships and restaurants. As they drove by Sausalito, Sarah looked wistfully at its sun-washed beauty. Boats, restaurants and buildings were nestled artfully on a hillside, which overlooked the bay. The town quickly disappeared out of sight with the curve of the road.

Soon they were climbing the mountain road that led to Steve's house. Sarah was silenced by the profound beauty that met her eyes. Tall second-growth redwood and fir trees dwarfed the dirt and gravel road. A brilliant blue sky towered overhead and hawks circled lazily above the forest. One of the powerful birds screeched out a call to its mate, and Sarah shivered with awe at its beauty. They passed several other small cabins, and then arrived at Steve's house at the end of the road.

Steve carried in her bags, while she stared in wonder at a giant redwood tree that stood several yards from his quarters. The tree's girth was half as wide as Steve's home, almost fourteen feet across. She tilted her head backwards and followed the trunk upward as its top disappeared beyond her sight into the sky.

"You're going to hurt your neck," Steve joked from the deck.

"It's huge!" Sarah said as she circled the tree.

"You see how twisted the middle section is? The loggers couldn't use it with this odd shape. So, they left it. It's one of the last old-growth trees on the mountain."

Sarah didn't answer because she was speechless.

"Come on, Sally. I'd better show you around before I leave."

Steam rose up from the water as Sarah lowered herself into the hot tub. A quarter-full moon rose over the tall trees and cast a dim light over the dark forest. The two candles Sarah had found in the bottom drawer in the kitchen cabinet were now lit, and flickered faintly where they sat on the picnic table on the deck. She sipped from a glass of merlot that she had poured a half hour before. Steve had instructed her to let the wine breathe for at least a half hour before she drank any. She wasn't sure why this was necessary, but followed his instructions anyway. She had to admit, the wine was flavorful and delicious.

As she soaked in the tub and sipped the rich wine, a shadow moved toward her through the forest. At first she did not see it, but when she did, she looked about herself for a place to escape. The forest came up to Steve's cabin on all sides, except for where the deck and hot tub lay. The road from which the shadow now approached was the only way out. Sarah wondered if she had time to run to the house, but she did not, as the dark shape and the sound of footsteps moved quicker now and headed directly toward Steve's place. She took a deep breath and slid underwater. She tried not to move or splash and kept herself from floating to the top by bracing her knees against the underwater bench on which she had just sat. She doubted that she was visible in the darkness, and then remembered the candles.

"Oh, shit!" she thought to herself as she struggled to hold her breath longer. Her lungs began to ache. She felt as if the air was being torn from her lungs. Finally she had no choice but to emerge for fresh air. She poked her head out and exhaled silently. No one was visible from this limited view. As she slowly raised her head a little to look over the edge of the hot tub, a large form jumped up in front of her.

Sarah gasped ... and then began to laugh. Two upright, pointed ears were cocked forward in intent interest. Dark eyes and a large, wet, black nose stared back at her. Two big furry paws held onto the wooden frame of the tub, as a dog stood on its hind legs to peer at Sarah. The dog had jumped as Sarah had. He now resumed a more relaxed pose and began to sniff her. Sarah patted the large head with her wet hands, and long, red strands of hair stuck to her hands. As she leaned forward to attempt to read the dog's name tag, he licked her face and neck.

"What's your name?" Sarah asked as she scratched him behind the ear. His tags were unreadable in the dim light. Now that they had met, he backed off, jumped down from the platform on which the hot tub sat and trotted over to Steve's door and barked twice. Sarah wondered why Steve had not told her he had a dog. She climbed out of the hot tub, toweled off and wrapped herself in her bathrobe. She blew the candles out and took the dog inside. After her eyes had adjusted to the brightness of the indoor lights, she squatted down to read the dog's name tag. He licked her face again.

"Rusty. Okay, boy," she said as she flipped the tag over to check the owner's name and address. She saw that the dog belonged to someone named "Thomas...." The last name was worn off the tag. Whoever he was, he lived on the same road as Steve.

"Oops. I'd better let you out. You must belong to one of those cabins up the road."

She opened the door and coaxed the large dog to go out,

but instead Rusty circled three times and lay down. He stared at Sarah with large dark eyes and panted happily. She again tried to coax him, but he refused to move. Sarah had just decided to call the number on the tag, when a loud whistle echoed through the forest. The dog jumped up and ran out the open door, and Sarah smiled as she watched him disappear into the darkness.

The next day Sarah awoke early and baked a pan of cinnamon rolls for her cousin. Steve was due to return later that morning. Steve was a friendly and gracious host, but it was never easy to have someone else living in your home. She set the hot rolls in the middle of the table with a note, and then left to enjoy the coolness of the morning.

Sarah walked up the driveway and stopped for a moment to pat Rusty, who stood guard in front of a cabin. He was even more beautiful in the daylight. As Sarah petted him, she stared at the house, which seemed vaguely familiar. Although, she could not place where she had seen it.

Soon Sarah found a narrow path that led away from the road and through the undergrowth. She sighed contentedly as the peace of the forest settled over her. There was nowhere else where she felt as peaceful. The ocean offered her wonder in its churning power, the city offered excitement with its chaotic mix of mirth and dimension, but only forests offered her the depth of peace she now felt. She hiked on happily, unaware of time, life's problems or any other human entrapments.

Suddenly, the forest opened to a hillside vineyard, and Sarah took a deep breath as she looked at another kind of beauty. A vineyard reservoir lay at the base of the hill, reflecting the vineyard, forest and gray sky in a perfect mirror image. A storm had rolled in during the night.

A wind gusted up the hill and around her, blowing her hair across her face. For a moment before it did, she saw a man hiking along the base of the hill with a dog. The dog barked happily, and she recognized Rusty. She was about to call out or wave to the man, when the wind picked up, became intense in its strength and the cloud above her opened up. Sarah laughed and sputtered as streams of water poured down her face, into her mouth and over her. A shaft of sunlight came through a hole in the cloud and down onto her shivering body. She hugged her arms to her sides, shook her wet hair and then ran the rest of the way back to Steve's cabin.

The following days were a combination of social activities and quiet introspection. She and Zoie went shopping and talked away hours in long visits. Steve took her hiking and sailing, after he had borrowed his neighbor's, Thomas', sailboat.

After a few days with her friend Zoie, she decided to return to Steve's house for another visit before she returned to New England. When she arrived at Steve's house, she found a hastily scripted note that explained that he had been called away to a fire, and that Thomas would be by to check on her. The name Thomas had been written in large letters and underlined. Sarah shook her head as she read the note. Steve was more of a big brother than her own brothers were. She settled in, read a mystery novel for awhile and then drank a glass of wine that made her sleepy. She decided to take a nap out on the chaise lounge on the deck. As Sarah slept, a series of strange dreams visited her.

A tall man, with pale blond hair and striking blue eyes, looked into her eyes. He held her and spoke about things that made no sense to Sarah. She pulled away from the man and saw a pastel purple sky above her. The sky began to ripple, and then turned into an ocean. She felt herself pulled into it, and the purple became a blue-green, which darkened to a grayish-green as she went deeper. She held on tightly to something. She looked, and saw that she held the dorsal fin of a dolphin. In her mind, she heard the dolphin speak to her, and was startled awake. As she awoke, she found she was lying on her side with one arm slung over the side of the lounge. Her hand was clasped tightly on Rusty's collar as he lay asleep on the deck next to her.

Rusty stayed with Sarah for the rest of the afternoon. They walked together and, as evening drew on, she fed him and herself sourdough bread and cheese. Finally, Sarah decided to walk Rusty back up the road to his home. She hugged him once tightly, and then strode up the driveway.

From the cabin music came that was soothing and familiar; Sarah recognized Andreas Vollenweider's "White Winds" as she knocked on the door. The man who opened the door left Sarah confused and breathless. His eyes met Sarah's, and for a moment the dream rushed back to her. Clear and piercing blue eyes looked into hers, and she felt strangely dizzy. His long blond hair was pulled back and accented his blue eyes. His features were handsome, and became more so as he smiled. Where had she seen him? She started to talk, but only stuttered as the dizziness became worse. Suddenly, bright flashes of light exploded around her in a brilliant and confusing display of star bursts, their appearance merry and oddly comforting. Sarah shook her head, but the pinpoints of light remained. She focused on the man in front of her, hoping she would become lucid again.

"Are you all right?" he asked.

"Yes. I'm fine," Sarah answered. She felt extremely foolish and hastily continued. "Hi. I'm Steve's cousin, Sarah. I've been staying with him. This dog, Rusty, was down at his house." Rusty wagged his tail at the mention of his name.

"Yeah, Rusty does that. He thinks this entire neighborhood is his territory. I hope he wasn't bothering you. Oh, yeah, I'm Thomas. I've been trying to reach you by phone the past few days, but no one answered. I was going to go down in a few minutes to introduce myself." He thrust out his hand for Sarah to shake.

As she shook it, the small pinpoints of light blazed and Sarah's sight was temporarily blinded. She closed her eyes and tried to erase the image. But as she opened her eyes again, spots and lines were burned into her retina, as if several strobe lights had flashed in front of her. Thomas stared at her as if he was trying to make a decision. He opened the door wider and invited her into the house.

"Listen, I was just about to have a glass of wine. Would you like one?" As Sarah hesitated, and as she tried to clear her vision, he rushed on. "We could sit on the deck, if you like. That way Rusty can join us. He's not allowed inside. Are you, boy?" He rubbed the big dog's head affectionately.

Sarah nodded, and Thomas disappeared inside, returning a minute later with two glasses of chardonnay.

They began to talk and Sarah immediately felt more at ease. Her head was swimming, but at least the wine had cleared away the bright pinpoints of light. Thomas openly talked about himself, his separation, his life, in a way that was disarming. Sarah found herself telling him things that she rarely told anyone. She was a private person by nature and did not reveal herself easily. Yet, there she was, effortlessly talking to a stranger. She felt a strong desire to reach out and take Thomas' hand, but put it aside. The talk continued for hours, long after night had fallen. Finally, Thomas excused himself.

"I hate to end this, but I have to leave to meet a date in a few minutes."

A clock was visible through the large picture window of the

house, and Sarah saw that it was now after 8:00. She had come up here shortly before 5:00, and was surprised to see that so much time had passed. It seemed as if they had only talked for a few minutes. She thanked Thomas for the glass of wine and then walked back to Steve's cabin under the shelter of tall trees and the starry sky. That night as she slept, she had another confusing dream.

She found herself watching a scene as if it were on a movie screen, but she seemed to be surrounded by a dense white fog. She wondered where she was, and vaguely noted that someone next to her was watching the movie also. On the screen, a gaunt-looking man with wavy, black hair and a plump, attractive woman worked together on a farm. They looked poor, as if they were peasants. The two people worked to repair a wall of a small cottage with plaster. They worked companionably together, laughing often. Then the scene changed. The woman played with a little girl and boy in the surf with a pale blue sky overhead and many sea birds calling around her. Sarah viewed this as if she stood near them. A great feeling of contentment overwhelmed Sarah, and the scene changed once more. She watched as the woman bent over a shallow, miniature grave on a green hillside. Her view was blocked by tears as the scene changed ... and now the woman stood in a barn lit by lamplight. She hovered over the body of the man, who was obviously dead. Sarah could feel the woman's deep sense of sorrow. The view changed, and the woman lay in a bed surrounded by many people, adults and several children. Sarah awoke in the middle of the night, confused, but feeling strangely peaceful. Why such graphic dreams of poverty, joy and sorrow would offer her peace was baffling. She fell back to sleep, and this time Thomas' face filled her mind with a quiet serenity.

The next morning, Sarah heard a knock at the French doors which opened into Steve's cabin. Unconsciously, she wrapped her bathrobe tightly around her waist and then looked out through the glass. Thomas and Rusty stood side by side, looking in through the door. They each wore such similarly expectant expressions, that Sarah laughed. Thomas wore a pair of jeans and a light turquoise-colored shirt, which intensified the color of his eyes. Again, the feeling that they had met somewhere before washed over her. She almost remembered where ... but then the memory quietly slipped away. Sarah opened the door.

"Hi. I know it's early, but I thought I could take you out for breakfast, and then to the wineries," Thomas began to explain.

"Would you like a cup of tea and a muffin? I just finished baking," Sarah said, and then smiled again. Suddenly, it occurred to her that she was standing in her robe.

"Let me change first. I mean, come in and make yourself a cup of tea or coffee. Steve's at the firehouse for a meeting. I'll be right back."

A few minutes later, they carried a tray of hot muffins and mugs of tea out onto the deck and sat down to enjoy the peace of the morning. Sarah noticed that she felt as comfortable in silence with this man as she did in conversation. Before she understood why or could stop herself, she told Thomas about her dream. As she completed her narration, she felt self-conscious and awkward.

"The woman died in her bed, surrounded by people who I think were her family," she said. Sarah looked down into her empty cup.

"There's something about ... your dream, about you. Sarah, I would swear we've met. You've never been to California before – have you?"

"Once. Years ago. You seem familiar to me, but I don't see how we could have possibly met. I worked for a summer in the valley. My friend Zoie and I lived together that summer. I did go to some of Steve's parties back then. I don't remember meeting you at any of them, though. Those were fun times...." Sarah's voice trailed off. "No. I don't think we've met before now."

"I guess we didn't, then. Still, there's something about your eyes," Thomas said.

Sarah blushed deeply and looked at her feet. Rusty came over to her, as if he sensed she needed some support, and placed his large head on her lap.

"He's beautiful," Sarah said to change the subject.

"Do you believe in past lives?" Thomas blurted out.

"What?"

"Do you believe you have lived before – before this life-time?"

"Yes," Sarah answered. "I do. I don't know how or why. I'm just certain I have. I've never felt as if I belonged on this plan-et. I know that sounds crazy," she said apologetically. Why was she telling Thomas these thoughts, thoughts that she did not share with anyone?

"I feel the same way," he said quietly.

"For many years, as far back as I can remember, I've had these – odd memories," Sarah began. She quickly looked up to see how Thomas reacted, but his expression showed only interest.

Slowly, she continued.

"I see things...."

"What do you see?" Thomas asked.

"Visions, like movies. I'll go to a place, somewhere I haven't been to before, and it's as if I'm watching another time. The place is there in its modern form, but ghost-like images act out another scene. This probably sounds crazy."

"No. It doesn't," Thomas insisted.

"The place where I work in New England is an old tavern and restaurant. It was built in the early 1700's. The first time I went there for my interview, I saw men and women working in the restaurant."

"That's not unusual," Thomas said.

"No. You don't understand!" Sarah said with passion. These people were translucent! They were wearing clothes from another era, from hundreds of years ago. Their accents were not modern."

Thomas smiled and nodded. Sarah rapidly continued before she lost her courage.

"This has happened to me all my life. I see and hear people from other times. Perhaps they're not from other times, but from other dimensions."

Thomas sat quietly. His hand rubbed the stubble on his chin and he stared thoughtfully into space.

"I haven't had these kinds of experiences, but my own have been just as strange," he said, and then chuckled. "I have dreams about the other side. Once, I was awakened by three spirits."

"Really?" Sarah said. She was happy to have the attention diverted from her. "What did they say? Why did they come to you?"

A smile crept across Thomas' face, and then he spoke.

"They told me to lighten up. The three spirits said they were guides, and that I needed to stop taking things so seriously. I did – lighten up, that is."

Thomas smiled widely now. Sarah found herself laughing as she listened. The conversation drifted on in this way. For hours they talked about spiritual ideology, which Sarah had never talked about before. She had heard of many beliefs and concepts, but did not know much about the popular and unpopular concepts of metaphysics. They talked about religion and God. The lunch hour passed, and neither she nor Thomas noticed.

Sarah was intrigued by Thomas' depth of knowledge on many subjects. Again, she found herself telling Thomas about other paranormal experiences she had had. He listened quietly sometimes; other times he leaned forward, keen interest in his eyes. They moved on from the metaphysical to the physical. Sarah learned that Thomas had served in the Vietnam war, and that he was twelve years older than she. This one fact sobered her, and moved their talks into a new light. Thomas was almost a generation older than she, and with twelve years of experience beyond hers. She felt acutely inexperienced as she listened to him. Suddenly, Thomas looked down at his watch and cursed.

"Damn! I've got another date tonight. I wish I could cancel it, but I don't want to hurt this woman's feelings. It's been great talking with you. When do you leave. Maybe we can get together again?"

"Tomorrow."

As Sarah said the word, she felt a sincere sadness to be leaving, not just California and this beautiful forest, but something else. She said good-bye and watched as Thomas and Rusty headed back up the driveway. Rusty looked back several times, and Sarah was surprised that tears blurred her vision.

The next day, Thomas watched as Sarah walked up the driveway. Rusty barked happily as she approached and greeted her with a wagging tail and several soft whines. Her dress was pastel blue, calf-length and loose-flowing. The smile she wore seemed open and inviting, as if she were an old friend.

Thomas stood next to his roommate Cliff. Cliff's hands were shoved in his pants pockets for warmth, and his fair skin and light brown hair looked washed out in the morning light.

"Hi," Sarah addressed Thomas. "I wanted to say goodbye to Rusty and to thank you for your hospitality."

"Sarah, this is my roommate, Cliff. Cliff's moving to Seattle in a few weeks. Cliff, this is Steve's cousin."

"Hey, nice to meet you," Cliff said, and stuck out his hand.

Sarah took Cliff's hand, and then turned toward Thomas.

"Thanks for the great talk yesterday. I'm sorry we didn't have more time to talk again," Sarah said sincerely, and then shook Thomas' hand.

The three of them spoke for a while longer, and then Sarah turned to leave. As she did, the sun crested above the trees and shone upon her. Her long chestnut hair was illuminated, the sun silhouetted her slim figure and mud kicked up from her sandals. Thomas stood transfixed. His mouth became dry. His hands shook slightly, and soundlessly he mouthed,

"She's the one...."

Chapter 19

*T*homas sat down at his desk to write once more and, after a moment, tore up the first page he had written. He crumpled the torn sheet into a ball, took aim at the basket and threw the wadded paper deftly into it. The basket was almost full.

Evening's shadows crept into his small office, and Thomas reached over and turned on a desk lamp. Bookshelves lined one wall, and were filled with books on cabinet making, photography, travel and art. An easel, which had not been used in many years, lay against another wall, with old paintings stacked haphazardly nearby. Two filing cabinets took up the third wall. His work desk was crammed into one corner of the room, under a window that looked out into the forest.

There was nothing to stop Thomas from writing ... but his own fears. Cliff was with some friends at another farewell party. The house was pleasantly still and the forest had fallen asleep with the onset of dusk. He took out another sheet of stationery and began again. This time he crumpled the first sheet up before he had finished it. He got up in frustration and decided to go for a walk. Rusty bounded up and followed his master unbidden.

The two walked silently together through the forest, and through the vineyard that followed. A crescent moon hovered in a pale blue sky that was darkening at the edges as dusk gave way to night. They stopped at a cliff top and looked out over the Valley of Seven Moons. Thomas rubbed Rusty's head absentmindedly as they looked at this peaceful view. Lights came on one by one in the valley, but offered no illumination to Thomas' problem.

He wanted to write to Sarah, but could not. Every time he sat down to write, his mind became cluttered with thoughts and words. Who was this woman, and what was she to him? Why was she familiar, and in a way that was unsettling? He knew that in meeting her – his life would never be the same again. Rusty yawned loudly and then stretched, as if he had grown bored with Thomas' inner wanderings and itched to move on through the hills. They set out again and took a long loop back through the forest to the cabin.

The next day Thomas received a letter from Sarah. She had written a brief thank you note that was unusual and direct.

Dear Thomas,
 I wanted to thank you again for your warm hospitality while I was in Sonoma.
 I don't know why, but I keep thinking about you, three thousand miles away. I believe – know somehow – that you are thinking of me. Are you?
 Affectionately,
  Sarah

Her letter jolted Thomas out of his inertia. That evening he sat down and penned a two-page letter. After he had written it, he read it out loud to himself and Rusty, who panted happily as he listened. As he finished reading the letter out loud, he looked at his four-legged friend in alarm.

"I can't send this. This is a love letter!"

Rusty barked once, wagged his tail and put his head on Thomas' knee. He smiled up at Thomas as if he were mocking him and calling him a coward. Thomas quickly folded it, stuffed it in an envelope and addressed it. He went out to his truck, opened the passenger door for Rusty to join him and then drove down the mountain road to the closest post office, where he dropped the letter in a mailbox outside. As he did, he muttered to himself.

"She's going to think I'm crazy."

A few days passed, and he did not hear from Sarah. He was sure she had received his letter and wondered how she had responded. He worried about this until his sleep was interrupted, and he became agitated with self doubts. Why had he written a love letter to a woman he hardly knew?

Finally, he could stand it no longer. He got her number from information and dialed it. He did not know what he was going to say, but he had to talk to her. Maybe he would apologize. What came out of his mouth surprised them both.

Sarah arrived at the post office and found Thomas' letter. An inner knowingness and calm, which surprised herself, settled over her as she drove back to her cabin. Once she had made a cup of tea and settled in her rocking chair, she opened and read Thomas' words.

Dear Sarah,

How perfect to receive your letter today. Last night I sat down to write to you, but couldn't find the words.

I have a very strong connection with you. A day hasn't passed that I didn't think about you. You are in my dreams and I hear your sweet voice in my meditations. There was so much I wanted to say to you while you were here. There never seemed to be enough time. It took me several days to realize you were gone. So much left unsaid.

I flew up to Washington with a friend in a small plane and landed the job of my life. I now do the artwork, photography and videography for a company that customizes airplanes. They fly me to work from here! This has been a welcomed change from my normal cabinetmaking work. All this feels good and right.

You are special, Sarah. What can I say to make you understand how I feel about you? I must see you! I believe it is quite possible that I would drive across the United States just to talk to you.

From the first time we met I have felt our spirits fly together. I can't help but think you feel the same way. Please understand I am feeling very strong these days and my words come directly from my heart. I am happy to be just your friend.

The last day we talked on the deck, I looked up and saw

you in a "different" way. For one perfect moment between breaths, looking at your pretty face, I felt I had always known you. You looked back at me and smiled shyly, as if you knew what I was feeling.

I felt warm and wonderful!

I have enclosed a photograph of myself. I would love one of you. It is time for sleep now.

Love, Thomas

Sarah smiled as she read the Thomas' letter. Then, she slipped quietly out of her body, as she had done so many times during her meditation classes. It was as if her spirit had taken flight by reading Thomas' words. She wondered at this, and suddenly found herself back in her body again.

Sarah knew she needed to answer Thomas' letter, but did not know how. She started to write to him, but her words were awkward and stilted; something felt wrong, and quickly she tore up the letter. As she threw the torn shreds of paper into the basket, a voice whispered behind her.

He's the one. The one you have waited for. The one with whom you will spend the rest of your life.

She started, and turned to see who whispered, but found no one. Sarah was alone. The cabin and its rustic walls were silent. The sound of her heart pounding loudly in her chest was the only noise, and Sarah realized her breathing had become ragged. She drew a quivering breath and picked up her pen. Quickly, Sarah wrote another letter and kept the words light ... in case she was mistaken about Thomas' intentions.

She mailed the letter before work that day, and returned home in the evening to her cabin, where the ringing of the telephone broke the silence in her home and the forest beyond. Sarah ran the last few feet of the grassy pathway, past the spring flowers, daffodils and lilies of the valley in the yard, and into the cabin. Megan sat by the ringing phone and stared at it intently. As Sarah picked up the phone, a voice accosted her.

"Sarah? Is it you?" a male voice asked with passion.

"Yes. Thomas?"

"Yes. It's me. Why haven't you answered my letter? Do you know how long I have waited for you? Don't you understand how long it took me to find you?"

Sarah was stunned, but not as surprised as Thomas. She burst into laughter that was filled with relief and wonder. They talked for two hours about what they felt, the strangeness of these feelings and the intensity behind them. As they talked, each revelled in the ease they felt together. When they hung up, there were, for the moment, no further questions. That love existed was evidenced through their words and tones as each spoke. They both knew that something had started that went beyond time and themselves, beyond their limited understanding of life.

Three months later, Thomas arrived on a plane at Logan airport in Boston. He and Sarah packed up her sparse belongings. Sarah had sold most everything she owned, and what remained fit in the back of her car. Megan was with a neighbor who had asked if she could keep the sweet cat. All of Sarah's previous life had been carefully attended to and settled. They said their good-byes to family and friends and, as they drove west, Sarah tearfully watched as her home, the life she had lead, disappeared from sight with the bend in the road.

Their life together had begun, but this life would contain more than either Thomas or Sarah expected.

Chapter 20

*T*he first year held wonders that Sarah had never known existed. Thomas shared his world of adventures with her, and they traveled together throughout the Southwest, Mexico and California. He took her flying, ballooning, hiking through canyons and ruins, canoeing and to museums. They drove along the long, expansive California coastal highway. He taught her how to use a camera, and through it she began to see the world as a combination of light and shadow. Each day became a time of wonder, a time to discover life and each other.

Rusty accepted Sarah into their life as if she already belonged there. He became protective of her and guarded her tenderly. Thomas and Sarah had made an agreement to live together for one year before speaking of marriage. During this agreement, Thomas expressed his desire to marry Sarah, but she answered him with a silent look that said, "No. Not yet." Therefore, neither brought the subject up, until one day when Sarah watched Thomas change a flat tire on the car, she spoke.

"Yes, Thomas."

"Yes, what?" he asked, then grunted while loosening a lug nut.

"Yes. I'll marry you."

"You know I would have changed a tire sooner if I'd known you'd react this way," he joked. They agreed to marry the following spring, after the winter rains had passed.

The yoga class assembled on mats on the floor, and Sarah grunted as she tried an especially difficult position. Cool air blew across the floor as someone opened a door in the hallway. A slamming sound echoed into the room, and with it another gust of cold air was felt, as whoever it was left the building. Sarah peeked at the clock and thankfully saw that class was nearing an end. Thomas saw her look and laughed at her from across the room. Then, the teacher announced that this position was done. As the teacher stopped to help a student who had asked a question, Sarah murmured under her breath.

"I can't believe I let Thomas talk me into this class."

Her attention was abruptly diverted from her sore muscles when the teacher began a guided meditation as a cool-down to the long workout. Sarah fell easily into a meditative state and let herself relax. Her mind became still, and the quiet noises of the teacher's voice and of the breathing of the other students slipped into the distance. Suddenly – Sarah found herself in a strange place. The teacher, the students, Thomas and the yoga center were gone.

Sarah looked around herself and saw that she sat by a waterfall with a small pool at the bottom. Bubbles were churned up by the cascade of water; a few escaped into the air. The thick velvety moss beneath her ran along the edge of one side of the pool. Plants floated on the other side, away from the fall of the streaming water. A rainbow of colors met her eyes and the flowers glowed a beautiful, whitish-pink hue. Sarah recognized the flowers as lotus blossoms. Next to the pool stood the most beautiful woman Sarah had ever seen.

"Hello, Serra! Do you remember me? I am Quan Yin."

Small in size and encompassing in her beauty, the woman tranquilly stared at Sarah. Two coal-black eyes carried Sarah in their warmth. The smile that lay across Quan Yin's lips was dazzling and hypnotic. Thick black hair was plaited and coiled on top of her head. Small flowers were strewn through her hair and fell down over her shoulders. The flowers became part of the pattern of the soft blue robe she wore, and Sarah could not tell where one began and the other ended.

Slowly, Quan Yin reached down and picked one of the pink lotus blossoms from the pool. She turned and smiled at Sarah, and then walked over and handed Sarah the flower. Sarah cupped the flower in her palms and wondered at its beauty.

Next, Quan Yin reached into the air, as if she were picking something – but nothing was there. Quan Yin smiled secretively and held out her hand with her palm facing upward. In the center of her delicate hand was one perfect pearl.

"Watch, Serra!"

She dropped the pearl into the center of the lotus blossom, and the world around Sarah changed. A mass of rock floated before her in the blackness of space. Stars, planets and the sun shone brightly in the background. The pearl landed on the surface of the rock. A seedling sprouted from the pearl and grew into a giant tree. The roots of the tree split the rock into many pieces, surrounding and compressing the pieces into a tightly woven ball.

The lotus blossom appeared again, and Quan Yin's enchanting smile met Sarah's as she dropped yet another perfect pearl into the center of the blossom.

Sarah watched as the pearl touched the base of the tree and burst into a crystal-clear, blue liquid. The liquid filled the spaces between the rocks and surrounded the globe in an expansive blue.

A third time, the lotus blossom appeared before her eyes and the guide's smile turned into laughter as she saw Sarah's wonder. Quan Yin dropped a third pearl into the center of the lotus blossom, and the globe with the great tree in space appeared before her.

The pearl touched a tree limb and burst into air, wind, animals and life! Sarah gasped with awe at the beauty before her. She looked up and saw that she was back with Quan Yin by the waterfall. The lotus blossom lay perfect and whole in her hands.

"What is happening?" Sarah asked.

"It is time for you to begin your work!" Quan Yin said joyously.

Sarah felt someone shaking her, and the vision vanished. Her yoga instructor's face loomed in front of her, seeming strange and out of place.

"Sarah? Thomas is waiting for you. Class is over."

Winter had a way of slamming against Sonoma valley with cold-pelting rains that raged against the hills. Often these storms occurred with little warning. There was none the day the first storm of winter darkened their small cabin. Thomas built up the fire in the woodstove and started working on designs for a new hutch for a customer while he waited for Sarah to come home. A few months ago, she had started working in a winery in the valley. Sarah said her job was enjoyable, and it provided them with an ample supply of wine. In fact, their wine cellar had grown quite full, because neither of them drank much. With this thought, Thomas stood, went to the kitchen to pour himself a glass of wine and then turned up the dimmer switch on the light.

The forest had become dark and moody as the storm had gathered in strength.

He mused over the past year as he sipped on the wine. Sarah had fit into his life, his home, as if both had been waiting for her. He felt more sure of himself than he ever had. He was debating a bigger change but had not spoken to Sarah about this change yet. He wanted to sell his cabinetry business and work as an artist and photographer full time. The temporary job in Washington last year had given him the confidence he needed to take this step. Art and photography were the subjects he had studied in college, but after meeting his first wife, he had felt that he needed a more stable income than an art career provided. Sarah and he were independent and happy, very happy. The timing seemed opportune and appropriate. He decided to think this over a few days longer and then talk to Sarah. Something happened that night that postponed his decision.

Sarah returned home from work in the midst of the storm. They ate dinner, went to bed, made love and fell asleep. The evening was typical. Sometime during the night the storm abated, and Thomas awoke to an uninterrupted and absolute silence. He got up, noted that it was early, very early in the morning, and sleepily he went to get a drink of water. When he returned to their bed, he heard a voice which brought him completely awake.

"Hello, Thomas," a deep male voice spoke from Sarah's sleeping body. Thomas froze where he was, half in and half out of the bed. He whispered in response, "Who is it?"

No one responded. His heart's beating began to slow and he reached gingerly for Sarah. "Sarah?"

She remained unconscious, but rolled over and into his arms. "I love you, Thomas," she sighed from her slumber. Thomas brushed a strand of Sarah's dark hair from her cheek and watched her as she slept. He cautiously crawled into bed next to her, and then lay wide awake for the next couple of hours. Finally, with the coming of dawn ... he fell asleep.

"No. I don't believe it," Sarah said firmly and got out of bed. Sunshine streamed through the window and highlighted dust particles that drifted by aimlessly. The storm had rolled eastward and the bedroom looked warm and bright. She was angry and frightened by this joke Thomas was now playing on her.

"Sarah, please. This isn't a joke!" he pleaded.

As Thomas called her name and begged her once more to believe him, Sarah suddenly knew he was not kidding. Fear replaced her anger and she cursed silently to herself. Her hands trembled slightly, and Thomas took them in his.

"You don't remember anything?" he asked again.

"No, and you're frightening me. I did what? Channeled? What is channeling?"

"Channeling is when a person leaves their body and allows another spirit to use their physical being."

"You're making this up!"

"No. I'm not. You lay right here last night and channeled a male entity. He said, 'Hello,' and called me by name."

"What does this mean?" she asked him.

"I don't know, but it was wonderful. I was afraid, but at the same time felt an enormous love coming from whomever it was."

Sarah shook her head and leaned against Thomas' chest. He kissed her on the top of her head and she put her arms around his waist. Soon she began to cry, and Thomas tried to comfort her.

"Don't worry, Sarah. This is a gift. I am sure."

"I don't know. I just ... it's just that – well, I don't want it to happen again!"

"Then it probably won't."

For the following two nights Sarah did not sleep. She read and watched movies late into the night to ensure that she stayed awake and that no "entities" trespassed her body. On the third day, as she meditated in the late afternoon, her body gave up its exhausting vigil and she fell into a deep sleep. As she slept, she felt a strong and powerful presence move toward her. An intense white light surrounded Sarah and she felt herself gasping at its power. The light drew closer to her and a face suddenly loomed up close to hers. She recognized the man who had appeared to her many months ago in her cabin. A love, so vast and intense that it left her breathless, surrounded and filled her. The man's breath seemed to calm and nourish her. His voice boomed over her in resonant shock waves.

Serra! It is time for you to begin your work.

"Who – who are you?" she asked inbetween gasps. His voice was powerful, and yet soothing.

Don't you remember? Serra, it is me! Orryka.

His name brought back memories, without images, of a peace and love that was limitless. Sarah burst into tears and, at that moment, watched as a cloak of gentle white light surrounded her. The distinct feeling of being hugged followed and Sarah felt her heart and mind assuaged. Orryka's voice sounded in her mind again, but softer and gentler.

*Do not worry, Serra. I shall help you awaken slowly. I shall
be with you always.*

Tears flowed down Sarah's cheeks. Suddenly the entity was
gone. She cried harder as she felt his embracing warmth leave
her. At that moment Sarah awoke and found herself sitting
upright. She had lain down when she had finished her meditation. When had she sat up again? Her face was damp with tears
and her body ached with the need to cry harder. She gave herself up to this need and held the pillow to her chest.

Thomas arrived home from his workshop and found Sarah
asleep on the couch. When he woke her, she began to blubber out
a story all at once. He suggested they sit outside in the warm
afternoon breezes, and she quickly assented. A moment later,
they sat on the deck and Thomas listened as Sarah told him
about Orryka.

Hot spirals of steam rose up from her teacup and curled the
soft ends of her hair. Her large brown eyes looked troubled. The
sound of the hot tub recycling gurgled in the background. Rusty
snored at their feet. As Thomas stroked Sarah's arm, she ended
her narration with a question.

"What is this all about, Thomas?"

"I don't know, Sweetie. How did it feel?"

"Frightening at first, and strangely wonderful. I have never
felt so loved," she said awkwardly, and then continued with
another question. "Do you think I'm going crazy?"

"No. You're the sanest person I've ever met. What's the
name again? It sounds very familiar."

"Orryka."

"Orryka ..." Thomas said out loud. "I don't know what's
happening, but the name is strangely familiar."

"I felt as if I'd known this entity for a long time, and rather
than being relieved when he left, I felt sad."

"I wouldn't worry about it, then. He's probably your
guardian angel."

"Guardian angel? Maybe...."

"Don't be sad, Sarah. This is exciting!" Thomas said opti-
mistically. "Give yourself some time to digest these experiences. I
think we'll learn soon enough what they're all about."

During the following month, Sarah became edgy and con-
tinuously questioned her sanity. She wondered what she could do

to stop these strange experiences, and then the next moment questioned if she really wanted to stop them.

If insanity was the cause and she was truly crazy, then she was a remarkably lucid lunatic. Thomas seemed to trust these experiences and awaited the next joyously. Often Sarah wished she had Thomas' simple trust and understanding, but all of this was new to her. Meanwhile, her sleep and daily routines suffered.

"Sarah, what's this?" Thomas pointed to their salads.

"Hmm?" she asked distractedly.

"You know, I really do like chocolate, but this is something I never thought of trying," Thomas said as he bit into a cucumber covered with chocolate syrup.

"Oh my gosh!" Sarah said as she looked down at her plate.

Thomas broke into laughter, and then continued to eat his salad. Sarah put her head in her hands and began to laugh.

Then, one day as Sarah meditated on the couch, she had an experience which helped her to find a place for the visitations she had been having. As she meditated she became more and more calm, and soon lost focus of the room, her body, her breathing and her surroundings in general. She looked around and saw that somehow she had come to be in a long dark tunnel. At the end of the tunnel was a bright white light, to which she felt mysteriously drawn.

Sarah walked with measured steps toward it, until she was right at the edge of the tunnel, looking into a deep chasm of brilliant white light. She had an overwhelming desire to dive headlong into this illumination, to immerse herself in it. She looked behind and saw, off in the distance at the end of the tunnel, the room where her body sat on the couch. She hesitated only a second, and then leapt into the white blaze.

A blast of light and love filled her being. She felt as if every molecule in her body shivered in joy. Brilliant white fog drifted around her in soft cloud-like formations. One spot in the cloud grew brighter, and suddenly a person emerged, a man. Orryka.

Hello, Serra! You made it.

"Where am I? I cannot see you very well. It's the light ... it's very bright," she said as she squinted.

Take my hand, Serra.

She took his outstretched hand, and they raced onward

through the light. Fog drifted past them in wispy brightness. Ahead, the fog seemed to separate and, suddenly, Sarah and Orryka burst through the clouds into a sky above a meadow.

Purple flowers covered the meadow on one side. On the other side a forest lay, lush and deep. The meadow ran up a hill to a cliff, where a stand of trees lay. All about her, Sarah saw health and vitality in growing plant life. She looked up and noticed for the first time that the sky was purple. Orryka saw the astonished look on her face and broke into laughter. His laughter awakened a merriment inside of her, and she began to chuckle.

"Where am I?" she finally asked.

In the between. *We're observing a meadow on our home world.*

"The between? Our home world?" Sarah asked in confusion. What Orryka said made sense, but she could not remember or explain why. Her mind felt weighted by all she was experiencing.

Yes. We are between dimensions. The home world is the planet where we – you, Thomas and I – originated.

"Why am I here?"

To learn, dear, Orryka said very gently.

Dear? she thought. *At least I am hallucinating kind spirits.* Her thoughts were abruptly, but gently, interrupted by Orryka's kind voice.

You are not hallucinating, Serra. You are in a different dimension. This place exists in a way you cannot yet comprehend and – you are not crazy.

"What will I learn?" She asked, hoping for a clearer answer.

First, coming here is enough. I shall eventually teach you how to develop your telepathic and empathic abilities, but for now you shall learn how to consciously go back and forth between your dimension and others. Now you need to return to your dimension, your body.

Orryka held out his hand, and she took it. A wonderful sense of well-being filled her as they raced back through the light. She burst through the light, into the tunnel and raced toward her body. Orryka was still with her and led her. Just as they entered the room, he let go of her hand, and she was back in her body. Sarah felt her breath, which was deep and even, and she noticed that her body trembled slightly, that she had a strange sensation of shivering although she was not cold. In fact, she felt peaceful and content. The fears she had had before her meditation were gone.

Thomas had covered her with a blanket sometime during

her meditation. She yawned, and then slowly opened her eyes. The room was dim as the evening light was fading. Thomas and Rusty were both gone, probably for a walk. She stretched slowly and wondered what would happen next.

The phone rang, and Sarah answered it automatically, as if she were at work. Because she stood in the middle of their kitchen at home on a Sunday afternoon, the answer was humorously inappropriate.

"Hello, Clair de Lune Winery, Sarah Clark's office"

"What'd the winery do, Sally – open a branch at your house?" her cousin Steve teased her, and then laughed.

"Sorry, Steve. I was distracted."

"So I've noticed. Cous, I'm worried about you. You haven't been yourself in some time."

"I know. I ..." Sarah began to explain, but somehow she could not tell Steve about the channeling.

"You what? Thomas isn't hurting you – is he?" Steve's voice became instantly hostile.

"No! God, no. Steve, Thomas is the best thing that has ever happened to me. Honest."

"Then what is it?"

Sarah hesitated. She had to tell him sometime. Perhaps now was a good moment.

"Steve, maybe we should talk."

"Right now? I was going to go for a hike before work."

"I could go with you," she suggested hesitantly, unsure of herself and this decision.

"Okay. I'll meet you out front in five minutes."

They walked companionably through the forest and toward a canyon named The Devil's Basin. At the top of a cliff, a river, which was narrow in the summers and deep and wide in the winter, fell over the edge and then plummeted a hundred feet into a carved stone basin on the canyon floor. Sarah walked faster to keep up with Steve as he strode through the forest and toward a clearing at the edge of the cliff, which would give them a spectacular view of the waterfall and canyon beyond. As they came to the end of the worn dirt path, Sarah sighed as she looked out over the view.

Dark gray clouds hung in the sky and the waterfall ran rapidly with the added waters from the winter rains. A slight drizzle began to fall, and Sarah pulled up her hood on her rain jacket. Steve picked up a stone and threw it into the canyon.

"Well, Cous, what's the big secret?"

Sarah blushed and avoided answering by asking a question.

"How long have you lived on the mountain, Steve?"

"Ten years. Now – answer my question." He threw another stone.

"I've been having unusual experiences. Thomas and I...."

"Wait!" Steve held up his hands. "This isn't going to get kinky – is it?" This broke the tension, and Sarah burst into laughter. She picked up a stone and threw it after Steve's.

"No. Steve, I began channeling a few months ago. I don't know how or why. It just happened."

"Hmmm ..." he said without commitment.

"I'm not kidding. At first it was ... weird, but then I began to notice how good I felt after the spirits visited us."

"When do they visit you?" Steve said. His expression showed nothing of what he felt, and Sarah began to feel nervous.

"So far, they've only come at night. I don't remember much because I sleep through the visits. Thomas tells me about them the next morning. He said a French woman – or spirit – has been visiting us, and a man." Sarah waited for Steve to respond, but he remained quiet. He bent, picked out another handful of stones and began throwing them into the canyon like the others.

"Steve? What do you think?"

"I think that what you're telling me is possible," he said, and shrugged his muscular shoulders. "I dated a woman for a time who claimed to be a channeler. I don't know if she was a good channeler, but she had other talents," he said, and grinned. He continued, "Listen, Sally. This is California. This woo-woo stuff is popular and normal here. I'm not into it, but you can't spit and not hit a psychic here. If you tell me you're channeling, then who am I to argue?"

He stopped for a moment and examined her. His green eyes crinkled as he stared into hers. "Just answer me this: Are you okay, Sally?"

"Yes. I think so."

"Okay," he said, and nodded his head. He turned back to throwing stones and spoke over his shoulder. "Just let know if you're ever not."

✳

"You woke me up speaking French again," Thomas said, and yawned as he stretched in the early morning sunlight. "I wonder who the woman is, and why she needs to come through you?"

"I don't know," Sarah said as she handed him a cup of tea. "I don't remember anything."

These midnight channelings were taking place frequently now. Sarah didn't feel tired by them, but she did awake hungry. She had come to know when they had occurred by how hungry she was when she awoke in the morning. She often felt as if she had swum fifty laps in a pool and worked up a hunger. She began to dress for work and tried not to think about these strange events. She kissed Thomas good-bye a few minutes later and left for the day.

Later, at work, as hard as Sarah tried, she could not put the events out of her mind. Finally, at lunch, she told a friend what was happening to her. Holly had expressed her interest in psychic phenomenon before, and Sarah felt she *might* be sympathetic. Although Holly listened with compassion, something in the way she looked at Sarah made her feel uncomfortable. As Sarah finished her story, Holly backed away from the table and quickly made an excuse to leave. Sarah realized in that moment Holly had become afraid of her.

That night she told Thomas what had happened.

"Holly acted like I was ... a leper. I don't understand!" Sarah complained while she fixed dinner. Thomas stood and leaned against the door frame as he listened. The smells of olive oil and garlic drifted up from the pan. Sarah furiously chopped carrots, scallions and broccoli to add to the stir fry. She put down the knife and cursed.

"Damn it! Thomas, I wouldn't hurt a spider!"

"Sarah, you'll have to be patient. Holly probably reached her boggle point."

"What?"

"It's a term in metaphysics. *Boggle point* is the point at which a person's mind shuts down. Holly might have been open to other forms of paranormal events, but channeling was probably her boggle point. For example, she was – from what you say – interested in ghosts and visitations from Mother Mary. But, the channeling of ghosts or spirits may be too much for her to digest right now. She may come around."

Sarah wiped the cutting board with a clean rag. She began to carefully peel a piece of fresh ginger root with her knife as she listened.

"Give her a chance. She'll probably think about it and want to ask questions later," Thomas tried again.

"Humph. I don't know," Sarah said stubbornly. Thomas walked across the room and kissed her on the cheek. She let him kiss her on the mouth, and then he reached over and turned out the flame beneath pan. Thomas kissed her on the neck, and she said, "Okay. I'll try."

The following night, as Sarah meditated before dinner, she once again found herself in the dark tunnel, rushing toward the light. She had become accustomed to this and no longer wrestled with the experience. In a split second she was surrounded by the bright white fog, and after another few seconds she found herself bursting into the meadow, into *the between*. Orryka waited there for her.

You have a question? he asked her gently as she sat next to him on the thick, green grass which ran up the hillside.

"Yes. I told a friend about my experiences. This ... channeling. She acted as if she was afraid of me. Why? Why would she be afraid of me? I am not evil. I wouldn't harm her or anyone. I try very hard *not* to harm or hurt anyone ever...." Sarah's voice trailed off at the end as she spoke of Holly's reaction to her. Orryka answered her consolingly.

You were chosen to do this work, Sarah, because of this intent, that you truly do not wish to harm anyone. Your friend is afraid because she thinks you will see into her heart and mind, where she hides secrets from herself and the world. She does not understand that you would not trespass that privacy. She does not know that, even if you would, you could not without her permission. It is easier for her to believe that this is not true and that you are crazy.

Sarah, do you wish to continue to channel? As we've told you, this won't be an easy path, but there will be many gifts contained within this path. The choice is yours. If you do not want to continue, you may stop now. This work needs to be done. If you cannot continue, I shall have to find someone else with whom to work. Do you understand?

"Yes. I understand." She thought about the prejudices and hardships she would have to face on this path. "Could I continue coming to *the between*, if I stopped? If I chose not to go on?"

She gestured to the beauty of the meadow where they sat.

No. You would come here again, someday when your body

dies, but for now these experiences would stop.

She sat and stared at the thick handfuls of grass she held. Its green hue vibrated with life. She gazed across the meadow and breathed the sweet air. The air was neither cool nor warm, but perfect. The purple sky above her caused a singing in her heart. Here she felt content, whole and safe. With Orryka everything seemed perfect and serene.

"Would I see you, talk to you again?"

Yes, but not here. Your natural abilities will not be taken from you, Sarah. Your telepathic and empathic abilities would remain intact. Your clairvoyance is a part of your make-up.

Sarah continued to breathe in the perfumed air. She hesitated, and then bravely made a decision.

"Yes. I'll go on."

Orryka smiled at her, as if he already had known her answer.

Chapter 21

*R*usty walked by Sarah, who sat on the couch, and to his corner of the room. He circled three times on his bedding and then lay down. A loud yawn escaped Sarah's mouth and she put her hand over her lips to stifle it. The day had been a long one. Channeling in the late afternoon, when she arrived home from work, was beginning to wear on her. While she readied herself by getting into a comfortable position, Thomas rummaged in a drawer of the couch-side table.

"Why do you need a pad of paper?" he asked.

"I don't know. Orryka said to keep one in my lap while I meditate. Can you hand me a pen?"

"Sure. Hey, I wonder if you're going to autowrite?"

"What's autowriting?"

"Some channelers channel the energy of a spirit through their arm and hand, and use writing as a way to communicate."

"It doesn't sound good. I'm not sure if I can go through with this."

"Ah-hah! See, Sarah. You just came up against your own boggle point. I wish you would read up on this subject. There are many well-researched books on the subject of channeling. If you did, you might feel better about what's happening."

"If I did read them, then how would I know the difference between what is really happening and what I might make up from what I read? I wouldn't. I'd just think this was my imagination working with material from 'well-researched' books. Each time I come to a new step I just become a little nervous. You know that," she ended. This was an old argument between them.

"You'll be fine," Thomas reassured her.

He kissed her quickly on the forehead, and then sat down next to her on the couch. A few minutes later, each was lost in the private peace of meditation. When Sarah awoke an hour later, Thomas sat before her on a chair he had pulled up to the couch. His face beamed with wonder and excitement.

"Look down!" he instructed her. On her lap were two pages of scrawled notes. The handwriting was very different from her own; it was quite large and had a childlike simplicity to it. The message itself was not what astounded Sarah. What surprised her was that the one and a half pages of writing were completely backwards. Thomas laughed as he held up a mirror.

She read the words slowly, out loud.

Hello, Thomas.

Do not be afraid. I mean you no harm. I am here to guide you. I am from the light. You may choose to be afraid or you may choose to respond with love. Remember light and love surround you always. If you choose, I shall guide you toward love.

Jonah

"It was the only way I could read it. I came out of my meditation, and when I turned to look at you, I saw an old man sitting in your place. He had a long beard and white hair. His hand was moving across the paper in slow motion, as a very old person might move. Do you remember anything?"

"Not much. I remember a ball of white light, and someone asking my permission to use my body. That's all. I felt at ease with whomever this entity was. He felt like an old and close friend. I wish I could remember more," Sarah said. Frustration tinged her voice. "I wonder what religion this spirit follows. Jonah? He drew a fish like the Christians use. Do you think he's a Christian entity?"

"I don't know, but that's a good question," Thomas answered.

Thomas came out of his meditation quickly, as he again heard the sound of pen scratching across paper next to him. The room had become dark with the onset of evening. He quickly got up, turned on a light and retrieved the mirror he had placed on the coffee table nearby. Again, he glimpsed the image of an old man. A long white beard covered his face and deeply wrinkled hands held the pen. The old man, Jonah, scribbled across the sheets of paper slowly and, again, backwards. Thomas decided to try to speak with the entity.

"Who are you?"

Your guide, he wrote.

"Are you a Christian? You drew a fish the last time you were here."

There are not the limitations of religion in the light, he scribed slowly.

"Why are you here? Why do you write instead of speak?"

To guide you, and to assist in opening Serra. Writing is the tool I use to open her. It connects her intuitive brain functions to her intellect. Later someone will speak through her, when my work is done.

"You spelled her name wrong."

No. I did not, he wrote backwards.

Thomas decided not to argue with the old man, and waited silently as he continued to write.

Another wishes to communicate.

"Who?"

Yerraba wishes to speak.

Thomas' heart began to pound loudly in his chest. Speak? Another entity was going to speak through Sarah. Someone named Yerraba. Somehow, when he was fully awake during the daylight hours, this experience seemed different. His hand shook slightly with anticipation as he picked up one of the sheets of paper that had fallen to the floor.

Sarah's body slumped forward, and suddenly Thomas had the distinct impression that someone had just left the room. Just as suddenly, Sarah sat bolt-upright, as a new entity entered her body, and her hand began to fly across the sheets of paper. In this brief moment, Thomas glimpsed the figure of a tall blond woman sitting in Sarah's body. Her face was brilliantly lit with her smile, and she was definitely familiar to Thomas. Thomas leaned over and studied her indiscernible scribblings that covered the page.

As this newest entity finished, she stared directly up at Thomas and smiled proudly. Her expression was filled with

enthusiastic pride that was childlike. The smile was contagious, and Thomas began to laugh. The vision faded quickly and Sarah's body slumped over. A few minutes later, Sarah fell asleep. Thomas covered Sarah with a blanket, watched her for a while as she slept and then began to make dinner.

✳

The following days brought repeated attempts at communication by the woman they now called "Yerraba." Each time, when Sarah came out of her trance, pages of scratching lay in her lap. They had no idea what the scribbles meant, and Sarah began to joke that Yerraba had been either a doctor or an editor in another life.

These events seemed so strange and non-purposeful that Sarah again became afraid that she was losing her mind. Also, she could not recall these channelings, as related to her by Thomas. She could only trust what he told her and trust that Yerraba's presence had meaning. Orryka continued to visit with her in *the between*, and in this she found comfort.

Two weeks later, as Sarah meditated, she found herself floating on the ceiling above her body. She looked down and saw Thomas meditating on the couch and her own body sitting cross-legged next to his. She smiled as she watched Thomas' attractive features in repose. His mustache and beard were beginning to turn auburn and his cheeks were pink from spring's first sunny days. Her own body looked slight and relaxed. Three months ago she had cut her waist-length hair in a pixie style. Somehow this short haircut made her look much younger than her thirty years. Next to her, Orryka hovered with benevolent serenity.

"What am I doing here?" Sarah asked.

We have decided to let you watch the channeling, so that you will feel more comfortable.

At that moment a translucent image of a woman appeared before her. Intense blue eyes stared back at Sarah out of a long, narrow face. The woman was dressed akin to Orryka, in a long, pale robe that shimmered slightly. Something about the woman made Sarah feel buoyant and excited. Sarah felt as if this woman was an old and dear friend. Impulsively, she moved forward to embrace her. As she moved through the transparent apparition, the woman's laughter rang throughout the cabin, and Thomas came out of his meditation abruptly. He looked around, saw that Sarah was sitting quietly and seemed puzzled. Orryka began to explain.

Sarah this is Yerraba. You were close friends a long time ago.

Yerraba suddenly spoke to Sarah in a foreign tongue, and Orryka carefully translated her words. The words sounded as if each flowed into the next in round syllables and phrases. *Sarah, Yerraba is asking your permission to try a different form of channeling today. She said, "I would like to try to speak using Serra's vocal cords." How do you feel about this?*

"I'm not sure."

If you are not ready, then that is fine, dear. There is no rush. The choice is yours.

"Okay." Sarah made her decision swiftly, and then watched as Yerraba floated down into her body. Thomas watched aptly now as Sarah's body gestures changed. He recognized the amazed delight of Yerraba's countenance as she moved Sarah's body awkwardly. Suddenly, Yerraba began to speak using Sarah's vocal cords. Thomas' shocked expression caused Sarah and Orryka to laugh. Sarah laughed harder as Yerraba proceeded to have a conversation with Thomas – in fluent French.

"I don't understand you!" Thomas threw his hands up in a gesture of defeat. "I don't speak French."

Neither did Sarah. Orryka began translating Yerraba's French dialogue for her.

Serra, Yerraba is saying to Thomas, "My name is Yerraba. We came to this planet long ago in a spaceship from across the galaxy. We came for anthropological studies of the people on Earth, and to research the ancient civilizations here. You, Serra, Orryka, myself and others came here together. Don't you remember me?"

At this point, Orryka interrupted Yerraba; he spoke to her telepathically.

Yerraba, this is not France. They do not remember. You must speak English.

"I do not speak English."

Yerraba answered in French, and looked up at the ceiling. Thomas understood this one phrase, and nodded his understanding. Yerraba then spoke telepathically to Thomas in the strange language she had used when speaking to Orryka. Orryka reminded her that Thomas was not telepathic and could not hear her.

Even if he did hear, he would not understand the language of our home planet. He does not remember yet. You will have to learn to speak English if you wish to speak to him.

"Oui," she said, and drifted out of Sarah's body. Sarah smiled at Yerraba's ghostly form, and then was startled as Yerraba disappeared. Just as Sarah was about to ask Orryka where Yerraba had gone, an old man appeared.

He looked Native American, seemed familiar and was translucent and glowing, as Yerraba had been. Unlike Orryka and Yerraba, he wore Native dress, a long leather tunic and pants with intricate beadwork and feathers sewn all over them. His gray hair was cut bluntly across his forehead, but hung thickly over his shoulders. His eyes were so black that they seemed to disappear into the background as Sarah stared into them. Suddenly, his ancient-looking figure floated down and into Sarah's body. Thomas jumped as Sarah's body gestures and posture changed once more.

The ancient man began a beautiful story, told in hand signs, that Thomas could not understand. Orryka translated once again for Sarah, but Thomas could not hear his translation.

This is Red Elk. He is communicating in an ancient sign language used by Native Americans. He is now telling Thomas the story of when we first came to this planet.

"First came to this planet?"

Shh, yes ... listen.

"*Once a race of Giants in flying discs came to our people.*" Orryka translated. "*Our people lived by the great waters then, before tribes from the north conquered us. Many of our people gathered to meet with the giants. The giants stayed with our people and taught us to speak with our minds, instead of using words or signs. Then, one day the giants left us. They said they would return someday, when all people would become one tribe.*"

The native man's beautiful dance of hands ended and Sarah's body slumped forward. Before she could question Orryka, she felt a rushing sensation that was gentle and yet intense, and then she was back in her body.

Sarah came out of her trance abruptly and stared through blurry eyes about the room. The evening had grown dark during the channeling session and Thomas had turned on a lamp that cast stark shadows across his face. She yawned and stretched slowly. Thomas leaned over and kissed her on the cheek.

"Back yet?" he asked softly.

"Hmmm ... almost," Sarah answered with a sleepy voice.

"Sarah, this was the strangest channeling yet!"

"Yes. I know," she said, and then yawned again.

"You remember? That's great! What did you see?" Thomas asked excitedly. Sarah told Thomas what she had seen, detail by detail, including Orryka's translation of Red Elk's story. As she finished, Thomas stared at her in disbelief. It was the first time he had responded this way, and it made Sarah acutely uncomfortable.

"Space beings!" Thomas exclaimed. Sarah winced under his response.

"Remember the boggle factor ..." she began to joke, but Thomas' expression stopped her. This wasn't a joke to him. He looked completely stunned by this news.

"Well, maybe I am going crazy. These experiences are getting too intense. I don't know, Thomas. Maybe I should stop channeling."

"Stop? Why?"

"Well, look at how you are reacting. You're having a hard time with this. I'm having a hard time with this. I don't know if anything I experience is 'real' or not. I lie awake at night wondering if I am hallucinating this whole experience. Then I wonder, *why* I would have these hallucinations? Now *you* are questioning the validity of these experiences."

"Yes. I am, but that doesn't mean I want to stop. I just have to get used to the idea. Really, Sarah. Space men! Native American spirits! It's hard to digest."

"I know and I think we should stop. Let's quit. All I have to do is say, 'No.'"

"Don't. Please, not yet. Sarah, give me a few days to think this over before you decide to quit. Space beings ..." Thomas said again and shook his head.

Thomas sat on the couch and stared at Sarah's stiffened posture. The light on the side table cast shadows over her feminine features. Several minutes elapsed and the stiffness passed as Yerraba adjusted to this physical form. Yerraba's awkward and unique gestures came through, although Sarah's face looked back at him. He quickly focused on Yerraba's presence and began questioning her about their lives as spacemen and spacewomen. After a time, Thomas stretched and looked at the clock. He had been questioning Yerraba for almost an hour now. She answered his most recent question about whether extraterrestrials were visiting Earth in this modern day.

"Oui."

"We have an underwater space station, there, in the ocean?" Thomas pointed to a place on a world map he held.

"Oui."

"Yerraba. Who else came with us on the ship?"

"Many," she said in a thick accent that made her words barely intelligible. "Some you know now. Some you do not know now, but will meet."

"Who? Who do we know now that came on the ship?"

"Your friend Diane and her fiancee Dave. Your friends, Jon, Karen, Steve and Jim – as well as other friends you have not yet met."

"Sarah's cousin Steve? Are you sure? We just met Diane a few months ago. We barely know her." Thomas tried to understand these connections.

Yerraba chuckled for a moment, and then answered simply, "Oui. I am sure. You will be, too, Thomas. You will remember your connection with them – someday."

"Where did we come from?"

"L'ours."

"Yerraba, English please."

"The Bear. A galaxy near this constellation you call The Bear, no?"

"No. I mean, yes. Your English is getting better," Thomas said, and then smiled.

"T-t-thank you," she stuttered over the words.

"Why are you coming to us in this form, through channeling?"

"Ah, oui. I came to learn from you as you learn from me."

"Then it's mutually beneficial?" Thomas questioned. He scratched his chin thoughtfully.

"Oui."

"Where is Sarah?"

"In the light with Orryka." Her tongue slid over Orryka's name and pronounced it with extra syllables that Sarah and Thomas could not say.

"Do you have a message for us? You live in another dimension and must have a larger view. Do you have anything you might wish to tell us?"

Yerraba's face split into a wide grin.

"No," she said.

Thomas broke into surprised laughter.

Over the next several months, as Yerraba continued to learn English and Thomas learned about other dimensions and space travel, Sarah was put into intensive spiritual training. Each time she channeled, she went into the light, where she was met by Orryka. He gave her lesson after lesson, each linked to the next by one common bond ... love.

On one day, as she and Orryka sat in the meadow in the midst of the bed of flowers, Orryka began to review her lessons. A warm breeze blew over them and up the hill. Sarah sighed, and then leaned back into the thick grass before she answered his questions.

Your task is to learn to love yourself again, Serra. Describe to me what you have experienced today, but do not use words of judgment.

"Sure," she began, "I went to work and called back a difficult client – who has been obstinate and a general pain in the neck...."

Orryka held up one hand.

Difficult, obstinate, a pain in the neck? These are all judgments on your part. Perhaps the person you judge sees you as unreachable. Try again.

They went on this way until Sarah grew weary and humbled.

"I understand."

Yes, Serra. **When you judge another, you hurt not only them, but yourself. Really, those whom you judge are you, since each person reflects back to you a quality in yourself – or a quality that you believe about yourself.** *In this way you are not practicing self-love. When you return, you may wish to begin a journal in which you practice describing your world without judging it. This is your choice.*

Sarah returned and began a journal. The task proved harder than it was in the light, in the meadow. Orryka and she had humorous and confusing telepathic dialogues, which she transcribed into her notebook. He asked questions and she did her best to answer non-judgmentally.

How do you view me, Serra? Orryka asked, as Sarah sat at Thomas' desk in the studio. It was her day off from work and Thomas was at a job site. The house was quiet and still around her on this summer morning.

You're good, kind, intelligent ... sort of like God, she answered.

I am not God. I am, like you, part of The One. *What is "good?"*

Good is what is right, Sarah answered practically.

What is "right?" Orryka questioned.

Sarah didn't answer, as she was stumped. *I don't know,* she finally answered.

Right is a judgment. Right and wrong do not exist except in judging. What is right for you may be very wrong for another, Serra.

If you were one of the earlier settlers of this country, you might have felt it was right to take the Native's lands. How do you think this would feel for them? Right? No. They would see this as painful and wrong. Do you see how judgments are, at best, subjective views and, at worst, dangerous to the others upon whom we inflict them?

Yes, Sarah said humbly.

What is God? Orryka tried again.

God is what is good ... Sarah began. *Oops.*

Serra, use your empathic abilities to find the answer.

This time Sarah tried to *feel* for the answer instead of using the practical, judging side of her brain. Sarah sat quietly and thought about *the light.* The beauty of *the between.* The answer came to her in a wash of emotions.

Love! she said triumphantly.

Are you sure that is all? he asked gently.

No! Sarah said with emotion. *I feel all emotions, all thoughts in this feeling of God. Love, envy, trust, hate, innocence – and beyond that – much more! Yet, in the center of all this I feel a solid core of love. That is all. It was this core I first felt. This core of love is the glue that holds all together.*

Is this good or bad?

Neither! Sarah said immediately. *It simply exists.*

The learning went on in this way. Sarah learned not to judge the world around her. And as she learned *not* to judge the outer world, she stopped judging her inner world. Eventually, she was able to laugh at her own growth and, as she did, she began for the first time to truly love herself.

Chapter 22

*T*he peg board on the wall held winery schedules, bulletins of up-coming events and the newest wine label designs. Florescent lighting made the pinned papers look yellowish. On her desk, Sarah had a framed picture of Thomas and Rusty. Both were smiling. Sarah drew circles on a pad of paper while she stifled a yawn and listened to the voice on the other end of the phone. This buyer for a local restaurant was taking an unusually long time to make his selection and to place his order. Suddenly, Sarah felt herself lift out of her body and begin to float above her desk. As she struggled to stay in her body, her hand jerked and knocked over a cup of tea she was drinking.

"Damn!"

"Excuse me?" he said.

"Sorry! I just ... spilled some tea on my desk. Where were we?"

A co-worker sat in the background, idly at her desk. Sarah felt Holly's gaze resting on her as she mopped up the tea with a napkin, and Sarah turned and winked at her. Holly's eyes narrowed slightly in response and her pretty mouth turned downward on her round and pleasant face. She pushed her hand through thick brown curls and went back to doing paperwork. When Sarah placed the phone on the hook, Holly questioned her.

"You feeling okay?"

"Yeah, just a little lightheaded," Sarah said. She was reluctant to explain about the side effects she was having from the channeling, because Holly was the one who had first reacted in fear when Sarah had confided in her months ago.

"This doesn't have to do with ... you know?"

"The channeling?"

"Yeah."

"Maybe."

"Sarah, maybe you should see someone," Holly said as she brushed her thick hair out of her face again. She wrinkled her freckled nose as she stared at Sarah and awaited a response. Sarah sighed and answered.

"Someone?"

"Yeah, a shrink," Holly said cautiously.

"A shrink – you mean a counselor."

"Yeah. How do you know that what is happening to you is good? These spirits could be bad spirits trying to hurt you."

"They're teaching us to be better humans and to love ourselves. How can that be bad?"

"I don't know, but you're acting kind of naive by just trusting them."

"I didn't 'just' trust them. We're slowly building a relationship of trust. They never push me," Sarah answered. Irritation tinged her voice.

"Well, you ought to be careful. You don't know. They could be evil."

"Evil?"

Sarah was dumbfounded. She could not imagine less likely evil beings then Orryka, Yerraba and Jonah. She remembered what Orryka had told her about each person reflecting some part of her. Obviously some part of her was still afraid, not just of this experience, but of the insanity that might be incurred in the process. She decided to talk this over again with Thomas that night at dinner.

Steam rose from the marinara sauce as Sarah poured a large spoonful over Thomas' plate of linguini. She put a smaller portion on top of her own dish of pasta, put the pan back on the stove and then sat down at the table. Thomas poured Cabernet into their glasses and listened as Sarah talked about what was troubling her.

"Holly thinks I need psychiatric help. I want you to tell me the truth. Don't lie to me, Tom. Do you think I'm crazy?"

"No. Listen, Sarah." He held up his hands as he talked, and began counting off on his fingers.

"One. If you are crazy, then this is the most fun I've ever had, and I'm glad you are.

"Two. If you are making this up and it's all you, then I'm honored to know such a wise and loving person.

"Three. None of that matters, because all that we are learning about life and love is more than most people ever get to experience, and we're not hurting anyone! I'm really grateful for this experience," he finished.

Sarah sipped from her wine, feeling somewhat better thanks to Thomas' practical words, but was still not convinced.

The sky was brilliant purple on this day that Sarah sat with Orryka in the meadow. *The between* felt especially surreal in that moment, although Sarah did not know why. She twirled a blade of grass between her fingers and sighed as Orryka reviewed the same lesson for the the sixth time that month.

We are all one, Orryka said again.

"Yeah, yeah...."

What is bothering you, Serra?

"Sarah. S. A. R. A. H."

What troubles your heart, dear?

"I'm afraid I am crazy!" She stood suddenly and began to pace. Orryka stared up at her with his kind blue-green eyes. She sighed once more, and then continued. "I'm afraid that you're some manifestation of my subconscious, due to some narcissistic neurosis, and that I'll regret all the time I'm spending with you."

Check your heart. What does your heart say?

"That you're real! That I'm not crazy. That there are more things in this world and others that cannot be explained ... more than anyone knows."

What else, Serra?

"That I love you ..." her voice choked with tears, "and for the first time in my life, I'm beginning to see clearly, feel happy and love more wholly. I just can't find anything bad about you."

This disappoints you? he said and then chuckled.

"No. But, you're breaking apart everything I have learned, and forcing me to view everything, EVERYTHING differently! Nothing is familiar anymore! I don't know what to do with all that I'm learning. Why am I going through all of this training anyway?"

Orryka smiled at her. He hesitated for a moment, as if he was deciding something, and then spoke.

Serra, I am limited in what I may tell you at this moment, but I can tell you that you are learning what each person on this planet is here to learn – to love themselves. **Whether a person is a banker, a housewife, an artist, a mercenary, a child in school or a tribesperson, does not change their basic lesson. Whatever style or form the souls choose, the lessons remain the same, to learn to love themselves.** *You are no different.*

"Orryka, why, then, is there so much pain in the world?"

This, dear, is the other end of the equation, the lesson. **Wherever there is pain, there is a lack of love.** *Many on this planet do not know how to love. Each time a soul chooses to heal a part of his or herself that is in pain, he or she is choosing to love. Whenever this happens, the world is brought closer to healing itself. This, in turn, touches the entire universe. All – all – life, Serra, is connected. Do you understand this?*

"Yes. I'm beginning to, at least."

Let me give you a new lesson, dear.

As you go through your day not judging, I would like you to take this act one step further. Each person you meet is to be treated without judgement and with compassion. Stop, take a moment and feel what it would be like to be that person!

The meadow vanished and Sarah found herself standing in her office at work. Orryka stood next to her. Before them a scene played out. Her boss entered the room and told her that he needed the paperwork on one of the winery accounts – immediately. Orryka whispered in her mind, *Observe, Sarah. How would it feel to be in your boss' position?*

Sarah watched her boss. His brow was furrowed with tension. His fingers drummed on the back of her chair impatiently. His breath was slightly rancid from a nervous stomach condition. Sarah imagined that she was the boss. She felt the pressure this man was under, the impossibilities he faced in trying to please his supervisor and those who worked for him. She saw the stress this created in his life. She felt the weariness of those pressures. At the same time, from the moments when he did meet and conquer the demands of his daily work, she could feel a small satisfaction that lived within the tension. Sarah looked at Orryka with an expression that was both humble and amazed.

He smiled at her again, and Sarah felt a profound wonder at what she had learned and would learn. Her earlier frustrations vanished as her heart was opened in a new way. She felt a gratitude that went beyond words as she looked up into Orryka's eyes. From their blue depth, his eyes twinkled back at her, and he nodded as he spoke.

You don't have to explain, dear. I understand.

"Quit your job," Thomas said reasonably as he climbed into bed next to Sarah. He picked up a book on boating he wanted to read, but placed it on his lap while they finished their conversation.

"No. I can't."

"That's ridiculous. Sarah, I make enough money to support us both. I think the work you're doing through channeling is more important than selling wine. You can't do both. Since we returned from our honeymoon six weeks ago and the channeling was increased from twice a week to every day, you've been having a hard time keeping up. You've admitted that this schedule of working all day and channeling at night is exhausting you. You have to make a choice.

"When I decided to quit my cabinetmaking business last winter and I started my photography business, you supported me. This new business is exceeding both our expectations. Actually, I need help. You could work part-time as my assistant. We have plenty in savings. I think you should do it."

"I don't know. Let me think about it," Sarah said reluctantly.

From the day Sarah left her job, their experiences intensified dramatically, as if the entities had waited to begin the real work so as not to tax her. She channeled two to three times a day and meditated in-between. Orryka increased her lessons and asked her to write down what she experienced. A few times a day Sarah and Orryka met in *the between,* where they discussed lessons, other worlds and life.

On one such occasion, Sarah and Orryka sat on the ridge that looked out over the lake and watched the second moon in its quarter phase rise above the dark surface of the water. Night had fallen over this strange world, stars shone throughout the sky like fireflies and Sarah felt especially peaceful. Sarah smiled at this beauty and listened as Orryka informed her that he had a new lesson for her.

Serra, when you go back, look at your world as if you created everything in it. Everything! Ask yourself why you would create each object that you view, he said so simply that Serra felt that this particular exercise was probably not as powerful as the others. Orryka heard her thoughts and laughed.

Don't underestimate the power behind this lesson, Serra. It WILL be life-changing.

A half hour later, Sarah awoke on the bed and sleepily looked about the room. The bed, in its antique oak frame, surrounded her in a wooden nest. Her cranberry-colored bathrobe hung next to Thomas' green one on hooks on one wall. The antique oak dresser had stacks of film canisters on top of it and, next to these, a framed picture of them on their wedding day. Sunlight filtered in through the window and showed the slight film of dust that had built up on an antique maple wardrobe. Sarah's eyes trailed to a pile of dirty clothes that had fallen from the clothes hamper in the corner.

Next, her eyes came to rest on the bedside tables. Piles of books on boat building, photography and architectural design sat on Thomas' table beside a lamp that should have been thrown out and replaced years ago. On her bedside table was a stack of cloth-bound journals and notebooks for her work, an FAA flight manual, two flashlights, two pens, a pencil and a vase of poppies. On this table, beside the poppies, was a beige-colored telephone with a long, dirty, tangled extension cord.

One by one, Sarah looked at the objects again and asked herself why she had created them. Many of the answers were obvious, but others surprised her and caused her to stop and think.

"Hmmm.... The antique furniture is here because I love beauty from all eras. I like a sense of history around me," Sarah said out loud, and then hastily scribbled this in her notebook.

The picture of our wedding day reminds me of the joy in my life, she thought.

The clothes in the hamper and the dust on the wardrobe.... Perhaps I created this because I've been trying to relax more, not worry about being so perfect in all that I do.

Thomas' books symbolize an interesting partner.

The poppies.... Sarah smiled and reached over to touch one of the delicate peach-colored petals. *Because ... I love to have at least a small part of nature with me always. Somehow I don't feel complete when I am totally cut off from nature.* This last thought surprised Sarah, and she continued, more curious now.

Why would I keep this lamp, which works, but is old, worn and ugly? Sarah laughed as the answer came to her. *Because my poverty background won't allow me to throw away anything that still functions! I'm making a decision based on old patterns and not based on what I want!*

Quickly, Sarah looked around the room, excited by what she was learning.

The FAA airplane manual caused her to laugh aloud. When she had trouble sleeping, she read this dry manual and quickly was bored into sleep.

Only the FAA could make something as wondrous as flight so dry and dull! she thought.

The notebooks and journals were evident to her. *How much I love to learn!* she thought. Her eyes came to rest on the phone and swiftly her mind answered, *Communication.* As she looked at the long tangled cord attached to the phone her thoughts became quiet.

"Now why would I create such a tangled mess?" she said out loud. Sarah stared at the cord, but no answer was found. The cord drove her crazy by wrapping itself around chair legs and the bed frame. It was a large, dusty knot of wiring. *Why? Why would I create this in my life?* she thought, truly puzzled by this one item. Suddenly, the answer was clear. The words echoed loudly in her mind as if someone else spoke them.

Because you are afraid to let go of chaos. Chaos has distracted you through most of your life, shielded you from facing yourself, from creating your dreams ... from experiencing what you truly want. You've been afraid to let yourself have what you want.

"What?" Sarah said out loud, startled by this revelation. "What do I truly want?"

To live in joy – to experience love – to know peace.

Chapter 23

*W*eeks had fled by and the summer season had passed into fall. The harvest was underway. The grapes were picked by seasonal migratory workers, and the sound of Mexican folk songs drifted across the vineyards and toward Sarah and Thomas' small cabin in the forest. The heady smell of crushed fruit, which had fallen on the roads from the gondolas, permeated the air, and the grape leaves had turn bright gold and scarlet.

Thomas walked down the dirt road toward the neighboring vineyard with his camera pack strapped around his waist. He whistled to the pickers' song and stepped up his pace. A few moments later, he stood just inside the vineyard gate and watched as the setting sun began to cover the world with deep rosy tones and golden halos. A worker in a Michoacan straw hat stopped to watch the sunset. His hat glowed with warm yellow tones and his dusty brown skin turned to a deep bronze color. Even his worn, patched jeans looked rich in this lighting. Thomas dropped to one knee and photographed this stoic man with the vineyard as a backdrop.

The grape picker came over and spoke with Thomas for a few minutes in broken English. As the worker turned to leave, Thomas looked to his left, toward a breathtaking view of the mountains, which rolled one after another northward. The Mayacamas mountain range traveled all the way to the Oregon border and beyond.

Because the view was so striking, Thomas did not at first notice the object that flew across the sky. When he did, he thought his eyes were playing tricks on him. A large craft, in the shape of a triangle, flew soundlessly from horizon to horizon far above the northern mountains. The distance it covered meant the ship was flying at hundreds of miles per hour. His mouth fell open as the ship suddenly increased its speed and disappeared in a bright burst of light.

Thomas looked down at his camera, which sat idly in his hands, and cursed.

"Damn! I could have photographed it!"

The following night, Thomas awoke when he thought he heard something, a noise, coming from the living room. Quietly, he pushed back the covers and crept down the hallway. At the end of the hallway was something so startling that it left Thomas speechless.

Where the doorway of their living room usually stood was a porthole that led to outer space. The porthole was rectangular in shape and framed stars from the floor to just above Thomas' head. Gone was the couch, the coffee table, the lamps, the wooden walls and television. For as far as Thomas could see, space, in all its dark, vast beauty, lay in front of him. He knew that, if he wanted to, he could step through this opening and be transported ... but to where? And how would he get back?

He quickly walked back to the bedroom and tried to wake Sarah, but she seemed permanently lost in sleep. His mouth was dry as he tried to call her name and no words came out. Silently, he leaned against the headboard of their bed and tried to fathom what he had seen. As he decided he would go back and look again, he suddenly and heavily fell asleep.

An hour later, Thomas was awakened again by another noise. Through closed lids, he could tell that a light was on in the room ... but this illumination did not come from their bedside lamp. The color was different. A strange, amber lighting filtered through his lids, and its oddity reached his sleepy brain. He opened his eyes slowly and gasped at what he saw. Three tall beings stood by the bed. Giants! A man who had to be at least seven feet tall, with pale hair and eyes, stared back at him. A mind probed his, but he could not quite get the message. Another man, equally as tall, with the same Nordic coloring, spoke.

"Thomas? Can you see us?"

Wordlessly, Thomas nodded yes. His breathing was shallow and his heart rate had slowed, as if he were drugged. He didn't feel afraid, but more curious and startled. *Who are these beings? Am I dreaming? Shouldn't I be afraid? Why am I not afraid? Why are they in our bedroom?* These questions shouted in Thomas' mind. His concern was suddenly for Sarah. *Sarah, is she safe?*

He turned to see her sitting peacefully beside him. She smiled gently at him; something in her look said, *Don't be afraid, Thomas!* Then, Sarah looked back at the tall men by the bed and said, "Yes. I'd say he can see you!" Her laughter floated over Thomas in comforting waves. His head turned in slow motion, back toward the giants.

At that moment, a small being floated into the room, the tiniest creature Thomas had ever seen! Dark, large eyes, which appeared to wrap around the being's face, stared back at him. Bone-white skin covered his large skull. No nose was on his face, but a slit of an opening was below where a nose would have been. Thomas guessed this was the being's mouth. For some reason, although Thomas could not say how, he knew this small being was male and that he was smiling at him. A warmth of emotions spilled over Thomas, and then, swiftly, he became unconscious.

The following morning, Thomas shook Sarah awake. The light coming in the window angled over the dresser and onto her face. She stared up sleepily at him, and then looked around.

"What time is it?"

"9:30 a.m."

"9:30! What happened?"

"Do you remember any of last night?"

"No."

"Sarah, you won't believe what happened!"

"Wait. Let me wake up."

Thomas darted out of the room, and returned a few minutes later with a steaming cup of tea. As Sarah sipped the tea in bed, he proceeded to tell her another of many amazing turns of events.

Thomas took a deep breath and began to pace by their bed.

"Space beings, Sarah, extraterrestrials. Tall men, and a little being with large eyes, were in our room! I woke up and the bed was surrounded by them. You were sitting up and talking with them. I was sitting up, too! Then I lost consciousness. Jeez! I can't believe you don't remember any of this!"

Sarah took another sip of tea and stared at Thomas over the lip of the cup. Steam rose in curly wisps and made Thomas' handsome face look surreal. She asked him a question.

"Are you trying to tell me that I slept in because we were up all night talking to extraterrestrials?"

"Yes."

"I don't believe it."

"Oh, come on, Sarah! Do you think I'd lie to you?"

"No. Maybe it was a dream," she suggested calmly.

"I did not – not – I repeat, dream this."

"I know you wouldn't lie to me or make this up, Thomas, but – what were we talking about, anyway?"

"I don't know. I was hoping you could channel so that we could find out."

"I thought you had a photography session this morning."

"I did, but my client called while you were sleeping and asked to postpone his appointment."

"Okay. Let me take a shower first to wake up."

An hour later, Sarah settled onto the couch nervously. It took her longer than usual to calm herself and begin the steps she had been taught to put herself into a trance. Fifteen minutes later, she was gone. Thomas waited impatiently for Yerraba or someone to come through. A few more minutes passed before he heard a soft voice spoken with a French accent.

"Hello."

"Yerraba! I'm glad you're here. I have many questions...." Thomas rushed forward. He proceeded to describe the previous night's activities. Yerraba listened patiently.

"What do you wish to understand?" asked Yerraba.

"Why? Why were they here?"

"The beings you describe are descendants of our race. They have followed you throughout your experiences in order to learn. They are here on an anthropological study and to assist, at times, in the human evolution of this planet. They study you to assist other races and the human race."

"Wait a minute, Yerraba. Aliens are here – studying humans?"

"Aliens? **No one is 'alien,'**" Yerraba said seriously.

Thomas sat back, stunned, embarrassed by a statement that was obvious. He had separated himself from these beings and others. He humbly continued.

"I apologize. You're right. 'Alien' is an unfriendly and derogatory term. What shall I call them?"

"Thomas, there is no them or us! There is only *us*. You are part of *them* as much as they are part of *you*. As long as humans separate themselves from each other with these beliefs of *them and us* or *alien* they will not know peace, because, in doing so, a separation or isolation takes place. *We are all one*, part of a whole. You could try calling these beings, 'friends.'"

Thomas reflected quietly for several minutes. In elementary school, it was boys against girls, us against them. In high school, it was "surfers" against "cowboys", again another them and us. In college, it was the rich against the poor. Always, throughout his life, it was one faction against another. That he might be fighting some part of himself, an important and necessary part of the whole, was not something he had thought of before this moment. That he might be acting in prejudice against something, someone, he should love, needed to love ... was a new concept. His own ignorance shocked and humbled him.

"What is wrong, Thomas?" Yerraba asked in her thick accent.

"I feel like a fool."

"Why?"

"Because of what you have pointed out to me."

"Thomas, you are not acting in self-love now."

"What?"

"Why do you criticize yourself for learning something new? Can you not congratulate yourself for having the courage to see the Universe in a new way?"

"I hadn't thought of it like that."

"You do not help the universe or yourself by putting yourself down. I am happy for you that you are able to learn, to see where you could not before. Do you understand?"

"Yes. This is all new. It is going to take a while for me to adjust to these new concepts. Can you tell me more about these 'friends?'"

"Oui, bien entendu...."

"Jonah, how long have Thomas and I been in contact with these beings?" Sarah asked. She had been surprised upon arriving in the meadow to find Jonah, instead of Orryka, awaiting her. He sat next to her on the grass and serenely answered her questions.

All this life, as well as during other experiences and times. Do you remember when you were a little girl and you believed in angels?

"Yes." One of Sarah's first memories was one in which she

explained to a playmate that angels existed and visited her at night.

The beings you referred to as angels were extraterrestrials, Jonah said simply.

"Then who are you?" Sarah asked.

You see me as you are most comfortable in seeing me. I take a form that you are most likely to accept, a biblical one you were taught to trust.

"What are you? What do you really look like?"

Just one moment, please, Jonah said.

He stared off into the distance and appeared to listen to something, someone whom Sarah could not hear. He cut off the communication abruptly and turned to stare at Sarah with a peaceful smile.

We believe you are ready.

The air shimmered around him and the old man dissolved. In his place stood a petite being who was maybe four feet in height. Pale, grayish-white skin stretched over a skeletal frame. Two huge, dark green eyes stared at her, out of a hairless skull. An intense love filled Sarah as her eyes met his.

"Jonah?"

Yes. I am Jonah. You see me in the form I took when I was alive.

Something about the small man was familiar. He reached forward, placed one long-fingered hand over her eyes and said, *Look!* A series of images flashed before Sarah's closed eyes. A spaceship with carved metallic walls, that looked like stainless steel, came into view. On the spaceship, in a room with concave walls, a variety of creatures worked together. Tall blond women and men stood by a screen and discussed an intergalactic star map. Several of the petite beings moved about the room quickly. The scene changed.

A large room with the same metallic walls lay before her eyes. In the center of the room was a long table. Around the table sat beings of several races. Sarah recognized six of the tall blond men and women; with them was an unusual-looking being, humanoid with blue skin and gills across his cheeks. Black hair covered his head and chin. At least, she believed the blue-skinned entity was male.

Next to him were two taller, more substantial versions of Jonah. Next to these beings was another human-type being with unusual eyes. The being's eyes looked like a cat's without whites and were a deep amber color. His face was bearded with thick brown hair. In the middle of the table was a holographic image of a technical device that was a part of the spaceship. She knew, somehow, that this group had been brought together to find a solution for a mechanical problem. No one used words, as all present spoke telepathically. Sarah watched for a moment more, and the scene changed again.

She saw herself, years younger, sitting at a table on the spaceship. On a panel behind her, brightly colored lights flashed on and off. A window in one wall looked out at a starry heaven in the galaxy. A tall blond man stood next to her by the table. Across from her, on the other side of the table, stood two of the petite beings with large eyes. One of them was Jonah. The images disappeared as Jonah took his hand away.

For a while Sarah was quiet. She did not know what to think, what to say or what to question. Jonah waited nearby patiently. Finally, she began by asking him a question.

"Is this what is happening at night? Thomas and I are going to – a spaceship?"

Sometimes, yes.

"What do we do on the spaceship?"

There is not one answer for this question. You study and learn. You also teach us what you have learned here, on Earth.

"What could we possibly teach you?" Sarah was surprised by his answer. "Why do we not remember these experiences?"

You teach us much, about plants, about people, about animals, about whatever you learn here. You do not remember more, Sarah, because you would become distracted by what you learn on the spaceship, and that would make your learning on earth difficult, if not, in some ways, impossible.

"I understand that. The spaceship, the beings I saw in those few, brief images were fascinating. It makes what I am learning here seem mundane and unimportant."

Serra, you must remember that everything you learn is important! Jonah said firmly. *Your life here is as important as anything you do on the ship. One does not preclude the other. Each and every lesson is valuable to you, to us, to the universe. With each step you take toward peace, you heal all of us. You heal* The One, *the whole. Do not dismiss this life, your lessons here, so easily!*

"Yes. I understand," Sarah said. Jonah looked at her, and though his small mouth did not change, she knew he was smiling.

Thomas had been quiet for days. This revelation, that extraterrestrials actively existed in his daily life, had been hard for him. The boggle point he had taught Sarah about now threatened to close him off from their experiences. He questioned Sarah about everything she had been told, everything she had learned from Jonah, until Sarah refused to answer any further questions. She did not keep anything from him; she simply had run out of information to give him. Thomas reflectively went about his work and, by joint agreement, Sarah stopped channeling for several days while they both adjusted to this new information. When she did channel again, they both had many questions.

Thomas waited impatiently for Sarah to go into a trance. The sound of his fingers tapping on the side of his chair was the only noise in the living room. From outside, birds could be heard singing a morning song. Sarah opened her eyes to just a squint and whispered, "Thomas, please?" He forced himself to sit quietly and waited. Sarah fell back into her meditative state, and he watched her peaceful face.

Her hair had grown out and was worn in loose waves over her shoulders. She had begun to fill out, and this added weight looked good on her. The weight gain was a natural side affect of the channeling and seemed to improve her health overall. Sarah seemed to glow all the time now.

Sarah's head dropped forward, her shoulders relaxed and then her body stiffened as an entity came into it. Yerraba's bright and happy gestures filled Sarah's body and created a defined and unique presence.

"Yerraba, what am I learning on the spaceship?" Thomas asked before she could speak.

"Flight training," Yerraba said simply, as if everyone on Earth went to flight school on a spaceship.

"I'm learning to fly a spaceship?" Thomas asked in astonishment.

"Oui."

"I don't believe it!"

"Pourquoi?"

"Why? Because —"

"Bien entendu. One moment please, Thomas."

Yerraba appeared to be talking to someone else and then she turned and addressed Thomas.

"Do you wish to see?" she asked.

"Yes. Definitely!"

"Close your eyes."

She reached up with Sarah's hand and placed it over his forehead. A flash of white light blasted the darkness behind his closed eyes, and he was sitting behind a control panel. A view of star-filled space lay before him through a window. Multi-colored, diamond-shaped panels flashed on and off on a control board in front of him. Thomas reached forward and placed his right hand over one of the diamonds. He felt himself move from his body, into the ship. He told the ship where to go, how to move as if *he* were its brain. The ship glided effortlessly through space in a graceful arch as he instructed it to navigate to his right. He took his right hand away and placed his left hand over another diamond, and again moved into the ship from his body; he instructed the ship to go into orbit. As the ship settled into its repetitive pattern around Earth, Thomas backed away from the panel and turned to look at another display window, a four-by-six-foot window, which showed Earth in all its splendor.

"The Blue Planet!" Thomas heard himself whisper.

Yerraba removed her hand, and Thomas was yanked back to the reality of the cabin in the mountains of Sonoma. He sat in the chair and gasped. After he got his breathing somewhat under control, he turned to Yerraba.

"Yerraba, I think for once I don't have any further questions."

"Oui," she said, and then smiled.

Serra, you made a commitment to do this work. That is why you are here!

"It's that simple?" Sarah asked.

She sat in the ambrosial bed of purple flowers. Orryka sat next to her, as he had for the past hour. Their fragrance offered the solace of peace during a confusion of thoughts. She tried to understand their connection to extraterrestrials, to this life and to other lifetimes ... but it was a struggle.

"I don't understand," she continued. "Why would we come here to do this work, and over many lifetimes? Why not just one? This world, Earth, is difficult. It is not an easy place in which to live."

You needed many lifetimes to gather the information you will take back to our home planets and other worlds. Each lifetime has difficulties, but each holds gifts and wonders, as well. Each lifetime is fleeting and brief. Each is a gift to be cherished. This you taught us! It took many lifetimes for you and Thomas to

353

learn what you sought to learn.

"If this life, in which I am now living, is an example of other lifetimes, then they must have been difficult and ... odd."

Serra, it is not so simple. You have gained much through each brief lifetime. **You may look upon each life as a short difficult task, or you may look upon each as a brilliantly lighted moment.**

"You're saying that we traveled through lifetimes for over three thousand years, that during that time you followed and learned from Thomas and me. That's a long time, Orryka! Were we slow to learn or something?"

Orryka's laughter spilled over the meadow and into Sarah's heart. She also began to laugh.

Serra, you describe three thousand years as if it's a long time. It is brief and momentary in the duration of this world and the universe. Look!

Suddenly a pond lay before them. The purple flowers ran up to the edge of the pond and the water lay clear and picturesque before her.

This pond is the Universe. Look again!

A single shaft of sunlight fell on the surface of the water, and hundreds of reflections bounced off it. The effect was startling and beautiful.

Each lifetime is like a sparkle on the water, brief and fleeting. It remains for a short duration of time. Each moment is precious and important, not to be dismissed. Each life is gift-filled with wonders, if you will open your eyes to them. *Enjoy your life, Serra, for it is only a sparkle on the water of time!*

Chapter 24

*T*he car rumbled to a stop in front of a brightly lit house. Night surrounded the house, hiding the scenery, and only the sound of waves breaking on the shore told Sarah that they were close to the ocean. Seal's barking echoed through the blackness as Sarah stepped from the car.

"Do you have Guy's birthday gift?" she asked Thomas.

"Right here." He held up a brightly wrapped package.

"You're sure he wants to play Trivial Pursuit again?" Sarah said, and shivered in the cool night air. She wrapped the red wool shawl she wore tighter around her shoulders.

"Sarah, we've been over this a half-dozen times. You don't have to play."

"If I don't play, Guy will be disappointed," she answered through chattering teeth.

"Tell Guy the truth," Thomas said, and then grinned mischievously. "Tell him you're dyslexic and have trouble reading the cards after only one glass of wine. He'll understand."

"Very funny ... and all the jokes will start about my being a moron, or he'll become overly solicitous. I'd rather struggle through the game."

As Sarah finished her statement, the door opened and a backlit figure, a woman, greeted them.

"Sarah, Thomas, come in!"

The inside of the house was decidedly warm when compared to the outdoors. Dinner was over, and people sat on couches, in chairs or on the floor as Guy's wife June served cake and coffee while each person took a turn roasting Guy. Each person told a story which contributed to Guy's quickly dissolving reputation. Guy drank a glass of wine and coaxed one story after another from his friends. A ruddy color had spread over his cheeks as the wine had spread through his veins and the jokes had spread over his soul. The contrast of this color against his dark brown hair and blue eyes made him look feverish or giddy.

Sarah and Thomas sat comfortably on one of the couches. Laughter warmed the room and Sarah smiled often as she listened. She did not know Guy well enough to tell a story about him.

"Come on! One of you must have something nice to say about me!" Guy teased. His arm came down around June's plump waist as he spoke.

"Okay. I've got one!" yelled a friend of Guy's, a man Sarah had never met until this night, named Louis. Louis jumped up and began an animated story about when he had first met Guy. He towered over his audience at six-and-a-half feet, and Louis' brown eyes twinkled as he poked fun at his old friend. The light reflected off his coal-black skin, his white teeth and the glass of wine he held in his large hand.

"Once, when Guy and I were on campus – we had only known each other for a couple of weeks – he decided he wanted to check out the local bar...."

Sarah's mind wandered as she quickly lost interest in yet another drinking story about Guy. Her thoughts fell into a reflective place.

I wonder why Guy needs this kind of attention? Why do he and his friends hold onto old drinking stories? Guy is so nice and intelligent – why does he need to focus on drinking? Perhaps he is hiding a shyness. He admits that he's hardly ever home during the football season because he's usually at a bar watching a game with his friends. How does June handle this? Does it make her lonely, angry or sad? They seem happy together. Look at how she smiles at him. This is such a great group of people, but I'm restless. How do people manage to sit for hours, telling drinking stories and not get bored? I wonder when we can politely leave?

"Sarah?" Thomas shook her gently on the shoulder. "It's your turn to tell a story about Guy."

The entire room of people stared at her and waited. She swallowed and began haltingly.

"I met Guy – that is, Thomas introduced me to Guy about a year ago, and I remember thinking...."

Sarah felt her cheeks turning red as she realized she did not know what to add to what she had begun. Guy jumped in.

"You remember thinking what a handsome man I was. Right, Sarah?"

"No," Sarah said, and then blushed more deeply as she realized what she had said. The room broke into laughter. "I – I thought how nice you were," she tried to say over the laughter.

"No. You had it right the first time, Sarah. Guy is one ugly cuss," Louis said, and laughed.

"Almost as ugly as my dog," another man joined in.

Orryka! Please get me out of here! Sarah thought in frustration.

Another person took her place in storytelling and began to talk about Guy's inability to miss a sports game. As Sarah sighed with the relief of not having to finish her story, Orryka came through.

Yes, dear?

Orryka, I'm so sorry. I just failed miserably.

Failed? Failed what?

I've been sitting here judging a very nice group of people. All your teaching was for nothing. I blew it!

A pain knotted in her throat and suddenly she felt like either running from the room or crying ... or both.

Serra, you did not judge. You watched and learned and asked questions, but you did not judge. You observed. Do you know the difference?

No.

Did you ever once think less of these people for their choices?

No, Sarah answered slowly.

Did you feel that even one person in this room should change and become more like you?

No, of course not! How could I expect anyone to be like me when we're all individuals?

Sarah felt Orryka's warmth spread over her as she answered. His hug comforted her as he continued.

Did you think that Guy should be nicer to his wife, that he should drink less, should be a certain way? Orryka asked gently.

No.

*You observed and, by doing so, learned about yourself. You saw what works for you, what makes you happy and what does not, by watching others. There is a difference a – big difference – between observing and judging. **"Observing" is a way to learn, a form of seeing and practicing awareness of your reality. "Judging" is a way of managing or controlling others with your opinion, a way of passing your opinions on to others.***

Do you understand how important it is to practice awareness of your world so that you can learn? Do you see how placing judgment on others can hurt them?

Yes. I understand, Sarah answered.

At that moment, June touched her shoulder and said, "Sarah, we're playing Trivial Pursuit. You're on my team."

Orryka spoke in her head in the next moment. *Don't worry, dear. We'll help you read the cards.*

Shadows of the tall fir and redwood trees lay over the deck and kept the worst of the late fall, or Indian Summer's, heat at bay. Sarah and Thomas sipped iced tea and ate cookies in the afternoon as they read their mail. Rusty sat at Thomas' feet and waited expectantly, to see if perhaps a treat was forthcoming.

Thomas watched Sarah's face and the emotions which crossed it. Her brown eyes first looked kind and curious, then stormy, and then a tear fell down her cheek as she read the letter he had just handed her. It was the reaction he had expected. Without words, he reached forward and pulled Sarah into his arms.

"Why?" Sarah said the one word that expressed all her emotions.

"I don't know," Thomas began. "Maybe she's afraid. Perhaps Holly will never accept that there are other worlds, other realities than the one we see here."

Sarah sat up abruptly and read the letter out loud.

Dear Sarah and Thomas,

Although it was fun to see you last week, I have made a decision that I can no longer socialize with you. I have finally confessed about my friendship with you and the work you do to my pastor. He has explained that you are doing the Devil's work, that I would be forsaking Jesus Christ, my Lord, by associating with you.

Please do not call my house ever again, and do not tell anyone that I have known you. I will pray for your souls.

– Holly

"Why, Thomas? Why do people react this way?" Sarah demanded. "We're not that different. We drink vanilla creme soda, eat grilled cheese sandwiches and tomato soup. We watch television, go grocery shopping, work, shower and...." Her voice trailed off into a sigh.

"This isn't the first time, Sarah, and it probably won't be the last, as our friends discover that you channel, that we have visitations from extraterrestrials," Thomas began. He meant to approach this practically, to offer comfort, but his voice was tinged with the sadness he felt from this latest rejection.

"I know. Your friend Quinn hasn't called in months! We haven't heard a word since I channeled for him and the information proved so accurate that he accused of us of spying on his private life. I don't think we'll ever hear from him again!" Sarah said with passion. "I'm beginning to think we won't have any friends left!"

Sarah stopped as she began to cry in frustration. Thomas held her again as she mourned the loss of a someone she had come to love.

Orryka's voice interrupted Sarah's tears. *Sarah, some people are deeply afraid, as is your friend Holly. She always has been. She couldn't move beyond her fears. Send her your love, and then let Holly go the path she has chosen with your blessing. Other friends will come to replace those that are afraid. A woman named Anne, a man named Harvey and many others will fill your life with friendship and warmth.* Sarah repeated the message to Thomas.

"Ask Orryka: When will people stop being afraid?" Thomas said into her hair. He kissed the top of Sarah's head as he awaited an answer.

Serra, please tell Thomas: **Fear leaves the soul as the soul learns to love again. As this world awakens and learns to love again, fear will be abated.**

Sarah again repeated Orryka's words, and Thomas murmured, "I have a feeling we have a long wait ahead of us."

A cloud, white and billowy, drifted by Sarah. She blinked and wondered how she had come to be in the light. Usually this took place through a series of well-rehearsed steps. Today, she had sat down to work on one of Orryka's exercises in her journal, had suddenly lost consciousness and then found herself in *the between.* As if in answer to her question, a figure began to take form in the clouds.

Serra! Come. I have someone who wishes to meet you!
Orryka spoke with excitement.

Clouds began to drift by in increasing movement. A richness of feelings swept by and through Sarah as she and Orryka
raced deeper into the light. As they did, the light became more
intense, brighter and more encompassing. It seemed to fill every
ounce of Sarah, until she felt certain she would burst from its
beauty. After a while, she realized that she was blinded by its
luminosity; she could no longer see Orryka or her surroundings.

At last, they reached a place where even Orryka seemed
diminished in size, in being. Before them lay a presence that was
at once familiar and foreign. Sarah searched her mind for memory of this being. As she did, memories flooded her. Lifetimes of
experiences overwhelmed her.

Sarah saw herself as a young, male French painter, as a
woman in early Colonial America, as an Island woman off the
cost of South America, as a Native American Pueblo woman ....
on and on the memories played, until they swirled around her in
a pattern of shapes, colors and beauty, all mixed into one being,
one soul – herself.

The vision ended as suddenly as it had begun, with an
implosion of light, and she found herself back at the birth of her
soul. All sound, sight and thinking was gone. She had only sensation, a soul reaching out in its infancy to *The One,* reaching for
its parents. Such wonder, such grace and freedom was in this
moment. The purity of sensation was astounding. No guilt lay
here. No pain or suffering or prejudice. She was purely and wholly loved. She was love.

The vision of her soul's birth ended.

Sarah felt the physical sensation of being in *the between,* of
being a developed and experienced soul again. She whispered to
the being before her.

*Who are you? What do you want with me? What do you
want me to know?*

The voice that answered was deep, resonant and powerful.
It cast its words over Sarah as a fisherman casts nets into the sea.

Serra, please bring this knowledge to your world.

The being stopped for a moment, and Sarah felt as if she
were being gusted about by the force of his words, the importance of his meaning. She felt the being's intense scrutiny and the
love behind him ... or her – no defined sex came from this being,
but, instead, a blending of both sexes. An array of images filled

her consciousness all at once and Sarah felt herself gasping at all she was shown.

Trillions of souls, all reflecting against one another, all sharing the universe, each perfect and balanced and sharing the next soul's energy and experiences, filled her sight, mind and her heart. All souls were touching and equally sharing the whole. All lives came together in a dance of perfection. One soul was never better than the next – ever. One person experienced what the next would in another lifetime. The man who was a priest in this lifetime might be a murderer in the next incarnation. Each soul gathered and joined *The One*, bringing its beauty, what it had gained. This mass of energy spun into a starburst of light and brought Sarah to a place of wonder and love she had never seen on Earth or in *the between*. It brought her back to this being.

The being spoke once more, the last words it would say to her in this moment before she was sent back to the dense reality she knew as Earth.

All – all – *souls are equal.*

A few moments later, Orryka pulled Sarah back through the light. As she was carried along, Sarah asked Orryka a question.

Who – what was that?

Orryka answered solemnly, but with love.

Serra, do you really think that God, The One, *can be named?*

Chapter 25

*T*he room was dark and the night especially still when Thomas awoke. What had awakened him? He looked about the room for some clue, but found none. Perhaps the porthole phenomenon was back in the hallway. He yawned, and then pushed back the covers and walked down the hall.

No. The living room was there as it always was; shapes of furniture were darkly visible in the unlit room. He crossed the room and stepped through the front door onto the deck. Stars peeked out between tree limbs and a soothing breeze blew over Thomas' bare back. An owl hooted somewhere in the trees to his left, invisible in the night's shadows. A furry object moved toward him, and then leaned up against his legs.

"Hey, Rusty," Thomas murmured softly.

The owl called again, as if it, too, were greeting the dog.

Thomas had turned and had begun to walk back inside when an astonishing sight froze him. Through the large picture window of the living room, Thomas watched as a narrow band of light from floor to ceiling opened into a doorway. Two small beings, the ones with large eyes and pale white skin, stepped out from the opening. One of the beings turned and stared back into Thomas' blue eyes. Rusty's ears cocked forward in interest.

For a second, Thomas suddenly saw himself through the extraterrestrial's eyes, although he could not say how this happened. He saw himself as slender, but muscular in build and size, standing naked on the deck, with just a hint of starlight playing off his features, his shoulders and arms. The night hid the lines that had formed more deeply around his eyes as he had aged.

And the first hints of grey, a few strands at the top of his head, stood out and ran long and silvery over his shoulders.

He felt the extraterrestrial's curiosity about such a large and bulky body, compared to its own. He felt a warmth and humor – and then Thomas was again looking through his own eyes. He tried to move, but could not. Instead, he stood silently and watched as the extraterrestrials stepped back into the doorway and disappeared. A split second later, the doorway shrank back to a long vertical line of blue light, and then it, too, faded away.

✳

Sarah flipped the pancakes as she told Thomas about her latest extraterrestrial memory. The smells of pancake batter sizzling in butter wafted through the room, and Thomas found it hard to concentrate as he watched her. Sarah's long, dark hair tumbled down her back, and she was wearing only a flannel shirt – one of his – as she cooked. Although one of the side-effects of channeling, weight gain, caused Sarah to complain often, she still looked good to him. Her roundness was pleasing and her legs were as attractive as ever. He had recently found a picture of her from when they had first met, and was surprised to find how much he enjoyed this newer, sensual version of the woman he loved. He smiled unconsciously at this happy image and tried to bring his mind back to listening to Sarah's story.

"Back up, Sarah. I wasn't listening," he admitted.

"I was explaining about the inside of the ship again. There were some kind of ... I guess you would call them 'hieroglyphics,' on the walls. I don't know what they meant, but they were very familiar."

"What type of room were you in?"

"I don't know. There were tables – metal tables – and seats around the tables. Some others, human others, were in the room with me. I sat next to a petite, pretty woman named Annie, and next to her were her parents. Annie's father was a nice man named ... Bert, Robert? No! His name was Bob. Her mother was a vivacious and funny woman named Missy. In any case, I've never seen them in my waking state," she said, and handed Thomas a plate stacked with pancakes.

"What were you doing there?" Thomas asked as they sat down at the table.

"I remember learning about transportation, about the porthole. I can't remember the face of the extraterrestrial who taught us, but I remember he said this was a common technique they used to transport themselves around the universe."

"Like on Star Trek? They transport through objects and walls?" Thomas asked as he poured maple syrup over his pancakes.

"No. I asked the same question. The extraterrestrial said that this didn't make sense, that it is far easier and more efficient to go around something – around molecules – than through them. He used the comparison of driving around a mountain instead of tunneling a hole through the mountain to get to the other side. He said one way was time consuming, dangerous and a lot of work, where the other was simpler.

"He explained that they used dimensional doorways, like the one in our house, to go around matter and space."

Sarah stopped for a moment and concentrated on eating before she continued. Thomas thought over everything Sarah had said. It all made sense, and he seemed to instinctively understand the information on a deeper level than his consciousness. Sarah sipped her tea, and then continued.

"They said they also use this concept to navigate the ships. Rather than parting or separating the molecules to move through space, they ride them or bounce off them to change direction. He called it 'riding waves of molecules' – like surfing."

"Space surfing – I like that," Thomas said, and then laughed.

"What about you? Do you remember anything from last night?" Sarah asked, her full attention upon him.

Thomas stared back into Sarah's questioning, brown eyes, remembered the strange doorway and the two small extraterrestrials, and then smiled.

Several weeks later, Thomas and Sarah sat in one of their favorite restaurants and enjoyed breakfast. They talked about plans for the day, a photo shoot Thomas had, and then Thomas dropped Sarah off at their cabin before heading out for work. When Thomas returned home later in the evening, he looked pale and drawn.

"I'm going to bed early," Thomas said after he had explained about suffering from an upset stomach, vomiting and cramps earlier in the afternoon. He seemed to feel better now, but looked and felt tired. Sarah's stomach had begun to churn about an hour ago, but so far wasn't too bad. Maybe they both had light cases of the stomach flu. She looked at the clock after Thomas lay down: it was nine in the evening. She settled down on the couch to read and tried not to focus on her stomach.

An hour later, the cramps began. Her lower back throbbed with pain and her stomach tensed involuntarily as each cramp hit. Sarah decided that maybe soaking in the hot tub would help. She walked onto the deck, down the stairs and out toward the hot tub on the lower deck. As she lowered herself into the hot water, the cramps intensified. She tried to get back out of the tub, but could not move, as one after another the cramps seared through her. She fell onto her side, paralyzed with pain. She called weakly to Thomas, but realized he'd never hear her. The hot tub was too far from the house.

Slowly, she pulled herself out onto the deck and lay there trembling as the cramps continued, until she managed to get up on her hands and knees and then onto her feet. As she began to walk back to the house, she knew then that something was very wrong; she was more sick than she had realized. There was no way she could make it back to the house. The cramps were filling her body with mind-numbing, agonizing pain. She was frozen, doubled over on the path in the forest. Frantically, she began to call for help.

"Orryka! Somebody! Please help me!"

A breeze blew around her and Sarah felt herself lifted under each arm, dragged down the path and up the stairs. She did not move her legs. Someone lifted her up the stairs and into the house. She reached the bathroom and began to vomit. There was little left in her stomach because she had eaten only a small bowl of yogurt for lunch. Sarah suffered the misery of dry heaves for another fifteen minutes, and then collapsed on the floor. She tried to drag herself out of the bathroom, but could get only as far as the studio floor. There she passed out.

Sarah's release from pain was only momentary; the toxins in her body awoke her just a few minutes later. She stared up at the ceiling with glazed eyes as cramp after cramp continued to assault her.

Then she began to hallucinate, or so she thought. The room filled with small Chinese men who moved quickly and spoke even faster. Sarah watched their dizzying movements, and then realized that these men weren't Chinese, but the small men and women from the spaceship.

One of the beings came over to her head and placed one long-fingered hand on her brow. She heard a gentle voice in her head.

Sarah, you must not move!

She nodded silently. She could not move, because she was

in too much pain. The being disappeared from her sight as he moved down her body. Suddenly, the pain stopped and Sarah felt an overwhelming sense of relief. She thought about how good it would feel to stretch. The being returned and again placed its long, thin hand on her forehead.

You must not move!

Again she nodded and lay still. Finally, Sarah fell asleep. She awoke several hours later, there on the floor. She stood slowly, noticing that now there was no more pain. She went to the bathroom and splashed cold water on her face and then sat on the toilet to urinate. When she looked down she was surprised to see that her urine was orange with bright purple streaks in it. She shook her head and remembered the strange dream. Orryka's voice came into her head.

Sarah, you will need to rest for the next two days. You must not eat any solid food for twenty-four hours.

Why?

You had emergency surgery last night. A section of your intestine ulcerated and became caustic when a food toxin entered your system.

"What?" Sarah asked out loud.

Look at your stomach, Orryka answered.

There, on Sarah's abdomen, was a long, thin scar that looked old rather than new. It had not been there yesterday. As she crawled into bed, Thomas was just getting up for the day.

"Sarah, are you just coming to bed? What did you do, stay up all night reading?"

"I was sick."

"What happened?"

"Oh, you know, UFO-HMO."

"What?"

"I'll tell you later. I need to sleep."

✳

Two nights later, Sarah drafted a thank you note to the beings who had helped her. She placed the note on the desk in their bedroom and ignored Thomas' teasing.

"Sarah, just tell them you're grateful the next time you see them."

"I know. I just want to do something more ... tangible."

In the middle of the night, Sarah awoke when she felt a presence in the bedroom. Over the desk hovered a ball of white light. A quiet voice filled her mind.

You're welcome.

Chapter 26

A day came when Orryka informed Sarah that she would not channel for several months. She had been channeling for almost three years and, Orryka explained, they did not want her or Thomas to become dependent on this source. He further explained that he would be with her. Although she would not see him, she would be able to hear him. Both she and Thomas were saddened by this news, but they had learned to trust Orryka enough to believe that this was an important and necessary part of their learning.

During those eight months, Orryka did keep contact with her, and at the most unusual times. Sarah could not control this telepathic communication. She could call him and hope that he would answer, but most often Orryka's voice suddenly appeared and spoke with her about whatever she was experiencing.

Once, during a dinner party, he interrupted her gently. She and Thomas had been invited to a party by a mutual friend. The friend, Jeffrey, one of Thomas' old clients, was giving a pool party at his house. He particularly wanted Sarah to meet his neighbor.

"Gwen has so many things in common with you, it's amazing. She's from New England. She's a chef. Gwen has the English-Scottish and Native American heritage that you have. She's your age, and has recently begun studying photography, like you!"

Sarah admitted at the time that the coincidences were interesting. But, as she and Thomas entered Jeffrey's house, she felt uneasy and nervous. Jeffrey happily introduced them to his neighbor, Gwen. Sarah shook Gwen's hand and smiled in welcome, but Gwen scowled at her in return. Gwen was tall, almost six feet, slender and attractive. Her waist-long, thick gold hair was tied back with a beaded barrette and the clothes she wore were Native American in their accent and design. Sarah recognized the patterns of thunderheads and an eagle in the beadwork on Gwen's cloth jacket. Gwen moved with an intensity of purpose that made Sarah feel as if she had been somehow dismissed. Still, Sarah tried to make light conversation with Gwen ... but the conversation failed.

A long table had been set casually with plates, knives and forks and wine glasses in Jeffrey's back yard. Soon barbecued swordfish was piled onto the table, and the group of twenty or so people sat down to eat. Jeffrey sat at the head of the table and Gwen sat near him. As Sarah and Thomas approached the table, Jeffrey called them over to him.

"Hey, Sarah, Tom, sit here! I want you and Gwen to have a chance to talk."

As Sarah sat down, Orryka's voice suddenly appeared in her head.

Do not talk, dear. Listen. You are being given a gift today.

What? Sarah asked telepathically.

You will see, dear. Relax. Enjoy yourself.

"So, Sarah, isn't it amazing how much you and Gwen have in common?" Jeffrey asked as he speared salad with his fork.

"I don...." The words came out mumbled and unclear. "Ecsxuse...." Again she could not pronounce a word. Jeffrey continued unaware. Sarah realized he probably thought she was drunk.

"Gwen, what tribe was your grandmother from?"

"Seneca," Gwen answered, and then pursed her lips in a frown. "I have decided to do a photo essay on the Seneca tribe. I've been in contact with a member, and am going to try to exhibit my work locally."

"Nice that's, really?" Sarah was shocked by what was happening. She had tried to say, "Really, that's nice," a polite retort. Yet the words came out backwards. Orryka's voice boomed in her head.

Sarah, we have asked you not to speak. Dear, listen – just listen. There is something important here for you to learn.

Gwen stared at Sarah as if Sarah were crazy, and then continued to explain about her search for her lost Native American heritage. Her words were angry and said almost as a challenge to Sarah. Sarah listened, ate salad and sipped on wine. Every statement that came from Gwen was tinged with anger or criticism.

She openly criticized her friends and Native American-blood mixes who did not uphold their ancestry. She criticized parents and their child rearing. She was a mother of three daughters and knew the proper way to raise a child. Gwen angrily described the prejudice against Native Americans, and called Caucasians, "ignorant white people." At that point, Sarah choked on her wine as she attempted not to laugh. Thomas patted her on the back as she coughed, while Orryka patted her mind with his kind words.

Do you see, dear? You come from similar backgrounds, education, class structures, the same part of the country, similar ancestry ... and look at the differences. You were given love, where Gwen was not. Without that love, negative thoughts would have been fostered in you, as they have been in her. Your life has not been easy, dear, but you have been given more than you know. You could be like this. Listen, Serra. This is important. Observe, but do not judge. See the differences. Learn, and don't speak.

"Well, what are you going to do about it?" Gwen directed the question at Sarah. Sarah had been listening to Orryka, and had no idea to what Gwen referred. Gwen continued.

"Sarah, don't you think drinking amongst the natives of our country is a sad and debilitating plight?

"Races all by suffered plight sad a is it."

Sarah covered her mouth with her hand and she felt herself blush. Orryka spoke in her head as the people at their end of the table turned to stare at her.

Dear, we have told you not to talk, he said gently, and then chuckled.

"Drunk!" Gwen said, and she wrinkled her nose as if Sarah were something she had stepped in which stank. Thomas put his arm around Sarah's shoulder. Sarah tried not to laugh, but she could not control herself. She began to chuckle, and then openly laughed. Her laughter brought another angry stare from Gwen. Thomas whispered into her ear.

"Sarah, what are you doing?"

She shook her head as she laughed helplessly. When she looked up at Thomas, his eyes were smiling and puzzled. She squeezed his hand, and then silently finished her dinner.

Another time, as she and Thomas drove up the mountain road that lead to their home, Orryka came through unexpectedly.

Do not stop for your mail.

What?

Do not stop at the mailboxes! Orryka said more firmly.

Sarah told Thomas what Orryka had said, and they drove by the row of mailboxes in perplexed silence. Thomas pulled into their driveway and, as he did, a car raced down the hill, going much too fast for the narrow roadways in the mountains. At the same time, another car raced up the road, going uphill. A screech of tires sounded as the two cars swerved to miss each other – directly in front of the line of mailboxes. Thomas looked at Sarah with an expression of shock upon his face. Sarah began to tremble.

"Thank you, Orryka," she whispered.

✴

You could make that choice, but another will bring you more pleasure. You will find the choice you now make will be disappointing.

Sarah chose a salad and pasta instead of the baked fish entree. Strange. Orryka came to talk to her at the oddest of times. No detail was unimportant. No moment was inadequate for his attention. From ordering lunch, to saving their lives, and everything inbetween, he was there for them. His patience seemed limitless, and he never criticized them for wasting his time with a question, no matter what the question was. He displayed a genuine love and caring about all that they did and experienced.

As time went on, Sarah began to wish that each person could feel the love she and Thomas experienced. The wonder that was in their life through the channeling and their contact with extraterrestrials was astounding. As she and Thomas discussed this one day, the phone rang.

"Thomas Locke?"

"Yes."

"Hi. I'm Rowena Garnock, from the Center for Applied Hypnosis and Intuitive Studies."

"Yes?"

"We have heard of you and your wife; Sarah, is it?"

"Yes. Sarah."

"We've heard of the work you're doing, and we have a question for you. We have a series of clients here who are experiencing paranormal phenomenon. We have a trained and licensed staff of counselors and hypnotherapists here at the center. The therapists agree that a support group for paranormal phenomenon is needed, but none of us have any personal experience with this subject. Would you consider leading it? You need to know beforehand, that you would not receive compensation for your time. The work you'd do would be strictly on a volunteer basis."

"I don't know. Sarah and I would have to talk about your offer."

"Well, please do. Let me give you our number here at the center...."

They decided to join the group on an equal leadership basis. Sarah would do the paper and organizational work while Thomas fielded phone calls. The group would lead itself. They placed an ad that stated simply that they were forming a group where the paranormal would be seen as a normal aspect of this world. The calls began to come in slowly. After four weeks of interviews, a small but solid core group was founded.

"The group" met weekly to discuss experiences and speculate on what was happening. They offered support to each other, and through this each found a place for what they were experiencing in their lives. Each person's experience was vastly different, yet all shared a common bond. They each had had a visitation from extraterrestrials or a spiritual phenomenon; in many cases, both. Also, as Sarah and Thomas learned later, their group was based on love. Everyone in the group, except one, saw the experiences as loving and wondrous events. They were not afraid of these experiences. The one person who did not necessarily see the events in this light acted as an important catalyst and kept the meetings lively. The only fear the group members shared was of ridicule from the public. Therefore, the meetings were held privately and no member was allowed to mention another by name. The fear of exposure was real. Ridicule was not the only cost to the members. Being labeled as "crazy" or "sick" or "delusional" was also a realistic possibility. Each member was a solid, functioning citizen in the community around them. The possibility of losing that safety was something the group carefully sought to avoid.

Sarah and Thomas began to travel to meet with other groups, and to hear lectures when they could. The difference between their group and some others became pronounced. The fear-based groups fascinated them, and Sarah began to question why her and Thomas' experiences were not fearful. The group discussed this at length, but did not find any answers.

One night, when Sarah was in the presence of the extraterrestrials, she spoke to them about this subject. Two of the small beings floated in their bedroom. Sarah gazed into the depth of their large, reflective eyes and asked what she had been unable to comprehend on her own.

"Why do so many people have terrifying experiences, while others experience love? Our contacts sound very much like those of some people we meet. Yet, while I feel loved and grateful, others feel anger and fear during a similar experience."

One of the small beings with pale, translucent white skin and large dark eyes floated toward her. She heard tranquil words in her mind.

Come, Sarah. We will show you.

She accompanied this being, and others, as they traveled on a small spaceship to different houses under the dark sky and starry atmosphere. When they stopped at each house, the little being telepathically asked a sleeping person if they wished to experience an extraterrestrial contact on a spacecraft. Each person was told what they could expect to experience, and where they would go. After a time, a group of thirty people or so were gathered and brought to a larger spaceship. Once on the spaceship, the people reacted in a variety of different ways. Some became indignant. Others were disappointed and angry that the experience wasn't more mystical. Still others became frightened by the differences they saw. Sarah heard one of the small beings in her mind.

Watch, Sarah, and remember!

As one woman stood up and began to yell in anger, her energy hurtled out from her body toward the small beings. Sarah noted that the beings glowed a clear white light. They seemed to move in this light as if they were in a cocoon. The woman's anger bounced off this white shield and reflected back to the woman. She was met with her own fierce anger.

Another woman stood up and began to scream. Her terrified energy poured forth from her and out into the room. As it met one of the little beings, the energy bounced away effortlessly and back to the woman. She came face to face with her own fears.

A man stood up and began to question the extraterrestrials with humor. His energy was sent out in loving waves, and as it reflected back from the little beings, he saw humor and love in their actions. One of the little men began to speak again in Sarah's mind.

Do you understand, Sarah? Each person sees what they bring with them. They bring their own love or their own mon-

sters. We mean no one any harm. The woman who yelled had a difficult day at her job; her life is angry and tumultuous. She brought that with her. She sees herself through us. She sees her own monsters.

"I understand," Sarah said, and then she remembered no more.

✳

Even after Sarah's explanation to the group of what she had been taught, the one member who had always acted as a catalyst questioned the benevolence of the beings. He pushed and questioned Sarah and Thomas.

"How do you know they are *good*? What proof do you have? Channeled beings, extraterrestrials, what good do they do? How can you be so sure?" he persisted.

Sarah knew that this man represented some doubt that she still had deep inside her. That night as she fell asleep, she asked these same questions to herself.

Wake up! a voice echoed in her head.

"Leave me alone. I'm not going to channel now," Sarah mumbled sleepily. She then felt a shove on her left side, which woke her up, because there was no one on her left side. Only the small side table separated her side of the bed from the wall. She looked about the dark room in confusion.

Hurry, hurry, the voice persisted. *You must go to the field in the forest.*

"Please, leave me alone!" Sarah tried to ignore the voice. Orryka had told Sarah, months ago, that she would have an experience in an open field which lay in the forest a half-mile from their cabin. He had told her it would happen at four in the morning and that she need not be afraid. No harm would come to her. Now that this moment was here, Sarah was afraid. Again, the voice pursued with an intense urgency.

Sarah! Get up. Quickly!

The urgency filled her, and she climbed out of bed. She looked at their digital clock – 4:35 a.m. As she dressed herself with shaking hands, she called Rusty to her. Step by step, Sarah walked up the dirt road, toward the meadow, with Rusty by her side. Her breath was ragged, but from fear, not exertion. She imagined all kinds of outcomes as she walked: a spaceship that hovered over the field, perhaps extraterrestrials floating about the tall grass there. What would she experience there?

Her experiences had always been dreamlike when she was half-asleep. Now fully awake, she didn't have the dreamy buffer to make these experiences easier. She began to shake as she drew closer. She saw the pathway that led through the woods and started up it.

"God, what am I doing?" she muttered to herself. As she drew closer, her shaking became worse, and she reached down to hug Rusty before continuing. At last the path through the woods led her to an open field.

Nothing.

Sarah began to laugh with relief.

Then anger arose.

"What the hell is going on?" she said aloud.

Just then, a bright flash of light, approximately four feet in diameter, burst at the opposite end of the field. Sarah stepped forward into the field to investigate it. As she did, with the first light of dawn, a strong wind blew across the field. As the wind blew over the grass, to Sarah's left a flame leaped into life. Sarah hurried toward it, and found a three-foot bed of coals that had lain smoldering through the night. Two empty wine bottles lay near the abandoned campfire. Just before they had fallen asleep, Sarah and Thomas had talked about the loud party they had heard out in the forest. The flames increased, and Sarah hurriedly scooped dirt from the ground to cover the fire. She managed to cover the coals with dirt, but she realized it was not enough. She ran with Rusty back to the cabin and shook Thomas awake. A few minutes later, she and Thomas dragged ten gallons of water back to the field. They doused the coals and waited nearby for the next hour to make sure the fire was truly out.

Covered with ashes, soot and dirt, the three of them arrived back at the cabin, tired and excited. Sarah was shocked and pleased by what had happened. Thomas brought up the obvious.

"We have to report this."

North Bay counties were under a fire watch. The long summers without rain left the forest and fields in a tinderbox state. If the fire had caught, the whole mountainside would have been ablaze in minutes. On these narrow, winding roads, escape would have proved difficult. Sarah, Thomas and the others in their community could have lost everything, possibly even their lives. This was a serious offense.

"What shall we tell the Fire Department? I can tell my cousin, Steve, but what about the people he works with? How can I possibly explain this?" Sarah asked in a bewildered voice.

"I don't know. Maybe we can tell them Rusty smelled smoke and woke us up."

"Okay. That might work."

Later that night, on television the news reported the Santa Barbara fires had struck. People and homes were devastated. As Sarah watched, she broke into quiet sobs. If the beings had been using Sarah and Thomas for their own selfish needs, they would have simply told Sarah and Thomas to leave, without preventing a far-reaching and disastrous catastrophe which could have affected countless lives. At the very least, the wildlife, forest and the homes of dozens of people had been saved. Perhaps many more lives had also been saved. Sarah shuddered as she thought of the probable scenarios. At last they had their physical proof that the beings were benevolent. The irony was, they could tell hardly anyone, because most would not hear or believe.

Chapter 27

*D*ear, we would like to teach you how to act as a
guide to others on the astral plane. Would you
be interested in learning this? Orryka asked
Sarah calmly.

How? How would I do this?

I shall take you with me, and you would learn from me.

Sarah lay for a while longer in the hammock on their
porch before she agreed. Once she had, Orryka asked her to go
indoors, to lie down where she would not be disturbed. Sarah lay
on the bed and wondered what would happen next. The windows were open and warm air moved through the room in gentle breezes. The day was going to be hot because it was already
ninety degrees at ten in the morning. Rusty had dug a hole under
the deck and had fallen asleep in the cool shadows there. The
heat seemed to bother him more now that he had become an old
dog. Thomas was in Santa Rosa photographing a wine tasting
event. Sarah had arisen at six, cleaned the house and cooked the
food for the day before the heat struck. Orryka interrupted her
peaceful reflections.

*Dear, let yourself fall asleep. You will come with me while
your body rests.*

As Orryka spoke, Sarah felt suddenly drowsy. Her eyes
became unfocused and heavy. She felt herself slipping away....

Are you ready?

Yes, Sarah answered as she looked around herself. She was
floating above their cabin in the open sunshine next to Orryka.
Yet she was not hot. Strangely, this did not seem unusual.
Instead, she felt perfectly at peace in this extraordinary circum-

stance. She watched as her neighbor got into his small sports car and drove away. A black and white cat strolled lazily down the driveway; he made a nest in the cool shade under one of the tall redwoods, where he fell asleep. The wind chimes tinkled sweetly where they hung from a tree branch by the deck. The sound was distinctly familiar. Sarah heard Orryka's voice as if he were far away, instead of right next to her.

Take my hand.

Sarah took Orryka's hand. And as she did, a burst of white light blocked out the sunshine, and they were gone. They flew soundlessly over mountains, valleys, rivers, lakes and towns. The scenery blurred by so quickly that Sarah barely had time to notice it. Above her, the sun shone and a pale blue sky stretched on endlessly. They passed an airplane, and Sarah wondered if the passengers or pilots could see them.

No. They cannot see us. The most they would see is a strange or inappropriate reflection of light in the sky. The pilots would think that they were seeing sunlight reflected through water vapor, Orryka answered.

The world below her continued to change. Sarah knew that they had left the North American continent and had traveled south. Tall mountains loomed up ahead. *Where are we?* Sarah wondered.

South America. We are going to the Andes. I am to help a child there today. You will help, also, if you choose to; if not, you may watch and learn.

The mountain loomed up, large and unreal. They moved more slowly now, and Orryka pulled her toward a small village. A few miles outside the village on a narrow mountain road, he stopped. Sarah hovered next to Orryka and took in the breathtaking beauty. Mountain peaks, draped in snow, stood regally against a royal blue sky. Beneath them, a narrow dirt road wound dangerously around the base of one of the peaks below the snow line and down the slope.

Sarah waited patiently and wondered again what would happen next. This time no answer was forthcoming from Orryka. Time passed slowly, or not at all. Sarah felt transformed by the beauty and by what she was experiencing. Then, down the road, a small child came into view.

A little girl walked, by herself, on the shoulder of the road. She wore a school uniform and carried books in her small arms. Her dark hair was in two long braids that hung down her back. She seemed lost in concentration and did not notice as a car sped around the curve toward her. Before Sarah could cry out, the car hit the little girl and drove on. The driver never saw or noticed the little girl. Somehow, Sarah could hear the driver's thoughts. He thought he had just hit a rock with his car. His thoughts were elsewhere. He did not look in his rear-view mirror, because he did not have one. The old car rushed down the mountain road as if a strong force pushed it and its driver along. Orryka moved instantly to the little girl's side.

Come, Serra. She will not live without our help!

As Sarah stood over the little girl, she was struck by how small and fragile the child was. Her left leg was bent backwards, under her, at an unnatural angle. A large gash on the back of her head seeped blood. Her arm hung limply to the side and was broken between the elbow and shoulder. Orryka bent and put his hands over her head. His hands began to glow, and the little girl's head shimmered beneath them. Sarah watched, transfixed, as the wound in her scalp healed and she began to come to consciousness. Her eyes fluttered, and she stared upward toward Sarah. She groaned in pain, and then gasped.

She sees me! Sarah thought in astonishment. Orryka continued to focus on the little girl's head. As the light that came from his hands intensified, the little girl became more lucid. She stared up at Sarah in wonder. Sarah wished fervently that she could do something to lessen the little girl's pain. Suddenly, Orryka spoke in her mind.

Put your hands over her arm. See the bone in your mind. See it whole and mended.

Sarah did as she was told and focused intently on the little girl's arm. Her entire being began to shiver as a loving, electrifying energy coursed through her. She visualized the bone whole and strong. She saw the small arm strengthened and vibrating with health. She closed her mind to all else, until she heard Orryka again.

Serra, look!

She looked down and saw that the arm lay mended and whole. The little girl looked up in wonder and awe. Sarah felt an intense love flowing from herself into the little girl. The little girl murmured two words softly.

"Santa Maria."

Orryka took his hands away from the soft brown hair, and the little girl's eyes closed in sleep. He moved back and directed Sarah to look up. A car had stopped several yards away and two men were running toward the child. They cried out loudly in alarm, in Spanish. Sarah watched as they gently picked up the little girl and her books and put both in the back seat of the car.

They moved quickly and gracefully. Only a minute had passed before the men drove back toward the village. Sarah was left breathless and felt strangely tranquil after the experience. Orryka began to explain the experience as the car drove out of sight.

She could see us, but not hear us. Accidents – traumas – often open neuro-pathways, which allow senses that are normally closed to function. Also, she is a child. Often children have the ability to see and hear other dimensions, because these pathways frequently remain open during childhood. As children are taught to deny what they experience, their pathways close through lack of use, practice or belief. In your country, these experiences are often referred to as a child's make-believe world or as an invisible friend. She will remember the work we have done, but will translate it into something she will understand. Because you were here, she will tell the adults who helped her that she was visited by the Virgin Mother – Mary – and an angel.

Orryka, why didn't you stop the accident? Why did this little girl have to suffer? Sarah asked with passion.

Serra, there is more to this story than you can see here. This little girl's father was in an accident last month. He broke his arm and has been unable to work. Lately, he has begun to drink, because he feels he has failed his family. He was heading down a path of self-destruction. His daughter's accident will awaken him to what is truly important.

A second story is unknown to you. This little girl is the third of six children. She has felt discouraged herself, unseen by her parents. After her accident, she will see how much she is loved. On a soul level, she agreed to have this experience to help not only her father, but also herself.

Sarah looked into Orryka's blue-green eyes, humbled by what she had heard. Only love and compassion was reflected there.

Orryka, who are you? What are you ... an angel?

Yes. In a sense, by the definition of some, I am. But, so are you. **We are all angels and guides for each other.** *Sometimes angels take astral form and other times they take a more tangible, physical form. You learned today how to act as a guide, an angel, on the astral plane. Humans do this on a daily basis, but are not aware that they do.*

I don't understand.

Many humans choose to act as astral guides.

How?

Just as you did today. While they sleep, they leave their

bodies and do work from the astral plane. Have you ever had a dream, Serra, in which you were with someone you did not know, doing work that you did not necessarily remember?

Yes. Many times.

Some of those dreams were experiences taking place on the astral plane, in which you did work like you did today.

How do I know the difference between dreams and these experiences?

As a rule, for millennia most humans were not ready to know, and so these experiences were masked as dreams. Humans on this planet are beginning to wake up, to come to the consciousness that we are all connected. They are beginning to understand that they are part of a larger whole, and not just a part, Sarah, but an active part. They are enacting many of the roles, such as angels, from which they had before separated themselves. Humans are a part of the God they choose to see as separate. They are not only a part of the world of angels, but men are angels! You and the race of beings you now live amongst are an important part of the universe, not more important than or separate from, but part of a whole.

Sarah floated silently by Orryka's side as he explained this new view of Heaven and Earth. The proud Andes Mountains surrounded her. Blood had congealed in a dark mass on the dirt roadway, proof that what had transpired moments ago, had really happened.

Would you like to learn to act as a guide on a conscious level, Serra?

Yes. Of course.

No, dear, not of course. Many choose not to do this, because it is not an easy path. Your sleep will be interrupted at times – more than it already has been – and the following day you will experience fatigue and listlessness. Some of the tragedies you will see will leave you depressed or exhausted. This work is not done without an expenditure of energy.

However, you will always find the experiences rewarding, peaceful and loving. After each you will need a few days to rest and rebuild your energies. Also, most times you will not remember the circumstances, as this would allow you waking memories of another's life and would cause an invasion of privacy which cannot happen. Therefore, most often you will not remember, and in doing this work, you must accept that fact.

Sarah was aware of an intense sense of well-being. She said, You make it sound grim. I cannot imagine anything more wonderful. How will I know when I am doing this work?

You will know, dear. Come, it is time to return. Serra, this time you will remember all that you have experienced. You will awake tired. Let yourself sleep later today if you can. You will need to rest.

Why, Orryka, do I need to remember at all?

Because someday you will share this information with others.

She took his hand and began the magical flight back over the mountains, valleys, cities and plains. When Sarah awoke sometime later, she awoke tired, as if she had worked for hours in some distant place. She remembered a vivid dream of a little girl in Peru and wondered what it all meant.

"Sarah?" A female voice questioned on the other end of the phone line.

"Yes, it's me. Ioanna?"

"Gabe and I – we've separated. Sarah, I had the strangest dream about you last night. "

"I'm so sorry. I know how painful that is," Sarah said with genuine concern. Ioanna was a friend she had met during the previous year.

"Sarah, it has been hard, too hard. I didn't leave Gabe. He left me. I've been ... not coping. Last night I drank myself into a stupor. I actually considered killing myself, but fell asleep instead. You came to me. You talked me through this. You convinced me to go on. I don't know what to say, except thanks."

Sarah was speechless. She had had a dream in which she had spoken to Ioanna. She had not remembered what they had talked about, but had been left with a vague feeling of sadness and wonder when she woke up. She started to speak, but emotion choked the words in her throat. Ioanna continued, while Sarah was silent.

"You think I'm crazy," she said flatly.

"No. No, I don't," Sarah spoke once she had cleared her throat by coughing. "I'm stunned. That's all. I dreamt about you last night, too."

"Wow!" Ioanna exclaimed. "Then it was real! This is exciting, Sarah."

"Yeah, I guess it is."

"You don't sound excited."

"No, it's just that right now I feel ... humbled. Do you understand?"

"Yeah, I sure do. Listen, my boss just walked into the room.

Can I call you later?"

"Yes."

"Sarah, thanks again.

Later that night, as Sarah told Thomas about what had happened, he listened pensively. When he did not respond, she questioned him.

"What's wrong, Tom?"

"Nothing. I had a dream about your friend Ioanna, too. I heard her calling. I woke you and told you that she needed help, and you left the house to go to her. That's all I remember."

They looked into each other's eyes and neither spoke. No words seemed adequate.

Over the next several months, Thomas and Sarah repeatedly had dreams in which they were together, or separately, assisting different people. Sometimes they remembered their experiences, and validation occurred during the following days.

On one such occasion, Sarah awoke with a clear and vivid memory of riding in an RV with a couple who were in their late sixties. The couple, exhausted from the long day of travel, drove down a local highway looking for an RV park. They had become hopelessly lost, and an argument ensued. The exhausted wife accused her husband of not listening or paying attention to her directions. The weary husband blocked out his wife's voice and continued in a direction that took them farther away from their intended destination.

Sarah hovered between them and stared at the map in the woman's hands. She recognized the road the couple were on and knew that they would not reach the park by traveling in the direction the couple now took. Sarah firmly and quietly began to direct the man behind the wheel.

You must turn around, she said.

"Henry! Where are you going now?" his wife screeched. The man silenced her.

"Shut up, Ester. Let me concentrate!"

Go down this road. Now turn right. Keep going. Take this left. Go straight. Up ahead is the highway you want. Go south. Sarah directed the man, who drove on, unaware of her presence. He did not exactly hear her as much as he "felt" he should go in a certain direction. *Now, here. Take this exit. It's just up ahead. On your left. There. Look! Do you see the sign?*

The following morning, Sarah awoke groggy and wondered about the dream. Thomas suggested they go out for breakfast, and she agreed. They drove across town to a favorite restaurant and took seats in a booth. The waitress recognized them and teased Sarah about looking so sleepy. As they sipped hot tea while waiting for their breakfasts, they observed two people seated in the booth next to them: the couple from her dream, Henry and Ester. Sarah put down her tea; she closed and opened her eyes several times to make sure they were real. Henry and Ester were unaware of her and proceeded to argue about the previous night's trip. Sarah stared at them, until she realized that she was being rude. She ate her breakfast, but did not taste the food.

Chapter 28

*S*arah sat on the forest floor in front of the house and brushed Rusty's thick red coat. Leaves stuck to her the legs and the seat of her jeans, and she ignored them as she ran her hand through Rusty's fur to see if she had missed any mats. He whined softly and tried again to escape this necessary grooming. Sarah kissed his muzzle, which had begun to turn gray, pushed him back down and resumed her search. As she did, her hands came across a lump under Rusty's leg, up near his rib cage. She massaged the mass – it felt like a fatty tumor – and made a mental note to call the vet that afternoon. Just as she reached for the mat comb, the cordless phone, which lay on the ground near her, rang loudly in the quiet forest surroundings.

"Hello?" Sarah answered it and released her hold on Rusty. He jumped up, ran several feet out of her reach and then began to roll in the dirt.

"Hey, Sal," her cousin Steve greeted her. "Can you pick up my mail and check the house for one more day? I won't be back tonight after all. I'm covering for a co-worker."

"Sure. No problem," she answered and then groaned as Rusty found a moist patch of ground and began to roll in the mud. "I have to go. Rusty's destroying my grooming job. I'll talk to you when you get home."

A few minutes later, Sarah and Rusty, who was caked in mud, walked up the road to the row of mailboxes. Sarah picked up Steve's mail, and then walked back down the road, past their cabin and to Steve's house.

She opened the door, and shook her head as she saw the mess Steve had left before leaving for work two days ago. After placing his mail on the table, she got the broom and began to sweep the kitchen floor. Rusty lay outside in the shade and waited patiently for her.

A half-hour later, as she finished washing the pile of dirty dishes, the phone rang. Without thinking, Sarah automatically answered it.

"Hello, Steve Clark's residence."

"Hi. Who's this? I'm trying to reach Steve."

"Steve's at work. This is his cousin."

"Sally? Is that you?"

"Yes?"

"This is Ian. Do you remember me? We dated a couple of times, many years ago, when you first graduated from high school."

"Ian? Yes. Of course I remember you! How are you? Where are you?" she asked cheerfully. The image of a young, fair-haired man with striking green eyes and an especially strong Harvard accent came to her as she listened to his voice. The accent had softened and his voice was more refined.

They talked for the next hour, only as two people who had not seen each other in fifteen years could. Ian still lived in Cambridge, was married, but was currently going through a divorce. He'd never had children, but had become a college professor and looked upon his students as substitute children. Sarah had not known Steve still kept in contact with Ian, and she soon learned that Steve had also kept Ian up to date on her life, as well.

"Steve tells me you've become a channeler," he began. "Why did you decide to do this? I never knew you had an interest in psychic phenomenon. You always seemed too sensible for that sort of ... hobby."

Sarah felt herself blush. She had never adjusted to the title of "channeler", and Ian's reference to channeling as a "hobby" made her feel uncomfortable. She stuttered her reply.

"I d-didn't want to be-become a channeler. It just sort of happened. So, have you seen anything of Joel?" She tried to change the subject, but Ian ignored her question.

"Did you start hearing voices? I'm really curious." His voice was slightly mocking.

"Yes -- no. An ... an entity appeared to me. I could see and hear him."

Ian began chuckling softly at the other end of the line. Their friendly phone call was quickly disintegrating. Ian pushed the subject further.

"Why did this 'entity' come to you? Why you? You're not that special, Sarah. I mean, aren't channelers or prophets supposed to be monks or saints or something? You hardly fall into that category."

"I don't know," Sarah whispered, "I never asked." She was rapidly remembering why she had stopped dating Ian. All the awkwardness of being a young girl, the painful memories of being one of the poor kids, who had had to work hard in high school to keep up with the more affluent students, like Ian, was flooding back to her. She was surprised to find that these feelings of inadequacy still existed. A minute later, after a hasty excuse, she hung up.

As she stepped outside and closed the door of Steve's house, her reflection stared back at her from the glass in the door.

"Why?" Sarah asked her serious face. A sadness had crept into her dark eyes during the conversation with Ian. He was right. She was not special. In fact, she was quite average: average in height, in weight, in beauty, in intelligence.

Nothing in her past could have foretold the unusual life she now lived. She had been a bright student who had been shy and never fit into the more popular groups in school, who had never really fit in anywhere. The natural empathic abilities she had, had only caused her to stand out as different, as if she had a red light on her forehead that blinked on and off and spelled "O-D-D." She had gone on to a series of bad relationships and a cooking career once she had graduated.

Why would Orryka work with someone so terribly average – a cook? She had never stopped to ask why. The question left her feeling hollow and confused. The more she thought about it, the more flaws she found in herself, the more reasons that Orryka should have chosen someone else, someone more God-like. In that moment, she realized how completely human she was – with every human frailty.

A deep sigh escaped her lips and she turned to walk away. A shimmering ball of light glowed faintly before her on the deck, and Orryka's kind voice filled her mind.

Serra, that which has labeled you as different has also made you special.

Sarah shook her head and choked back a sob. Her words were spoken telepathically. Even if she had wanted to verbalize them, she could not have. The lump in her throat was too large.

Different? You mean "odd." I am terribly human, Orryka. I get angry. I cry and get impatient. Ian is right. There is nothing unique about me – except my oddness. Why didn't you come to a New Age seeker or a monk or someone who was into all – this spiritual stuff – or at least to someone who was more perfect?

Serra, do you really believe someone else would be more

perfect than you?

*Yes – most anyone would be! I have made countless mis-
takes in my life. I feel scarred and wholly unsuited for this work!*

**Every soul is God-like. You, with what you call your
frailties or scars, are perfect.** *Every soul has a guide. A soul
does not have to be physically and emotionally perfect or have a
special talent to receive guidance, to be loved by God, by The
One. Every soul is perfect and is loved. This is a fact of existence.
All are loved equally. You cannot see how the very things you
consider flaws are gifts given to you by The One. You cannot see
this because you cannot see a bigger picture.*

I don't understand, Serra said, and then she sat down on
Steve's deck and put her head in her hands. Tears fell down her
cheeks unchecked. Rusty licked her cheek and whined. Sarah
laced her hands around his neck and hugged him for comfort.

Let me tell you a story.

As Orryka began his story, images filled Sarah's mind, the
deck dissolved away and his words filled her heart.

*One day, a man awoke and saw that it was a glorious day.
The sun was shining. The sky was clear and blue, and the birds
flew through the sky in sweeping arches of wonder. The man
decided to go for a long walk, in an area he had not trespassed
before. He set out happily.*

*He had walked for hours when he came to a large meadow
with green grasses that bent lightly under the gentle breezes. On
the far side of the meadow was a giant oak tree.*

*Never before had the man seen such beauty or perfection
in a living tree. He was so struck by the tree's perfection that he
decided to sit in its shadow and rest. As the man drew near, there,
in the shadow on its trunk, was a large scar.*

*The man became angry, and said out loud, "How ugly!
The tree would be whole and perfect without that scar! How disappointing. Who could have done this? The tree is not as lovely
as it was before."*

Sarah gasped out loud as the image of the scar filled her
mind. The scar was deep and mangled in the trunk of the tree.
The sensation of being held, a warm hug, surrounded her, and
then Orryka continued his parable.

*You see, Serra, the man did not know how the scar was
made. He did not know that, hundreds of years ago in that place,
two farms had existed. While erecting a fence, the farmers had
nailed boards across the tree, which had then been young. They
had braced the fence against the tree to make the fence strong.
The young tree had grown around the fence and held it upright.*

Now, dear, because the fence stood strong, one farmer's sheep did not go into the other farmer's crops, and these two farmers knew peace and happiness together. Because these two farmers knew peace, their families knew peace. Because their families knew peace, the whole village felt this peace and prospered. The man could not see this. He could not see the whole story.

Sarah, **sometimes that which we consider ugly and horrible is truly beautiful and wondrous.** *You are like that man. You do not know the whole story. Dear, you are whole and perfect with your scars.*

Sarah was silent for a long time.

If this story was true, then the problems or frailties of each soul held a purpose, were perhaps important in ways the individual could not see. No soul was ordinary, and each life was perfect. A smile began to creep across her lips as she thought of her many flaws: her dyslexia taught her patience in learning, her sensitivity allowed her a depth of compassion for others and her empathic abilities had led her to work with Orryka, to experience *The One.* Each had been a gift! Again, she felt Orryka's warmth surround her and his voice whispered in her ear.

Yes, Serra! **Each soul is a perfect aspect of The One!**

Chapter 29

*T*he smell of oil paints filled the afternoon air and sunlight glinted across Thomas' multicolored palette. He dipped a long-stemmed brush into the Prussian blue paint on the board, and began to mix this with a dollop of Chinese white. Sarah leaned against the door frame and studied Thomas' latest emerging work. Several finished paintings were propped up against the walls in the studio.

Somehow Thomas was able to capture the feelings of what they experienced, with the channeling and the extraterrestrials, in his paintings. No matter what the subject matter, whether outer space, oceans, marine life or people, the love they experienced poured through and into his paintings. Whenever Sarah felt out of sorts, all she had to do was step into his studio and she felt better, as if Thomas' paintings caused a healing for anyone who looked on them. A peace that was gentle and penetrating filled her as she looked at Thomas' work.

His latest painting was of a moon in a starry sky, as viewed from the surface of an ocean. Two dolphins poked their heads above the ocean's surface, and your eye was drawn to a spaceship which floated in the background. She sighed as again this peace settled over her. Thomas looked up from his work.

"Hey, kid, what's up?"

"The vet called."

Thomas put his brush down and gave Sarah his full attention.

"What were the test results?"

"Rusty has cancer."

Thomas nodded once, and then took Sarah in his arms. He held her while she cried and stared over her shoulder at

Rusty, who slept on the deck next to the French doors that opened into his studio. At last, Thomas spoke with a broken voice.

"What are our choices?"

"Not many. We could try treatment, but it may not work. Rusty would have to go through the pain and frustration of multiple visits to the vet's office. The vet said he could live for another year without treatment, and with treatment, well, it might give him a few months more than that."

"I can't do that," Thomas said emphatically.

"I can't, either. Rusty hates the vet. He's almost twelve. I don't want him to spend his last few months in misery."

They both looked at Rusty, who slept innocently while his future was decided. Sarah wiped tears away from her face. Thomas squeezed her hand, and then picked up his paintbrush.

"Sarah, I saw a wolf in our house today," Thomas said over dinner. She stopped, her hands in mid-air above a large bowl of Caesar salad from which she was about to serve them, and looked into his blue eyes. In that moment, Sarah realized that what Thomas referred to was not physical or tangible.

"What kind of wolf? Where?"

"In the living room. A white and red animal with gold eyes. The wolf was transparent, and walked across the room, turned to stare at me and then walked through the wall."

"What do you suppose it means?"

"I don't know. Perhaps it is a symbolic message."

"Thomas, I've been thinking. Maybe we should get a second dog – for when Rusty dies. Maybe this is a sign."

"I don't know, Sarah. Think of Rusty. I doubt he'll like having a puppy around at his age, especially since he's sick."

"You're right. It was just an idea."

The wolf spirit, as Sarah and Thomas came to call it, visited them for two more months, and then the apparition ceased. They each wondered about this strange event. One of the paranormal group members had validated this ghostly, animal visitation, when she had commented on seeing the spirit in their house during a meeting. She had gone to the bathroom, and had been met by the wolf spirit in the hallway. By then, Sarah and Thomas had become use to this apparition, and were not surprised by the woman's startled description. When this pooka-like spirit had left them, Sarah felt an odd mixture of emotions: sadness and elation. She questioned Orryka about this when she next met with him in the meadow in *the between.*

"Orryka, why is there a wolf spirit in our home?"

This is the spirit of a sled dog you once lived with in another life. She watches over you and is a guide for you.

"Where did she go?"

I may not answer this now, Orryka said simply. Sarah had learned to trust Orryka and why he answered at some times and not others. She knew he never refused to answer one of their questions – unless it would alter a future event – or a lesson they were currently experiencing. There was a purpose, reason, behind everything Orryka did, and Sarah had learned to trust those reasons completely.

She and Orryka sat on the cliff edge, overlooking the lake. The lake caught her attention, and she stared appreciatively at this spectacular view. The lavender sky reflected on the water in tones of gray, blue and purple. The first moon rose, a crescent moon, and was reflected on its wavering surface. Sarah questioned Orryka further.

"Orryka, I've only seen short scenes from this life with this sled dog. Could you help me remember more?"

Yes, dear. Orryka placed one hand over Sarah's eyes. His words echoed in her mind and called forth her forgotten memories. *You lived as an Eskimo, and this dog was called "Blue Eyes." I lived in that life with you. I was your grandfather.*

As he spoke, a series of vivid images filled Sarah's mind and heart. She looked up at Orryka and felt a profound love, a wonder at their connection.

"I remember," she whispered.

Yes. It was then that I made a promise to watch over you. In a sense, so did Blue Eyes. She has returned, as I have, to guide you.

Sarah did not respond. How could she put into words the depth of love she now felt? The wonder of all she had experienced was intense and satisfying, on levels that had no description, had no limits. She smiled at Orryka, and he spoke for her.

Thank you, Serra. You have given me more than you know or understand.

"We'll just look."

"Sure!" Thomas said in disbelief as he steered the truck around a tight bend in the road. Trees shaded their path and their old truck struggled as they headed up an especially steep part of the mountain road.

"I promise," Sarah said unconvincingly.

They had stopped to pick up Rusty's medication at the veterinary hospital a half-hour ago. For some reason, each time Sarah had called to see if Rusty's medicine had come in, she was told the shipment of medicine had been delayed. The vet supplied them with samples in the meantime. Two weeks late, the order had finally arrived. While Sarah had waited for the receptionist to finish with another client, she had read the bulletin board. There she had found the ad she and Thomas now discussed.

Wolf-hybrid puppy, free to **good** home only! Call....

With her concerns about Rusty, Sarah had forgotten about her conversation with Orryka months ago, and now she could not explain what had compelled her to copy down the ad or why she pushed Thomas to look at this puppy. A wolf-hybrid was not what they had planned. They had talked about getting a retriever once Rusty died, or maybe a sheep dog, never a wolf-hybrid. Thomas shook his head as he pulled into their driveway.

"Okay, Sarah. Remember that we are just looking."

Two days later, a green sports car pulled into driveway, and before the driver could stop, a white and auburn head poked out through the open window. Two intense golden eyes stared back at them as Sarah and Thomas walked down the steps from the deck. Thomas looked at Sarah.

"Look familiar?"

"Yes! It's the wolf spirit!" Sarah said in surprise.

Before them, in solid, living flesh, was the very wolf who had visited them months before in ghostlike fashion. The only difference was the animal before them was smaller because she was a puppy. Thomas laughed as the puppy ran up to them and grabbed onto the hem of Sarah's skirt. She playfully tugged on Sarah's dress until Rusty walked around the corner of the house. The puppy whined with delight and ran forward to chomp on Rusty's legs and tail. The owner, a young man, looked on in surprise.

"This is amazing. I've shown her to a half-dozen people, but you're the first she's reacted to like this. It's as if she knows you."

They made plans for the young man to bring the puppy back in three days. He was moving out of state, and explained that he could not take the puppy with him. He called the puppy to him and, as he did, Sarah questioned the foreign-sounding words. The young man explained.

"It's Spanish, and means, 'Yellow Eyes.'"

Sarah and Thomas looked at each other, and then at the puppy before them. The puppy appeared to be laughing at something ... perhaps it was them.

The young man dropped off the puppy three days later, as planned, along with a bag of dog food. After he had hugged the puppy goodbye, he turned to leave, and then turned back to them once more. He yelled to Sarah and Thomas from where he stood next to his sports car.

"This is going to sound strange, but I feel as if I've been taking care of her for you – like she was never mine, but was just waiting to go to her true home."

He waved as he drove off. The puppy sat between Sarah and Thomas, and did not try to follow.

"Sarah, I know you're attached to the coincidence of her name, but 'Ojos Amarillo' is a long name for a puppy. We need to shorten or change it."

"What do you have in mind?"

"How about 'Dancer?' She is graceful and moves like a dancer," Thomas said.

"That sounds like a reindeer."

"How about 'Yerraba?'" Thomas joked.

"Funny," Sarah said dryly.

"Well, you come up with a name."

"Let's just leave her name as it is," Sarah said.

"Watch. Amarillo! Ojos! See," Thomas reasoned, "no response. Even she doesn't want this name. I know – 'Okami.'"

The puppy's ears perked up, and she ran over to Thomas and sat down at his feet. Rusty, who lay nearby, growled at her as a warning to get no closer. The puppy whined and wagged her tail.

"What does that mean?" Sarah asked.

"It's Japanese for *wolf*."

"Okami," Sarah tried out the new name. The puppy ran to Sarah, wagged her tail and promptly began to chew on Sarah's pant leg. "I guess that's your new name. Okami," she tried the name once more. Okami looked up at Sarah with a content and playful expression.

✳

Months passed and Rusty's health declined rapidly. He still went on hikes with Thomas, Sarah and the puppy, but he no longer led their walks, and often he needed to stop to catch his breath. Thomas and Sarah knew the end was near, and spent more and more time with Rusty.

One morning, Thomas shook Sarah awake. Slowly, Sarah responded; she opened her eyes reluctantly. For the past week, each morning had been difficult to face, because each day offered the question of whether or not to put Rusty to sleep. His health was failing dramatically. He could only walk a few feet at a time, and often his body did not respond to his own commands.

He did not seem to be in any physical pain that they could see. Rusty had always been a baby about even the smallest of cuts. While he was fiercely protective of Sarah and Thomas, he was, at the same time, sensitive to pain. Since he did not whimper or cry out, they each hoped he did not suffer physically. What tormented Sarah was the look in Rusty's large, brown eyes. Every time his body failed to function, he looked up at Sarah with a pleading and confused expression. His mental faculties were completely intact, and this made his physical demise more difficult to take. Sarah had watched old dogs fall into ill health, but they all had been senile and unaware of what was happening to them. Rusty knew, and his pained expression hurt Sarah and Thomas profoundly.

"Sarah, I have to tell you what happened just a minute ago!" Thomas shook her again as she started to close her eyes.

"I woke up because I heard Rusty come into the bedroom. I opened my eyes, and he was sitting by the bed. He looked great – just like he did when he was the young dog I found by the side of the road!

"He looked happy and energetic. I lay here thinking that Rusty had had some kind of miraculous cure. Then I realized that I put Rusty in the pen last night. He couldn't be in the house. I knew his spirit had come to me to ask to be released. Then the vision ended. Sarah, he doesn't want to be in that old, broken-down body anymore. We have to let him go."

Sarah nodded as tears fell down her cheeks. She knew

Thomas was right. She quickly dressed, and ran out to Rusty. She found him collapsed on the ground. His body had failed completely during the night. His eyes looked into hers, pleading for an answer. Thomas came up behind her and a tear fell from his blue eyes into Rusty's fur.

"I'll call the vet," he said quietly. Sarah held Rusty's head in her lap until the vet arrived. While the vet injected Rusty with the medicine that would put him into one last and final sleep, Sarah fell into a blurred world where tears washed over everything she saw and her heart cried out in agony at the loss of such a friend. Thomas patted Rusty's large head and his tears mingled with Sarah's and the vet's. They buried Rusty in the forest, beneath a dogwood tree that somehow had magically grown beside tall redwoods and firs.

The following morning, Sarah and Thomas awoke simultaneously from identical dreams. They each had seen Rusty running in a meadow. He was strong, alive and joyful. Orryka's voice interrupted their conversation.

Rusty is fine, dear. He has made the transition and is free once more.

Where was he? What happens to animals when they die? Sarah asked telepathically.

Orryka's voice sounded surprised as he answered her.

Serra, what do you think happens? Rusty is a part of the whole, The One. *He is in* the light, *where all souls eventually go after death.* **Animals are not different or inferior to humans in spiritual matters. They are part of the whole of the universe. Each animal has a soul that learns and grows, as other life forms do.** *Rusty is contented and loved. You may be happy for him, dear. He is in* the light.

Sarah repeated what Orryka had explained to Thomas and, although they continued to grieve their loss, each felt at peace with Rusty's death.

Chapter 30

*T*homas joked with Sarah, who sat on the living room floor as she brushed out Okami's coat. An early spring rain made grooming outdoors impossible. Beside the beautiful adult wolf-mix was a large Golden Retriever puppy they had picked up shortly after Rusty's death. Okami, in wolf-like fashion, had gone into an intense mourning for Rusty. She had refused food and water and would not play until Sarah and Thomas had brought home a new companion, a fat and playful Golden Retriever puppy. The puppy was large for his breed and, at seven months, stood almost as tall as Okami at two years.

"Maybe we shouldn't feed Kelly so much. Look at the size of him."

The puppy wagged his large tail as Thomas said his name.

"Come here, Kelly," Thomas called him to his side.

Kelly got up quickly, wiggling as he came, and knocked over a lamp on the side table. The lamp crashed to the floor, but miraculously did not break. Sarah laughed as she reached over and replaced the lamp in its former position. As smart as Okami was, Kelly was as dumb. He became the comic relief in their life on a daily basis, and through his humorous antics, the pain of Rusty's death had healed. Their home was again happy and peaceful.

Thomas stood and went to the kitchen, where he filled the tea kettle and put it on the burner to heat. He yelled to Sarah from the kitchen.

"What about Idaho?"

"Too cold," she answered without hesitation.

For months they had tried to decide what turn their life would take next. They had decided to move out of California, but where would they go?

"Texas?"

"Forget it. Texas has the opposite problem. It's too hot and humid."

"I was kidding, Sarah," Thomas said as he leaned through the kitchen door.

Sarah stared at Thomas and realized she appreciated his presence, who he was, as much as they day they had met. His beard had two wide, gray streaks running through it. The little weight he had put on over the years looked good on him, as he headed toward fifty. And his eyes twinkled with a keen sense of humor, a sense of the wonder of life, as they always had. She was as much in love with him now as the day they had married. No. She was more in love. From the smile on his lips, she knew he felt the same about her.

The tea kettle whistled and Thomas called out another choice.

"What would you think about moving to the Southwest – to maybe Arizona or New Mexico? I know it's dry, but the winters are mild."

"That sounds good to me," she yelled back.

Thomas carried two steaming mugs of tea into the living room, placed both well above Kelly's height on the table and they continued their discussion.

"The Southwest is beautiful, Sarah. You would love it. We could move to the the mountains or the desert."

"Okay," Sarah said, and then smiled. "Let's plan a vacation to check it out."

Moonlight spilled through the window and onto Sarah's face. Her face was peaceful in its sleep and a smile lay quietly on her lips as she dreamed. Thomas rolled over and put his arms around her waist, drawing her closer to him. He, too, slept peacefully.

In Sarah's sleep, a dream, a visitation, occurred.

She was on the ship, surrounded by people she loved. They were in an amphitheater where a large communication device, which translated the many languages of all who spoke into one universal tongue, stood on the center of the stage. The instrument glowed with energy and light, like a giant crystal, as Sarah listened to different people speak. Everything and everyone about her held a luminescent quality. She turned in slow motion and saw Thomas sitting next to her. Near Thomas were their friends Diane and Dave. Next to them were other friends, some of whom they now knew; others, Sarah realized she would soon meet: Jon, Karen, Jim, Steve, Anne, Harvey, Jeffrey, Mavis ... the list went on. All races from Earth were represented: Black, Asian, Hispanic, Caucasian and others.

A speaker rose, a tall extraterrestrial being with ice-blue eyes and pale yellow hair. His name suddenly came to Sarah's mind. She remembered speaking with him on other occasions, one to one; she had called him "Ikon." Slowly, he spoke about peace on this planet, about Earth's part in the galaxy.

"Each person here will have the opportunity to teach peace," Ikon finished simply. "When your work is done, you will have a choice whether to continue working on this planet or to return to your home worlds."

The meeting broke up and people began leaving the amphitheater. Sarah turned toward Thomas and took his hand.

"It's time to go home," Thomas said, and then the dream ended.

After what seemed like minutes later, Sarah awoke in the bedroom. Moonlight flooded through the room and Thomas' breathing changed and became more shallow, as if he, too, was waking up. He stirred, rolled over and sat up in bed.

"Sarah?" he called to her in a sleepy voice.

"I'm here," she answered softly.

"I just had the strangest dream. We were on the ship in an amphitheater and...."

They compared dreams and found that the dreams matched – exactly.

"How strange that we both had the same dream," Thomas murmured as they lay down again. He was quickly drifting toward unconsciousness.

"I don't think it was a dream," Sarah answered, but Thomas did not hear her because he had already fallen asleep.

A knock sounded on the front door. Thomas looked at the obstacle course of packed and unpacked boxes which lay between himself and the door and yelled, "Come in!"

Steve pushed the door open and stared about the room. Thomas smiled and watched as Steve pushed a path through the heavy boxes, moving them aside as if they weighed nothing. When Steve reached him, he stuck out his large hand and shook

Thomas' in a tight grip.

"You're almost done packing, I see," he said. "I came by to say goodbye. I just got called in to the firehouse to cover for someone this morning."

"Then you won't join us for one last lunch. Sarah will be disappointed," Thomas responded.

"Yeah, well, the truth is, Tom, I've never liked long good-byes," Steve said and shrugged.

At that moment, Sarah walked out from the bedroom carrying a box. She saw Steve and her face broke into a large grin. Thomas watched as Steve smiled widely in return. After crossing the room, he took the box from Sarah, placed it on top of another and then pulled her into a bear hug.

"Steve has to go to work," Thomas explained as he watched their farewells. Steve's now gray-haired head was bent over Sarah as he held her, and for someone who did not like emotional goodbyes, Thomas noticed that his back shook slightly , as if he suppressed tears. Sarah patted Steve's shoulder tenderly, a much smaller woman comforting a giant. When Steve stood up, Sarah smiled gently, wiped away her own tears and then reached up and wiped a stray tear from Steve's cheek. Thomas smiled again, and then turned away from this private moment.

A moment later, the three of them stood out on the deck.

"It's been great having you two as neighbors," Steve said hoarsely. "I'd better get going. You take care of her, Tom. And you –" he hugged Sarah one more time. "Don't take any wooden nickels from bad spirits."

Sarah laughed softly as she cried and hugged Steve in return.

As they watched Steve walk slowly off the deck, Thomas put his arm around Sarah's waist. He pulled Sarah closely to him and whispered in her ear.

"It's alright, Sarah. We'll see Steve again."

Sarah packed the last box and looked about the cabin that had been their home these many years. California had offered them a richness of experience and beauty, for which she would always be grateful. Thomas entered the room and saw her teary-eyed gaze, and smiled knowingly. He took the box and went to place it in the moving truck.

He and Sarah climbed into their old pickup after Sarah had checked on the dogs. They were in their kennels, and each seemed content and excited. They sensed that something new awaited them. Sarah slammed the truck door, rolled down the window and looked one last time at their home. The brown wooden walls of the cabin, which had always looked warm and inviting, looked strangely plain and quiet. The richness of the wood had somehow faded without their presence attached to it.

Their home, she realized, was something they took with them, not a house or structure, but a place in their hearts where they shared the life they had built together.

"Don't worry, Sweetie. Home is where the dogs are!" Thomas joked. "Let's go!"

They drove down the mountain road, and Sarah, sadly and happily, said good-bye to the forest that had been their home. She thought of all the experiences they had had there. The many friends they had known. Her cousin Steve, who had been tolerant, supportive and kind.

Sarah remembered the time she had been brought to put out the fire, the long walks with Rusty and the moonlit sky that had covered their snug little cabin. A profound sense of being blessed by riches and wonders that were endless settled over her. She wished in that moment that she could share these gifts with the world. Orryka's voice entered her reminiscences.

Hello, Serra.

Hi, Orryka. I was just thinking of you. I wish there was some way I could thank you – give you what you have given us.

You may.

How?

Tell your story. Share with the world what you have learned.

How, Orryka? How can I do that?

Write.

Write?

Yes, dear. Write this story for others to read.

I'm not sure I can, Sarah said doubtfully.

Orryka's voice filled her with peace and love as he answered.

Don't worry, dear. We'll help you....

Epilogue

arah awoke from a heavy state of sleep in which she had had a vivid dream. She shook Thomas awake gently. He leaned over and switched on the light by their bed in their new home in the Southwest. The light glanced off the stark white of the walls, which were still unfamiliar. He squinted at the clock and mumbled sleepily to Sarah.

"Sarah, it's four in the morning. What is it?"

"Thomas, I –" She began to cry soundlessly, and then went on, "I had a dream about a memory, or a memory itself from long ago. I was in my mid-twenties."

She proceeded to tell Thomas about this dream that had touched her so profoundly.

"I was on the ship, the spaceship, and in a room with many other beings. Tall men. The short beings were there, also ... the ones with the pale, translucent skin and large dark eyes. One of these small beings was lying on a bed. I was sitting next to him.

"I felt as if he were a very old and dear friend. I held his hand, and knew that he was dying. Sadness. Oh Thomas, there was such sadness. Coming not only from me, but from him. I could feel him filling my mind with emotions. As he realized we were saying goodbye to each other, his sadness filled me. He was sad that he was leaving me here, because the people of our planet don't understand about our universe, don't practice tolerance of other lifeforms.

"Thomas, there were other emotions! Love. Joy. Gratitude for having been able to live. Compassion for our species and others! The emotions I felt coming from him were strong and real. Then, he spoke to me. He told me how important it is that the people of this planet understand."

"Understand what?" Thomas asked solemnly. His voice was quiet and tears hung on the edges of his beautiful eyes.

"That we're not alone! Other lifeforms, countless lifeforms, exist in the universe. As he spoke, images flooded through my mind. Thomas, the beings that exist are ..." she fell speechless again. Thomas rubbed her shoulders and encouraged her to continue.

"The beings that exist are what?"

"They're us! They are part of us! Like family, but bigger," she struggled with the words. "We are part of something that is so much bigger than anyone could know. He wants us, this world, to know that they are not here to hurt us or anyone. They are here to help. They need this world to know this, to understand.

"Then, Thomas, he raised his hand and touched a place on my forehead. As he did, I heard him speak clearly in my mind. He told me to remember. I felt as if someone had suddenly filled me with such an abundance of knowledge and feelings, which were so wonderful and loving.... I don't know how to explain everything I was shown and felt," she ended.

Thomas pushed himself up into a more comfortable, sitting position, and asked, "Sarah, why did he show you this?"

"He said they needed our help. He asked me to tell the world what he had shown me. He asked me to tell the world that they mean no harm, and that they are part of us. I promised I would, and then, while I held his hand, he died. As he died, he told me he loved me. Thomas –" she choked over a sob and continued. "It was Jonah's death I saw."

Sarah looked into Thomas' eyes through her own blurry, tearful gaze. Tears fell onto her cheeks and down her neck. Thomas reached over and wiped one away.

"It's time, Sarah."

"For what?"

Thomas stood up and walked across the room. He rummaged through the desk drawer until he found what he sought. He returned to the bed, and handed Sarah a yellow writing tablet and a pen.

"You promised."

The End

A note from the author ...

Although *A Sparkle on the Water* was written in a fictional format, it is in some aspects autobiographical. To protect the privacy of friends and family members in "Part Three", all names and places have been changed. The remaining characters throughout the book are either wholly fictitious or composite characters, and any resemblance to living or dead persons is accidental. However, all the paranormal events in "Part Three" were kept intact. The other exception to this is the character known as Orryka. I have described him completely as we have known him and have not changed his name.

The paranormal events in "Part Three" were carefully guided, and I do not recommend that these experiences be sought after or tried at home. If you choose to do so, you act at your own risk and with full responsibility for yourself.

I do sanction letting the love of the universe enter your life in every way. This may be accomplished by simply accepting it. You do not need paranormal events to feel or be loved. Love is waiting for you in this very moment! Open your heart, let your mind welcome it and then trust. Love will come to you ... and you may be surprised at how it appears.

Lastly, there are a few people I want to thank more personally.

To my husband Joseph ... what can I say? You listened for hours, gave when you were tired of giving and designed a beautiful cover. Je t'aime, Amoureux.

To my two favorite editors, Kim Rufer-Bach and Shirley Harvey, thank you! Kim, your clarity and insight made *Sparkle* shine. And, Mum, you are simply the best.

J'envoie mes bons souvenirs a mes amis des planetes au loin; Soneyan, mon cher ... Yink-ka et autres, je vous aime.

To Orryka, thank you – for guiding with patience and love, for bringing light to the darkness and for existing.

To all who read this book, thank you for sharing in our journey. If any of you would like to share your experiences, we invite you to either write or e-mail us at:

"Sparkle"
P.O. Box 1339
Cedar Crest, NM 87008-1339

StarPath@aol.com